A retired chef of over 40 years, James Miller has finally achieved his dream of becoming a writer. This is his second book written during the Covid shutdown. Married for 32 years to Jill, he has three children and two grandchildren. James enjoys travelling and meeting people along the way, which helps to inspire his writing creativity. Having achieved a lot as a chef, James hopes one day to write a piece of work that will propel him forward in the literary world and hopefully make him a bestseller.

I have a big 'thank you' to go out to Chris and Ruth Whittaker, who were responsible for my falling in love with Kalkan. Their encouragement for me and my wife to give the resort a try is gratefully acknowledged. I would also like to express my heartfelt gratitude for their friendship and generosity, taking us out and about to discover the true wonders and beauty of this region which has inspired me to write this book.

James Miller

A Kiss Under a Kalkan Sunset

Austin Macauley Publishers
LONDON · CAMBRIDGE · NEW YORK · SHARJAH

Copyright © James Miller 2023

The right of James Miller to be identified as author of this work has been asserted by the author in accordance with sections 77 and 78 of the Copyright, Designs and Patents Act 1988.

All rights reserved. No part of this publication may be reproduced, stored in a retrieval system, or transmitted in any form or by any means, electronic, mechanical, photocopying, recording, or otherwise, without the prior permission of the publishers.

Any person who commits any unauthorised act in relation to this publication may be liable to criminal prosecution and civil claims for damages.

This is a work of fiction. Names, characters, businesses, places, events, locales, and incidents are either the products of the author's imagination or used in a fictitious manner. Any resemblance to actual persons, living or dead, or actual events is purely coincidental.

A CIP catalogue record for this title is available from the British Library.

ISBN 9781398461581 (Paperback)
ISBN 9781398461598 (ePub e-book)

www.austinmacauley.com

First Published 2023
Austin Macauley Publishers Ltd®
1 Canada Square
Canary Wharf
London
E14 5AA

Thank you once again to the team of editors at Austin Macauley that has deemed my book worthy of publishing and to all the staff there that will be working on it.

Sunday Day 1

Kelly awoke from her deep sleep, stretching and yawning as she arose from her bed; with great excitement, she rushed to open the curtains to see what wonderful sights may await her through the window.

She had arrived in Kalkan, Turkey, in the early hours of the morning, it was wonderfully warm but the view from her terrace high up on the mountainside overlooking the town offered her only a scene of beautiful lights.

There was a great gasp of excitement as her jaw dropped open at the sight before her; fumbling in her hurry to open the patio doors, she screamed out, "Anyone awake yet?" Walking out onto her terrace she is taken aback by the view before her, the sun is rising up over to her right and she is amazed at how warm it is already given that it is just after 9am.

Kelly's sister Alice appeared on the balcony next to hers. "Oh my gosh, Kelly, it's so beautiful; look at that view!"

Kelly turned to her sister and agreed, "Yes isn't it just, where are the others?" The sisters were soon joined by Emma and Lacey who were quick to show their approval at the vista on offer; all four were really happy and so full of excitement they had quickly forgotten all about their tiredness having travelled for so long to get there.

The girls from the Taunton area of Somerset are all in their mid to late thirties and have been friends for many years; they all lead very different lives but the one thing that connects them is that they are all single and terribly distraught at the fact they may stay permanently that way upon the ever expanding shelf of life.

Kelly and Emma have both been married to cheating husbands and are now divorced while Alice and Lacey have had a number of, shall we say, unsuccessful relationships. A little while back, a friend of Lacey's came to Kalkan for a holiday and met someone whom she is now in a relationship with and so it was

Lacey who suggested that they should come here in the hope of finding some romance of their own.

They have booked a beautiful four-bedroom villa with private facilities that included a large pool and sun terrace to the rear and a wonderful sun terrace overlooking the town and harbour at the front, the view stretched way out to sea past the large islands in the bay that was flanked by the headland on both sides. The foursome strolled around the property, appreciating the quality on offer and all agreed it was a wonderful base for a terrific holiday.

After a few moments more of revelling in the morning sunshine and taking in the view, Alice suggested they get themselves ready and head out down to the town and explore what's on offer and find somewhere for breakfast. The others agreed and they all went inside and sorted themselves out. Lacey found a taxi number on a fridge magnet and called to arrange a pickup to take them down to the town. Soon enough, they were all heading on their way down the hill towards town in the taxi. Memhet the driver took the time to point out the supermarkets, banks and suggested some places they may enjoy in the evenings before handing Kelly a business card saying to call him anytime if they needed transport.

Emma asked the taxi driver if he knew a good place for breakfast and he said he knew the perfect place for them with a view over the harbour and proceeded to take them there. "Here we are, ladies, please enjoy your day." The girls thanked him as Kelly paid him for the trip.

The girls sat down at a table on the edge of the restaurant looking down over the harbour where there were many large sailing boats and pleasure craft. Alice said that they should all go out on one of them one day as she had read several reviews saying what a great day out it was; they all agreed it sounded a good idea.

A waiter came along after a few moments and took their orders for breakfast and the girls sat there chatting amongst themselves as they awaited their sustenance, taking the odd picture of the view as they waited.

Breakfast duly arrived and the girls tucked in whilst discussing what they should do after; they all came to an agreement that a pleasant stroll through the old town with the odd bit of retail therapy followed by essential shopping at the supermarket for basic necessities and then a relaxing afternoon around the pool to plan their evening.

With breakfast finished, they thanked the waiter and set off, slowly walking up through the old town which was not particularly busy at that time; they often stopped momentarily to check out the merchandise on display. The cobbled road was a little steep in places and they started to notice it in their calf muscles and lower back; especially Alice who gave out a loud groan; a passer-by smiled at her in acknowledgement at her grief, offering that she would get used to it after a while.

Before long, the girls arrived at a supermarket where they stocked up with their needs before heading outside to call a taxi. There were many taxis zipping by in both directions. Emma tried unsuccessfully to flag one down as Kelly searched for the earlier driver's card. A lady standing close by pointed out to a button on a board and instructed them to press it, saying it was a taxi call button. Moments later a taxi arrived and once on board, the driver asked where to; the girls froze as they looked at each other then burst into laughter. Lacey asked if anyone remembered the address and Emma said she knew it was Sunset Villa number 1 but that was it.

"Ah yes ok, I know Sunset Villa up the mountain," the driver said smiling as he pulled away.

The girls looked in disbelief as Kelly asked him how he knew without an address, the driver added that he knew every villa in Kalkan as did majority of the drivers and explained that British people cannot pronounce Turkish streets well when they are sober so they have no chance at night after drinking too much; he laughed out loud, causing the girls to chuckle in agreement.

The temperature was rising; it was almost 1 pm and the girls were truly feeling the heat, Emma said it was the hottest she had ever been in as the sun beat down from a clear blue sky. Lacey said she was glad they came in September as it was even hotter in July and August; the girls gathered their shopping and made their way up the steps to the villa entrance; once inside they were relieved to feel the coolness of the air conditioning as they put away their wares.

Alice had bought a couple litres of vodka on the plane and put them in the freezer box last night after arriving and asked the girls if they were up for a drink. Kelly and Lacey were quick to agree but Emma said she was ok with a beer for now. With drinks all sorted, the girls quickly changed into their swimwear and headed for the pool. Alice was first out and could be heard crying out that the floor was scorching hot and shouted to the girls to ensure they wore something on their feet.

The girls settled down on the sunbeds and relaxed with their drinks in hand. Emma said it would probably get even hotter later on and advised her friends to make sure they were well protected as she reminded them of a ruined holiday she had some years back after getting severe sunburn on her second day; Alice said she remembered the photos she had showed her.

"So who is going to be first to try the pool?" Lacey asked with a big grin.

"Well, I think that's going to be me," Alice said confidently as she adjusted her bikini standing at the side of the pool before launching herself in.

The others laughed as the water splashed up from the pool and the sight of Alice wearing her bikini top up around her neck from the impact. "Oops, forgot about that!" Alice laughed as she pulled the top off and threw it to her sunbed. "Oh it's wonderful in here," Alice declared as she swam around the pool; her sister Kelly decided to join her but preferred to walk in down the steps gently and it was not long before all four of them were enjoying the respite from the heat the pool afforded them.

One by one the girls returned to their sunbeds and dried off in the hot afternoon sun; they all heeded Emma's earlier words and applied plenty of sun cream before settling back under a little shade provided by the sun parasols.

Kelly said the wine she put in the icebox should be cold enough by now as it was already slightly chilled and asked who was up for a glass of rose; as expected, there were no refusals and so off she went to fetch the wine.

Returning a few minutes later, Kelly passed around the glasses of wine to the very appreciative girls. "That sun is getting seriously hotter," remarked Lacey as she pulled the shade over her a little more. Emma meanwhile was sat cross-legged on her lounger, combing through the various literature on the sights to be seen around Kalkan.

"Oh, this looks like a nice place to try for dinner tonight," she said excitedly as she passed over a leaflet showing one of the many rooftop restaurants in the town overlooking the harbour.

"Oh yes, doesn't it look fab, the place looks great all lit up, I am really excited about seeing it at night," Kelly said passing the leaflet on to Alice who smiled and nodded in agreement looking at the pictures.

"Can we all promise not to go too crazy tonight; after all, it's our first night and we don't want to spend all the next day suffering in bed and missing out on all the excitement," Emma asked the others in a pleasing way.

Kelly laughed and although she agreed with the sentiment, said she would do her best but pointed out she was here for fun and excitement so could not give any guarantees. Alice raised her glass in support. "I'll drink to that, sis," she giggled away.

The four friends spent the rest of the afternoon relaxing by and occasionally in the pool, regaining their vigour from the long journey and lack of sleep the previous night. It was around 5 pm that Emma said she was ready to go in to take a cold shower and a little nap in the coolness of her room before getting ready to go out later.

It wasn't long before all of the girls were in and getting ready for their first night on the town, music was blaring out from the sound system, drowning out the noise of the multiple hairdryers hard at work helping transform the young ladies into objects of desire. The girls fumbled through their wardrobes, looking for the ideal outfit for their first adventure into Kalkan night life. Alice, who was arguably the most sparkling jewel in the box, held up a pretty mini dress in front of the mirror and smiling, said to herself, "No, I don't think so; a bit too much of a statement for my first night," then proceeded to walk to her sister's room wrapped in a towel.

Knocking on her door before entering, she asked Kelly what she was thinking of wearing as she didn't want to glam up too much if the others were going casual; Kelly was sat at her dressing table wrapped in her towel and told her to do as she felt and not to worry about others, adding that she was going to stand out in anything she wore with her gorgeous figure and good looks anyway.

Alice laughed. "Aww thank you sis, but seriously, are you dress or shorts tonight? I can't decide."

"Dress for me I think, Al, that nice strappy one you like, not too bold and will help keep me cool."

"Don't want to overplay on the first night; leave them wanting more, eh kid?"

"That's exactly what I was thinking; oh my, we are so alike, aren't we?"

"Well, we are cut from the same cloth, sis, as they say."

Alice returned to her room gleefully smiling to herself as she knew exactly what she will wear; she headed to the wardrobe and selected a skirt with a coordinating blouse. Moments later, Lacey appeared at her door.

"You decent, Al, coming in?"

"Hey Lace, what's up?"

"I was wondering if you were going all out tonight or cas…but I can see from what you're holding, it's cas."

Alice laughed saying that she and Kelly had just had the very same conversation just as they heard Emma call out, "Hey everyone, what's the dress code tonight?"

Alice and Lacey were in unison, shouting back "CAS", then laughed together and once all the girls were ready, they gathered on the patio and Lacey suggested that they all have some shots while waiting for the taxi; they raised their vodka shots and toasted to a wonderful evening as Kelly said that she hoped they all had a wonderful night and wished them luck on finding some romance.

It wasn't long before they were arriving at the top of the old town, the area was bustling with holidaymakers, Lacey remarked how busy it was but the taxi driver said that this was quiet as it was only 7.20 pm; it was early, wait until later, he added, saying that the area would be packed.

The girls thanked the driver and made their way down the street they had walked up earlier that day, they all commented on how different and more appealing it looked at night. Many of the street side restaurants were getting busy; music blasted over head from various bars and the sound of cheering fans could be heard from one of the bars showing live football.

Many restaurant employees tried to entice the group into their restaurant with promises of the finest service and quality of food but the girls politely refused their advances and headed down the street to the old town. Lacey paused for a moment at the top of the old town itself as she checked the map for directions to the restaurant they had seen in the leaflet around the pool.

After several minutes of being dazzled by the beautifully lit shopfronts en route to their chosen restaurant and constant appeals from various other establishments to try their place, they arrived. They were greeted by a charming young man who enquired if they had a reservation; Lacey said she didn't realise they needed to book and apologised as the man said it was not a problem, he could fit them in as it was early.

The girls were led up a number of flights of stairs to the roof terrace where they were very warmly greeted by more staff and shown to their table. They all marvelled at the view across the rooftops; there were other restaurants in every direction you looked. Emma pointed out at the boats in the harbour all lit up and they all took pictures of the scene and each other.

A waiter approached them saying his name was Seckin and that he would be looking after them. He took their drinks order and left them to look at the menu. It wasn't long before Seckin returned with their drinks full of sparklers lighting up the table and bringing forth a lot of cheer and amusement from the girls and other diners alike.

They were quick to capture the moment on camera before raising their cocktails in a toast to themselves then sampling the wonderful creations they had ordered. Seckin soon took their food order and left them to chat amongst themselves as another younger waitress supplied them with some bread and a pre starter of some form of a patè mousse.

The girls appreciated the little taster as they eagerly tucked into it. "Do you realise, girls, this is the first thing we have eaten since breakfast apart from some nibbles around the pool?" Alice commented.

Emma agreeing said that she was a little apprehensive about taking the shots before coming out because of that very same reason and was happy now that they were getting something to eat. Kelly nodded in agreement adding that the heat can subdue your appetite and that they should make sure they drink plenty of water to avoid dehydration as she reached for the water and filled everyone's glass.

A smiling Seckin arrived soon after with their starters and the girls wasted no time in tucking in to them savouring and enjoying every mouthful; the conversation turned to what they should do after dinner and it was agreed by all that they should probably take a gentle stroll around the old town and allow their food to go down before finding a lively bar.

The main course was served and again eaten with much enthusiasm and appreciation and washed down with a nice glass of well chilled wine; at the end of the meal, they asked for the bill as they had no room for dessert but to their astonishment, a little sweet treat was given them anyway by a cheerful Seckin as he left the bill.

The girls thanked the staff for their service as they paid the bill and left the restaurant, making their way down towards the harbour and stopping off on their way to look into the shops as they were passing. Kelly commented on how beautifully lit the place was; brilliant white buildings shimmering in the golden shade of light brought out a magical quality in the place. There were many narrow alleyways leading off to other parts of the town to the left and right as they made their way closer to the harbour. Smiling faces greeted them at every doorway with a kind gesture of hands inviting them to enter within to sample all manners of ware, from carpets and rugs to t-shirts and mugs, ceramics and paintings were strewn across every available surface.

Having descended a number of steps, they made the harbour promenade just above the harbour itself, to the right there was a walkway strewn with bars and restaurants and to the left something similar. Emma commented on how lovely the nearest bar to them was having these large throne-like chairs all brightly coloured.

Lacey said they should go down and look at the boats and get some info on a day trip for themselves; everyone seemed happy with idea and so they progressed down to the lower tier and surveyed all the vessels that were available for day trips and private hire. Many of the boat owners called out to them offering to take them on a wonderful experience out in the bay. Emma was quick to spot a group of what looked like British men making arrangements to go on a trip on one of the boats. She nudged Alice. "Look over there, they look a bit of alright, don't they?"

Alice looked in the direction she was intimating and nodded in agreement, "Ooh yes, come on ladies, this way." She beckoned the others to follow her as she headed over towards the group of men.

Alice approached one of the men. "Hi, I wonder could you tell if the trips are any good?"

Kelly held her head in her hands wondering if that was the best line she could come up with. The man, a good-looking chap around mid-thirties, responded that they had been on the same boat last year and it was fantastic and so they were booking again to go out the day after next, he added that it was a good day out saying that they fed you well and entertained you as well.

Alice thanked him for the information and turned back to the girls and recommended that they book the same trip now in case it filled up. Kelly was watching the man Alice just spoke to return to his friends who were all laughing and gesturing to him as they all looked up in the direction of the girls.

"Bloody hell, they are all looking over here," Kelly whispered to her friends who in turn looked up in the direction of the men. "Don't look now; oh my god, they are all looking at us."

Emma said she wasn't complaining; "Nice to have some attention for once," she claimed; the men smiled back in the direction of the girls as they walked away.

"Right, come on, let's get this booked," Lacey insisted, marching them towards the young lady taking the bookings. "Hi yes, we would like to book four places please for the day after tomorrow if we can; that's um Tuesday, isn't it?" she asked.

"Yes that's right, ok thank you," replied the young girl then explained to them about the trip, what took place and what they should bring along with them and the time; once everything was paid and they had their receipt, the girls went on their way and started the climb back up the old town in search of a lively bar.

The girls stumbled upon a bar that was reminiscent of a Bedouin tent with large cushions to sit on and a lively atmosphere; they made their way inside and got themselves comfortable and ordered a round of drinks. Alice asked Kelly what she thought of the men they had just seen in the harbour; she answered laughing that she would have taken any of them as she was way past the stage of being too picky now; the others laughed, Emma giving her the thumbs up and adding that she couldn't agree more, she knew that feeling well, making the girls laugh even heartier.

Kelly had been divorced almost four years after her husband left her for someone else, she had two failed attempts at making a fresh start; both had cheated on her and left her feeling she had no hope. Emma was divorced 18 months ago after catching her husband cheating with a work colleague, she had a one-night stand and a two-week fling with someone she discovered was married so ended that and now, having gained two sizes, felt that maybe that was her lot.

Alice had been engaged for two years having already been together for four years then discovered he was seeing her best friend behind her back, he came home one day to find a huge bonfire of all his clothes and certain possessions in the garden and her gone, since then she had struggled to find anyone she could trust to start a relationship with so had thrown herself into her work as an office manager for a high-end company.

Lacey had been engaged since leaving university twice, both very different individuals with one common trait—untrustworthy; both cheated on her before they were engaged and she never discovered either until planning her weddings. Lacey had not dated seriously since even though she had had suitors because she found it hard to trust men; an attractive 33-year-old in her own right, she felt men just wanted her for her looks and the added bonus that she ran her own small business and had her own home.

The foursome sat and enjoyed each other's company, talking about all things under the sun and the conversation was occasionally broken when one of them alerted the others to the odd good-looking chap that passed them by. Lacey, who ran her own interior design business, enjoyed monitoring the outfits being worn by the more fashionable ladies passing by, sometimes being a little critical of the choice of the accessories they carry with them.

"Oh have a day off, Lace," Alice said, reminding her that she was on holiday now. Lacey just smiled back and nodded in agreement and acknowledged that Alice was right but said she found it hard especially when the outfit was so perfect. The night was moving on wonderfully and was approaching 10.30 pm when Emma suggested they move on elsewhere and so the girls thanked their hosts promising to return again sometime and moved on through one of the narrow streets where they were greeted by a charming bar owner who enticed them up to his rooftop bar.

The girls were shown to a table that was quickly cleaned and prepared for them; they were seated and given a menu to choose their drinks. Emma pointed out to the girls the cocktail bar at the rear where the mixologist was creating some amazing cocktails with fireworks and everything.

They all looked on in amazement as the waiter delivered the drinks to the customers who ordered them, the bar was full of light from the fireworks and sounds of gasps of approval from other customers. Kelly suggested that one of the large cocktail bowls for four to share looked good and it had everything in it; she said with relish, "Come on girls, let's go for it; sounds right up our street."

Emma enthused and the others agreed so they ordered their drinks, some minutes later with a fanfare of fireworks and appreciative applause all around, a large bowl arrived with a fish bowl of glass inside on ice filled with a wonderful cocktail and four straws.

The girls clicked away with their phone cameras eagerly, full of smiles and in awe at the creation; Lacey asked the waiter if it came with snorkel and flippers, causing the others to burst into laughter, the waiter replied that unfortunately not but he would be happy to dive in and rescue anyone if they should fall in.

He gave a cheeky grin and wink as he left them; Alice commented that there was hope for them yet before encouraging them all to get stuck in.

Sucking away on their straws, the girls enjoyed the delicious infusion of flavours of the cocktail, sitting back in absolute delight and satisfaction, Emma said that it was a great choice as her palate was alive with a symphony of sweet exotic flavours that she had not known before. Moments later, the owner came over to check on them and sat with them for a short time asking about their holiday and what they hoped to do in Kalkan.

He told them that he was known as Mussie and offered them a lot of suggestions as to what was on offer in the town; he also gave them recommendations for dining and where to book trips. Alice was quite taken by his tanned well-toned physique and good looks but was also aware that men in his position saw a lot of female holidaymakers throughout the season so kept her thoughts about him to a minimum.

The group were very appreciative for the kind attention he had shown them and thanked him saying they would highly recommend his bar to anyone they met as he got up to move on to another table. "Well, he was a bit of alright, wasn't he?" Lacey suggested. Alice agreed and shared her thoughts about him with the others and they all gave a disappointed nod of agreement.

"Right ladies, we are approaching the midnight hour, do we have a final one here or shall we find another place?" Emma asked, feeling really happy about the evenings events so far and ready for some fun. Kelly said that she was ok and felt she had drunk enough for one day then suggested that she may head back but was fine if the others wanted to carry on.

Lacey thought she had enough as well and that maybe a coffee on the patio in her nightie was the ideal end to a wonderful first day. Alice clutched Lacey's hand, giving it a little squeeze. "Yeah that sounds perfect, Lace, mind if I join you?" Lacey told her that would be fine as Emma interrupted with the fact that they could have their coffee but she would join them with a glass of wine. The foursome made their way down the stairs and out of the bar into the street where Mussie was talking to some people; they waved and thanked him as they made their way up the slope towards the taxi rank.

As they neared the taxi rank, a familiar voice called out to them, "Hello ladies, how was your evening?" It was Memhet the driver from earlier; he asked about their evening and if they needed a taxi. The girls happily told him about their night and said that they were now ready to return home; the driver led them to the front taxi and said that the driver was his cousin and that he would tell him where to take them as he was now off duty. Thanking him, the girls got in the taxi and returned to their villa.

Kelly told the others that she was ready for bed and said goodnight, giving them all a hug before she went and thanking them all for a great first day. Alice and Lacey sat with a coffee as Emma enjoyed a glass of wine on the patio all in their nightwear. Emma commented on how warm it was still as they sat looking out over the brightly lit Kalkan town; even the headland was lit up to a point. Soon the trio one by one said their goodnights and went to bed to dream about what tomorrow might bring on their holiday adventure.

Monday Day 2

Kelly awoke early the next morning as she had left her bedroom side window ajar through the night and the morning call to prayer from the town mosque aroused her from her sleep; she walked jadedly from her room to the kitchen to make some tea; everything was so still and almost silent except for the humming of the fridge and the faint snoring sound coming from one of the bedrooms. Kelly made herself some tea and gathering her robe went out onto the front patio, there was a pleasant coolness in a gentle breeze cutting through the morning warmth. Kelly could see the sun obscured mostly by the headland to the left start to rise, the faint noise of traffic occasionally passing by on the main road at the foot of the hill and the distant bark of a dog were the only sounds to be heard other than the odd bird twittering away. She sat there for some time pondering her life to date wondering what she could have done differently and whether it would have made any difference.

Kelly smiled to herself as she thought in her mind that the past was now behind her; she can't change that but her future was hers to decide and whatever happened or whoever she met whenever, it will be on her terms, it will be her decision as to how her future went. With a positive mindset, she got up to go and replenish her tea returning to the kitchen where she found her sister pouring out a glass of juice.

"Morning Al, how you feeling, did you sleep well?"

"Hey morning sis, yeah great thanks, that bed is so comfy. How about you, have you been up long?"

"Oh about forty-five minutes. I've been out on the patio watching the sun rise, it's so peaceful and relaxing here at this time."

"I'm making tea, want some?"

"No thanks sis, I will do with my juice thanks; are you going back out to the patio?"

"Oh yes, come and join me, maybe get your dressing gown there is a cool breeze out there at the moment."

The sisters sat together on the patio watching as the sun moved further into view, Alice asked what time it was and Kelly said it was somewhere after eight but she wasn't concerned about time; she just wanted to live for the moment.

Kelly confessed her earlier thoughts to her sister who agreed earnestly with the sentiment adding that all four of them were in the same boat and should adopt the same view. Emma soon joined them on the patio with a bottle of water in hand saying she had put the coffee machine on; she greeted them asking if they slept well and confessed that she should have not had that last glass of wine.

"Good morning girls" rang out as Lacey joined her friends saying kudos to the person making the coffee, what a lovely way to wake up she said, adding that she was like one of the bisto kids getting out of bed with her nostrils full of the scent of freshly brewing coffee; the others chuckled at her comment. Emma said she would organise coffee and asked who wanted a cup. Alice and Lacey raised an enthusiastic finger with big smiles.

While Emma was sorting the coffee, Lacey asked if there were any thoughts about what they should do that day, Kelly and Alice looked at each other shaking their heads answering that nothing had been discussed. Alice said that they should consider they were out on a boat trip tomorrow so suggested nothing too heavy.

Emma returned with the coffee and asked what was on the agenda, Kelly said they were thinking about what they should do that day considering they have a trip the following day.

"Yes good shout, we need to be tip top tomorrow, especially with a boat full of gorgeous hunks; the hungover look is not a good look for us girls, eh." The girls all laughed at Emma's comment.

Alice skipped off to the information table in the lounge where there were loads of brochures of places to go and an activity folder filled with ideas for spending a day in the area. Lacey found a section on the various beach clubs they could visit saying they had great facilities, restaurant bar and water sports and passed it around; all the girls thought that the one in particular looked good.

Alice grabbed her phone and rang to reserve four spaces saying they would be there around midday; when she gave the villa's address, she was told that they get VIP service staying there and told they would be collected and dropped back free of charge if they wanted; this delighted the girls and so they arranged a 11.45 am pickup.

Feeling excited at getting VIP treatment, the girls sorted out breakfast then got themselves ready for a beach club day out, before long their car arrived and whisked them off to the beach club. The foursome were full of smiles and anticipation as they were greeted and led to the sunbeds by a charming young man who explained about the club's facilities, rules and regulations before finally leaving them with a menu for drinks and snacks to be enjoyed on their sunbeds and a menu for the restaurant.

"Please, lovely ladies, anything you need, just wave to us over there and we will come to you. From time to time one of my colleagues if not myself will come by to check everything is ok with you and attend to your needs if you have any. Please enjoy a lovely day, thank you."

The girls thanked him as he walked away, Alice was quick to say she felt there were needs she had that he could attend to anytime, the girls laughed nodding in agreement as Kelly gave her sister a playful slap on the backside giving her an unconvincing look of disapproval, tut tutting as she did.

Once settled, the girls sat back on their sunbeds admiring the view out to sea and back to the town and harbour of Kalkan, they all in turn commented on how beautiful it looked and how lucky they felt to be there to enjoy it. A man appeared saying his name was Mesut and asked if he could get them anything refreshment wise; the girls quickly surveyed the menu and decided they would all start with a cold beer, Alice said she would maybe have some wine with dinner later but thought a few beers would be best way forward today given the conversation earlier at the villa.

Mesut returned with the drinks that were ice cold a short time later and asked how the girls were enjoying their holiday; Emma said it was wonderful saying what a great villa they had booked and how beautiful and friendly the place was, Mesut smiled nodding with great joy to hear this positive feedback and asked if they had been anywhere yet.

Alice said they had a boat trip booked for the following day, Mesut enquired on what boat and after fumbling in her purse, Kelly showed him the ticket. "Ah wonderful, this is my cousin's boat; you will have an excellent time I can promise you."

Mesut then asked if they were going to do a sunset cruise as the Kalkan sunsets were magical to see, the girls shook their heads saying they didn't know anything about it.

"Oh ladies please, you must, it is incredible, the boat anchors out there," Mesut pointed to a spot out in the bay, "then you sit in beautiful calm silence as you watch the sun get lower over the mountains while you drink your champagne. Then the magic happens as the sun meets the top of the mountain with a beautiful kiss and she melts into his heart as she brings her dark curtain down around us to shelter until she rises again in all her glory to love another day."

The girls sat silent, their jaws falling on their sunbeds almost. Emma reached for her stomach as butterflies filled her with a sensation that caused her to whisper to Alice, "Oh my, I think I just had a bloody orgasm," then laughed as Alice confessed she may have just wet herself, laughing away as she said it. Kelly was mesmerised saying how beautiful it sounded and told the girls it had to go on their list of things to do.

They thanked Mesut for the beautiful way he told it, he replied that it was his pleasure and pleaded with them to try it as he went back to work. Alice told Kelly and Lacey what she and Emma had said; to their great amusement, Lacey confessed to being moved by it.

The girls got comfortable and enjoyed soaking up the sun until again it started to get a little too hot. Alice asked if anyone fancied joining her for a dip in the sea, Lacey and Kelly were quick to their feet but Emma seemed away from it all, lost in another world of her imagination.

"What's up, Emm, everything ok?" Kelly asked.

Emma was slow to answer but just replied that she was dreaming about that sunset, how the sun kissed the mountain and melted into it, she said, "I was thinking how much I would love to be kissed under a Kalkan sunset and melt into someone's arms."

The girls looked back at her; silently all of them feeling a little moved by their friend's heartfelt words. Alice agreed that it would be wonderful as Kelly said, "Well, I would be happy just to be meaningfully kissed even if in the middle of a thunderstorm never mind under a magical sunset." Again the girls all laughed as Emma said that they should all get in the water and stop the daydream nonsense even though she knew that desire would dig deep into her to fulfil it.

The day out at the beach club had been a great success, the girls enjoyed a nice light lunch there with a few more cold beers and stayed until around half four before heading back to the villa, they tipped Mesut before leaving and thanked him again, promising they would go on the sunset boat trip.

Back at the villa, the girls were talking about that evening and their options. Lacey said she was pretty worn out after all that sun and beer adding that she was surprised how tiring it could be enjoying yourself. Kelly said that they had plenty to drink in the villa and that they could always order in pizza or something as she rummaged through the brochures looking for takeaway menus. Alice thought it a top idea and was happy to go along with the majority and had that seconded by Emma.

That evening, the girls spent the night in to save themselves for the boat trip the next day, they enjoyed a mix of southern fried chicken and pizza with salad and some well chilled wine then relaxed on the patio until bedtime.

Tuesday Day 3

The next morning, the villa was a hive of activity as the girls had breakfast and prepared themselves for their adventure out at sea. Lacey seemed to take charge ensuring they all packed everything they would need including change of swimwear and the necessities for a trouble-free trip. Kelly had arranged the taxi and by the time they were all ready, the taxi arrived.

"Good morning ladies, how are you?" beamed a happy looking Memhet. "So the boat trip today eh; you have perfect weather it will be wonderful I am sure."

The girls all smiled, greeting Memhet with a good morning and looking really enthusiastic for this trip as they got in the taxi, then Memhet drove them down to the lower harbour deck. Memhet wished them a good day and said he would be on all day if they wanted him later then waved them off.

The girls were queuing at the gangway when Lacey prodded Emma in the back and using her eyes encouraged her to look over her shoulder, there making their way towards the boat were the men they saw the other day.

Once on board, Emma suggested they went up front as that was probably where the men would go, the girls found themselves a suitable spot and began to get comfortable just as the men arrived laughing and whispering to each other, the girls were greeted with nods and mornings as the men moved amongst them.

Alice smiled at the one she had spoken to before and said they had taken his advice booking the trip, the man smiled back pleasantly saying good and that he hoped they enjoyed just as a female called out "John".

Alice looked out to where the voice came from to see a woman standing with her hand out gesturing for the man to come to her and beyond there were other women with the rest of the men who were making their way to one of the upper decks. Alice looked at the other girls who were all bemused at the sight before them. "Oh well, that didn't work out too well, did it," Kelly scoffed as she adjusted her towel.

"Well girls, we may as well make the most of it; we are here now so let's enjoy; when does the bar open?" Emma laughed.

It wasn't long before they were underway making their way out of the harbour one boat at a time, the captain welcomed everyone onboard and explained the itinerary for the day as they made their way to the first stop-off point. Everyone had their phones and cameras out capturing the glorious views back to the harbour and town. Once there, the anchor was dropped and the captain encouraged everyone to take a dip in the warm sea and suggested the best areas for snorkelling and viewing the sea life jut as a giant turtle passed by to everyone's delight.

There was a good number of people on board all enjoying the day. Emma noticed two men sitting on the deck just above and caught the eye of one of them who smiled pleasantly at her and nodded as he was getting ready to go into the sea. Emma was taken by surprise and shyly looked away. The trip gathered pace stopping here and there until it was lunchtime, everyone took turns to help themselves to the plentiful buffet on offer as the crew went around taking drinks orders.

Emma was helping herself to some food when she stumbled backwards into another passenger; it was the man who had smiled at her earlier. Emma apologised for her clumsiness but the man assured her there was no harm done. He was quite tall and well built like a rugby player, Emma thought him to be in his thirties and was good-looking to boot.

She hurried back to her friends to tell them of her encounter, Alice glanced up at the man who had just removed his vest to reveal a slightly tanned muscular physique, she agreed he was fit looking and with another man just as good-looking, she added. Kelly said she had noticed him looking Emma's way a few times that morning and jokingly suggested she should go and talk to him.

Emma wasn't so sure saying that she doubted he would be that interested in her, especially now as she had gained so much weight. Alice was quick to tell her that she was a beautiful girl and he, and any man come to that, would be lucky to have her—a sentiment that was rapidly supported by the others.

Emma had such low self-esteem since her last relationship split followed by her weight gain that she lacked the confidence to think anyone would find her attractive again. The girls sat and ate their lunch all of them monitoring the two men sitting above them on the first upper deck. Kelly whispered across to Emma that the one she spoke to had gone to the bar and to go get a drink and start a conversation; she had nothing to lose. Emma paused before putting on a sarong and made her way to the bar.

Emma stopped just short of the entrance down into the bar as she saw the man exit with a bottle of champagne in an ice bucket;, a crew member smiled at him and laughed out. "Oh champagne time, is it?"

Emma was stunned at the man's response, "Yes well, it is my honeymoon, after all."

The man didn't notice Emma standing there as he made his way back up the stairs, Emma trudged back to her spot, head bowed low in disappointment as the others looked up at her asking what was wrong. Emma responded with a hand gesture and mouthed the words 'he is gay' to them, they all looked at her in disbelief, mouths dropping open to the deck as Alice asked if she was sure and how she knew.

Emma sat down and all the girls gathered around her as she relayed what she had just witnessed, Kelly and Lacey looked up at where the men were sat as the sound of the cork popped out of the champagne. The two men laughed as the one poured out the champagne and then they chinked glasses.

Emma was deflated and the sounds of the two above laughing out loud and talking made her decide to take a dip in the sea against Kelly's advice as she had only just eaten lunch; without further ado, Emma launched herself off the deck into the sea and began swimming around.

Alice took out her phone and began videoing Emma in the water as she playfully moved around, two jet skis were just passing by rather fast and Alice shouted, "That's what we should get, Emm," pointing out the skis. Emma turned to look and was hit full in the face with the wash from the skis and unfortunately swallowed a large gulp of seawater, causing her to splutter somewhat before taking in another mouthful that hampered her breathing slightly and in turn led to her losing control and going under the water.

Alice screamed out in distress, "Emma, no Emma!" she screamed frantically as the helpless Emma splashed about furiously trying to catch a decent breath; the other girls rose to their feet quickly to see what was happening as a huge splash was seen as someone had dived in to Emma's rescue. Emma felt an arm around her waist as she was pulled up from below the water spluttering and coughing as she tried to rid herself of the seawater in her throat.

A voice told her that she was ok and that she was safe. "I have got you, don't worry, you will be fine, I won't let you go I promise," the reassuring voice told the slightly disorientated and distraught Emma as he pulled her towards the boat.

Two crew members had also jumped in to assist and helped get Emma back on board where her frantic friends waited for her with a towel and fresh water.

The Captain checked that Emma was ok and didn't need any medical assistance saying that she needed to drink plenty of fresh water and that she would eventually bring it all up. Her friends all gathered around her supporting her as she eventually threw up all that she had ingested and sat back feeling a little foolish creating all that commotion.

"How are you feeling now, any better?" a familiar voice sounded from above.

Emma looked up; it was him, he was the one that rescued her his voice so distinctive. "It was you, you're the one who saved me, aren't you"

"You gave us all a bit of a shock especially when your friend screamed out. I spilt my champagne," he laughed, "but you're ok yeah?" Emma nodded and confirmed that she was fine thanking him for his actions. The man smiled back at her saying that he was happy to have been able to help just as the other man almost mockingly patted him on the head telling him he was such a hero and deserved a medal. Emma didn't much appreciate his attitude and snapped that he was her hero and she would be forever grateful, he smiled back at her raising his glass thanking her.

The boat made another stop before afternoon tea was served, Emma was feeling much better now but didn't want to go back in the sea just yet so just lay there soaking up the sun recalling to mind the moment that man had his arm around her holding her tightly telling her that she was safe and he would never let her go. She glanced up through her sunglasses at where he was stood and saw him dripping wet drying himself down his rippling muscles dancing across his body as he wiped here and there.

Emma flung herself over onto her front in a huff thinking to herself that here was the perfect answer to the search for a wonderful man—good-looking, muscular and a hero to boot—and he was gay; she huffed away as she assessed that she was destined to be alone forever. Lacey asked Emma if she was sure the men were gay because she confessed that since the incident, she had hardly taken her eyes off the pair of them and that she had not seen anything about their nature or mannerisms that would suggest they were gay. She also pointed out that she hadn't seen them intimate with each other, Kelly supported Lacey on that point saying that it was odd, especially on honeymoon.

"Look, I was there. I heard him say quite clearly that he was on his honeymoon, do you see a woman with him? Anyway, look at that Welsh rugby player; he is muscular, fit and no one knew he was gay."

The day cruise came to an end and the boat headed back into port, the girls all agreed that apart from the disappointment early on and Emma's little drama, it had been a very enjoyable worthwhile trip, soon they were making their way ashore the captain and crew thanked them as they left, checking Emma was fine before she went.

Once ashore, the girls decided a stroll up the hill for a nice cocktail before taking a taxi home was what they would do and so made their way to a bar just down from the rank. As they approached the bar, Lacey spotted the two men from the boat and suggested they invite them for a drink to thank the one for saving Emma, Alice made a beeline for the pair and asked the hero if he and his husband would like to join them for a drink as a thank you.

The two men looked at each other in total bewilderment before bursting into laughter. "Husband, what the hell makes you think we are gay let alone married!" demanded the one as the other struggled to contain himself with fits of laughter. The other girls looked on in wonderment as to what was going on from the table they had taken in the bar, they watched Alice join in the laughter and questioned what was happening as Kelly said she would investigate.

Just as Kelly was about to make her way over to Alice, she and the two men walked towards where the girls were seated, all three still laughing. As the trio arrived at the table, Lacey asked what was so funny and so Alice told the girls the men were not gay and that the one who was named Gavin would explain all.

Once drinks were ordered, Gavin explained that he had been due to get married just over a week ago but he had split up with his partner of several years four months prior, he told them that they had planned to honeymoon there and booked and paid for everything from the villa, car hire, boat trips everything well in advance so decided to come out and enjoy it best he could and brought Jeremy, his best man, with him.

The girls sat there in disbelief. "Oh my, so it's not just us that suffer this; men do as well," Lacey commented. Emma confessed she was the one that started the gay assumption because of what she heard him say about being on honeymoon, Gavin laughed saying it was funny and not to worry adding that the trip with champagne was paid for so they were enjoying it and that he was making light of his situation.

Jeremy was paying a lot of attention to Alice and asked where they were staying, Alice gave a reasonably brief idea where their villa was high up on the mountainside. Emma asked where they were staying. Gavin quickly pointed over towards Kalamar bay area, saying it was a stunning villa, two bedrooms and great facilities adding it was only 10 minutes or so in a car or taxi.

As the group sat and chatted getting to know each other, Jeremy asked what the girls were up to that evening, they hadn't planned anything special other than coming into town for dinner and seeing how the evening went. Jeremy suggested they should come over to the Kalamar area as there was a restaurant with one of the best ratings in Kalkan having live music there tonight.

The girls looked at each other smiling and nodding as Kelly suggested nothing ventured nothing gained and so they agreed, Gavin produced a business card for the place saying he would book a table and asked if 8.30 would be ok adding that if they got there earlier, they could have a drink beforehand, they all agreed that was a good idea as Alice suggested they finish their drinks and return home to get ready.

Gavin stood up to leave just as Emma stumbled over a chair leg and fell his way; Gavin caught the startled Emma in his outstretched arms, grabbing a little bit more than he had bargained for. Rather embarrassed, he apologised saying he was acting on reflex; a slightly red-cheeked Emma just smiled assuring him it was fine, she looked into his eyes and said that it was the second time he had saved her that day to which he responded that he hoped it would earn him the first dance that night.

Kelly glanced at Alice with a pleasing smile and look, nodding in Emma's direction just as Jeremy said to Alice that even though he was not a hero that day, he hoped she would save him a dance later. With a big grin on her face, Alice said that she would see and beckoned the others to get a move on as they made their way over to the rank, telling the guys they would see them later.

Back at the villa, the girls were getting themselves sorted out for the evening ahead, the decision had been made that it would be full on glam night tonight as they now had a little bit of colour and they were itching to get into the new outfits they had brought with them. The foursome sat in the air conditioned lounge in their bathrobes painting their fingers and toes discussing what they were going to wear and their hopes for the evening.

Kelly told Emma that she thought Gavin was a real gentleman and that she got the impression he liked her, she asked her what she thought of the situation.

Emma was very dismissive of it saying that he was nice but didn't think he would be interested in her in a romantic way, Lacey told her to stop being so negative about herself as she was a beautiful girl and she believed Gavin could see that and the way he asked her to save the first dance for him that was so sweet, she added.

Alice laughed out agreeing with Lacey saying he even grabbed her boob, Kelly joined in laughing saying she agreed pointing out his embarrassment showed what a gent he was. Emma wasn't pinning her hopes on anything romantic happening but she couldn't deny the feelings of desire she had for him burning deep within her.

As the early evening progressed, the girls were on the verge of dressing when Emma appeared at Kelly's door. "Hey Kell, can you help me decide please? I can't choose between outfits." Kelly was happy to help her friend and went to Emma's room where she was shown two outfits—a dress and skirt with blouse.

"Definitely the dress, darling, you will slay him in that."

"You don't think it too desperate do you? I don't want to go overboard."

Kelly called out to the others to join them; they both agreed with Kelly the dress was killer making the best of Emma's curvaceous body and showing just the right amount of cleavage to keep them wanting more, Alice said.

The girls all gathered in the kitchen glammed up to the nines; they looked fabulous and took many selfies and group shots of themselves, Kelly poured out some shots and they toasted to a wonderful night ahead as they slung the shots back. Lacey said that it was almost certain that Emma and Alice were sorted for the night and suggested that if they wanted to carry on elsewhere later with the guys, they should do so and not worry about her and Kelly, that was agreed by Kelly and her earlier, she added that this holiday was about finding some magic back in their lives and they should not waste time or opportunities and asked the girls to agree.

Looking at each other, Alice and Emma rather timidly agreed, Alice looked at her sister for reassurance and was given it with a smile and nod, Kelly called Memhet, the taxi driver, to come and collect them soon as and before long they were on their way to the restaurant over on the Kalamar road, Memhet complimented the girls on looking so fabulous and wished them a wonderful evening before arriving at the destination.

The girls made their way into the venue and were greeted by a staff member who asked if they had reservations, Alice spotted the guys in the bar and said they were meeting with them as she pointed over. Gavin's face was a picture as he saw a nervous Emma walk towards him. Kelly looked back at her. "Wow, look at that for an expression of delight," she told Emma before telling her to relax and smile saying she looked gorgeous.

The two men stood up to greet the girls saying how wonderful they all looked, Gavin approached Emma with a beaming smile and a glint in his eye.

"Wow Emma, you look amazing, truly amazing! I knew when I saw you on the boat that you were pretty but wow, I was not expecting to see you this beautiful."

Emma felt weak inside with butterflies flying frantically all around her stomach, a tear started to form in the corner of her eye as she looked at Gavin and thanked him saying he must have something in his eye as she tried to offer a faint attempt at a laugh. Kelly heard his comment and felt a little moved by it herself as she smiled and winked at Emma; meanwhile, Jeremy offered Alice a seat and complimented her in his own way. "Well very nice, I must say you scrub up very nicely, don't you?" he said very approvingly as Alice in her elegant white trousers and black top stole the show with her shapely figure and ever so pert bottom that had all the males in the bar turning their heads.

The men arranged drinks for everyone as they sat around a table in the bar perusing the menu for dinner, Gavin spoke up saying how he wished he had two other friends as he was conscious of the situation and didn't want anyone to feel left out. Kelly put him at ease saying everything was as it should be and not to worry about it.

All six sat at a table in the restaurant close to the bar where the entertainment would commence around 10 pm, Jeremy said it was the best table as most of the bar will be used for the band and dancing then asked the girls if they liked Jazz. They all responded differently but were of the consensus that they were out to enjoy themselves whatever.

Dinner was started and they all sat chatting to each other and often Emma would be cornered by Gavin who wanted to know everything about her and paid her great attention and often signs of affection that didn't go unnoticed by her, it made her feel special again something that she hadn't known for some time, the food as promised was the finest they had enjoyed in Kalkan so far and the evening was going in a wonderful direction.

It wasn't long before the band started to warm up and the compere came out to announce them and asked people to get up and dance if they felt so inclined, the warm evening air was filled with cheers and applause to the music as people wined and dined the night away and some threw some jazzy moves on the dance floor.

Gavin stood up and, offering his hand to Emma, asked her to dance; the other girls clapped and cheered as Emma accepted, they all enjoyed watching the couple move across the dance floor laughing and smiling at each other as they danced away. They were soon joined by an enthusiastic Alice and Jeremy who made for good watching as both were good movers and made a handsome couple; as the night moved on Kelly and Lacey sat watching the others dance away and were approached by two men who looked to be a lot older than themselves.

The one man smiled pleasantly at them offering a "good evening ladies" the man behind him smiled pleasantly and asked if they would like to join them on the dance floor and as he was about to introduce himself and his friend to the pair, Kelly had leapt to her feet telling Lacey to get up and thanked him as he led her to the dance floor. Emma nudged Alice and pointed across the floor at the girls, they both smiled seeing them up dancing with smartly dressed slightly older men and seemed to be having fun.

Kelly was happy to be up enjoying a dance with a man instead of having to share the floor with Lacey; it made her feel more included in the event going on; Lacey on the other hand wasn't overly bothered.

"Hi I'm Matt, what's your name?" The man asked Kelly, she introduced herself and asked him how he was enjoying Kalkan.

"Kalkan is wonderful. I have been coming for years, I've had my own holiday home out here now for seven years and been coming for about twenty."

"Oh wow, twenty years! This is my first time," Kelly replied.

"So how you finding it; have you been bitten by the bug yet?" he laughed.

"I'm not sure I've been bitten but it is a beautiful place and this is my first week so we will have to see."

The music got a little louder and the mood was faster, making it difficult to talk. Matt gestured if Kelly would like a drink and accepting, he led her off the dance floor. Lacey was sat back at the table with Matt's friend who was called Giles and they had been joined by the other four, Kelly introduced Matt to the others and in turn was introduced to Giles who asked if anyone minded if they joined their table.

Everyone seemed pleased with the idea and Matt asked a waiter to bring the chairs from his table so they could all sit together, once sat they all tried to chat amongst themselves but it was difficult with the music blaring out so close to them but it made for some amusement when things were misheard and taken out of context.

Soon the music slowed down and softened, Gavin looked longingly at Emma smiling as he did and asked in a gentle tone if she wanted to dance, then taking her hand led her again to the dance floor to join other couples who were dancing up close to each other. Gavin put his arms around Emma and pulled her in close as she wrapped her arms around him.

Emma laid her head on his chest and was totally immersed in the moment of feeling appreciated, wanted and even feeling echoes of love. They swayed gently side to side to the music; her hands moved over his shoulders and she could feel every ripple of his muscular frame as they slowly made their way down his back.

Alice and Jeremy had joined them on the dance floor and were happily smooching away whilst chatting and laughing together, Kelly and the others looked on with approval, Kelly told Matt about earlier on the boat how they met the two boys and he was surprised as they looked like a couple that had been together a while and looked to be very much into each other.

Emma and Gavin shared a few more slow dances until it was announced that the band was finished and they re-joined the others, Giles had taken the liberty of ordering more wine for the table and they all sat there enjoying the warm night air laughing and joking. Lacey had everyone laughing when she recounted the story from earlier when Emma was convinced that Gavin and Jeremy were married and on honeymoon together; Matt and Giles applauded Gavin for his heroics saving Emma in the sea.

Emma defended herself saying she saw a man with a bottle of champagne telling someone he was on honeymoon sitting with another man, she asked what was she supposed to think. Matt agreed that would cause similar rationale in most of them in all honesty. Jeremy blurted out it could have been worse as they were going on the romantic sunset cruise tomorrow afternoon; champagne and all that followed by a candlelit dinner at a hotel that overlooked the town and harbour.

The table burst into laughter. Matt argued that would definitely raise an eyebrow or two, Emma looked at Gavin and asked, "You're doing the sunset cruise tomorrow, are you?"

Gavin smiled back saying yes as it was one of the things prebooked and he didn't want to waste the money.

"Why don't you come and join us; it will be fun and maybe we won't get so many funny looks from others?" he asked her excitedly. Emma wasn't sure and as she looked up across at Alice, she could see her nodding and making eyes at her to say yes. Emma looked at the others as Jeremy suggested that all the girls should join them. Gavin laughed. "Oh no, sorry mate, I was going to dump you and take Emma instead." The others joined in the laughter as Gavin said that he was joking and agreed that all the girls should join them.

Kelly commented that they had intended to do the trip at some point so why not do it tomorrow, Gavin said that he would make arrangements in the morning for the extra places and Lacey insisted that they would reimburse him for the tickets. Kelly and Emma went to the bathroom where they discussed the evening so far, Emma said that she was still finding it hard to accept that Gavin was into her and confessed that she would love for something to come of it but it was their first day and they knew nothing about each other.

Kelly said that she thought he was a genuine guy and didn't strike her as a rogue type that would hurt her, she said just watching the way he looked at her and his body language suggested that she may be pleasantly surprised. Jeremy said he wanted a cigarette; he had given up but enjoyed the odd one especially when out enjoying himself and managed to cadge one off a chap on a nearby table before walking out into the street to smoke it, Gavin took the opportunity to ask Alice about Emma saying that he felt she was a little unsure about herself, lacking confidence he thought.

Alice gave Gavin a very brief history of Emma's former husband and what he had done and said she found it hard to trust men, her last encounter had turned out to be married, she added. Alice pointed out that Emma had gained some weight the past year and that wasn't helping her self-esteem, she said, "You can see she is an attractive woman, a very pretty face but she is not happy with her newfound curvy figure."

Gavin was a little surprised; he said he thought she was perfect and that her curves did her proud, Alice asked him if he was really interested in her and he said honestly that he had not come away looking to find any romance, he said that his ex had hurt him deeply and not unlike Emma, had trust issues but he felt good in her company.

Just then Emma and Kelly returned as did Jeremy who asked what the topic of conversation was about, Gavin laughed. "Oh nothing really, we were just talking about idiots that smoke."

Jeremy just responded "oh ha ha" and gave him a funny look. Alice said that he was only joking and that it was about nothing special, Lacey was engrossed in talking with Giles who turned out to be an accountant and was busy discussing her business situation with him as Matt returned from the gents asking if anyone was up for a nightcap as his villa that was less than a 10-minute walk away from where they were and well stocked.

Jeremy was first to say the idea sounded great and was quickly supported by the others and so they all finished up their drinks and followed Matt back to his villa. "There is a little bit of a climb ahead, ladies, I hope your shoes are up to it," Matt said rather apologetically.

The sight of the villa raised a few eyebrows amongst the girls as they looked at each other with looks of surprise and amazement, they walked through the security gates and up the steps to the side door marvelling at the beautiful frontage of the property.

"Do you actually own all this?" Lacey asked with a sense of amazement in her voice, Matt just laughed and said that he did adding that he had worked very hard in his life for it. Giles jumped in on the conversation saying that although he couldn't deny Matt's years of hard work as a property developer, he felt the sizeable chunk of inheritance his father left him helped out a lot.

Matt, although nodding in agreement, wasn't too happy with Giles' chipping in with that comment and gave him a funny look to let him know. Giles responded putting his hand on Matt's shoulder and saying, "Come on, it was only a joke." Matt just nodded with a telling glance.

Once inside, the girls gushed with praises for the look of the place as it was a dream pad, beautifully fitted out and decorated, Matt led them up a flight of stairs then out onto a balcony that had its own built in bar and plush seating area. Matt pointed out where to find the bathrooms before getting behind the bar and attending to everyone's drink requirements.

Gavin and Emma sat with their drinks on a comfy sofa at the front of the balcony, Gavin said that the view must be amazing during the daytime as all they could see was the tops and outlines of the buildings below in the foreground and the beautiful lights of the town and headland out to the left.

As the rest of the group settled together laughing and talking, Gavin asked Emma if she was comfortable sat there alone with him as her body language caused him a little concern, Emma smiled and assured him she was ok but confessed that she was finding it hard to accept that anyone would want to show any interest her. Gavin asked her why she had so little confidence in herself as he thought she was an attractive woman with a great personality.

Emma laughed. "Really Gav, you honestly think that, well, you're a rarity, I must say," she said unconvinced.

Gavin was unsure how to respond; he recalled the conversation with Alice earlier but didn't want to let on he knew anything about her past so just commented, "Boy, someone has done a number on you good and proper, haven't they?"

Emma replied he had no idea but Gavin said that he probably did as he was hurt very badly recently himself, Emma apologised saying it was a little insensitive of her; she wasn't thinking due to the amount she had probably drunk that night. Gavin said it wasn't a problem and asked if she wanted to share stories, Emma said ok and asked him to go first.

"Well, where to begin, her name was Jess," he started and then went on to tell Emma how they had met several years ago at a country fayre show, he told her that Jess was into horses and was helping show some farm horses with a friend of hers. Gavin explained that his family were farmers of six generations in south Gloucestershire and often showed cattle at the fayres, he added that he was one of four brothers the youngest in fact and that he and his next brother helped run the farm whilst the two much older brothers had a veterinary business. Emma looked surprised she said she had never thought him a farmer, she said he looked more like a professional rugby player.

Gavin laughed and nodded saying that he had been a rugby player some years back but had to give up, with so much work on the farm as his father was getting on he and his brother Luke had to take on more responsibility.

Gavin told Emma how he and Jess met at the fayre saying it was love at first sight, she was from the Cheltenham area and worked in IT. Gavin said she was beautiful, intelligent and great fun to be with.

"So where did it all go so wrong?" Emma asked.

"To be honest I am not sure, I thought everything was going great; we came out here for our first holiday, we came here four times in our six years together. The last time we came was a little over a year ago and that's when I proposed."

"Oh right and you never suspected anything then?"

"No nothing, she was over the moon, she rang home immediately all excited to tell her parents and it was her idea to come here for the honeymoon."

"Can I ask when or how you erm…parted ways?"

"Yes it was back end of April this year, Jess had landed a top job with a big company a few months before we came out last time, it was based in Cheltenham and I suppose when I look back on it, I shouldn't have been so blind. Her company had a Christmas party that we were due to go to staying overnight and all that but the day before my brother Luke was struck down with the same bug my father was suffering with, so I had to look after the farm and couldn't go and I couldn't ask her not to, so she went alone."

"Oh right, I am not sure I need ask what happened next."

"Yes, although I never knew straight away, I was blinded by my love for her I suppose you could say but it came out in the end; she apparently hooked up with one of the senior managers; a one-off fling she claimed at first but she said he offered her a life of living in a luxurious house in the elite part of Cheltenham with great future prospects."

"She compared that to the thought of living on a working farm miles from anywhere and anyone else, it made her rethink what she wanted out of life and decided that it wasn't going to be on a farm."

Emma could not help feel for him as she knew very well the heartache of losing someone you were very much in love with and thinking that your future was all sorted only to have it ripped away.

Gavin explained how the day after his proposal, they went about planning ahead for their honeymoon out there, he said that the rest of their holiday was spent going around looking at places and sites for ideas of things to do.

"She was so excited about it agreeing there and then to book and pay for the villa, the boat trips, even a champagne candlelit dinner at that lovely hotel overlooking the town and harbour."

Gavin broke into laughter as he said that he thought he came out with more vouchers for things than actual money. "Seriously, apart from some meals and drinks, everything was paid for upfront, I have a folder full of all the vouchers and receipts," he scoffed, shaking his head almost in disbelief.

Emma laughed and added that there was nothing like being prepared. "She was very organised I must say, I remember still organising things for my wedding right up to the day before."

Emma asked him how he was coping with it all saying that for her finding out her husband's betrayal ripped the heart out of her and that she went downhill rapidly.

Gavin said that at first he was distraught and felt humiliated by it, he said he and his brother Luke fell out as he blamed him for getting sick being the cause of everything. He went on to say his eldest brother Harry pulled him to one side one day and laid out some home truths that Jess would have probably left him at some time being the way she was, saying she had shown her true colours in doing what she did and that it was better for all that she did it before they were married rather than later. He also pointed out that if they had had children, how much worse it would have been. "I love my big brother; he really helped me get through it, it was he who suggested I didn't waste the honeymoon money and come out and enjoy it and send Jess a postcard telling her what an amazing time I'm having."

"Are you having an amazing time, Gav, really?" Emma asked him looking at him sympathetically.

Gavin responded honestly saying that he wasn't, he said that as much as he put a brave face on it, the reality was very much different, he said that he and Jeremy were doing things he should be doing with the love of his life and that it just was not the same.

"Don't get me wrong, Jez is my best friend, has been for years; we talk about anything and everything, there is nothing I can't share with him, hell he was the person I called first after Jess gave me the shove. I guess I came out here thinking that enjoying what Jess had mostly paid for would give me some kind of payback but it hasn't, it has been a silent nightmare that I can't express openly, I have hated every minute of it almost."

"Almost, what do you mean by almost?"

"Well, I met you, didn't I, and you kind of lit a little spark back into me, I know we have only just met but you make me want to smile and feel a bit better about myself. Oh I'm sorry, have I gone down the old corny road with this?"

Emma laughed and gave Gavin a reassuring rub on his shoulder as she shook her head smiling at him. "No don't be silly, you are quite a sensitive person under all that muscle and brawn, aren't you?"

"Oh he is not being a boring old soppy git, is he?" the voice of Jeremy sounded from behind them as he approached to replenish their wine with a bottle in hand.

"No, quite the opposite actually, he was telling me about how he and Jess split."

"Really, look, I've told him countless times no one wants an ugly farmer with a dick the size of a maggot." Jeremy laughed out loudly even Gavin smiled as he shook his head in disbelief at his friend's comment.

Having refilled their glasses, Jeremy said that he was sorry for the comment as he hugged his mate from behind saying that he would always love him if no one else would, ruffling Gavin's hair as he stood to walk away laughing.

"You will have to forgive my friend, Emma, I'm sorry but he has always been one to speak his mind, he means well but sometimes his choice of vocab can be a little off if you know what I mean. I will say one thing for him though; for all his lesser qualities there is no other I would want by my side in times of trouble; he is a true and solid friend."

"Well, that's an endorsement of friendship if ever I have heard it, he is definitely the livelier of you two and as you say not afraid to say what he wants."

Gavin smiled at Emma as he recalled a time in the summer some years back when all his college mates and some girls were meeting up at a pub by a river in their area, he said that he had been working in the fields when he got a call from Jeremy saying he was on his way to collect him and went on to say that he rushed inside, had a quick wash of face and hands and changed his top as Jeremy pulled up.

"Well, I ran out of the house quick as I could and jumped into his car that he was revving up fast smiling and laughing as he did before spinning the wheels and pulling away, well, we hadn't gone 100yds and he slammed on the brakes and looked at me saying, 'Mate, you bloody well stink.' He spun the car around and drove back to the house, ordering me to shower as quick as possible before we could leave."

Emma held her hand to her wide open mouth as she gasped in disbelief. "Oh my gosh really, haha," she laughed.

A smiling Gavin nodded. "Yes really," he replied. "That's when you know you have a real friend, when they are not afraid to tell you when you stink." The pair sat there enjoying the moment and it didn't go unnoticed by the others who were sat across the patio behind them.

Kelly smiled, seeing her friend enjoying herself and said, "Well, those two seem to be getting on well together; maybe the start of a holiday romance," she raised her eyebrows at the other girls as she rubbed her hands together.

"Well, she could do with some good in her life at the moment," Lacey commented nodding in agreement with Kelly's observation.

Giles asked if Emma had some situation going on and Lacey just said that she had been through a few years of heartache and betrayal that has left her with low self-esteem with a bleak outlook for the future.

"Oh poor girl, that's no good, can we do anything to help brighten up her holiday, give her a bit of a lift?" Matt asked with genuine concern.

"I may be wrong but I think she may have found just the thing to brighten up her life and in doing so, pull my mate's head out of his butt hole at the same time," Jeremy added to the scenario.

Kelly said that she hoped that he was right and that Gavin wasn't going to be another let-down for her, Jeremy was quick to his friend's defence saying that Gavin was a good bloke with a big heart who knows what it was like to be messed about and that he didn't have it in him to be unfaithful or untrustworthy. Alice joined in saying that she thought Gavin was a decent guy, pointing out that after all he was a hero diving in to save their friend. The other girls laughed and raised their glasses in turn to acknowledge the fact.

Kelly said that they were all out there looking for something to put that magic back into their lives, she said they had all suffered breakups of a sort in the past; they had all been cheated and mistreated in various ways.

"It is difficult finding the right person for you, someone you truly believe you can trust who will be loyal and faithful through thick and thin," Kelly echoed as she had a melancholy moment drifting deep into thought.

"When you have been betrayed, really let down, then the barriers spring up forcing you behind them and even though you can access the button easily to drop them there is always something to hold you back, something unseen that keeps you just far enough back to prevent you experiencing more hurt and who knows maybe you are being kept away from your true soulmate."

"Whoa, that was deep, Kell, true I know what you mean but deep," Alice commented.

Matt and Giles looked at each other, Matt puffing out his cheeks then saying that it sounded like they had all been through the wars but now they were on holiday and that they should put it all behind them and enjoy themselves.

"Yes come on, Kell, we said before we came out, no mentioning the past; we live for the future," Alice reminded her sister with the backing of Lacey.

Giles asked Lacey what her plans were for the following day and she said they hadn't arranged anything for the morning but were doing the sunset cruise later in the afternoon then would go for dinner later.

"Oh yes, the sunset cruise, I remember it being mentioned earlier and what about your friends Emma and Alice, will they be joining you for dinner or out with the lads?"

"Well erm, I'm not really sure, we haven't discussed that and to be honest, I have not even given it a second thought."

"Oh well, I don't wish to jump the gun here but I was wondering if Alice and Emma were going to leave you and Kelly then perhaps maybe we could take you out for dinner, there is a wonderful little restaurant just out of the town only five to ten minutes away just off the bend of the road; it has the most wonderful setting that is above the shoreline views out to sea better in the daylight I must say but nonetheless very pleasant at night with great home-cooked food."

"Right well, that sounds very nice and all that but I am not sure what is happening yet, I will have to check with the others."

"One for the road anyone, it is almost 1.30 am and I have a rather nice brandy for a nightcap if any one fancies one," Matt offered.

Jeremy said he would gladly join him for one as did Giles but the girls declined.

Matt went over to check with Gavin and Emma but they both declined thanking him for the offer, Emma commented on how the time had passed by so fast saying that she was enjoying the night and Gavin's company.

"Gavin, I really hope I can make a difference to your time out here I mean it really but please don't say or do things just too make me feel good about myself. I would appreciate your honesty."

"Emma, I promise you from the first moment I saw you on the boat, I couldn't stop looking at you, watching the way you organised your towel and the others and then the way you rifled through your bag looking for stuff was so comical it warmed me towards you. I watched you swimming in the water; I thought to myself that you looked so peaceful and happy, then I looked away to grab a drink and heard Alice scream out. I couldn't get in the water fast enough."

Emma felt the same butterfly moment she had experienced earlier that evening as she felt her throat slightly tighten and a little light headiness. Gavin's heart felt words truly struck home with Emma stirring feelings inside that had been silenced for so long, she took a deep breath as she fidgeted away with her hands whilst she sensed a tear or two form in her eyes.

"Oh Emma, you ok, was it something I said? I'm sorry if I've upset you somehow."

Kelly looked across Emma's way, a little concerned having slightly overheard Gavin and sensing her friend's unexpected distress and the body language of Gavin. Kelly arose to go over but halted seeing that Gavin was happily smiling at Emma and things seemed ok.

Emma told Gavin that was one of the nicest things anyone had said to her in a very long time and after the trauma she had been through of late it was just too good to be true and caught her by surprise, again she thanked him for his kind words still wondering if he was genuine.

Gavin asked how long Emma was in Kalkan for and she said she was in her first week and not going home until Saturday week; she asked Gavin the same and he replied that he was going home in a week on the Wednesday. He explained that the wedding had been planned for the Saturday and as they were having a late wedding, they couldn't make the Saturday flight so booked the Wednesday after instead.

"Well, I hope you feel the same, Emma, but personally, I would like to spend as much of the next week getting to know you better, I don't want to come between you and your friends but I know I want to see as much of you as possible; what do you think?"

Emma's pulse raced at the wonderful things she was hearing, she paused for breath before agreeing with Gavin, saying how nice that would be but she would need to speak to the girls first.

Gavin beamed a huge smile back at her promising that together he was sure they could blot out the past hurts and move forward with their lives and really enjoy this holiday; Emma said she hoped so whilst still harbouring a little doubt; the barriers were definitely falling slightly but were nowhere near down yet.

Kelly had arranged for a taxi with Memhet a few minutes earlier and it had arrived, she waved down from the balcony to the driver that they were on their way as she summoned everyone to gather their things together. Saying their goodbyes to each other with pecks on the cheek, they all thanked Matt for his hospitality and said they hoped to see them again soon. Giles gave Lacey his business card saying to call him for dinner tomorrow if things go the way he suggested earlier.

Jeremy had arranged a time to meet the girls the next day for the sunset trip at the bar they met earlier, Gavin walked down the path with Emma saying how much he looked forward to seeing her the next day as Emma agreed smiling back and thanking him for a lovely evening. There was passion welling up inside her eager to explode with such ferocity, oh how she yearned for him to take her in his arms and kiss her. Prying eyes looked out of the taxi window hoping and waiting for that magical moment, and as they wished each other goodnight, Gavin bent forward, all heartbeats stood still for a moment in the taxi with great expectation only to beat sadly again as he kissed Emma on the cheek.

The taxi pulled away with Gavin and Jeremy waving them off, Emma sighed saying she thought she was going to get a really nice big kiss goodnight as Memhet looked at her in the rear-view mirror asking her why she was so sad.

"He looked like a nice man, you like him I think yes?"

Emma could only nod with a disappointed look on her face wondering if her thoughts of doubt had any relevance here.

"Then I think, young lady, you are in luck, I watched this young man, he is gentleman I think yes very much, when did you meet him?"

Kelly stepped up saying they met on the boat that day and explained how and then said about going for dinner and back to Matt's place.

"There you are, if he is not gentleman you have no, umm what you say here in the throat," Memhet pointed to his throat saying doctors take out if bad.

Alice roared out with laughter. "TONSILS!" she exclaimed.

"Exactly; if he is no gentleman tonight, you have no tonsil," Memhet laughed asking if she understood.

Emma was in fits of laughter with everyone else and nodding in agreement. Alice commented that would only work as well as that in a Turkish taxi, just would not be as funny back home.

It was just after 2 am when the girls arrived back at their villa, Memhet said they were his last call and he was going home, he said he would be back on midday next if he was needed and wished them all goodnight.

Lacey said that it had been a day to remember, even though it was so late she felt full of energy but knew the morning would probably tell her something different.

Once inside the villa, Kelly said she fancied a cup of tea before bed and Alice along with Lacey decided to join her, Emma happily settled for a bottle of very cold water.

"So Emma, everything was looking very cosy over on the edge of the balcony with you and Gavin, so come on, spill girl, tell us all what's the score there then?" Alice smiled with a quizzical look on her face.

"Oh well, we talked about his breakup with his fiancée at first and then he told me some things about Jeremy…"

Kelly interrupted, "Oh come on now, Emm, it looked pretty intense at times from where I sat; there must be more to it than that, come on girl tell all; you know we will find out eventually, don't you?"

"Well, he did say he liked me and that he thought me attractive."

"And why wouldn't he?" Lacey commented with assurance in her manner.

"He gave me butterflies and a feeling of umm…" Emma paused searching for the right words to describe how she felt as all the girls sat on the edge of their seats with their tea firmly clutched in their hands awaiting Emma's next sentence with bated breath.

"A feeling of what, Emm, tell us," Kelly asked with great urgency as the others nodded in agreement with an expectant look etched across their faces.

Emma smiled before continuing and with a faraway expression said, "Excitement I suppose, you know of what might happen between us, as I looked into his eyes I just wanted him to grab me and kiss me so I would know it was real. Does that sound stupid?" she asked her friends, looking for a supportive response, the others were momentarily silent as they gazed at each other, all sporting affectionate smiles and looks of approval.

"No not at all, Emm," was the emphatic response from them all in turn, they were all really happy for her and said that they hoped he would be what she has been looking for even though they have only just met.

Emma expressed her disappointment at not getting a proper kiss at the end of the night with an air of sadness until Lacey had them all laughing saying that at least she still had her tonsils.

"And what about you, Alice, how did you get on with Jeremy, now he would get into your pants in a flash given half a chance!" Kelly laughed looking at her sister raising her eyebrows as she did.

"Well, there is no chance of that happening, I can assure you, well, not any time soon that's for sure." Alice giggled, adding, "Jeremy is a typical man's man, a player even, don't get me wrong he has qualities—good-looking, well-b~~ a little too cocky at times, perhaps needs to think a little more before speaki~~ you know what I mean."

All the girls nodded in agreement, sighing with the odd yes of acknowledging the type of guy they all knew too well. Lacey asked if she would snog him and Alice was quick to give a positive yes in answer adding that he looked to have a very kissable mouth.

The girls sat there for another ten minutes deciding a lazy morning and lunch by the pool would be good in the morning to recuperate for what was promising to be a good late afternoon and evening later; slowly, they got themselves up wishing each other a goodnight before going to bed.

Wednesday Day 4

The next morning, all was silent in the villa as the girls lay in their beds, the shutters on the windows hid the brilliant sunlight that was beating down on the resort outside. Alice was first to stir as she stretched out her body in the comfort of her bed, running her fingers through her hair and gently rubbing her eyes as she then sat up, yawning out loud.

Gingerly rising from her bed, she made her way to the window where she opened the blinds, the shock of sunlight bursting through causing her to shield her eyes away was intense as was the heat she felt opening the window.

Alice glanced down at her watch on the bedside table. "Oh my gosh, it's 9.45 am already," she uttered as she made her way out of the bedroom and to the kitchen. After setting up the coffee machine, Alice made her way to her sister's room and opening the door gently peered inside whispering, "Are you awake yet?" There was no response as she made her way over to Kelly's bed.

Kelly was sleeping on her front as Alice cuddled up to her on the bed putting her arm around her and again asking if she was awake. "Morning sis, what time is it?" Kelly mumbled out.

"It's almost ten and no one is up," Alice replied.

"Coffee. I need coffee, lots of coffee," Kelly groaned as she turned over.

"Coffee is on, Kell, won't be long, should I wake the others do you think?"

"Nah leave them; they will get up when they are ready, how's weather outside today?" Kelly asked jokingly, knowing full well this time of year it was usually full sun everyday as it was one of the first things she had checked before deciding to come here. Alice smiled walking over to the window to open the blinds saying it was the usual rain, wind and thunder as every day, then she let the sunlight burst in to fully illuminate the room as Kelly pulled her blanket over her head.

Alice said she would go and sort out the coffee and met Emma on her way to the kitchen. "Morning Emm, how you doing?"

"Morning Al, oh yeah I'm ok all good, can't believe I slept so late; how long you been up?"

"Oh not long, I put the coffee on and just went to wake up Kell."

The girls set up the cups ready and just as the coffee was ready, they were joined by a sleepy yawning Lacey, "Hey girls. Kudos to the coffeemaker; just what I need right now."

Alice and Emma greeted Lacey and as the coffee was being poured out, Kelly joined them. "Morning ladies, how we doing, what a night eh can't believe we have all slept in so late," Kelly said scratching her head and yawning.

The girls sat drinking their coffee and Kelly said that they had better get a move on if they were to get any sun before going out later, Emma asked what time were they meeting Gavin and Jeremy and Alice said it was arranged for around 4.30 pm at the latest.

Kelly looked at Emma and asked her almost teasingly if she had sweet dreams about Gavin and was she excited to see him later, Emma rather shyly just said no unfortunately and then gave a positive yes to the second question.

With coffee out of the way, the girls got themselves comfortable around the pool all of them oiled up they sat planning the night ahead.

Lacey asked Emma if she thought that Gavin might invite her and Alice to join him and Jeremy later, Emma said that she had no idea and that it had not even come up in conversation.

Emma asked Lacey why and Lacey responded by recalling what Giles had asked her about her and Kelly joining them for dinner if she and Alice were going out with the lads.

Kelly responded that it was news to her and enquired why she hadn't said anything earlier, Lacey explained it was very last minute last night and with the taxi and tonsils and all, she had forgotten until now.

That comment brought smiles to everyone's face remembering the trip home last night with Memhet, Alice asked Lacey if she fancied Giles and Lacey replied that he was good-looking for an older man but she really couldn't see anything between them. Alice then turned to her sister. "Well, what about you, did you fancy Matt, sis, I mean him not his obvious wealth," she laughed with a big grin on her face.

"I think he is an attractive man who obviously has looked after himself, but like Lace, I can't see any romance there but I'm happy to enjoy his company, especially as he is someone who respects women and knows how to treat them."

Alice couldn't help but agree she said that the pair were very decent, well-spoken and educated, she pointed out that they had helped make the night finish on a high.

Lacey said she was feeling hungry and asked about everyone else, the others said that they were all thinking about breakfast although it were nearer to lunchtime, Kelly commented.

Lacey said that there was plenty in the fridge, especially a large tray of eggs so offered up scrambled eggs with what she could find to go with it, Emma offered to help and went in with her.

A short while later, Emma and Lacey appeared with the food, scrambled eggs, tomatoes and mushrooms and a shed load of toast, Alice and Kelly were very appreciative of the gesture thanking them both as they all sat cross-legged on their sunbeds devouring and savouring their food.

The early part of the afternoon passed by slowly with the girls relaxing and resting in the sun, only getting up for some light refreshment or the bathroom.

Soon enough though, they were getting ready for their boat trip, Emma was very conscious of what she would wear, she didn't want to look too full on or desperate and then Alice appeared to help her choose a pretty summer dress that had a classy look that didn't scream "look at me."

Once all were ready, Kelly called Memhet to collect them, he was on another call but promised to be there ASAP so the girls had their first bit of alcohol of the day with a shot of vodka each while they waited.

Alice proposed a toast "to holiday romances may they find us all wherever we are"; the others laughed in agreement as they chinked their glasses together and knocked back the spirit.

The sound of a car horn signalled the arrival of the taxi and so the girls made their way down to the front of the property smiling pleasantly as the awaiting Memhet greeted them with wonderful comments on how beautiful they were all looking. "Where do we go now, ladies, it is early for you to be going out I think?"

Kelly explained that they were meeting the two men from last evening and going on the sunset cruise with them, she said they were meeting for a drink prior just across from the taxi rank.

"Oh my, the sunset cruise you say; oh my oh my," he laughed. Alice laughed at him asking why he was saying that, Memhet looked up into the rear-view mirror at her and said, "Tonight I will prophecy many a tonsil will be lost on this boat, please believe me it is impossible such beautiful women as you can escape the magic of the sunset, please trust me, many tonsil will sing tonight."

The girls could not contain their laughter, tears rolling down their cheeks as some of them experienced tummy cramps from the laughing, Memhet just grinned widely as he continually nodded his head to reassure them that he was right in what he was saying.

"Oh Memhet, we will have to take you home with us you are so funny," Kelly muttered through her laughter and tears of joy.

The taxi pulled up at the rank and the still laughing girls got out, other drivers in the rank looked at them in wonderment at their demeanour, Memhet spoke in his native tongue to them explaining the amusement to which they all heckled and cheered back, smiling and laughing, some waving.

Memhet wished the girls a wonderful trip before they left him to find the lads, Jeremy spotted the girls walking his way where he was sat with Gavin and waved to them, Alice purposely held back from acknowledging him as she was playing it cool but Kelly and the other two did.

Gavin jumped to his feet as the girls neared them, his eyes firmly fixed on the beautiful looking Emma, she smiled pleasantly back at him as he greeted her and boldly kissed her on the cheek telling her that she looked stunning.

Emma said thank you for his compliment and said that she was impressed with his sense of style for the evening decked out in chinos with a smart short-sleeved shirt and sweater draped over his shoulders. Gavin explained that there was a dress code at the restaurant later so he had to wear trousers, then offered Emma a seat before greeting the other girls.

Having ordered drinks, the group sat talking and Alice was busy chatting away with Jeremy explaining about the taxi driver last night and just; Jeremy laughed and as was his custom said that he hoped Memhet was right as he would love to tickle her tonsils and make them sing. Alice sat back playfully slapping him on the wrist saying that he should calm down and rather tongue in cheek claimed she was not that sort of girl; Kelly hearing her words falsely coughed muttering the word liar then laughed.

Alice asked him if Gavin had mentioned anything about his feelings towards Emma at all, Jeremy laughed shaking his head and quietly replied that he had not talked about anything else since last night adding that impossible as he thought it may be, he truly thought Gavin was smitten with her.

Alice told him how disappointed Emma was that Gavin didn't kiss her goodnight last evening, Jeremy responded saying, "That was typical of Gavin, he is not like me, if I thought I had a chance with you, I'd be straight in but not Gav; he is more of a thoughtful caring person, a bit soft if I'm honest but that's him and I know he wanted to because he ain't shut up about it all day." Jeremy chuckled.

Alice told Jeremy that Emma had one wish on this holiday and that was to be kissed under a Kalkan sunset and asked him to discretely let Gavin know just in case the opportunity arrived later; Jeremy assured her that she could rely on him to sort that out.

Gavin checked his watch and suggested they make their way down to the port and get on the boat early to get the best spot, he said the top deck would be perfect but there was only so much room. He added that when he got the girls tickets earlier, he arranged for extra champagne for them, Lacey apologised saying she forgot about the tickets and asked to reimburse him but Gavin said it was his treat and to forget it.

Kelly said that she insisted on paying for the cocktails they just had and that they would get the next round later after the trip, Gavin tried in vain to say it was ok but the girls were having none of it. The party made their way down to the port Emma and Gavin walking closely together, there was a cool breeze blowing around the harbour as one of the locals noticing Emma shiver a little said quite simply, "Thunder tonight yes," the local pointed skywards, smiling and nodding, "Yes, thunder tonight."

Emma just smiled back thinking he was either drunk or just very much mistaken, the party arrived at the boat and Gavin handed over the tickets as they all got on board.

They all headed up to the top deck under Gavin's direction as he went to speak to a crew member to arrange some champagne to be brought up, there was about forty-five minutes before departure so everyone got comfortable.

Jeremy had held back waiting for Gavin and when he had the chance, he told him what Alice had said earlier, Gavin smiled as he thanked his friend and said he would try to make it as special as possible.

A crew member appeared with champagne on ice and six plastic champagne flutes, he duly opened the bottle and poured out the content emptying the bottle and asked who the happy couple was as Jeremy stepped forward, pointing at Gavin and Emma. "Them."

The crew member offered Gavin and Emma a glass each with his and the captain's congratulations before handing out the rest, everyone laughed at the situation as Emma stood almost in shock lost for words. Jeremy raised his glass toasting Gavin and Emma saying "to the happy couple", Gavin looked at the shocked expression on Emma's face and apologised for the situation whilst giving Jeremy a look of disapproval.

The other girls rallied around Emma checking she was ok trying to make light of the situation, Jeremy apologised to Gavin saying it was only a joke and he didn't think it would upset anyone. Emma turned to Jeremy and told him not to worry about it that it was just her, she said she knew it was all in fun, it was just for a moment very surreal and caught her by surprise then lifting her glass, she said cheers to everyone then with one hand on her chest took a sip.

Having reassured everyone that she was fine, they all began chatting amongst themselves, Gavin placed a gentle hand on the small of Emma's back as he leant in to check that she was ok really, Emma touched him gently on his side thanking him saying she was feeling wonderful as she looked into his eyes and felt the butterflies returning to her stomach.

The boat was filling up fast and though there was some space for a few more on the top deck, no one joined them and it turned out to be because the captain told everyone that it was a private party up there.

The sun was disappearing over to the west as the boat chugged its way out of the harbour towards its docking point, there was much anticipation and excitement in the air amongst the group and on the decks below as couples huddled together with their champagne in hand looking forward to that much fabled magical moment when the sun kisses the mountain.

The captain announced over the speaker that they were about to drop anchor and that everyone had about fifteen minutes before the magic moment to get their cameras and video recorders ready, Alice told Lacey and Kelly what she had arranged with Jeremy earlier and they were so excited to see what would happen.

Moments before the magic was about to happen, Alice asked Emma to give her her phone so she could take a picture of her and Gavin with the sunset behind.

Everyone on board held up their phones, cameras and video recorders to capture the special moment, the sounds of oohs and aahs gushed forth as the moment happened. Gavin stood there with Emma and in a flash pulled her into himself, planting his lips firmly on hers, they embraced for what seemed like a lifetime to Emma as her body tingled from head to toe with fireworks exploding in her head. Lacey nudged Kelly to look Emma's way; the pair of them welled up with tears in their eyes with so much joy for their friend. Alice joined them wiping away a tear as she showed the pictures she had captured perfectly with the sun kissing then melting into the mountain.

Emma and Gavin finally ended their embrace with Emma almost gasping for air as she tried to compose herself with so many emotions running wild through her veins, it was all so unreal she was floating on air as she gazed across to her friends who were all looking at her with so much love, affection and happiness.

Emma looked up at Gavin they gazed into each other's eyes in silence before again embracing in a show of true passion and deep-rooted affection for each other, the friends watching on smiling as Jeremy whispered that he thinks he got his message well, Alice tapped him on the shoulder saying well done through a choked up voice before grabbing his arm and the back of his neck and then pulling him in close to her, she said "oh come here" then planted a big kiss on his lips, taking him by surprise.

Jeremy wasted no time in taking control of the situation and holding Alice around her waist, pulled her in close and passionately kissed her back, much to her enjoyment. Kelly and Lacey stood open-mouthed as they looked at the pair full on in the grip of eager passion, Lacey laughed saying that she thought Memhet may have a point with what they were observing and Kelly laughingly agreed.

When Alice and Jeremy finally parted, Kelly asked him about their plans for dinner later, she asked if he thought that Gavin may now want to take Emma along and possibly Alice to make a foursome.

Jeremy paused for thought as he looked over towards his friend who was holding Emma's hands and talking to her. "I haven't seen him like this for a long time, he looks like his old self." Jeremy turned to the girls and said leave this to me and walked across to Gavin and Emma, "Hey mate that was great, got some awesome shots of that sunset and you and Emma together. Look I hope this isn't going to be awkward but with all that champagne and the stuff earlier, my guts don't feel up to a champagne dinner, why don't you take Emma instead and I will chill with the girls; we can meet up later or I will see you back at the villa."

Gavin smiled back at his friend patting him on his arm asking him if he was sure, Gavin knew his mate well; there was nothing wrong with his guts he thought, he knew exactly what he was doing and winked at him with a pleasing smile.

Gavin turned to Emma and asked her what she thought, "How about it, Emma, would you like to join me for dinner?"

Emma was ecstatic on the inside and fought not to show it, she said she would have to check with the girls but Jeremy said that they have already said she should go if Gavin was to ask her. Emma said she would be very happy to join him as she squeezed Gavin's hand, twisting herself gently side to side in excitement.

The other girls looked on. Alice said that it looked like something had made Emma very happy as she always twisted that way when something nice was about to happen. The group joined together as Jeremy told the others that Emma would be taking his place at dinner tonight with Gavin and asked if they minded him chilling with them later.

Lacey said that she and Kelly had been invited out by Giles and Matt and suggested that perhaps he could entertain Alice for the evening, it was music to his ears as he said he knew the perfect place that served great fish.

Emma asked him about his bad stomach, was he sure he was up to it as Gavin gave her a gentle tug and telling look that caused the penny to drop. Emma felt a sense of deep appreciation inside herself as she realised what Jeremy had done for her but said nothing and showed an appreciative smile his way.

Jeremy turned to Alice and asked if she was up for it, Alice told him quietly that after such a lovely gesture towards her friend, she couldn't say no; besides, she told him that kiss had pretty much sealed the deal.

As the boat neared the harbour, Lacey called Giles and made arrangements to meet at the junction above the taxi rank at around 7.30, Emma was concerned that she may not be dressed well enough for such an occasion that was quickly rubbished by Gavin who told her she looked perfect and was eagerly backed up by all the girls. The boat manoeuvred back into its berthing spot as Emma looked over the pictures Alice had taken on her phone; hand held to her mouth, Emma struggled to contain her emotion as she witnessed the evidence of her dream come true, not only did she experience her kiss under a Kalkan sunset but there before her was a clear record of something she could cherish and relive forever.

Emma thanked Alice as they made their way down to the disembarking point, she turned to wait for Jeremy and as he approached, she tiptoed up to kiss him on the cheek saying thank you. Jeremy just smiled back saying it was his pleasure and that he hoped she had a wonderful time. Gavin patted Jeremy on the back jokingly saying, "Well you and Alice eh, well done mate, you have a good catch there; now remember to be nice and polite at all times and leave your ego home, you know you are a top bloke when you want to be; let her see it."

Jeremy grinned back broadly at him with his usual swagger of self-confidence, "Don't worry mate, I shall be the perfect gentleman, I fancy a few more of those lush kisses from her before the evening is over. I won't jeopardise that." The boys enjoyed a laugh together as they made their way off the boat thanking the captain and crew as they went, Kelly raised the point that the key for the villa was in the key safe outside for whoever got back first and to leave the patio door unlocked.

Gavin said his table was booked for 8 pm so had time if anyone fancied a quick drink before Lacey and Kelly had to go, the group made their way back to the bar they met at earlier and enjoyed some tasty refreshing cocktails before the time came for Lacey and Kelly to start making their way up the slope to their pick-up point.

Gavin suggested that Matt and Alice should join him and Emma for a pre-dinner drink at the hotel before they set off for their night out; they agreed and wished Kelly and Lacey a lovely evening saying to call if any issues and then took a taxi to the hotel that was a few minutes away.

Lacey and Emma didn't have long to wait for Matt and Giles as they arrived minutes before expected; once in the taxi, they set off for the restaurant. Kelly asked where exactly were they going. Matt, who was sat up front, turned and said that it was somewhere he had been going to for years just out on the Kas road, a few minutes out of town.

"It really is a lovely setting during daylight as the views are wonderful, it has become a bit of a pilgrimage over the years; I have gotten to know the family who run it well. The food is simple but delicious with attentive service, I am sure you will enjoy."

Arriving at the destination, they were greeted by the owner with a wonderful welcome. Giles commented to the girls that the locals were such a friendly bunch as Matt was being greeted with such honest delight to see him.

The outside dining terrace was on split levels and they were afforded a table in prime position had there been daylight to observe the stunning sea views.

Matt recommended that the girls should come out here for lunch one day to take it all in, the pair nodded saying that it was such a lovely setting that they may do that. Matt asked the girls if they would like an aperitif or start with wine,

Lacey said that wine would be preferable as they had just been for cocktails; Kelly agreed.

Meanwhile, the other girls had arrived at the hotel with Gavin and Jeremy, as Gavin strode forward towards the entrance of the terrace restaurant, he was approached by Mohammed the restaurant manager, who had a puzzled look on his face as he greeted Gavin, looking at the others.

Gavin and Jess had been frequent visitors to the establishment over the years and gotten to know Mohammed very well, Mohammed said that he had been looking forward to seeing him again as it was to be his honeymoon.

Gavin understood the looks and put up his hand saying, "It's a long story, Mohammed, but Jess and I are over." Then he introduced the others before sitting at the bar and ordering some drinks. Emma was amazed by the view and encouraged Alice to join her at the edge of the terrace looking down over the harbour and part of the old town, the opposite headland was wonderfully lit up and Emma wondered if the day could get anymore magical as they both took pictures on their phones.

The girls joined the boys back at the bar and said how wonderful the views were and that it truly was a beautiful romantic spot, Alice said she could see why he chose the place and couldn't help but ask how he was feeling being there now with Emma and not his bride.

Emma looked at Alice in a dissatisfied way. "No Alice, you can't put him on the spot like that, that's not the right thing to ask at all, you really surprise me sometimes; it must have been a really difficult situation and decision to make."

She turned to Gavin giving him a friendly rub on his leg and apologised for her friend as Alice herself apologised saying she never meant to cause upset but insisted that it must be a surreal situation to a point for him.

Gavin spoke up saying he didn't mind the question and that in fact it helped him put things into perspective rather better than he had been able to prior. "My situation is what it is. I admit that I haven't been dealing with things inside as well as I thought I would and to be honest, I have been dreading tonight until Emma came along."

Emma smiled back affectionately at him as he took her hand and said, "Look Emma, I don't know where this is going, what if anything there is for us beyond this holiday but what I can say is that as much as I may have saved you in the sea, you have saved me in a different way. Having you here tonight seems so right, I haven't given Jessica a second thought other than to explain to

Mohammed why she is not here. Maybe you will forget me after a week or so when you get home but for now, you are here with me and I am going to make the most of the time we have together."

Emma sat there quietly as Gavin poured out his feelings to everyone, inside she hoped that something may come of their meeting but her barriers were flickering up and down with the torrent of emotions she was undergoing within. Emma's scars from previous relationships ran deep and she was very reluctant to submit to anyone's advances be they genuine or not. Gavin was the first person in a very long time to get anywhere near her affections that she was feeling for him right now.

"I keep telling you, mate, live for the moment, enjoy your holiday and if anything comes of you and Emma, great; if it turns out to be a holiday romance then you both have done well; go home happier than when you came out."

Alice agreed with Jeremy saying that all the girls came out not knowing how things would go but so far, it had been better than expected.

Mohammed appeared briefly to tell Gavin that his table was ready. Soon after, Alice and Jeremy said goodbye to the other two wishing them a great evening before leaving, Gavin and Emma were sat at the most perfect table that allowed them unspoilt views across the harbour, old town and across the bay.

A young waitress came along with menus as Mohammed stood by smiling with a bottle of champagne that he opened with professional gusto and ease then proceeded to pour out two glasses.

Gavin raised his glass proposing a toast to a wonderful evening and whatever the rest of the holiday may bring. Emma responded by repeating his words as she gazed at him with a warm feeling inside her, raising her glass to his before taking a sip. Mohammed said he would return shortly to take their order.

Ten or so minutes later, Mohammed returned to the table and took their order before he wished them an enjoyable evening and left them to continue looking at each other with much care and passion in their eyes.

Alice and Jeremy had gone back to the villa in a taxi as she wanted to freshen up and change; Alice told Jeremy to stay in the taxi as it would only take her a few moments and in a flash she was up the steps and in the villa. Alice wasted no time quickly refreshing herself and slipping into a rather sexy little mini dress showing a lot of cleavage; moments later, she was locking up and making her way back down to the taxi.

Jeremy could not believe his eyes at the sight of Alice getting into the taxi, giving him a real eyeful of her ample breasts; the expression on his face led Alice to state, "Ok calm down tiger, it's no more than you have seen in my bikini."

Memhet commented from the front that she looked very beautiful and told Jeremy that he was a lucky boy, Jeremy answered with a wide grin that he agreed as he looked at Alice telling her that she looked stunning.

Alice sat back feeling rather pleased with herself as that dress had gotten the response she was hoping for when she decided to buy it. Jeremy gave the name of the restaurant he wanted to go to; Memhet commented that it was a good choice as he pulled away.

Kelly and Lacey were having a fun time with Matt and Giles at the out of town restaurant, the wine was flowing and the food though simple was as enjoyable as Matt had promised. Kelly asked the men why they were not with partners of their own as they were obviously successful businessmen and certainly not unattractive, both had been married and divorced and had a few short-term relationships but had found life simpler being single.

Giles said that he had two children from his marriage in their early twenties and that his ex-wife had remarried, he said that strange as it may have sounded, he got on better with her now than when they were together.

Matt said that he was at fault for his breakup, he said he regretted his actions back then and that he had certainly learnt his lesson. He went on to say, "Look, I was young, affluent and full of myself, attracting all the wrong types to me and I paid the ultimate price, I lost the greatest thing in my life I ever had and I will never be able to replace her."

Lacey commented that Kelly had been cheated on and let down a number of times by men and that she herself was a victim of the same; although she had not been married like they had, it still hurt as much.

Giles chipped in, "Look, mistakes happen. I don't suppose people get into relationships looking to cheat on their partner but unfortunately, temptation is always there for the taking and some are not as strong as others, not that it excuses it in anyway."

Kelly said that she hoped Emma was doing ok as she was finding it hard to trust men and Gavin was the first bloke she had been on a date with for ages. "She has major trust issues; she struggles to lower her barriers. She is such a lovely girl that has lost all her self-confidence, hasn't she, Lace?"

Lacey looked at Kelly sighing as she nodded in agreement. Matt said that they should change the subject as it was a holiday and it should be about enjoyment and laughter not dwelling on past failures. Giles suggested they get another bottle of wine and then head back into Kalkan to one of the more livelier bars to finish the night off. Kelly and Lacey were happy with the idea but said they were going to have to slow down a bit on the drinking as it was starting to catch up on them.

Alice and Jeremy arrived at the restaurant and were shown to a nice table with great views of the marina and seafront, Jeremy said that he and Gavin ate there on their second evening in Kalkan and enthused on how good the fish was. Alice said she loved fish and seafood but was not a lover of fish bones so whatever they had must be well filleted. Jeremy laughed, assuring her everything would be fine as the waiter brought them menus and took their drink orders before pointing to the display fridge offering all of tonight's fresh seafood dishes.

Emma and Gavin were really settled into their evening; having enjoyed a delicious starter, they were now being served their main course, the waiter topped up the champagne finishing the bottle and asked if he could bring them anything else. Emma said she was ok for now maybe a small glass of wine later before tucking into her main course of the hotel's traditional lamb dish.

Gavin asked if she was enjoying it and Emma could only respond with "ooh um ooh", nodding in sheer delight as she savoured each morsel with such enjoyment.

"So Emma, I have told you about my past; what about you, how did things go so wrong for you?" Gavin was quick to see the horror on Emma's face at hearing the question. "Look, if it's too much for you, I understand, please you don't have to say anything; it won't change a thing I promise." Gavin got a little concerned that he may have hit a big nerve and was worried about Emma's response.

Emma could easily sense Gavin's concern and reached out her hand and clasped his saying, "No it's ok, Gav, I suppose it is only fair, you caught me by surprise that's all."

Emma started by saying she had married someone she met in college some years earlier, she told him that she had gone to a reunion where they reconnected and started dating before marrying a few years later. Emma said that she was two sizes smaller then and smiling gleefully to herself suggested that he should have seen her then, Gavin interrupted that he could not imagine her any more beautiful than she was at that moment.

Emma rose up and leant over to kiss Gavin for that comment. "Well anyway, we were married and I thought we were doing fine, we had a house, mortgage, etc.; both in good jobs with good salaries, you know, the normal everyday stuff.

"Like you, Gavin, I never suspected anything until one morning he left his phone home and a message came through from a work colleague of his arranging to meet at a motel that afternoon, I was devastated as he told me the previous night that he had a serious senior management meeting that afternoon, meaning he would be home late."

Gavin looked on as certain things reminded him of his own previous situation but encouraged Emma to continue, Emma took a large gulp of water before continuing.

"I took an overnight bag to work with me and cried all the way there, I rang Kelly and told her and asked if I could stay with her that night, she had been through the same and had been divorced a few years at that point and she suggested that we go to the motel and catch them together. I had only been in work ten minutes when Steven my husband rang me asking if I had seen his phone, I just said I hadn't and then said that Kelly was really upset and asked me to go over later so I wouldn't be home that night.

"He didn't seem bothered in the slightest as it probably made his deceit easier. I spoke with my boss who was really understanding and she said it was ok for me to leave early and so I did and met up with Kelly and we went to the motel in her car. We didn't have long to wait as Steven's car pulled in and then a leggy dark-haired girl pulled in behind him, my stomach churned as I saw them embrace outside the reception entrance before they went in, Kelly and I waited until they emerged, walking across the terrace to the rooms kissing and hugging as they went and just as he put the key in the door, I screamed out at him. Kelly had taken some pictures of them together on her phone. Steven was startled and tried to say it wasn't what it looked like until I told him I had seen his phone message."

Gavin sat back saying that he thought her brave confronting them like that, applauding her actions but Emma said she was with her best friend Kelly, who was nobody's fool.

"So anyway, I told him I wanted him out of the house by the time I was home the next evening and that I didn't care where he went but if he wasn't gone then my eldest brother James would come around and move him out. James is 6ft 4in and solid muscle; no one messes with him and he warned Steven at our wedding that he would answer to him if he hurt me in any way, he was only joking but I knew there was truth in it as he was very protective over me."

"So I guess having heard that, Steven didn't hang around, did he?" Gavin asked.

Emma laughed slightly, saying that he wasn't there when she got home, Gavin asked her what happened next just as the waiter came to clear away their empty plates and asking if they would like to see the dessert menu.

Emma declined as did Gavin but he suggested they have some coffee with hot milk and Emma eagerly agreed. "So you were saying, Emma?"

"Oh right erm, well, I had a few calls from Steven over the next couple of weeks trying to patch things up but I found out that he had been seeing this girl on and off for a while and there were rumours from the gym he used that she was not the first, so we ended up divorcing about 18months ago now."

Gavin said that he was sorry to hear of her situation and hoped that it was all behind her now, Emma responded that she wished everything was so easy as that.

"Several months after Steven and I were divorced, I went out with all the girls to an event in Taunton and met someone I had a drunken one-night stand with, woke up next day totally regretting it and it took several weeks to get over. That said, no sooner was I over it, I was swept off my feet by Aaron, whom I had met online; he was sweet, charming and very good-looking and lived down near Exeter. We had a wonderful two weeks together until I received a call from a woman claiming to be his wife and had found my number on his phone along with all the text messages we had sent each other, I confronted him and he initially denied it before confessing it saying that they were breaking up anyway so I ended it right there and have not dated since."

"Wow Emma, you haven't had much luck have you?"

The waiter interrupted them with their coffee and said that Mohammed had offered them two brandy on the house if they would like with their coffee; they both happily agreed turning to thank Mohammed who was standing nearby.

The pair sat there enjoying the coffee and brandy as Emma received a text message, it was from Alice saying she hoped she was having a wonderful time And that she was enjoying the best fish dinner ever. As Emma looked at her phone, her thoughts turned to earlier on the boat when she had her photo taken with Gavin and so scrolled through them until she found the best one kissing under the sunset, she passed it across so Gavin could look just as Mohammed passed by.

Mohammed could not help notice the picture and asked if he may take a closer look. Gavin gladly passed it up to him wondering why Mohammed was looking as he was. Mohammed spoke in Turkish to one of the elder members of staff beckoning them to come see, he turned to Emma and told her that the picture had magical qualities about it.

Emma looked up surprised and asked what magic as the lady assistant went over to her to explain.

"My dear girl, the Kalkan sunset can be a magical experience for some if they are lucky enough to catch it; look, see how the sun meets the mountain behind your head creating a ring around you, this means true love surrounds you but the magic is here, look see how on top of your head it creates like a flash that looks like a bright diamond exploding; that is the magic being sent to you, you are such a fortunate girl; much happiness is destined for you."

The lady smiled at Emma as she told her these things and gently placing her hand on her head telling her that she was very blessed; another waitress intervened to see what was happening and when she saw the picture, she put her hands together almost prayer-like and told Emma that she was so lucky.

Emma felt the surge of cascading butterflies fill her within, for a moment a feeling of light-headedness passed over her as she felt emotions overwhelm her causing tears of sheer joy to trickle down her cheeks. She struggled for breath as she fully took in all that had been said to her, wondering if there were any truth in it, Gavin took her hand with compassion asking if she was ok.

Emma sat back in her chair unable to speak for a moment before eventually asking, "Gavin, do you really believe all she just said, is there such a thing as true magic? I mean can a photograph bring you real happiness and blessings."

Gavin said that he had never given much thought to it but he believed that what was meant to be was meant to be, looking at Emma in a favourable way he told her that if those words made her feel better about herself and gave her some kind of hope for her future then she should hold on dear to them and see where it took her.

Gavin asked Mohammed to take a couple of pictures of them with his phone before thanking him for a great evening, having sorted out the extras on the bill.

Gavin suggested that they might take a walk back up to the main road to help the food go down just as they heard what sounded like thunder grumbles.

They hadn't walked 100yds when more rumblings were heard, Emma asked Gavin if he thought it might rain and he said it sounded like it was far away.

Gavin took Emma's hand as they walked up the steeper part of the incline to reach the main road, at the top he said that they could go left towards where they were yesterday or right back to town.

Emma said she fancied a walk down to town and although it was well after 10 pm, she felt wide awake and didn't want the evening to end, Gavin said he knew a nice bar they could go and chill in and while the night away.

As they walked to town, the rumblings got louder and more frequent and there was a pleasant coolness in the air as a gentle breeze picked up. The town was really alive bright lights in every direction with people walking, sitting, eating and talking, music of all types could be heard with every step they took. Emma shivered a little as they passed an open spot and was caught by the breeze.

Gavin put his jumper over her shoulders then pulling her close by her waist, he gently kissed her then more passionately as the kiss continued before just smiling and winking at her as he led her on into town.

Gavin led Emma up a flight of stairs to a cocktail lounge and were fortunate to arrive just as two couples were leaving their table situated overlooking the main street down to the old town; the place was lively with people enjoying themselves with the sounds of music pumping away in the background.

A waiter presented them with the cocktail menu making a couple of recommendations, he suggested they share a house speciality which was the Love Bowl and assured them it was the perfect drink for young lovers.

Gavin laughed and asked Emma if she felt that they were young lovers, Emma rather shyly smiled, dropping her head saying that she did feel like it at that moment before swiftly lifting her head to see Gavin's reaction.

Gavin looked longingly at her with a wry smile and told the waiter that they would take his recommendation and asked for extra sparkle in it, the waiter told them they would not be disappointed as he swiftly took their order to the bar.

"I am so happy to see you this way, Emma, you have definitely come out of your shell tonight, I feel I am seeing the real you for the first time and I must say I like what I am seeing."

"Yes Gav, I do feel more relaxed with you tonight, it has been an incredible day and you are really easy to talk to, I know it's only been a couple of days and I don't want to sound too clichéd but I feel like I have known you for ages."

"Yes Emma, I know what you mean, I feel exactly the same; it's crazy but you have really made a difference to this trip for me, I feel I can relax and enjoy this trip more when I am with you."

The pair fell into momentary silence as they held hands and gazed affectionately at each other, Gavin leant in to kiss Emma and thanked her for being there with him, adding that he hoped she didn't get bored with him.

Emma just laughed and squeezing his hand assured him that was probably not going to happen and that she herself had similar thoughts about him.

The pair sat chatting away while waiting for their cocktail, holding hands and looking at each other with a growing yearning for each other burning within that they both did well to hide.

Not far away down in the old town, Alice and Jeremy were finishing off their wine after their very enjoyable fish dinner, Alice thanked Jeremy for a wonderful meal and entertaining evening and asked what he had planned next as thunder rumblings roared out over the sea.

"Go and buy an umbrella by the sounds of it," he chuckled.

"Oh do you think we will have a storm?" Alice asked the waiter as he delivered the bill to them.

The waiter looked out seawards and said that he thought that within the next hour, the storm would break, he said that it was quite common at this time of year and that it would not last long but would clear up the air a bit better for sleeping.

Kelly and Lacey were just coming into town in a taxi with Matt and Giles as a big flash of lightning lit up the skies out in the bay, Matt said that it would no doubt rain shortly so asked the driver to get as close to the bar he wanted to take them to just in case. Matt led them out of the taxi across to the bar the girls had been previously, Mussie was standing outside and smiled very happily when he saw Matt approach, stretching out his arms to welcome him and his guests. Kelly said to Giles that Matt was a popular guy out here and he replied that Matt was co-owner of the bar with Mussie. Kelly and Lacey looked at each other wide-eyed.

Mussie recognised the girls and welcomed them both back, saying it was lovely to see them again, Matt ushered everyone upstairs where they ordered drinks whilst waiting for a table to become available.

Soon enough a table was ready and they sat down chatting as the storm rumblings grew more intense with more frantic flashes of lightning and bloodcurdling claps of thunder.

Emma and Gavin had not long been served their cocktail complete with sparklers and all manner of decorations and were eagerly sipping away together through their straws, Gavin suggested that maybe if she was up for it, they could go back to his villa and enjoy the storm from there as the views were incredible and they could sit with a coffee or something stronger if she fancied, watching it all unfold.

Emma could not believe herself as all her barriers were down; she gladly accepted the offer and eagerly helped finish the cocktail; having paid the bill, Gavin and Emma made their way down the stairs as a massive burst of thunder erupted overhead with almost immediate flashes of lightning.

The pair ran up towards the taxi rank as the skies opened up and a deluge of rain plummeted down upon them, Emma screamed out with a mix of horror and excitement as she was encompassed by the deluge.

Gavin threw his jumper over Emma's head in a valiant gesture but to no avail, the downpour was really intense, bouncing up two feet off the pavement as they approached a taxi. All around them people were running for cover, the screams of women could be heard all about them as they searched for shelter.

Emma tried to open a door of a taxi close by but was diverted to another further along all the while getting soaked through to the skin; eventually, in what seemed like an age, the pair clambered into the back of a taxi both soaked through to the skin.

The pair looked at each other and burst into laughter as the driver asked where they were going, Emma apologised to Gavin saying that she had better go back to hers as she was soaked through, Gavin said it was fine and Emma gave the address to the driver and they went on their way.

Although Gavin was disappointed that the evening had not gone entirely to plan, he couldn't help see the funny side of the situation and commented that they were like two drowned rats as the storm grew and intensified outside. The driver said that everything would calm down soon and things would blow over in about half an hour.

Arriving at Emma's villa, she went to get out of the taxi and looking back at Gavin, asked him if he was going to join her, Gavin had thought his night was over when Emma said she would have to cancel his plans and he couldn't get out of the car quick enough after paying the driver.

The rain was still beating down hard and the thunder rolled on with flashes of lightning as they both hurried up the steps, Emma screaming with laughter as she ran as quick as her feet would carry her; once she found the key, she let herself and Gavin in.

Emma went and got some clean towels and told Gavin to use the laundry room where there was a shower and a tumble drier to dry off his clothes while she went and showered herself; she told him to help himself to a drink adding that she would be as quick as she could.

Once Emma was ready, she walked into the lounge where Gavin stood wrapped in a towel looking out the window; staring at his bare back and muscular features, she felt a desire within her that had laid dormant for such a long time; clutching at her throat, her voice trembled as she asked him if he was sorted ok.

Gavin turned swiftly around to see Emma standing in a short dressing gown, her hair combed back wet and glistening. Emma marvelled at his tanned torso as the dormant feeling inside her begged to burst into life.

"Did you get a drink, Gav?"

"No I waited to see what you wanted actually."

"Well to be honest, I fancy a nice cup of tea, but please if you would rather a beer, wine or something stronger, that's ok; we have plenty of vodka and Bacardi."

"No thanks Emma, tea sounds good. One sugar please."

Emma went to put the kettle on and told Gavin to make himself comfortable, standing in the kitchen full of wanton emotion, Emma tried to supress her inward womanly desire she was feeling towards Gavin. Gavin sat on the sofa looking out at the storm through the open patio doors. "The storm seems to be giving up the fight now," he called out to Emma.

Emma joined him briefly to look for herself saying that storms could be beautiful to watch at times. Gavin just looked at her with doting eyes saying that he hadn't noticed. With the surge again rising in her, clutching at her dressing gown around her neck, Emma made her excuses to attend to the tea; standing in front of the kettle, she put both hands on the counter top as she threw her head back with a deep exhale of air.

Emma pondered what she was going to do to hold back this feeling that was tormenting her inside, Gavin had not physically shown her the same feeling and she was concerned that he may think less of her if she could not control her feelings towards him.

Unknown to Emma, Gavin was experiencing similar thoughts and feelings and was worried he may frighten her off if he came on too strong. Emma brought in the tea and said she would go and check on his clothes in the dryer.

Returning, Emma said that she had hung everything up to air adding that his trousers were still a little damp around the waist.

Emma sat by Gavin and drank her tea as she looked him over wanting to pounce on him with the passion she was feeling for him at bursting point, she put her cup down and as she turned towards him, he clutched at her arm and pulled her close to him. Emma was like putty in his arms and had no resistance to him; he kissed her with passion and tenderness as he ran his fingers through her damp hair.

Emma wrapped her arms around him as she welcomed his loving actions, all her worries of holding back had been blown away with the storm. Emma had had her own storm brewing in her the past hour or so and now had become saturated in her own torrents of passion and emotion as her heart thundered with unbridled pounding. Gavin's hands moved over her with intensity, finding his way inside her dressing gown and fondling her breast.

Emma was momentarily shocked as it had been so long ago that she had been this intimate with anyone, Gavin sensed her uneasiness and apologised stopping his actions but Emma told him it was ok and not to stop as the kissing continued with more fervour.

Gavin lent into Emma until they were both laying on the settee, Gavin slightly on top of her, the passion and desire between them grew and grew as they writhed around together; causing Gavin's towel to loosen around him.

They spent the next fifteen minutes in this way stopping momentarily for air; suddenly, an all too familiar voice shattered the moment.

"Oi oi, what's all this then; get a room, you two!" Jeremy laughed out as Alice apologised to Emma and tried to drag Jeremy out to the back patio, startling Gavin as he jumped up, causing his towel to fall from him exposing himself and the erection he had.

"Ha Ha, nice one, mate!" Jeremy laughed out as he was pulled from the room by Alice who herself caught an eyeful and couldn't resist a sneaky smile and faint laugh.

"Oh poor Emma, why did you have to shout out like that, she will be totally embarrassed by all this now," Alice reprimanded Jeremy.

"Oh come on Alice, what do you expect me to say; it was only a joke, anyway they should have gone to her room; anyone could have walked in on them as we did."

Alice regrettably had to agree that he had a point and said that Gavin must be well embarrassed having exposed himself like that, she couldn't resist a cheeky smile as she said it looked like he was ready for action, the poor boy.

"Poor boy! There was nothing poor about that boy from what I seen!" Jeremy chuckled back to a nodding Alice who hoped they hadn't ruined their chances of taking it to the next step.

More familiar voices were heard as Kelly and Lacey arrived back at the villa, Lacey walked out to the back where Alice and Jeremy were wiping down the chairs on the patio. "Hey guys, how was your night?" she asked.

Alice started to tell Lacey about the evening as Kelly joined them enquiring if everything was ok with Emma as she had just said hi but the response was somewhat muted. Alice was quick to fill the girls in on what they had walked into causing them to laugh but with concern, Lacey asked if Emma was ok but Alice replied that she hadn't had the chance to speak to her yet.

"Oh how awful, poor Emma and poor Gavin too, was he naked then?" Kelly asked with enthusiasm. Alice just responded with a nod and raised eyebrows.

"So you saw everything, Al?" an eager Lacey enquired and again Alice nodded and with puckered lips indicated with her index fingers the size of the situation, raising her eyebrows again.

Kelly and Lacey just looked at each other with big dirty smiles, Lacey said she couldn't believe it and again repeating what a poor girl Emma was, Gavin came out to join them looking rather sheepish.

"Oi oi, here he is, man of the moment, I knew you would rise to the occasion," Jeremy again rather cruelly suffered his friend to further embarrassment as the girls struggled to hide their amusement however cruel it was.

Kelly asked where Emma was and Gavin said she was in her room, Kelly marched off in a hurry to check on her friend. Knocking on Emma's door, Kelly asked if she could come in, Emma opened the door looking a little forlorn and embarrassed.

"Oh Emma, come her you silly sod; you have nothing to feel embarrassed about." Emma tried to smile then said that it was awkward for her, she had finally let all her barriers down and was really wanting Gavin then Alice and Jeremy walked in right when they were in total throes of passion.

Kelly said, "So what; you were making out with a hot bloke and one of your closest friends walked in, at least you were dressed; poor Gavin stood there starkers standing to attention and apparently very smartly." She grinned and winked at Emma.

Emma was forced to laugh saying she supposed that Kelly was right and that she was making a bigger thing out of it than she should, Kelly then joked that it wasn't as a bigger of a thing than Gavin had made causing Emma to laugh and tell Kelly that she was a cruel cow.

"Come on Emm, come out back with us and let's get this over with."

The two friends went and joined the others out on the patio, Jeremy stepped up apologising for his earlier actions as did Alice but Emma said it was fine as Gavin came over to her and took her in his arms.

It was almost midnight the friends sat there talking about their evening out in turn, Alice and Emma said that they all must go to the hotel where Gavin and Emma ate earlier, saying what a fabulous setting it was. Gavin said that he personally thought it the best in Kalkan and knew many that thought similar, Alice showed Kelly and Lacey pictures she had taken there and they agreed that they should give it a try.

Everyone was getting tired and Alice said she was ready for bed and the others felt ready too, Gavin asked Emma if he would see her tomorrow and she replied that she hoped so and gave him her cell number asking him to call her later in the morning once she had a chance to discuss things with the girls.

Kelly and Lacey left them to go to bed wishing everyone a goodnight, Jeremy had called a taxi and he and Alice went out to the front to wait for it while Gavin and Emma kissed and cuddled in the cool evening air out the back.

Emma kissed Gavin goodnight and waved him and Jeremy off in the taxi as they left, Alice put her arm around Emma as they trudged slowly back up the steps to the villa asking her if she was ok.

"Thanks Alice, yes I'm fine, I feel so happy like I haven't felt for so long, I really like him; he is so nice, different to other men I have met."

Alice replied that she agreed he was a nice man with good manners who came over as a thoughtful caring person. "Know they have been few and far between in our lives of late haven't they, eh?" Alice giggled.

Emma smiled and nodded as they went inside the villa. "Right Emm, I'm hitting the sack, this bod needs to revitalise and I'm thinking a lazy day is on the cards tomorrow without so much booze as today; maybe a detox day; what you say?" Emma only had one thing on her mind, tomorrow could be whatever it wanted as long as she was spending it with Gavin and feeling the way she was at that moment. Alice could see the love bug had certainly taken a massive bite out of Emma as she hugged her friend goodnight and wished her sweet dreams.

Emma smiled at Alice saying she didn't want the feelings she had to end before wishing her a goodnight and going off to bed. Gavin and Jeremy chatted in the taxi on the way back to their villa, Jeremy asked Gavin if he had fallen for Emma saying that he was a totally different person to the one he had come away with.

"Look mate, this is between us so don't go blabbing to Alice or anyone else for that matter, I feel a little mixed up at the moment; torn between what my head and heart are telling me. I do genuinely like Emma; she is a great girl with a fantastic personality and totally gorgeous."

"I'm sensing there is a 'but' coming here," Jeremy interrupted.

Gavin continued, "Yes unfortunately, you're right and it is about how we go on after the holiday is over. Look, she has made a huge difference to how I have been feeling these past couple of days; she has helped me deal with getting over Jess a lot easier than I was doing before I met her. I never planned to find a relationship out here, in truth I never even expected to meet anyone but I did and she has given me a different perspective on things and I honestly believe that I can now move on from Jess."

"So what you so worried about, Gav, look, you met a girl, she likes you, you like her; have some fun then when the hols are over, you go your separate ways; simples eh?"

Having now arrived back at the villa, Gavin continued explaining his concerns, "Look mate, what happens if over the next week we get even closer than we have already after two days, I mean I know how I feel inside and I can tell Emma feels similar but what happens if we end up really falling for each other; how are things going to work out then when we go home?"

"Whoa mate, you're jumping way too far ahead of yourself here, look this is just a little holiday fling, a bit of fun that's all, mate, at this rate you'll be ringing the vicar to meet you at the airport!" Jeremy laughed as he put his hand on Gavin's shoulder giving him a friendly squeeze.

Gavin shook his head and looked a little lost for a moment before saying, "This was not something I had planned for, Jez, and I can't say I have any idea where I am going with it, the only thing I know is that when I'm with Emma, I feel good and I want that to continue."

Having said that, Gavin told Jeremy that he was tired and was going to bed, Jeremy said he would see him in the morning and told him not to stress on things and to just see how things played out.

Emma and Gavin struggled to settle very well that night, lying in their own beds tossing and turning mulling over similar thoughts of hopes and worries. Emma occasionally gazed affectionately at the picture on her phone that had been such a spectacle at dinner earlier, the image warmed her heart as she recalled to mind the words of the waitress.

As the night wore on, both fell into deep sleep and dreamt the night away until the morning came around.

Thursday Day 5

At Gavin's villa, Jeremy was first up and refreshing himself in the shower feeling good about things and with thoughts of Alice in his head hoping that he could get a little more intimate with her. Back at the girls' villa, Lacey and Kelly were busy sorting out some breakfast as Alice joined them in the kitchen. "Morning ladies, how we doing, something smells good," Alice said enthusiastically, sniffing the air as she peered over Lacey's shoulder.

"I am making a sort of frittata out of some things we need to use up, be a love and see if Emm is up yet, will you?" Lacey asked as she poured in her egg mixture.

Alice gladly obliged and made her way to Emma's room then gently tapping on the door she asked Emma if she was awake, a faint reply of yes was heard as Alice opened the door and peered inside.

"Morning Emm, how are we, ready for another exciting day in Kalkan eh." Emma was sitting up in bed clutching at her phone looking at the same picture over and over since she awoke.

"Look, Lacey is making a frittata for us for breakfast; are you going to join us?" Alice asked an almost sad-looking Emma. "Hey what's up Emm, you look like you're carrying the world on your shoulders; everything ok?" she asked as she made her way over to her friend's bedside.

Sitting beside Emma, Alice looked down at the picture on the phone and said that was her favourite of all the ones she took, Emma commented that it was a beautiful photo that truly captured the moment and then told Alice what the waitress had said at the restaurant.

"Oh Emma, that is so beautiful! I hope that it all comes true for you, you really do deserve it to but why the sad face?"

Emma just sat there and gave a big sigh as she shrugged her shoulders whilst giving an expression of uncertainty, Alice encouraged her to get up and join them saying that she had to tell the others what she had just told her.

Kelly called out that breakfast was ready and they were having it on the front patio, it was another beautiful day just after 9 am and warming up nicely.

Alice and Emma soon joined the others and sat down to a lovely breakfast with them, Alice told the girls that Emma had something fantastic to tell them about last night and encouraged Emma to divulge it.

Emma took her phone and showed the girls the photo in question then went through the story with them exactly as it unfolded word for word, both Kelly and Lacey swooned at hearing it telling her that she was such a lucky girl.

Kelly turned to Emma and said, "Emma, that was really beautiful and I pray it really happens for you but please forgive me for asking but why the hell have you got a face like someone that has just been smacked with a smelly kipper."

The others agreed that she did look rather lost and forlorn, Lacey added that after the two unbelievable days she had just had, she thought she should be full of joy and happiness by now.

Alice and Kelly looked on in agreement at Emma who was sat there pushing her food around the plate, Kelly asked her to tell them what was bothering her as they were all friends and there to support each other.

Emma sat upright and with a deep breath explained all to her friends, "Look, I'm just a little scared ok or more like worried that everything is going to escalate up to a wonderful point before it comes crashing down around me again. It has been so difficult for me to let my guard down for so long now, I have refused to allow anyone to get this close to me in ages that I am worried I will do or say something that will ruin it all."

The others were silent as they first looked at Emma with sympathy before looking at each other all hoping one of them had the right words to offer their friend. Alice said that Jeremy had given Gavin tremendous praise as a friend and a person saying that he didn't have a bad bone in him and was not the type to cheat or mess you around.

Emma said that they all probably thought she was being foolish, something they all quickly refuted, she added that she never expected to have feelings like she did for someone, especially after only a few days.

Alice replied back, "Well, he did save your life, Emm, and you did get a one in a million picture with him on the sunset cruise, didn't you?"

Emma nodded in confirmation and managed a smile to go with it as Lacey asked what did everyone fancy doing that day. "Retail therapy is what we need, ladies!" Kelly cried out saying that she had seen in one of the brochures that it was market day in Kalkan on a Thursday, something apparently that wasn't to be missed.

"Well, I was planning on a quiet day today but I can always fit in a bit of RT so yeah I'm up for it, what you say, Emms, shop away the blues yeah, up for it, girl?" Alice asked.

Emma laughed. "Yeah come on, why not; a bit of RT may be what I need right now." Lacey was quick to say that she was game for it stating that she was never one to turn down an opportunity to spoil herself, Kelly suggested about half an hour to get sorted before they went meaning they would be able to get back and relax by the pool for the afternoon and plan out their evening.

As they cleared away the breakfast things, Alice asked Emma what her plans were regarding seeing Gavin next, Emma said that he was going to call her shortly to see what she was planning but she hadn't really had time to speak with them about it. Kelly interrupted on hearing the conversation and told Emma to do whatever she fancied; they would carry on regardless, Emma said that would mean Jeremy would be on his own and she didn't want to force Alice into having to go out with him every time she saw Gavin or force the girls to have to keep him company.

Alice said she didn't mind Jeremy's company but confessed she was not smitten with him as Emma was with Gavin, Emma asked Kelly if she and Lacey had planned on seeing Matt and Giles again.

"We said that we would call if at a loose end and Matt has my number now as he said he was planning a bit of a party at his place over the coming week and promised to invite us all once he decided when."

Alice told Emma that she must put herself first and not to worry about her or Jeremy, she added that Jeremy and Gavin had probably had a similar discussion themselves.

Kelly called Memhet to arrange pick up but he told her he was not driving today as on Thursdays he helped his uncle in the market. Kelly said that was where they were heading and Memhet said he would arrange for his cousin Rafa to collect them and bring them down. Memhet then told them where to find him and not to buy anything until they had as he would get them the best prices for whatever they desired.

All the girls were excited by that prospect and checked that they had enough Turkish Lira to enjoy themselves; once ready, they waited at the bottom of the steps for Rafa who arrived moments later.

As the girls climbed aboard the taxi, Gavin called Emma, "Hi Emma, how are you this morning?"

Emma answered that she was fine and told Gavin that they were on their way to the market, Gavin asked what her plans were for the rest of the day and she replied that at that moment, they were just going to do some shopping and then chill by the pool and decide on what to do that evening.

"Look Emm, how would you all fancy coming over here and chilling by our pool this afternoon, I can get some pizza and salad arranged with some wine or something else if you fancy, the views here are to die for and I'm happy to come collect you all if you would like."

Emma said that she would have to speak to the others first and promised to call him back in a while, she thanked him for his call before saying goodbye.

Emma told the girls of Gavin's proposal and they mulled it over as the taxi made its way down the hill to the town and the market, Alice said she was easy and happy to go along and then Lacey said that it sounded good adding that she was happy as long as she could just relax as the last two days had been mad.

As they neared the market, Emma texted Gavin back saying she would let him know when they finished at the market and that everyone was happy to go along with his proposal.

The girls were amazed at the size of the place and the amount of people mulling around looking at the various stalls that sold everything from shoes, clothing, handbags, to food, crockery and ornaments there was literally every sort of thing you could wish for.

Lacey shrieked with laughter as she pointed out to a sign that read "everything guaranteed authentic fake"; the other girls laughed as they looked on in bewilderment. Emma said she had to take a picture of it as it was hilarious.

"Ladies, Ladies," Memhet's voice called out as he walked to meet them, "good morning ladies, welcome to the Kalkan market; this is your lucky day, it is special price for beautiful English ladies day all day," he said with a cheeky grin and a laugh.

"Oh lucky us," Alice laughed as the other girls joined in the amusement chuckling along, Memhet led the girls along telling them that he would get them the best prices for whatever they wanted.

"We have beautiful handbags and shoes if you like," he said enthusiastically pointing out to a stall, Emma and Kelly were quick to say that they had enough of both of those items until Emma spotted something. "Wow look at that bag, oh my lord, it's gorgeous!" Emma rushed to pick it up and examine it closer.

"Same old Emma, she will never change." Alice laughed watching her friend enthuse over yet another handbag.

"What you think, girls, to go with my black and gold outfit, you know with the short jacket?" Emma asked as she posed with the bag in various positions and admired the design. The man on the stall was fast to step in with other options but was ushered back by Memhet with a stern look, waving his arms and speaking abruptly in Turkish.

The man backed off as Memhet encouraged the girls to look closely at the merchandise endorsing the earlier sign they had seen saying that the quality was excellent and that they were all authentic fakes, Emma asked how much they were as she picked up a little bag with a gold strap saying that it was perfect for nights out to carry the essentials.

Memhet assured them that the price would be favourable as the stall holder was his wife's cousin; Lacey asked if there was anyone in Kalkan that he wasn't related to. Emma had made up her mind that she was having both bags as the other girls found it difficult to resist buying one, once they had all decided what they were having, Memhet told them that each bag would be £20 each, the girls stood there in shock; even though they were not authentic, they still believed that they would be double that as they rushed to pay the man.

Emma asked if the small bag was the same price and Emma was shocked further to discover that she was being given it as a present for bringing good business. The other girls seemed a little envious of the fact but before anyone could react, Memhet spoke again in Turkish to the man who gave them all a Turkish silk purse each and that seemed to please them.

Memhet showed them around the market where Alice and Lacey bought some shoes at ridiculously low prices and he carefully ushered them away from the fake perfumes and DVDs; after they had satisfied themselves on their retail therapy session, they turned their minds to the fresh produce section where they stocked up on fruit and salad items.

The girls gasped at the size of the peaches and the quality of the produce in general but were totally amazed at how little it all cost compared to back home.

Soon the joyful shopping experience was over and the girls decided it was time to return to the villa, Memhet led them out of the market the back way and arranged for a taxi to collect them.

He waited with the girls until the taxi arrived and helped put their goods in the back of the car, the girls were huddled together discussing something as Memhet said that all was done and wished them a good day. Lacey called him closer so they could thank him and slipped a £20 note in his shirt pocket and gave him a peck on the cheek closely followed by the others who all thanked him.

This act of appreciation did not go unnoticed as a group of Turkish men smoking and taking shade beneath a tree cheered, waving their hands in the air with big smiles on their faces. "I will be much talked about now," Memhet smiled as he waved back at the men in acknowledgement; the girls got into the taxi, all smiling happily and waving goodbye to Memhet.

On their way back, they agreed that they would go over to Gavin and Jeremy's in about an hour or so, giving them plenty of time to get sorted, Emma eagerly called Gavin with the news and he agreed to collect them around 1.30 pm.

Time seemed to drag by for Emma as she waited on the terrace out front eagerly watching for Gavin's arrival, the others teased her a little about her eagerness to see him.

The sound of a car coming up the hill had Emma's head up and looking out down the road, hoping it would be him and there turning the corner he was, her heart fluttered as did her stomach as a beaming smile stretched across her face seeing him approach.

Lacey who was on the terrace waiting shouted out to the other two that lover boy was here, Emma gave her a funny look and asked her not to be so cruel.

The girls grabbed their bags and locked up and made their way down to the car where Emma had already arrived and was firmly wrapped in the arms of Gavin. "Come on, get a room, you two," Kelly giggled as they all got in the car.

The girls thanked Gavin for the invite, Kelly saying they had packed some wine and asked if they needed to get anything from the supermarket, Gavin politely said no as he had arranged everything already, adding that Jeremy was finishing off the last bits.

Gavin pulled up at the bottom of his steps and then led the girls up to the villa; the girls were very impressed with the location and the villa itself that was very grand, a little smarter than their own.

Entering the villa, they were greeted with hello's from Jeremy who got a little tongue-tied on seeing Alice; she was wearing a pair of rugged cut-off jeans shorts that were not fastened and a sheer white blouse tied under her chest over her bathing costume. Her hair just hung down somewhat dishevelled and even though she wore no makeup, she looked amazing to him.

Jeremy stepped up close to Alice to welcome her personally, she sensed his attraction to her and that pleased her, causing her to throw a hand around his neck and pull him down to plant a kiss right on his lips then saying, "I hear you have been a busy boy, what have you been up to?"

Jeremy was highly aroused by the kiss and asked Alice to follow him and led her out to the pool terrace; once there, Jeremy explained how he had laid out all the sunbeds having retrieved some from the solarium and blown up the inflatables, he also had set the dining table over in the shaded part of the garden for later as it was going to be a very hot day.

There was an outside kitchen and BBQ area that Jeremy showed Alice just as they were joined by the others, he proudly showed a well-stocked fridge with all sorts of soft and alcoholic drinks. Gavin pointed out that they had put out extra towels if needed and asked everyone to make themselves comfortable before asking Emma to join him up on the solarium to see the view.

Emma thought the view was stunning and even though she had a great one from her terrace, this one offered something different, the pair stood side by side as Gavin put a gentle arm around her and she rested her head against him looking out at the boats in the bay below and the jet skis racing out to sea.

Gavin asked how her trip to the market went and she was excited to tell him about the bags she had bought; Gavin laughed at her enthusiastic telling of the trip as he suggested that they re-join the others.

Around the pool, the others were moving their sunbeds into position and getting ready to relax in the heat of the day, Jeremy was entranced by the sight and vision of Alice, who having removed her blouse was now bent in half removing her shorts.

"Careful you don't drown in that drool, Jeremy!" Lacey cried as she watched him appreciate every little movement Alice made, the others laughed as they looked at his expression as Alice turned about to look at him with a puzzled expression.

"Right, let me get some drinks sorted, who wants what? We have everything from wine, beer, spirits and soft drinks. There is also coffee if you fancy it," Gavin joked.

After a few moments, Gavin was able to garner what everyone wanted and then instructed Jeremy to assist him, once everything was ready, the boys delivered the drinks to the girls who had just finished putting on their sun cream then joined them around the pool.

Emma had put two beds close together for her and Gavin and they lay there chatting away as the others settled down in the bright hot sunshine.

Gavin told Emma about a place he had discovered some years back with his parents the last time he holidayed out here with them, he said it was a nice drive away up through the mountains past the trout farms and the blue lake.

"So what is it exactly?" she asked.

"Well, it is a kind of restaurant outdoors set in little open-sided hut type structures where you sit on cushions and carpeted floorboards, it's really unique and it gives you a magnificent view of the Taurus Mountains across the countryside. We would go there for breakfast; you just make yourself comfortable on the floor and then they start bringing you fresh bread and Turkish tea, then an incredible amount of traditional Turkish breakfast dishes; it is unbelievable, there is so much choice."

"Oh wow, that sounds really nice, Gav, are you planning on going again this holiday?"

"Well, it was not part of the plan but I was thinking about it over breakfast earlier and thought that I would ask if you fancied going there with me one morning in the next few days, I will have to check for booking availability but what do you think?"

Emma didn't give it any thought and just said, "Yes oh yes please, it sounds wonderful," then in a whispered voice she asked what about the others.

Gavin said that he was sure they could spare her for a morning and perhaps they may all like to go together after he went back home; Emma's nature changed quite suddenly as she looked distant and troubled.

"You ok Emm, you look a little sad all of a sudden?" he asked her with a little concern in his voice.

Emma stood up and gave an unconvincing smile and nod saying she needed the bathroom and walked off wrapping herself in a sarong, Alice who was close by asked Gavin if everything was ok and he explained what had just been said.

"After you go home…oh no, it's not your fault, Gavin. Emma is a little fragile at the moment, you see, she has not allowed anyone to get this close to her for a long time in fear of being hurt again, she really likes you and knowing her, she probably has some fantasy going on in her head that this holiday will never end or perhaps hopes that is the case."

Kelly agreed with her sister and said she would go and check on her and got up to go find Emma and Gavin took himself off up to the solarium to think alone.

Jeremy then told Alice and Lacey that when he got up this morning, he found Gavin on his tablet working out how far it was from his home to Taunton and how long it would take.

"Do you think he will still want to see Emma then after the holiday?" Lacey asked him.

"To be honest, I don't know, Gavin is a top bloke, he won't mess anyone about but I think he is a bit confused about everything, he does genuinely like Emma and never stops talking about her when they are apart; it's just…"

"It's just what, what is it just, Jeremy?" a concerned Alice asked.

"Look, it's only my thoughts, nothing he has said or anything but I'm just worried this is a bit of a rebound for him, Jess really devastated him and he has not been the same since, all his banter and attitude is a front for the hurt he is supressing. Emma is a shield protecting him from it and I am not sure how he is going to react once we have to leave."

Kelly stood outside the bathroom door gently knocking asking Emma if she was ok in there, there was no reply.

"Come on Emm, talk to me babes, what's up eh?" Emma replied that she was ok and would be out soon, she asked to be left alone for a moment saying she needed time to think. Kelly agreed to leave her be, adding that everything would work out fine and not to worry herself too much.

Kelly returned outside and was met by Gavin coming down from the solarium. "Is she ok, Kelly, can I do anything?" he asked with much sincerity.

Kelly assured him that everything was ok adding she needed a few moments to sort herself out, the pair joined Alice and Lacey as Jeremy called out from the garden kitchen asking if they wanted top ups.

Emma emerged from the villa to join the others, feeling somewhat embarrassed, trying to hide her face behind her hand she made her way over to Gavin and apologised to him for being silly but Gavin said that he understood and that it was fine; he was feeling a similar way.

Emma was a little more positive hearing that from him and leant forward to kiss him saying thank you as she did, Emma looked up across to where Alice was sat on her sunbed giving her friend a smile and a nod, Alice raised her glass in response and mouthed the words "are you ok". Emma smiled happily as she nodded with enthusiasm.

The afternoon passed by slowly with everyone totally relaxed in the hot sunshine, Alice lay on an inflatable bed in the pool being playfully harassed by an attentive Jeremy while Kelly and Lacey added more sun protection to themselves as they lay back on their sunbeds.

The distant hum of the jet skis could be heard occasionally thrashing around in the bay below and the odd dog bark were the only sounds to break the silent peaceful atmosphere before Lacey asked Gavin to put some chill out music on.

It was a little after 3 pm when Gavin said that he would put out some snacks and nibbles for them to enjoy in the garden kitchen that was well shaded, he said that he would arrange for pizza delivery for around 4.30 pm once he found out what everyone liked.

"Well, very impressive, I must say, Gavin," Lacey commented entering the garden kitchen and seeing the trouble Gavin had gone to, there was a neatly cut up and arranged fruit platter, cheese on sticks, nuts and crisps and best of all, bite-sized prawn cocktails set on baby gem leaves.

Kelly joined her saying that they wouldn't need to order pizza after all that but Lacey said otherwise; saying this would be a nice starter before she tackled a spicy meat feast pizza. Gavin laughed saying that was what he and Jeremy always order, Kelly said that Lacey was a lucky girl who could eat anything and everything and not gain weight.

Lacey responded that she had an excellent metabolism and was quite an active person on a daily basis, which helped. Kelly pulled a funny face as she pinched at her waistline quipping that she had better ease up on all the cocktails she had been enjoying as she was certain she was gaining weight.

Alice was just joining them and hearing her sister's comment told her that she was fine and not to worry about it as she was on holiday and nothing should get in the way of her enjoyment.

Once everyone had snacked out and chosen their pizza, they all went back to their sunbeds, the sun seemed more intense as the stepped from the cool shade and the ground very hot as they scurried to get to the sanctuary of the beds. Gavin placed the order for the pizzas to arrive later then joined Emma on their sunbeds, Emma asked when Gavin was thinking of taking her to the mountain restaurant.

Gavin restated that he would have to check availability first and said that he would make a call shortly. Emma looked a picture of happiness as Alice commented that it sounded really nice.

Conversation was muted around the pool as the sound system played some soothing and relaxing chill out music, everyone just lay back and relaxed except Jeremy who found the heat a little too much and sought relief in the coolness of the pool.

Alice was returning from the bathroom and noticed her sister had dozed off and was getting burnt on the top of her legs at the back so applied some urgently needed sun cream to the area, causing Kelly to stir from her doze.

"You have caught it a little bad there, sis, I suggest you turn over and rest that area for a while and put plenty of aftersun on it later." Kelly thanked Alice for noticing and abruptly turned onto her back saying that it didn't feel too sore at that point and maybe she had caught it in time, Alice smiled saying she was glad before jumping in the pool and swimming over to Jeremy.

"How you doing then, Jezza?" Alice asked with a wide grin.

"Oh you know I'm just chilling here, that sun has really gotten intense since the storm last night, hasn't it?" he answered puffing out his cheeks before asking Alice how she was doing.

Alice said that she was glad they came over as it had been a nice afternoon and that the views were everything they were promised to be, Jeremy asked her if she had been up on the solarium yet and as she said no, he told her to follow him then led her up the stairs to it.

"Oh wow, look at that," she said as she gazed across the vista before adding that it was one of the nicest and prettiest views she had seen so far.

Jeremy smiled saying that it was beautiful but not as lovely as the view he was looking at right then, Alice turned to him giving him a pleasing smile and saying that she hadn't gotten him down as an old romantic type.

"Ah well, full of surprises me, I know when to turn on the charm when I have to."

"Oh really, do you, and when do you think you have to then?"

"Moments like this when I'm looking at a stunning girl that I want to take in my arms and snog the face off," Jeremy replied in full peacock mode brushing back his hair and puffing up his chest with his hands on his hips.

"So what you waiting for, big boy, an invitation, come on then let's see what you got."

Jeremy took Alice in his arms and proceeded to kiss her passionately on the mouth with full tongue action, the embrace took Alice's breath away almost as she enjoyed the moment. It wasn't the first kiss they had shared but the intensity was nowhere near as this before and it made Alice grow a little warmer to Jeremy, after a few minutes, they broke from the embrace and Alice expressed her shock at his intensity in the kiss adding that he must have been bottling that up for some time.

"You have no idea, Al, I think you are top class you know, I am well into you and think you're a stunner and someone I could easily go out with in a relationship. Forgive my crudeness but you are just my type, the sort of girl I always look for and I love your personal strength, not someone that will take any crap—you're solid."

"Well, I'm not sure I have been called solid before but I think I understand your reasoning. Look, I think you are a good-looking guy; need a little work on the personality front but nothing major but in your own words, you are a bit of a player and that's not what I'm looking for, sorry. Now that does not mean we can't have a little fun on holiday but honestly, beyond that, I don't think there is any hope."

Jeremy smiled turning his mouth downwards saying that was fair enough but there was no harm in trying to prove he could be different, adding that he hoped she may think differently before he left.

Alice said not to hold out too much hope but he was welcome to try, as they turned to return to the poolside, Jeremy asked for one more kiss before going down and Alice obliged as he gave her a cheeky squeeze on the buttock at the same time.

Alice gave him a look as if to say naughty boy but something inside her stirred as the reality of her enjoying it sank in. Jeremy led her back to the pool carrying with him a cheeky grin as they went.

As they re-joined the others, Kelly looked up at Alice and quizzed her on what they had been up to up there on the solarium, Alice a little flustered at the questioning just mumbled they were taking in the view.

"Oh so that's what they call it now is it, taking in the view!" Lacey chuckled as an unusually flustered Alice took to her sunbed.

Emma was about to question Alice on her disappearance when Alice was saved by a voice calling out "Pizza delivery"; Gavin and Jeremy rushed out to the front to meet the delivery man and once they had paid, they returned to the outside kitchen beckoning the girls to join them for the hot pizzas. Kelly asked how much they owed but Gavin said it was his and Jeremy's treat as they were their guests, refusing to accept anything from them.

The girls thanked them as they tucked into the pizzas and the side orders of chips that came with them, Jeremy opened some sparkling wine and handed the glasses around.

After finishing up the food, the girls insisted on doing the clearing up and told the boys to relax, Jeremy grabbed a beer and sat back at the pool side while Gavin went off to make a phone call before joining his friend back by the pool.

When the girls finished all the clearing up, they joined the boys and all agreed it had been a lovely day and wondered what they would do later, Gavin took Emma to one side and said that he hoped it was ok but he had booked the mountain restaurant for Saturday morning.

Emma smiled with pleasure telling him that she was sure it would be fine and rushed over to the girls to tell them the news. Kelly spoke up saying that she should go for it and enjoy herself, eagerly supported by the others who insisted that she should jump at the chance for a little early morning adventure.

Emma and Gavin only had eyes for each other as they hugged with delight, Lacey changed the subject back to what they were going to do that night.

Kelly said she fancied a quiet setting with some tranquil background music where she could kick back and relax without any fuss, Alice was easy about it and said she was happy to fall in with whatever and Lacey agreed adding that a chill out night would be good before the weekend started as she really fancied a wild party weekend where she could throw caution to the wind and see what happens.

Everyone laughed at Lacey as Kelly told her to be careful what she wished for, Emma asked Gavin if he had any plans but he had not given much thought beyond hosting them at his place and said that he was open to ideas.

Jeremy said that the beach club below where Gavin and Emma ate last night usually had some kind of music event on a Thursday night and that could be a bit laid back as it was usually acoustic and you could distance yourself as near or far away from it as you liked as the club was spread across the rock face.

"That's a bloody good shout, mate, it was pretty cool when we went the first night here, I have a business card somewhere for it. Shall I find it and give them a ring; what does everyone think?" Gavin asked as he looked around for responses.

Everyone sat there just nodding at each other until Lacey said that it sounded a good idea and asked Kelly if she felt it were chilled and laid back enough for what she was looking for, Kelly said that she was up for giving it a whirl adding that she could always leave if it were too rowdy.

Gavin disappeared to find the information and once he did, he called the club up and they confirmed they had a Blues Jazz saxophonist playing later. He took it upon himself to reserve a table for six not too close but close enough then returned to tell the others.

Everyone seemed pleased with the outcome and didn't bat an eyelid when he told them there was a small entrance charge payable on arrival. Gavin said they needed to arrive before 8 pm so asked the girls to meet him and Jeremy outside fifteen minutes before then gave Emma the card for the taxi's purpose.

"Ok ladies, I think on that note we had better get a move on; it's not far off six now," Kelly said as she started to gather her things.

The girls thanked Gavin and Jeremy for a lovely afternoon as they waited for their taxi to arrive, the sun was over far to the right of them about to disappear and the sight made Emma smile with delight as she recalled her sunset kiss with Gavin.

Back at the villa, they discussed what they were wearing out later. Lacey was in the kitchen making some tea saying she would take it easy tonight as she didn't want to spoil the weekend. Emma joined her saying she could do with a coffee and was asked by Alice to make one for her.

Emma carried a cup of coffee into Alice's room where she found Alice wrapped in a towel having just showered and sat at her dressing table, Alice thanked Emma and asked her if she was feeling better about things with Gavin now.

Emma said that she couldn't help feel a little stupid about the event but felt she was getting to grips with the reality of her situation and that she hoped Gavin and she may see each other after the holiday, Alice told her about what Jeremy had said to her about Gavin checking how far Taunton was from his home.

Emma was a little shocked but happy also and told Alice that they had not discussed anything about after the holiday yet. "To be honest, Al, I don't really want to think about it, I just want to enjoy each day that we have and then see how it goes." Emma paused before continuing, "But it is nice to hear that he is thinking about it, isn't it?" She turned to leave deep in thought.

Alice agreed but asked her in a caring way not to get her hopes up, she told her to enjoy herself to the full but not to get too far ahead of herself. Emma returned to her room where she started to prepare for the evening ahead, Kelly shoved her head around the door to ask her opinion on the maxi dress she had chosen to wear.

Emma responded very positively telling her that she looked fab, Kelly was grateful for the response but looked at Emma quizzically not expecting such a buoyant and lively reply. Walking past Alice's room, she poked her head inside, "How we doing, sis? I say what's gotten into Emma; she seems really chirpy a lot more than usual eh?"

Alice filled her sister in on what she had missed out on earlier and they both agreed that it would take her one way or another, Alice said she hoped it would be down the right pathway but you could never tell with Emma.

Once they were ready, the girls sat in the early evening warmth on the front terrace. Kelly had arrange for a taxi at 7.30 pm so they had ten minutes to wait, Lacey asked Alice if she had changed her mind about Jeremy and joked that they had spent such a long time up on the solarium quizzing her what went on up there. Kelly laughed adding, "Yes come on, spill the beans girl, we are all waiting."

Alice tried to say it was nothing that they were just looking at the view but the others were having none of it. "Oh ok, so we may have had a little kiss or two."

"Now we are getting there; come on, are you falling for him, Al?" Kelly asked with a beaming smile.

"Look he is a fit guy, fair enough and boy, his kisses can be intense but I erm I—"

"Yes great bod great snog, but you what?" Lacey interrogated her.

"I like him but what's the point, it's not going anywhere, I told him he needs to work on his personality in places and that he is a player and I can't trust men like that, so it's just a bit of fun unfortunately with a hunk of a guy who could kiss for England." Alice laughed then told them to change the subject.

Lacey asked Alice if she would sleep with him, Alice paused before answering in a reflective manner saying that she probably would in the right circumstances but it wasn't anything she was currently contemplating.

"How about you, Emm, would you sleep with Gavin?" Lacey asked as Alice chirped in, "Well, if we had been a little later last night, we may have known the answer to that, eh Emma."

Emma shyly said she didn't believe she would have allowed it to go that far as she considered that a major step forward for her, something she wasn't sure she was ready for at this moment.

Gavin and Jeremy were just arriving at the beach club, Jeremy asked Gavin how he was feeling about Emma now, saying that the mountain breakfast trip was a big statement and was worried Emma may get the wrong message given her actions earlier.

Gavin said that he was fine and that they were taking things slowly, Jeremy commented that if what he walked into last night was slowly, he begged him not to go any faster.

"What's your point, mate? Look, I've told you how Emma makes me feel, I don't understand what you're getting at."

"Ok Gav, hear me out; we have been best mates for years. I know you like a brother, I'm a little concerned you're getting all this on the rebound and in the end, you will end up worse than when you came out here, that's all."

"Worse! Worse than what, what do you think I'm some kind of sad arse that has lost it or something? What are you saying, Jez, come on tell me." Gavin started to get agitated with what Jeremy was saying mainly because deep down he knew he had a point.

"Gav, after you and Jess split, you went downhill fast and that was tough on you I know, as this holiday got closer, there was a change in you; something strange, not good and to be honest mate, I only agreed to come out with you so I could make sure you didn't do anything stupid."

"Stupid like what! Oh for fucks sake, mate, so you think I'm suicidal or something now, is that it?"

"No Gav mate, it was your brother Harry that said all your family were worried about you and even though it was Harry that suggested you use up the honeymoon as a holiday, he was still concerned for you so I agreed to come along. Mate, I just want to make sure you don't get hurt anymore or put yourself in a more vulnerable position, that's all."

Gavin walked off a little ways thinking to himself not understanding why none of his family had spoken of their concerns; at that moment, the girls arrived and getting out of the taxi, Alice looked at Jeremy's expression and sensed something was wrong.

Emma looked where Gavin was stood several meters down the pathway and turned to Jeremy, asking him what was wrong, Jeremy said it was something and nothing as Emma made her way tentatively towards Gavin asking him if he was ok.

Gavin turned to Emma and not with the best of expressions on his face that she had seen. "What's wrong, Gav? What's happened?" she asked sounding concerned."

"You think you know people, you know family, friends…" at which point he glared at a disconsolate Jeremy. Kelly jumped in and asked if they were going to sort out whatever was going on as she really wasn't up for a night of tension and bad feelings.

Jeremy apologised saying that their earlier conversation had gotten a little deeper than he intended and that some revelations that Gavin found hurtful came out, Jeremy assured them it was not his intention to cause his friend any distress and suggested that they continue on down into the beach club and give Gavin some space to get himself together.

Emma was quick to agree, ushering her friends away saying she would stay with Gavin, everyone made their way down to the club and were led to a spot reserved for them not too far from the bar or the music platform.

Emma comforted Gavin up on the roadside asking him if he wanted to talk about it, Gavin felt unable to disclose what had been said in case Emma may get offended or hurt so just said it was a personal thing that he would deal with as he wrapped his arms around her, thanking her for being there for him.

"Come on Gav, let's go join the others, try and put this behind you, look, I now Jeremy can be a bit of lad and perhaps a little thoughtless at times but he genuinely cares for you and I don't think he would say or do anything intentionally to offend or hurt you."

"I know you're right, Emm, it just came out of nowhere and I wasn't prepared for it, Jez has always had my back, I should have known he meant well and if I'm honest, there was probably some truth in what he was saying from his viewpoint."

Emma and Gavin joined their friends who were all sat comfortably listening to the relaxing background music and chatting amongst themselves, Jeremy got to his feet as the couple approached open-armed telling Gavin he was sorry. Gavin smiled saying that he too was sorry for his reaction as he hugged his friend.

"Ah, don't you just love a beautiful bromance!" Lacey laughed as the other girls looked on smiling and laughing at the two friends embracing each other.

"Go on Jeremy, give him a big kiss and make up like in a true romance," Alice added as everyone roared with laughter; even the people sat close by couldn't help laugh at the spectacle as Jeremy commented that he wouldn't do that, joking that last time Gavin had used his tongue.

"That's typical of you, Jeremy, to lower the standard once again," Alice said giving him a sort of naughty boy look.

The artist for the evening started his performance and the group sat back enjoying the melodic music that was relaxing helping them chill out with a little help from the social and very moderate alcohol intake. A little over halfway through the set, people were standing up dancing and swaying to the romantic tones emanating from the saxophonist's wonderful playing.

Gavin and Emma were entwined in each other's arms sharing the occasional kiss as were Alice and Jeremy although Alice was careful not to let Jeremy get carried away as he had earlier, Jeremy then plucked up the courage to ask Alice if she fancied staying with him at his place tonight.

Alice was a little shocked but not totally surprised as her knowledge of men, especially Jeremy's type, meant she had expected it to be on the cards at some point, something inside her stirred as she pondered his request because part of her wanted to.

"It is a lovely offer, thank you, Jeremy, but not tonight ok; maybe another time, let's see how it goes eh?" Alice knew the wonderful time she was having in Kalkan and all the alcohol she was consuming might make it happen but knew it was too soon and wanted to get to know him better first no matter how good his kisses and body were.

"Ah well, no harm in asking, is there, and there is always tomorrow and the next day and the next day…" he continued until Alice stopped him saying that she would see.

Kelly and Lacey looked on as their friends were embroiled with the two lads dancing and kissing. "Hey Lace, do you think it wrong to be sat here feeling a little jealous of those two having found some romance here on holiday and we haven't?"

"No, not at all, Kell. I think that is perfectly natural; although I feel kind of jealous in a way, I am still very happy for them, you know."

"Oh yeah I'm with you on that one, I wouldn't change things for the world and look at our Emma there; who would have thought it eh, especially after the year she has had; she looks so loved up. I hope it works out well for her."

"Well, at least we have Matt and Giles to fall back on, they may not be our boyfriend material but they are generous and know how to treat women correctly so all is not lost on us." Lacey chuckled as Kelly nodded in agreement.

Gavin and Emma strolled down to the water's edge where a cool gentle breeze caressed them as it rose up off the water, helping refresh them from the warm evening air, holding hands and gazing lovingly at each other. Gavin said he wished he could have a crystal ball to see how things would turn out for them but Emma said that she was happier enjoying the excitement of what every new day brought.

Alice and Jeremy had joined Kelly and Lacey back at the table and sat there looking down towards the other two, Alice wondered what they were talking about and hoped Emma was thinking straight.

Jeremy leaned over to Alice and whispered that he thought it would not be too long before Gavin and Emma were getting it on, the way they were together. Alice, unintentionally abrupt, sat up declaring no way saying that Emma was not ready for that yet as she had too many barriers and hurdles in front of her that no one could penetrate.

Kelly and Lacey turned towards them asking what was going on and Alice told them what Jeremy had said, Kelly and Lacey agreed with Alice saying that Emma was like Fort Knox when it came to that—something Jeremy found difficult to understand.

Lacey turned to Jeremy and said, "Look Jeremy, it's like this ok, Emma has built a fortress around herself over the past couple of years and every time something bad happened, she pulled up the drawbridge before lowering it again only to have to pull it up once more. Unfortunately, things got so bad for her that she pulled up the drawbridge and then shut the portcullis padlocking it and throwing the key in the moat—you get the picture?"

"Oh Lord, it's that bad?" Jeremy asked a little shocked.

"Oh there's more, now, as you can see, the drawbridge is lowered but Gavin will have to open the portcullis and even if he were able to retrieve the key from the moat, it will be all rusted and of no use. The portcullis is made up of square boxes and each one is open showing and reminding Emma of the hurt, betrayal, lies, abuse and so on. Gavin will have to close every one of those boxes if he is to get anywhere with her, that's if he is genuinely interested in seeing her after the holiday that is."

"Wow but the other night he was all over her and she seemed to be enjoying it; maybe he has closed those boxes," Jeremy said confidently.

Alice joined in saying that she thought they interrupted them at the right time, she said that Emma and she had talked about it and that Emma said that she would not have gone any further as much as part of her probably wanted to.

Jeremy sat there puzzled, rubbing his chin then jokingly turned to Alice saying he hoped her drawbridge was down and the portcullis open. "Oi cheeky boy, that's my sister you're talking to," Kelly reprimanded him before Alice said he was just having a laugh.

Lacey said that she would leave the key hanging outside if she could meet someone decent enough causing everyone to laugh as Kelly said she would gladly bulldoze her walls if she could find the same.

Gavin and Emma joined their friends back at the table and asked what all the laughter was about, Alice said it was one of those you had to have been there moments and quickly changed the subject to what they had been up to.

Emma just said they were talking and enjoying the view across the bay adding that it was only lights that could be seen just as fireworks started to explode lighting up the water over at the other side.

Everyone at the beach club watched the wonderful display go off for several minutes applauding and cheering as it finished, Gavin commented that someone must have gotten married as it was common out there for fireworks at night after a wedding.

Having settled the bill, they all made their way up to the road where several taxis were waiting, Gavin told Emma he didn't want her to go and hoped the evening could start all over again. Emma hugged Gavin and said that she had enjoyed their day together and felt the same but it was almost 11 pm and she was starting to flag a little and didn't want to spoil the next day.

Jeremy said that he was up for hitting the town if anyone was up for it but he had no takers, he turned to Alice holding her around the waist and asking if this was goodnight then. Alice smiled telling him to take it easy adding there was plenty of time to party, then winking at him, she kissed him goodnight.

Jeremy took full advantage, kissing her with the intensity she had experienced earlier that day and he finished it by clenching her right buttock to the shouts of "get a room, you two" from the others waiting.

Gavin reluctantly let Emma go promising to call her in the morning at first then signalled that he would text her later, Emma smiled back at him as she joined the others in the taxi and headed back to the villa. Gavin said it had been a long day and wouldn't mind an early one himself as he and Jeremy climbed into their taxi and head back to their villa, Jeremy was slightly disappointed but happy to go with the flow.

Back at the girls' place, Lacey said she was making a cup of tea before bed and asked if anyone would join her, Alice and Emma were happy to but Kelly said she had an urgent appointment with her pillow so declined as she said goodnight to everyone.

The three girls sat in the lounge drinking their tea and Lacey commented to Alice that she and Jeremy were getting really close, Alice assured her that it was all a bit of fun and that she was making the most of a situation that had presented itself.

"Look, I have made it clear he is fit and a great kisser but that is it honestly, although he did ask me to stay back at his tonight," Alice added with a big grin.

Lacey and Emma sat upright wanting to know more and Alice said that she had told him it was too soon, Emma asked her if she would sleep with him and Alice replied that she had already said that if circumstances and the situation was right then maybe she would but it was not something she was planning anytime soon before pulling a tongue in cheek face.

"Oh you little tart, Alice, you are going to, aren't you, you filthy tart, or should I say filthy lucky tart, haha!" Lacey giggled as she squirmed in her seat.

Emma received a text from Gavin and made her excuses to leave the other two, wishing them a goodnight as she went to her room where she spent the next half hour texting back and forth with Gavin.

Friday Day 6

The girls all slept well that night, waking up feeling really refreshed and full of energy, Emma had been first up making some coffee before returning to bed and waking Gavin up with a morning text.

"Well, that was the best night's sleep ever," Kelly said with a radiant smile. "I've had a wonderful shower and now feel ready for a good hearty breakfast down by the port; anyone up for it?"

The others looked at each other nodding in their usual way with Alice saying to go for it just as Emma joined them asking what were the plans for the day.

Lacey said that they were going down by the port for breakfast and suggested that they discuss it while down there adding that she was easy for the daytime but felt like really letting her hair down in the evening.

Emma was happy to go along with them but said she would be taking it easy that night as she had an early start the next day going off to the mountains for breakfast with Gavin; the others said that was no problem promising to be quiet that night when they returned.

Kelly called Memhet to collect them in half an hour as they all got themselves dressed ready to go, Emma texted Gavin to say what they were doing promising to let him know as soon as she knew.

Memhet pulled up pleased to see the girls all looking happy and well, he told them that his family and friends at the market had teased him all the rest of yesterday after they had left him and they all laughed.

Memhet dropped the girls at the same restaurant they had been on their first day in Kalkan and were warmly invited as Memhet shouted out something in Turkish to the manager who waved back at him with a smile. Memhet wished the girls a good day saying he was available all day if they needed him.

Over breakfast, the girls decided to go back to the beach club they had visited first out in the bay and relax before hitting the town later for dinner then some good raucous nightlife was on the agenda later. Lacey asked Emma if Gavin and

Jeremy would be joining them and at first Emma thought it may be a problem but Lacey assured her it wasn't; it was just that if they were then she thought to invite Matt and Giles along as well.

Kelly said it was a great idea and told Lacey to call Giles and see, Lacey made the call as Emma texted Gavin about the arrangements. Meanwhile, Kelly searched in her bag for the number of the beach club to reserve the sunbeds together and once she found it, she waited for Lacey to reply. Emma confirmed the boys would join them and asked what time would they be going down there as Kelly put up her hand for her to wait for Lacey who was talking rather excitedly to Giles.

Lacey told the girls with great enthusiasm that the party Matt had said he was arranging at his villa was for tomorrow and that it was no longer going to be there because he had hired a big yacht to take them out to the sunken city along with some friends and business associates of theirs who arrived early on Thursday morning and others that were arriving on Saturday morning.

Kelly and Alice screamed with excitement as did Lacey but Emma just sat there smiling happy for her friends, mindful that she was not going to be joining them as she would be away with Gavin.

Kelly realised this after a few moments, looking around the table at her friends. "Oh sorry Emm, you're off with Gavin, aren't you, look maybe you can get him to change it eh and then we can all enjoy the yacht trip together; what do you think?"

"No, it's fine Kell, really; I think it is meant to be as I already felt guilty about leaving you all now it doesn't matter and to be honest, I want some alone time with Gav while I still can, so no it is fine honestly."

Lacey then continued that the men would not be joining them today as they were entertaining their friends but promised to text them later the time to meet up for the trip.

"This is going to affect our plans for a raucous night tonight now so I think a major downgrade is needed so we don't ruin tomorrow's adventure," Lacey suggested, getting the thumbs up from Alice and a nod from Kelly.

Kelly arranged for six sunbeds at the beach club for around midday saying that would give them time to return to the villa and dress appropriately and get all the necessities needed, having called Memhet, they made themselves ready to leave and were soon on their way back to the villa.

They told Memhet their plans and he said that he had another call to pick up but would return for them in time to get to the beach club for noon, saying he could drop them close to the water taxi point.

The girls set about putting on their bathing costumes and covering themselves over with shorts and T-shirts before packing sun creams, hats and towels and everything else they needed.

It wasn't long before they were on their way to the port and getting on a water taxi over to the beach club, it was ten minutes before midday and the girls were feeling really excited about everything as the promise of a day out on a big yacht had really captured their imagination, filling them with much anticipation.

Arriving at the beach club, they were welcomed by a familiar face that recognised them immediately, Mesut showed the girls to their sunbeds asking where the other two guests were.

Kelly explained they would be joining them soon and then told him about the sunset cruise asking Emma to show him the now infamous photo, Mesut was stunned at the picture as he called a colleague to look, who applauded Emma.

Mesut was about to explain to the girls the significance of the image captured when in unison they all said yes we know; at that point, the boys arrived to the delight of Emma but Alice as always played it cool.

Mesut told Gavin he was a lucky man and congratulated him as he asked if he could take any drinks order, once he had taken the orders, he left them to settle down. Alice was wearing a rather revealing black and gold bikini and the lower part left nothing to the imagination at the back and when she stood and turned to adjust her towel, Jeremy's eyes almost popped out of his head.

In fairness, there wasn't a male in sight that hadn't admired the wonderful form that Alice cut as she stood there rubbing lotion over herself, she looked like a screen siren from some epic erotic blockbuster as she moved about with purpose, gently applying lotion to her now tanned toned body.

"Ok sis, you can sit down now. I think the world has seen enough eh, come on now, look at poor Jeremy; he is beside himself with amour for you." Kelly laughed as she again beckoned Alice not to make an exhibition of herself any further.

Alice was in total control of what she was doing as the sight of Jeremy's tanned muscle-toned body had turned her on as he and Gavin arrived, causing her to send out animal-based signals to catch his attention even though part of her knew she was wrong to do so and it was totally unnecessary because she had already won him over long ago.

Lacey told the boys about the yacht trip the next day with great excitement in her voice, a worried-looking Gavin turned to Emma who settled his mind before he had a chance to speak. "It's fine Gavin, don't worry. I want to go to the mountains with you that's all there is to it really, please don't worry about it." Gavin suggested that he may be able to change to another day but Emma said no and to leave it as planned.

Everyone settled down as Mesut returned with their drinks apologising for the delay as they were busy and short-staffed at that time, the girls thanked him and sat there enjoying their drinks as Gavin and Jeremy checked out the jet ski hire for later.

As usual, in Kalkan at this time of year, the skies were blue and it was lovely and hot, the sea was warm and inviting and there was always something to do or somewhere to go with the friendliest and most helpful locals you could wish to meet.

The boys re-joined the girls after booking a jet ski for later that day and sat down with their cold beer in hand, Jeremy asked Alice if she fancied doubling up with him on the ski later, something she found to her liking.

"Oh yes please, I have always fancied that but was not sure going on my own."

"Don't worry, you will be safe with me. I'm a bit of an expert on these things. I always book them when I'm away, you will have to hold on tight to me though," he finished with a cheeky grin.

"Oh so that's how it is, is it?" Then with an unexpected comment, she whispered, "And where exactly am I supposed to be holding on tight to?" Very much tongue in cheek that caught Jeremy off guard causing him to almost choke on his beer as he took a gulp.

With a confident swagger, he told her that he would leave that to her imagination and that he was not bothered where she held him; unfortunately, Lacey heard that comment. "Oh please, you two; it's a bit early for that kind of talk, if you're going to carry on like that, can I suggest you move away somewhere more private or better still, get a room." Lacey gave Alice a look of disapproval as she was behaving totally out of character, especially given all the things she had said recently about how she felt towards Jeremy.

Kelly had missed most of the conversation and asked Lacey what was up but Lacey just waved her away saying it was nothing. Kelly looked across to Alice as if for some explanation but Alice just shook her head nonchalantly and gave her a cryptic smile as she sucked on her straw taking a drink.

Meanwhile, Gavin was trying to convince Emma to join him on his ski but she was a little unsure as the near drowning escapade earlier that week had made her wary of deep water, Gavin tried to say it was like riding a bike, you fall off but you have to get back on at some stage and the sooner the better.

"Look Emm, how about I go out and have a mad run about for a while then come in and pick you up, you will have a life vest so it won't be so bad and I promise not to go crazy."

Emma pondered it for a moment and then said that maybe she would give it a try but made Gavin promise that he would go easy or she would not go at all, Gavin couldn't have promised any more devoutly, giving her every assurance that he would take great care of her.

There was a wonderful atmosphere at the beach club; the background music enhanced the mood as everyone chilled out on the sunbeds, out in the bay, jet skis patrolled the waters with revellers having fun as the tourist day boats sailed past, dropping anchor and allowing people to dive into the crystal clear warm water.

Around 1.30 pm, Mesut appeared with menus asking if anyone wanted to order food, he said that the kitchen wasn't too busy at that point so there should not be too much of a wait. "From 2 pm normally, people start ordering food then we have a crazy hour. 2 pm crazy hour for food, 5 pm happy hour for drinks!" he laughed.

Alice said that they wouldn't be eating until after 8 pm that night so a salad or something might go down well now, Mesut handed out the menus and promised to come back in ten minutes saying he would prepare a nice table for them in the meantime.

Jeremy said that the double chicken burger with fries was his choice and Gavin agreed that was a good shout, Emma said she fancied the chicken and avocado salad and was joined by Kelly and Lacey but Alice opted for the seafood mix salad. A short time later, Mesut returned to take their order and before they knew, they were being sat and their food was served.

Everyone agreed that the quality and portion sizes were excellent value for money, they all sat there in silence enjoying their lunch with some nice chilled wine for the girls and ice cold beers for the boys.

Once their lunch was finished, they returned to the sunbeds to let it settle, the boys had reserved the jet ski's for 4 pm so had time to allow their food to digest. There wasn't much conversation to be heard as they all applied more sun lotion, Alice taking a more conservative approach with her application this time but that didn't stop Jeremy from admiring her as she rubbed the lotion over her chest.

The afternoon sun was almost at its hottest and Lacey decided that a little shade was needed as she did not want to ruin her tan, she was aided by Mesut in putting up the sun shade and repositioning her bed so not to spoil it for those close to her that were happy as it was.

The time came for the boys to take to the water on the jet skis and so they made their way over to the hire point after telling Alice and Emma that they would be back for them in a short while.

The girls watched from their sunbeds as the boys roared across the water pulling tight turns and bouncing up and down crashing through the wash of the large vessels that passed by, Emma smiled poignantly at Alice as they witnessed Jeremy come a cropper pulling a stunt move, Alice just raised her eyebrows tutting as she said, "Boys and their toys eh."

It wasn't long before the boys signalled they were coming in for the girls who then made their way over to the jetty; having put on life vests, they climbed aboard the skis where Alice asked Jeremy if he had damaged anything in his little moment of madness.

"Well, I'm not sure to be honest, I think I may need a second opinion; what do you think eh?" he said cheekily, not expecting what happened next.

Alice pressed her hand just beneath his life vest on his abdomen. "Well, that feels fine to me, no damage there," she chuckled.

A slightly disappointed Jeremy was about to shrug his shoulders saying fine when Alice slid her hand down to his private parts, giving his penis a good squeeze then commenting, "Oh wow, now that feels promising" then burst into laughter.

Jeremy had a broad smile on his face as he gushed that he wasn't expecting that but thanked her anyway, Jeremy pulled away on the ski with lustful thoughts about Alice filling his mind as Alice herself was having a slight moment of regret. She could not quite believe what she had just done and wondered what was happening to her today as she recognised that she was not her usual self, it was a feeling that was slightly concerning to her but at the same time something inside her was enjoying it.

Emma wrapped her arms around Gavin the best she could with the life jackets in the way. Gavin pulled away at a steady pace, increasing as he went; he told Emma to say if it was too fast for her but she seemed content and safe in his charge.

The two couples revelled in the excitement of riding across the water on the skis joyfully, watched by Kelly and Lacey on the shore, Jeremy naturally made some risky manoeuvres as he tried to bring a real thrill to the moment.

Emma was surprised how much she actually enjoyed speeding across the water, she felt that Gavin had helped her overcome her deep water phobia and was really enjoying herself, actually asking him to go faster.

The fun and games were soon over and they reluctantly took the skis back in, they returned to join Kelly and Lacey who had just plunged themselves into the sea.

Alice and Emma joined the girls in the water and were eager to tell them about the fun they had, Lacey commented that she was surprised to see Gavin and Emma speed along as fast as they were. Emma responded saying how thrilling it all was and that was clearly evident in the way she was talking. Gavin and Jeremy were refreshing themselves with a cold beer discussing the recent bit of fun they had, Jeremy told Gavin what Alice had done to him grabbing his penis.

Gavin stood there open-mouthed totally shocked as the pair then burst into laughter, Gavin told Jeremy that he and Emma had discussed about him and Alice and he said that he asked her if she thought the two of them would hook up at all.

Jeremy was all ears asking Gavin what she said. "Well, to be honest mate, she said no, she said that Alice was not an easy target and like herself had been messed around enough before that; she was very particular who she got with.

"She did say that she would probably kiss you which she obviously has but that was it, but now she has grabbed your dick, who knows eh; maybe she has changed her mind," Gavin said bursting into laughter and chinking glasses with Jeremy.

The girls were in the water looking towards the boys wondering what all the laughter and chinking of glasses was about, Alice said that she had a good idea and told the girls what she had done.

Kelly was totally shocked as was Emma but Lacey just laughed out in bewilderment. "What! You actually grabbed his knob, what the hell are you on lately, Al, you are acting very strange, girl," Lacey added as Kelly said that she didn't know who her sister was anymore.

"Honestly sis, what has all that you have been saying about him meant, ok yeah, he is good-looking and all that but you know you will be just another notch on his bedpost, don't you?"

Emma just kept silent listening to them all because she knew how she was feeling inside herself and in a way sympathised with Alice, she knew part of her wanted her and Gavin at some point to be more intimate but she also knew there were several demons that needed casting out before she could be a true lover to him.

Alice tried to laugh it off saying it was just a silly prank but Kelly said that Jeremy may see it as some kind of come on. "Look, he is up there probably nursing a hard on for you right now," Kelly added.

The girls joined the boys back by the sunbeds and Lacey said that they should start to think about packing up as it would start to get dark soon, Gavin asked Emma what her plans were for later but she wasn't exactly sure other than they were going into town for dinner around 8 pm.

Alice told Jeremy that she had told the girls what she had done and asked him not to read anything into as it was only a silly prank, the problem was she had really enjoyed doing it and standing there looking at him caused a well-hidden emotion of sexual desire to rise up within her.

Jeremy, although gutted to hear those words, was surprisingly very understanding and gave his assurance that it was not a problem; giving Alice a gentle hug, he said, "Well, I suppose I can forgive you and if nothing else, I can go home in the knowledge the fittest girl in Kalkan grabbed my dick on a jet ski."

Alice laughed at his comment giving him a playful jab in the chest asking what she was going to do with him.

Kelly asked the boys if they were going to have the pleasure of their company tonight, Gavin looking at Emma said that he hoped so and received a nod of approval from her. Everyone thanked Mesut for looking after them, tipping him nicely, and made their way to the jetty to await the next water taxi.

On the water taxi, Alice asked openly if anyone had any suggestions for dinner later, Gavin said that there were a few places that he knew if the girls wanted to try something different. Lacey said that with over 100 restaurants to choose from, she wanted to go somewhere they hadn't been before with all the others in agreement with her, Gavin suggested that they meet at the usual cocktail bar around 8 pm and he would take them from there.

As they arrived in the harbour back in Kalkan, Lacey received instructions from Giles for the next day along with a picture of the yacht, Kelly's eyes lit up as Lacey, who was speechless, showed her the picture.

"Oh my goodness!" Kelly cried. "Look at that boat, it is enormous."

Lacey showed the picture around and then said they had to be at the port for 9.30 am and read out the rest of the instructions of what they needed to bring and then the footnote stressing no high heels, causing the girls to laugh.

Once they were on dry land, they all walked to the far side of the marina where they found the yacht moored up being made ready, they all took snaps of it gushing over how wonderful it looked adding that they were so excited looking forward to tomorrow.

Kelly said she couldn't face walking up the steep hill to the taxi rank and suggested she call Memhet to collect them, then she asked the boys if they wanted a taxi as well which they confirmed.

The two groups parted ways saying they would meet up later and returned to their own villas, Alice said that they had roughly two hours or so to get ready so she was going to take a little nap commenting that it was very tiring enjoying yourselves.

It was just after 7 pm when Kelly roused her sister from her nap, she was well aware that getting ready for a night out was something Alice could do in no time at all. "What time is it?" Alice enquired.

"It's just turned seven; you have forty-five minutes before Memhet collects us," Kelly answered her back.

Alice thought it ample time for a quick shower, fix her hair and a touch of makeup was not a problem for her, in the shower her mind turned to her earlier action with Jeremy and as she cleaned her private parts, the touch along with her thoughts caused her to feel strong emotions within herself; she pondered on them for a moment before abruptly pulling herself together and telling herself to get a grip.

The other girls were all ready and waiting out on the front terrace as Alice emerged looking a million dollars in a figure-hugging black mini dress that showed off her beautiful golden tan and long blonde hair wonderfully.

"Well, someone is out for the kill tonight," Lacey commented.

"What can I say, ladies, a woman has got to do what a woman has got to do?"

Alice smiled back at them full of confidence and ready for a good night out, Memhet arrived moments later and took the girls into town dropping them off and wishing them a wonderful night, he said to call him when they were ready to return.

As the girls neared the cocktail bar, they could see Gavin and Jeremy approach from the opposite direction, they had been down to check on reservations at a particular venue but could not get in. Gavin was able to secure another place but there was no table until 9.15 pm.

The girls didn't seem bothered saying that it was going to be a sensible night anyway so it just meant going home straight after dinner, the group made their way into a crowded cocktail bar where the girls were able to get seats but the boys had to stand until more seats became available.

A waiter that recognised them from previous visits welcomed them and took their orders soon returning with their drinks, they sat there for the next hour watching people pass by the girls commenting on some of the outfits other women were wearing and just generally chatting before it was time to head off to the restaurant for dinner.

They headed down the left side of the old town until they reached the rooftop restaurant and were taken up to their table; unfortunately, all the front-line tables overlooking the harbour were taken and they sat towards the back where there was a sound of lovely music coming from across the way.

Alice and Lacey peered over the wall into what looked like a large garden decorated with beautiful lighting and appeared to have an outdoor bar; they called the others to look and they too were impressed.

Gavin said that he had been in there in previous visits and explained a little more about it adding that they should all try it out at some point; once they had all ordered, the table talk turned to their expectations of what tomorrow may bring. Emma said that she was really excited to go to the mountains for breakfast with Gavin as he had told her so much about it, the girls all wished her and Gavin a wonderful day out.

Kelly said that she had always fancied being on a big yacht in the south of France sailing up and down the med and added that Kalkan was as good a place as anywhere to do it.

Just as the food was arriving, Lacey received another text from Giles about Saturday's event, she excitedly read through his message holding her hand to chest whilst smiling in disbelief at what she was reading.

"Ok guys, wait till you hear this, that was Giles he said that there will be a big seafood buffet with champagne, wine and every drink imaginable available on board and he is asking about any allergies or dislikes." Alice and Kelly squirmed in their seat with excitement eyes wide open as Lacey continued.

"He said they expect to be back between 5 pm and 6 pm then there will be a little party back at Matt's house and we are all invited to that later around 8 pm till late and he put very late in brackets!" Lacey laughed as Kelly and Alice looked on with great excitement.

Lacey texted Giles back that everything was perfect, they had no allergens and mentioned that Emma and Gavin wouldn't be joining them on the boat but Jeremy would.

Gavin asked Emma if she was sure she wanted to miss out on all that luxury for a Turkish breakfast in a wooden hut in the mountains, Emma took Gavin's hand in hers gently squeezing it saying that she was sure all the money in the world couldn't buy what they would experience tomorrow.

Gavin thought her response was beautiful as did Alice who overheard and gave Emma a pleasing smile and nod, everyone tucked into their dinner and talked away about their excitement until it was time to leave.

Walking up to the taxi rank, Gavin told Emma that he would pick her up around 8.30 am in the morning adding that it was a shame the day had to end, Emma smiled and answered that if it didn't end they couldn't share a beautiful one tomorrow alone together. Gavin took her in his arms and kissed her with great affection, once again stirring the flighty emotions of her innermost parts.

Jeremy said his goodnight to Alice not expecting much in return but was pleasantly surprised when she planted a big kiss on him, she said that it had been a good day and had enjoyed his company adding that tomorrow promised to be even better, winking at him in her alluring way and lingering before eventually letting go of his hand.

Jeremy smiled back at her with a look about his face almost as if he was expectant of them maybe really getting together, Alice was spot on sensing what he may be thinking and tongue in cheek raised her eyebrows to suggest he may be right.

Jeremy was really hot under the collar now; his hormones were raging with desire and his testosterone levels were probably through the roof, the girls returned to their villa as Gavin and Jeremy went their way discussing what had just occurred between Alice and Jeremy.

Gavin was a little confused suggesting that she was giving out mixed signals and that it must be playing on his mind, Jeremy agreed with his friend but added that he thinks she may be coming around to him, Gavin said that he would message Emma shortly and see if she had anything to say without revealing too much.

Back at the girls' villa, Alice was changing in her room when Kelly came in. "So sis come on now, out with it, what's going on with you and the bod then?"

Alice laughed at her sister's description of Jeremy before saying that there was nothing and that they were just friends with the odd benefit. "Oh come on, Kell, I've told you there is nothing going on."

"Well, it didn't look that way just now before we left and I heard what you said to him and saw the way you were acting, oh and please don't get me started on your actions earlier today on the jet ski."

Alice again giggled at recalling that moment saying that her sister had it all wrong. Kelly said she knew her well enough to know that something was not right and that she wasn't prepared to stand idly by and watch her younger sister embarrass and make a fool out of herself.

Alice started to get a little flustered, she knew Kelly only meant well but she didn't want to hear it right then as she had been in great place within herself all day and know Kelly was ruining it for her.

"Kelly, look, you're my big sister and you care for me thank you, I get that but listen, I am almost thirty-four years old and nobody's fool. I am well capable of making my own decisions about who I see and sleep with and quite sure I can handle things my own way without interference, thank you."

"Hey guys, what's all this; what's going on?" Lacey entered the fray.

"Well Lace, it seems that my little sister is intending on sleeping with boy wonder despite all her earlier protestations to the fact."

"Alice no really, but you agreed that you would just be another notch on his bedpost with us earlier."

"Look Lace, I'm not saying that I am definitely going to sleep with him but I had a sexual connection with him today and it is tormenting me. Bloody hell I haven't had sex for over six months and if I decide, and it will be me who decides, to have sex with Jeremy then it will be on my terms ok. I will be using him to satisfy me, not him using me. Maybe I can start putting notches on my bedpost; how would that suit, eh sis."

Kelly looked at her sister a little shocked but shrugging her shoulders, she said, "When you put it like that, it doesn't sound too bad I suppose and if I'm honest, I slept with my ex hubby on the second night and look how that turned out so I suppose if you feel that you're in control of it, you crack on, do as you see fit but please be careful, Alice, you have had more than your share of hurt already, heaven knows we all have; please don't put yourself in harm's way again, please promise me."

Alice hugged her sister before saying that she had already stressed that if she does so, it will be on her terms and that there will be no hurt to be had, the only thing maybe disappointment that he was not up to the mark but judging what she had felt down there earlier, no need to worry about that!

Lacey gave Alice a playful nudge telling her that she really was a little tart before saying that she hoped Jeremy gave it to her good and proper if the chance occurred.

Kelly stood up, raising her hands and saying, "Ladies enough please, no more this is my little sister. I don't want to think of a strapping hunk plundering her virtue, thank you very much."

Emma appeared at the door; she said that she heard the commotion but was busy texting Gavin and asked what was going on, Kelly said that her sister may have had a change of heart about shagging Jeremy that was all, then she said she needed a cold drink before she went to bed.

Emma stood there dumbfounded looking at Alice unable to say that she and Gavin had just been discussing the same topic to avoid breaking his confidence.

Alice told Emma that she never said she was going to; only that if she did, it would be on her terms, Emma replied that she thought Jeremy would gladly sleep with her on any terms she liked, causing both Alice and Lacey to laugh out loud.

The girls wished each other goodnight before going to their beds, Alice had a mixed night trying to sleep well as she was tormented by the invasive lustful feelings she was having towards Jeremy.

Saturday Day 7

Emma slept wonderfully and was up out of bed and in the shower at 7 am, she made her way into the kitchen after and put the coffee on and boiled a kettle for some tea for herself. Emma was soon joined by Kelly who thanked her for starting the coffee and asked how she slept, Emma replied that she slept well and woke excited for her mountain adventure with Gavin shortly.

Lacey entered the kitchen, scratching her head and yawning. "Morning all, how are we, looking forward to your romantic trip to the mountains then, Emm?" she asked.

Emma smiled nodding and saying she couldn't wait before taking her tea back to her room to get ready, there was no sign of Alice stirring yet so Kelly took her a cup of coffee to wake her up.

"Come on, sleepyhead, rise and shine, it's 7.40 am we need to be up fresh and ready for our day out; come on," Kelly urged her sister but only received a garbled response from a very tired Alice.

Kelly opened the curtains to let in the new day then sat next to Alice on the bed stroking her hair asking if she was ok. Alice eventually rolled over sheltering her eyes saying that she had an horrendous night, not sleeping too good at all. Kelly told her to drink her coffee and she would see if Lacey fancied knocking up one of her famous breakfast treats that would get her going. Alice thanked her for the coffee and sat up to drink it as thoughts of the night's invasive actions took a hold of her.

Alice wondered why she had allowed herself to get into this position to begin with contemplating that it was either meant to be or going to be a major disaster of a decision as she pulled a pillow over her face and grunted away to herself.

Kelly poked her head in again to say that there was good news as Lacey had suggested she would do them all a fry up except Emma as she would be leaving soon.

Upon hearing that, Alice's thoughts turned to Emma and she got out of bed to go and see her, knocking on her door she asked if she could come in and Emma encouraged her to do so.

"Oh Alice, sorry love but you look terrible; are you ok?"

"No I couldn't sleep much because Jeremy kept taunting me with his body and big cock," she moaned as she threw her heavy feeling arms around Emma, giving her a big hug.

Emma could not help but laugh. "Oh Alice really, was it all that bad?"

"No, the bloody opposite I think. I was enjoying it so much I couldn't switch it off!" The pair sat on the end of the bed laughing at her predicament.

"So not long now before your big adventure eh; although I wish you were coming on the boat with us, I think some alone time with Gavin may help you decide if you want it to continue after the holiday."

Alice told Emma that her hair looked nice the way she had put it up and asked what she was wearing so Emma quickly showed her the items she set aside and what she had decided on for Matt's party later giving Alice cause to raise an eyebrow of approval.

Alice said that she would leave her to get ready and joined the others in the kitchen. "One egg or two, Al, what do you fancy?" an eager Lacey asked.

"Oh um one, oh what the heck, give me two please, Lace," Alice answered as she returned to her room in search of her coffee that had cooled by now.

There was plenty of coffee in the pot as Alice refreshed her cup then joined her sister on the front terrace watching the sun come across from the east, Kelly asked her how she was feeling and Alice replied that she would survive just as Lacey called out for assistance carrying out the breakfast. The three friends sat enjoying their breakfast and chatting about the day ahead with all their hopes and expectations.

Shortly after, Emma appeared asking how she looked, she was wearing a pair of smart comfortable shorts with a coordinated top and sensible shoes for her day out, the girls all smiled in approval at her choice telling her that she looked a picture as Kelly took one of her on her phone.

There were still fifteen minutes to go before Gavin was due but the sound of an approaching car coming up the hill had them all looking out and they could see that he was early. Emma said that she needed the bathroom and to collect some things before she could leave and left the girls to greet Gavin still in their pyjamas.

Gavin came bounding up the steps full of energy and eagerness to see Emma, he stopped suddenly upon seeing the other girls still in their nightwear and apologised for disturbing them, not expecting to see them there.

Lacey had returned to her room behind Emma to collect a dressing gown and picked one up for Kelly from her room, Alice was wearing a t-shirt and bed shorts so wasn't bothered, the girls were touched by his shyness and apologetic nature then said that Emma would be out shortly.

Alice asked how Jeremy was and he replied that he was going to make his way down to the port and have breakfast then wait for them by the yacht. He added that he hoped they had a great day and was looking forward to hearing all about it later as the girls reciprocated the same feelings.

Emma emerged from the villa to calls of here she is and greeted the awaiting Gavin.

"I hope I'm dressed suitably," she said shyly.

"Wow Emma, you look more beautiful every day I see you."

The other girls loved to hear that sentiment as they looked on with doting love and care for their friend before wishing her and Gavin a fantastic time, Emma hugged her friends thanking them and wished them a great day before leaving with Gavin.

"You know what, girls, I don't think we could have hand-picked a better man for our Emma. He is so polite and thoughtful and the thing he said to her when she asked if she looked ok, oh my, how many times have we heard a reply like that in our time? Never is what I think; it really choked me up," an almost emotional Kelly said as the others nodded in agreement with deep sighs.

"Right then, ladies, let's get ourselves dressed, packed and ready for our high seas adventure; what do you say!" a buoyant Lacey cried.

The girls made their way inside and Kelly pointed out they had just over forty-five minutes before Memhet would be there to pick them up, having quickly showered, the girls attired themselves and packed their day bags checking they had all the essentials just in time as they heard the toot of Memhet's horn.

Gavin and Emma made their way to their mountain rendezvous going directly up out of town and across the main road straight over taking the road out past the trout farms and the blue lake, Emma was amazed by the scenery that route afforded them asking Gavin to stop occasionally to take some pictures.

Soon they arrived at the restaurant and Emma was struck by how much it reminded her of years back when she was backpacking with friends in Thailand, Gavin parked the car and they made their way into what was for all intents and purposes a large garden with a water feature and a number of roofed structures with open sides. They were led to their hut where they removed their footwear and sat on cushions on a carpeted wooden floor.

Gavin pointed out to Emma saying look there, Emma turned to see the most beautiful and wondrous site of the Taurus Mountains across the plain of lush green grass land that stretched for miles.

Emma commented that it truly was a magnificent and magical site to behold saying that the strength and power of the mountains could be felt in the atmosphere there, something Gavin was quick to agree with, saying he had always had the same feeling.

A young waitress appeared carrying water and glasses that Gavin said was drawn from their own spring; Emma said that it tasted so pure and fresh.

Next, a selection of homemade breads came with a plethora of homemade butters and spreads, honeycomb from their own hives with goat's cheese and fried eggs and so many dishes—too many to mention.

It was an incredible feast for breakfast topped off with a Turkish pot of tea, the pair sat there for ages slowly eating their way through everything, having the bread and tea topped up when requested.

Back at the port in Kalkan, Jeremy was waiting patiently for the girls when he was spotted by Matt and Giles who were already on board, they called out to him to come aboard saying that they could do with a bit of muscle moving things around. Jeremy thanked them for the invite and said that the girls should be with them any minute, Giles said it wasn't a problem as their friends were running fifteen minutes late.

The girls arrived at the yacht and were welcomed by Matt who showed them on board. Alice was reluctant to board as she looked around to see if she could spot Jeremy. A voice sounded out, "Hey gorgeous, you looking for me?" Up on the upper deck stood Jeremy in a pair of white shorts and his top off, the sight of his glistening muscular torso sent a shiver of excitement through Alice as she waved up to him as she boarded the vessel.

"So Emma and Gavin have hit it off big time, have they?" Matt enquired of Kelly.

"Well yes, sort of; it is really still in its early stages at the moment but it looks promising," Kelly answered.

"Oh good, good for them, they do make a nice couple. I am pleased, they both could do with something positive in their young lives, couldn't they?" he continued.

Kelly and Lacey smiled in agreement as he asked about them, wanting to know if they had any luck in finding some company, "besides us two old farts that is," he joked.

Kelly was quick to say that she and Lacey had agreed that they were two charming gentlemen that knew how to treat women and were happy to be in their company any time.

"Oh well, hope for us yet, Matt!" Giles remarked laughing.

The voices of people arriving at the yacht's gangway could be heard over the hustle and bustle of the busy port as other boats were welcoming their day trippers aboard, Matt and Giles welcomed their guests with a furore of greetings and gestures of delight in seeing that they had finally arrived.

Kelly and her group decided to make their way to the front of the yacht to find a good space, there were piles of padded cushions big enough to lie on as well as some really thick high quality towels and smaller cushions.

One of the crew advised them where to locate themselves and they wasted no time in getting settled, a throng of about fifteen people led by Matt and Giles descended upon them whereby Matt introduced everyone by name adding his and Giles' connection to them; some were friends of old and a few were business associates.

Lacey took note that there were a few more men than women in the gathering and noted that a couple looked quite handsome. Lacey turned to Kelly making eyes of delight having seen the few dishy looking guys.

"Hey Lace, it could be our turn today; a couple of real contenders there I think; what do you say?" Kelly whispered quietly, Lacey said that she had noted one chap give her a really pleasant smile when she was introduced so told Kelly it was hands off the one in the blue baseball cap until she had a chance to get to know him.

"Oh what you like, Lacey, come on now let's just enjoy the day; no planning or scheming in your case and see how it turns out yeah!"

Lacey nodded in agreement smiling and saying yes and that what will be will be as she made her pitch ready. Giles appeared saying that there was going to be a little toast on the upper deck in around thirty minutes once they were underway and told them not to get too comfortable adding that it was nice bubbly not to be missed.

Alice looked at her watch and pulling a face said that it wouldn't even be eleven o'clock by then and showed surprise that they were starting the day early. "We will all be pissed before we get to the sunken city at this rate," she scoffed.

"Well, I'm up for a bit of free quality bubbly anytime," Jeremy jumped in as he sat close to Alice.

"Well, there's a surprise I must say not," Alice said rather sarcastically.

"Whoa ok, calm down; it was only a meant as a joke, you're a bit tetchy this morning; you ok?" Jeremy asked as he looked at Alice with inquisitive eyes.

"Take no notice, Jeremy, our Alice didn't have a very good night, did you, sweetie, she had a lot on her mind apparently; well, according to Emma anyways," Lacey commented with a smug look on her face, grinning away at Alice.

"A nightmare was it, Al, bad dreams?" Jeremy tried to show some concern.

"No, it was more a STALLION than a mare!" Kelly screamed out, rocking back and forth in fits of laughter and joined by Lacey who couldn't speak for laughing and just nodded away frantically.

Alice was not amused at Emma betraying her trust like that and said she would be having strong words with her later, she sat there brooding for a few moments until Kelly told her to grow up, adding it wasn't as if it was something she wouldn't have told them herself.

Alice agreed saying she supposed she was right and tried to regain some positive composure, Jeremy suggested he gave her a neck and shoulder massage to help her unwind and relax as he hadn't seen her this tetchy and before she could refuse, she felt his strong hands gently squeeze into her neck in a soothing way.

"Wow Jeremy, you are a man of hidden talents; that feels so good, don't stop please, oh that's it right there." Alice sat there voicing her delight at Jeremy's touch as they felt the yacht's motor start up.

Kelly and Lacey looked on in awe. "Hey Mr lover, don't you think of going exclusive anytime soon; there are two more over here that could do with some of that, eh Lace, what you say?"

Lacey agreed with Kelly as she watched Alice exude total satisfaction at the treatment she was getting from Jeremy who laughed at the suggestion and said that he would see how things went.

Alice thanked Jeremy, kissing him sweetly with real gratitude for his attention and thoughtfulness; she apologised for her erratic behaviour putting it down to a restless and sleepless night.

Giles appeared again and beckoned them to join him and the others up top, he waited for them to gather and then told them that they must feel free to mingle and join in whatever was happening as they were all as welcome as their other guests.

The group thanked him as he led them up to the next deck, a crew member announced that they were about to leave port and the feeling of excitement was all around as people were visibly showing their delight as the wonderful yacht pulled away.

No sooner were they out into the open water of the bay that the popping of the champagne corks filled the air above the hum of the purring motor and joyous sounds of the passengers. Champagne was handed around and Matt gave a toast to his long-time friends and business acquaintances and acknowledged his newfound friends, asking all to have a wonderful time on board.

A happily smiling Matt said that there was plenty of champagne and other drinks available but asked them to save themselves a little for the party back at his villa later. He said they were going to make a few stops en route to the sunken city to allow for some swimming and snorkelling and that the Captain had estimated arriving at their destination shortly before 2 pm, he added that the crew would then prepare a wonderful buffet for them to tuck into.

Relaxing music started to play shortly after Matt's speech and Kelly noticed the man in the blue baseball cap head their way from across the deck. "Heads up, Lace, blue cap incoming," Kelly whispered as she made eyes at Alice and Jeremy to follow her.

"Hi, I'm sorry, I can't remember your name; Lucy, was it?" the good-looking chap asked as Lacey turned to greet him with a nervous smile. Oh my god, he is gorgeous, she thought, and his voice is like velvet. Lacey was mesmerised by him.

"Oh hi, no I'm Lacey, not Lucy," she said admiring him.

"Lacey, what a beautiful name! I don't think I have met a Lacey before, you know."

"Oh it was my parents into their American cop shows back in the day, mum was toying what to call me and in the show they were watching, the partner said oh Lacey you look beautiful and that was it. I'm sorry, what's your name again?"

"Oh Steptoe, yes my parents liked their TV as well," he joked to a giggling and now not so nervous Lacey. "Tristan, it's Tristan, but my friends call me Tris or Stan, I don't really mind to be honest, as long as I know you're addressing me."

"Well, it's very nice to meet you, Tris, the girls often call me Lace and so I know what you mean."

"Giles said you were an interior designer; is that right?"

"Yes, interior designer; I have my own business in the southwest near to Taunton."

"Ah I thought I heard a west country twang there for a moment."

"So what do you do, Tris?"

Tristan said she wouldn't believe it as he pulled a business card from his wallet and gave it to her. Lacey's eyes lit up when she read the card; he was a senior director of one of the country's top interior design companies.

"Oh wow, get out of here! You know, I love the work your firm does, I admit I often get a lot of my inspiration from your work," she said in absolute awe of him.

"Look, I don't want to keep you from your friends but I am going to get changed into my swimwear, how do you fancy joining me for a drink over on the seating up front thereafter?" he asked pointing to the plush thick-cushioned bucket chairs. "It will be nice to hear about your work and get to know you a little better."

Lacey wasted no time in agreeing saying she would let the others know and go collect a towel so she didn't get sunscreen on the cushions.

Tristan went off to get changed while Lacey went in search of her friends, she found Kelly being shown around by Matt in the lower deck interior, it had all the hallmarks of a top design team.

Lacey caught Kelly's attention and Kelly excused herself for a moment from Matt, Lacey explained her conversation with Tristan saying that she would be having a drink and a chat with him up top if she needed her for anything.

"Oh my lord, Kell, he is top drawer, I mean listen to his voice and his mannerisms and he is totally gorge, I mean totally."

"Oh good luck there, Lace, go on, go get him, girl."

Lacey disappeared to retrieve her towel totally unnecessary as there were loads provided up top had she noticed, Kelly smiled with joy as she continued her tour with Matt, who asked what all the smiling faces were about.

"Oh it's only our Lacey. I think she is a little smitten with your friend Tristan," Kelly answered with glee.

"Tristan eh, well she has made a good choice there, I have known him several years and I can honestly say he is a decent bloke with very high standards; she won't go wrong with him."

"If you don't mind me asking, Matt, how come he is here alone? I mean, not with a woman; after all, he is a very good-looking guy, isn't he?"

"Yes, yes he is but it is a very sad story unfortunately; you see, Tris was married to a beautiful girl that came from very high standing and they had two beautiful children; both girls, twins actually, sadly she was diagnosed with cancer about a year later and passed away quite quickly thereafter. Tristan has devoted himself to his girls; they must be about four years old now and of course his work that's what keeps him going, I think he has had a few dates since Penny passed but they have come to nothing; he seems content with his lot for now."

"That is so sad, Matt, he sounds like a really nice guy, why is it all the good ones suffer eh!"

Matt and Kelly continued looking around the yacht's exquisite interior as Lacey reappeared to see Tristan standing by the seats chatting to some friends and holding two glasses of champagne.

"Ah there you are," he said smiling and holding out a glass of champagne to her. "I took the liberty, thought you may enjoy a fresh one," he said in a charming way that made her feel somewhat special.

Lacey thanked him for the thought as he introduced her to his friends, Liz and Mike, explaining that he and Mike had worked on a few projects together over the years.

"Are you a designer as well, Mike?" she asked keenly after saying hello.

"No, I am in high-end construction actually, using alternate building materials in unusual ways, creating futuristic images and shapes."

"Oh wow, that sounds amazing! I would love to see some of those images sometime," Lacey commented as Liz suggested she and Mike leave them to get acquainted, winking playfully at Lacey as she said it was nice meeting her and telling them both to enjoy the day.

Lacey and Tristan sat down and Lacey commented that Liz seemed a nice lady, Tristan confirmed that she was and one of his dearest friends.

"The only issue I have with her is her constant attempt to set me up with someone whenever we are at a social event, I know she means well but believe it or not, I am well capable of sorting myself out."

Lacey laughed and nodded in agreement saying that she was sure he was and couldn't help ask why he was single saying that she thought he was a very attractive man with everything going for him.

"This is not what I normally start a conversation off with when I am first getting to know someone but as you ask so nicely, to put it simply, I am a widower of almost three years with two beautiful daughters and to be honest, with my work and the girls, I don't really have that much time to go courting again. I think if it is going to happen again for me then it will. I am just not fussed about going out searching for it."

Tristan reached down to a small bag and pulled out his phone whereby he showed Lacey pictures of his little girls then pointing at them, he said, "This is Mols and that is Pols; well, Molly and Polly that is, they are like two peas in a pod but Molly has her mother's tenacity and strength and Polly has a kind and thoughtful nature I like to think she takes from me."

"Wow, they are really beautiful; you must be so proud of them."

"Oh yes and then some."

"I am sorry to hear you have been widowed; it must have been terrible, especially with such young children, where are they now?"

"Penny's parents have them, that's my wife's parents, they always take them for a few weeks insisting that I get back out into the world and start living again, I am not sure what they expect me to find but it is nice to have a little me time without worrying about the girls or work but I do miss them terribly."

Lacey sat there full of admiration for Tristan not speaking for a moment just nodding in contemplation of his words, Tristan said that was his story and asked Lacey why was a young attractive lady as herself not attached.

Lacey said that he needed to fill her glass before she would continue and once he had done so, they sat back and Lacey began her story of betrayal and hurt. Alice and Jeremy were chatting with some people on the back lower deck as the yacht pulled out into the open sea and cruised along the coastline eastwards.

Alice was talking to a lady that looked like she was in her sixties, heavily draped in designer fashionwear. Alice knew it wasn't any fake stuff from Kalkan market as she gazed enviously at the various rocks that adorned her hands.

"So you are Alice, is that right, dear?" Alice nodded saying yes. "And this fine specimen of a man is your boyfriend and what is his name again?"

"That's Jeremy and no, he is not my boyfriend as such; we met out here funnily enough on a boat trip early in the week."

"Oh lucky you, my dear, you have done well, haven't you, a fine figure of a man I must say," she said looking at Jeremy in a lustful fashion as if she were about to devour him as she took a sip of her champagne.

Alice found it all so amusing to think this rather well to do woman probably old enough to be Jeremy's grandmother was contemplating sordid thoughts about him.

"Anyway, I'm Jennifer but please call me Jen and that chubby one over there is my husband Harry," she said rather disappointedly before adding, "Well, he keeps me in a fashion that I am accustomed to so I suppose we can't have it all, eh dear?" She laughed saying she needed a refill then called out to Harry, waving her empty glass.

Back up in the mountains, Emma and Gavin had enjoyed probably the most satisfying and eclectic mix of dishes for breakfast ever, Emma declared that she had never seen such an amount or choice before and to feast in such a way in picturesque surroundings was unbelievable.

She said that she would definitely arrange for her and the girls to come here one morning before they left adding that it was probably the best real Turkish experience you could get.

Gavin was so pleased that she had enjoyed the experience so much as the thought of what the others were doing at that time may have been more to her enjoyment, he asked her if she had any regrets not going on the yacht and Emma said she could do a yacht trip anytime but to have been here now with him feeling as she did was much better, then she said that she was sorry that their time there was almost over.

Gavin hugged her dearly, kissing her with so much happiness in his heart, he told her the adventure was not totally over yet as there was somewhere else he wanted to take her, Emma's eyes lit up with excitement eagerly asking where it was but Gavin said to wait and see, promising it would take her breath away.

They both thanked their hosts, Emma saying that she would be back next week with her friends and she was given a number to call to make a reservation being advised to book early as possible, the pair then returned to the car and Gavin drove off taking a different route to the way they had come and drove slowly through lush countryside so full of colour that it shocked Emma, who had imagined Turkey as a dry arid country and not the beautiful green paradise it was.

The yacht was ready to drop its anchor for the first time to allow some swimming and snorkelling in a popular area with scuba divers, Lacey and Tristan had been engrossed in each other's company with Lacey leaving no stone unturned in her revelation about her past disasters in the love stakes.

Tristan found it hard to understand how anyone could treat someone they claimed to love in those ways, drawing on his own past experience of finding everything he had ever wanted in his wife now deceased.

Tristan suggested that they put the past behind them and invited Lacey to take the plunge with him into the sea, Lacey wasted no time getting to her feet and holding hands, they jumped off the yacht together, watched by a very happy-looking Kelly and Matt.

Jeremy was soon plunging into the crystal clear warm blue Mediterranean Sea closely followed by a screaming Alice, a few others but not all took a dip to refresh themselves. Alice glanced up to the yacht where she spied Jen leaning on a rail looking over in the direction of where Jeremy was swimming on his back; it made her laugh as she swam up to him and told him of the earlier conversation she had had with Jen and what she had just noticed.

Jeremy looked up and confirmed she was still looking but she then turned and walked away as if she knew she had been noticed. "Oh well, maybe I will get lucky on this holiday after all!" he joked.

Alice, who found the whole thing ridiculously funny at first and knowing whole-heartedly that Jeremy was joking, found a little green monster was making an appearance within her, she quickly said without thinking that she hoped he had not given up on her yet, then giving him a cheeky grin swam back to the yacht, making her way up to the upper deck where Jen handed her one of the plush towels provided.

Jeremy arrived a moment later behind her dripping wet, Jen feasted her eyes upon him taking a deep breath as she did so, admiring his tanned well-toned physique that glistened in the sunlight. Grabbing a towel quickly, Jen made a beeline for Jeremy and dabbed at him with the towel. "Here darling, let me help you there; you are dripping wet all over the deck."

Alice was incensed; gently nudging Jen aside, she grabbed the towel from her grasp and said rather sharply that she was quite capable of looking after Jeremy.

"Oh my! Oh I mean, I'm sorry, dear, I never meant to offend, he was dripping water everywhere and I...erm...Oh dear." Jen was a little flustered by it all, well aware of what her intentions were and what she was doing, Alice just said it was fine and that she would take it from there as Jen made herself scarce.

Jeremy stood there with a grin of a Cheshire cat proportion, loving every minute of it and turning around telling Alice to do his back in a cheeky manner.

Too busy staking her claim to Jeremy, Alice gladly dried his back oblivious to the comment and the cheekiness of it—not something she would normally tolerate but then Alice had not been herself of late.

Alice went to find the bathroom and found her sister on the way, Alice told her about what had just happened with Jen and the comments she had made earlier. Kelly roared with laughter hardly able to believe what she was hearing just as Lacey was making her way to the bathroom. Lacey asked what all the laughter was about and as Alice made her way to the bathroom, she told Kelly to tell her. Lacey also roared, finding it hilarious adding that she had spoken to Jen herself moments ago saying she seemed a bit stuck up to her and was dripping with diamonds and other expensive jewellery going out on a daytime trip on a yacht.

Alice returned as Lacey made her way to the bathroom and was full of appreciation for the splendour and quality of the really plush fixtures and fittings. Kelly said that Matt had given her a really good tour of the facilities and said how informative he was about everything; she suggested they go find Jeremy before someone else did and get a drink.

Alice agreed and the pair made their way up top via the starboard staircase; meanwhile, Jeremy stood alone looking out at the mainland as Jen spotted him and seizing her chance to speak with him alone made her way over to him; as she was about to put her hand on his shoulder, Alice called out to him saying they were getting a drink and asked if he wanted anything; it was difficult to tell who was more shocked—Jen who had been caught red-handed or Jeremy, turning swiftly to see this hand about to descend upon him.

Jen was rather flustered and tried mumbling her way through some kind of apologetic gesture but couldn't find the exact words she was looking for other than she was only going to speak with him as he was alone; Alice thought it hilarious as did Kelly and Alice insisted it was fine and not to worry.

Kelly couldn't resist saying something and said talking was fine but touch the merchandise and she would be fish food before laughing hilariously and adding that she was only having fun and that it was the champagne talking.

Lacey and Tristan had just arrived behind them and were laughing at what they heard Kelly say. Tristan enquired what had happened and then said need he ask, noting that if form was anything to go by, Jen was probably up to her old tricks trying to sample the delicacies of younger men.

Everyone laughed except Jeremy who said she could keep well away from his delicacies as they were spoken for, raising a few eyebrows between Kelly and Lacey, Kelly glared at Alice who just smiled back, whispering 'on her terms'.

Tristan said that no one was drinking and asked what everyone wanted, Kelly said that perhaps she should hold off till later as she may end up too drunk before the fun started; she asked if there were any nibbles available to soak up the alcohol just as Matt and Giles appeared.

"Don't panic, my love, all in hand; we have some canapes and open Danish sarnies on their way to help us through until lunch is served," a joyous Matt announced.

Two crew members shortly appeared with some platters of the promised snacks and put them in the shade by the bar asking people to help themselves when ready, Lacey and Tristan took a plastic plate and helped themselves to some delicious looking fayre then with some well chilled rose wine went back to their seats where they sat and ate continuing their getting to know each other.

Alice whispered to Kelly that Lacey looked happy with Tristan and asked if she knew anything about him as in was he attached or anything like that. Once Kelly and Alice had plated their food, they grabbed some wine and found a quiet spot where Kelly divulged what Matt had told her.

Alice felt really sorry for him because he seemed such a lovely guy and she said that he must be finding it difficult alone with two young children, especially girls, she added that he had a much more difficult time ahead of him, especially when they hit puberty.

Kelly said that Matt had told her his wife was from a grand family and they had provided him with a full-time nanny to help him cope but acknowledged that it was no substitute for a real mother; Alice couldn't agree more.

There were two well-spoken men talking with Jeremy, Barry and Lester, asking him what he did as a profession. Jeremy said that his family ran a farm and plant machinery business in Gloucester and that he was the heir apparent. He said that he covered sales and services mostly but his father had been training him on all aspects of the job over the past few years as he was looking to take a step back.

Lester said that they were both major land owners in the Home Counties and Oxfordshire and would like to take his details at some point saying that maybe they could do some business in the future if he could be competitive.

Jeremy was very happy to do that, saying he had some business cards in the villa and would pass them on later that night, Barry and Lester thanked him before leaving to speak with some others in the group.

The yacht was now underway again; the sun was beating down from the clear blue sky and the temperature was rising, Jeremy said to Alice that he would see her down on the lower deck when she was ready as he was going to have a stretch out. Alice smiled back, saying she wouldn't be long.

Alice told her sister that she felt awkward now as Lacey had found a holiday buddy which meant that technically, she was alone. Kelly wasn't bothered in the slightest saying that there were plenty of friendly welcoming faces for her to chat with and told Alice not to worry about her but to enjoy herself and not meaning to make a pun, said not to go overboard with Jeremy.

Alice returned to where Jeremy was laid out soaking up the sun, bringing with her two bottles of cold water. "Here you go, big boy, thought you might need one of these," she said handing him a bottle.

Jeremy sat up, thanking her and asked what she and Kelly had been discussing, thinking it might be about Jen, Alice told him all that Kelly had said and he was a little taken aback recalling how a similar thing had happened to a close friend of his some years back; he said that it was a rough deal worse when kids were involved.

Alice and Jeremy settled back in the glorious sunshine as the yacht headed on to the sunken city of Kekova; the other members of the party on the other decks all settled themselves, chatting in little groups as the tranquil music played out relaxing vibes.

Soon after, they arrived at their destination and everyone stood up to admire the views of the coastline through the busy traffic of other vessels—Kekova was certainly a popular destination.

Matt gathered everyone together and explained that they would find a clear safe spot where they could snorkel in relevant peace and safety away from the masses; everyone was excited at the prospect and soon the captain announced that he was dropping anchor.

Meanwhile, up in the mountains behind Kalkan, Gavin was driving Emma to a secret beauty spot through some lush countryside that had so many hidden gems, Emma would ask Gavin to stop on occasions to allow her to capture some of the beautiful scenes on her phone camera. Emma said that she was so amazed at the diverse forms of landscapes and that she had no idea just what lay behind the mountains at the back of Kalkan.

Gavin told her to wait and see what was about to appear as they neared their objective.

"Oh wow! Gavin, that is amazing; it's almost taking my breath away!" Gavin smiled as he brought the car to a stop and inviting Emma to join him outside, he got out of the car.

Emma felt a little light-headed as she took in the view, it was literally breath-taking. Gavin had stopped at a clifftop carpark looking out to sea with views of small island structures and a busy coastline below.

Emma was afraid to get to close to the edge and hung on to Gavin telling him that they had gone as close to the edge as she was prepared, Gavin said how much he loved it at this place, saying it held good and bitter memories.

"Is this where you brought Jess, Gav?"

"Well yes, it was and at the time it was fantastic, we came up here and sat making plans for our future together, I am hoping that this trip might help erase those memories and I can form new ones. I love it here and I wanted to share it with you, Emm, I hope you don't mind after what I just told you."

"Don't be daft, of course, I don't; it's beautiful here! I am glad you brought me."

Emma put her arms around Gavin and hugged him as she kissed him with much affection, she said it would have been awful to have missed out on it because of what someone else had done even if it was a little scary up there.

Gavin chuckled, asking if she really felt that frightened, Emma said not overly but when they turned the corner and the view came at her almost a million miles an hour, she found it a little breath-taking.

Gavin agreed that it was a little moment of awe for him when he had first seen the view, he told Emma that she had nothing to fear when she was with him as he would always look after her.

A whirling stampede of butterflies filled Emma's stomach as Gavin spoke those words, it was something she had longed to hear from someone for so long that she gripped Gavin tightly to her and resting her head on his chest she asked him if he would always be there to look after her.

Gavin replied that he didn't truthfully know what the future held for them as the thought had crossed his mind several times before, all he would say was that as long as they were together, he would always take care of her adding that he didn't really feel right about making any future plans with her at this point seeing how they had only just met and that in the present location he felt it would be somehow wrong.

Even though Emma secretly would have loved to hear Gavin promise to be with and love her forever, she understood where he was at, she smiled at him saying she understood as the marauding butterflies began to settle.

Gavin asked another tourist close by to capture a picture of them at the beauty spot and he was happy to oblige, taking pictures on both their phones. Gavin thanked him then looking at the images said that he would study them long and hard until they replaced other images in his memory he had of that place. Gavin then led Emma to a vendor in a van selling all manner of drinks and snacks at the bottom of the carpark.

Gavin said that they would head back to Kalkan a few miles west of their spot taking the winding mountain road down from where they were and said that they could discuss how to spend the rest of the day before the others returned.

Having bought some cool refreshments, they drove down the steep winding road, Emma said that she was happy to relax by his pool if he fancied that and said that they would have to call in at hers first.

Gavin showed great pleasure at that, saying he could park up and enjoy a couple of cold beers whilst relaxing until what he said would be a glorious night at Matt's, if last time was anything to go by.

The pair headed back to Emma's to collect her bits and pieces before finally arriving at Gavin's villa; Gavin showed Emma in and offered her a room to get changed.

The pair made themselves comfortable by the pool with a couple of cold beers where they chatted and kissed, often embracing in heartfelt hugs for some time.

Over the sunken city of Kekova, many of the guests aboard the yacht were snorkelling in the crystal clear waters marvelling at the view beneath, there were all manner of building remains being eagerly investigated by the various schools of fish that navigated themselves with swift movements between them.

Tristan had an underwater camera and avidly caught many action shots of the ruins and the fish mingling within them. The captain announced that lunch was served and everybody got themselves back on board.

Matt greeted everyone with a fresh towel asking them to dry off before sitting for lunch; a makeshift shower was available for those wishing to wash the salt water off themselves beforehand.

The captain proudly presented a buffet fit for a king as there was every luxury you could want—fresh lobster, crab, king prawns and all manner of seafood and shellfish. There were plenty of fresh salads and cold meats also available with fruits and cheeses to round it all off.

Jen commented that it was one of the most sumptuous spreads she had seen in a while and probably not since Monte Carlo two years prior; she was very comfortable in name dropping a well-known celebrity who hosted that particular event, causing a few eyebrow raises.

The guests helped themselves to food and found a table to eat at, some stayed in the lower deck cabin as others opted for the shaded area on the deck above.

Alice and Kelly sat with Jeremy on the deck across from Lacey and Tristan who had taken the smallest table for themselves; Kelly commented that they seemed to be getting on well.

There were three other spaces at their table as they sat dining and were offered champagne by a crew member; a voice asked if they could join them and looking up, a girl of similar age to them smiled pleasantly as she and two slightly older men took the remainder seats.

Kelly said that she felt bad that having been on the yacht all this time, she had not spoken to them, something that Alice and Jeremy both sanctioned. Kelly introduced herself and the others and asked how could they have missed them.

"Well, I am Inga and this is Lars and Jake; we got into Kalkan early hours this morning having flown from Sweden, Lars is my brother and Jake is his partner; they own the villa next to Matt's and have been friends for a few years now. We were so exhausted when we came aboard that we decided to sleep in the cabins until we reached here; it was a well-needed rest, I can tell you."

"Well, that explains everything, I thought it strange how we hadn't met until now, I know it is a big boat but not that big you could miss three people!" Kelly laughed as she summarised it made perfect sense why Matt didn't show her some of the cabins.

The sound of happy diners tucking away at their delicious lunch and some going back for more filled the air as a crew member came around with more wine and champagne. Matt appeared to check everyone was happy with their food and received many thanks and congratulatory comments, he was so pleased that the trip was proving to be a great success and encouraged everyone to help themselves to more food as there was plenty still.

Lacey and Tristan chatted away about all things in the design world and Tristan took great interest in what Lacey had to say, he was aware that there was some kind of mutual attraction between them but didn't allow that to sway his opinion of what Lacey had to say.

"I can see you really do enjoy your work, Lacey, and I am serious when I say I would love to see some of your work portfolio at some stage in the future."

Lacey was flattered at the remark knowing that someone like her would not normally get a foot in the door with the company he worked for and she was happy to take full advantage of the opportunity she was being presented.

The subject soon turned to his home life and how he managed his time between work and the children. Lacey was impressed with his total commitment to work and family noting that was probably how he was still single.

"So Lacey, what does the future hold for you? Have you any aspirations in life now? I know it has been tough for you in the past but trust me, you have just been unlucky; not all men are as the ones you have known. Do you still hope to settle down and have a family, as you had previously planned?"

"The future, oh my god…to be honest, I have just been plodding from one day to the next; one contract to another, that's it. I have not thought about it, if the truth be told. Don't get me wrong; if the right opportunity arose and I met Mr Right, I have always thought of having children. I am thirty-four in November so the clock is ticking and there are no eligible suitors at the door at the moment so I won't hold out too much hope just yet."

"Well, I am very sorry to hear that, Lacey, I hope your fortune changes soon for you, after all, you deserve to be happy especially after all your former trauma and you work so hard I am sure it will come. Now, what do you fancy to drink?"

Lacey opted for some water as she wanted to save herself for the evening, thanking him as he went to the bar, his words were still ringing in her ears as she found herself warming to his charm and even contemplating how he could quite easily fit the eligible suitor needs.

"Oi Lace, what you smiling so happily about to yourself eh?" an inquisitive Kelly asked, noticing her friend sitting there like the cat that got the cream.

Lacey smiled back and just hunched her shoulders, giggling and giving Kelly and the other onlookers a joyful smile as she gazed upwards, wiggling her slender frame at the same time.

Kelly explained to Inga who Lacey was and Emma, who she would meet later at Matt's, Lars and Jake who had been relatively quiet over lunch speaking only to answer or when saying hello; they got up, thanking them for their company and went to find somewhere comfortable to rest up.

Once lunch was over, Jeremy and Alice returned to their favoured spot and made themselves comfortable allowing for good digestion while Kelly sat talking with Inga finding out a little more about her. Inga was a legal secretary back in Sweden and engaged to a lawyer a little older than herself, he unfortunately had some important work on so could not join her on this trip.

Gavin was returning from his outside bar with two cocktails he had made and proudly walked over to where Emma sat, slightly dazzled by the glaring sunlight, Gavin failed to see the plant pot base sticking out as he tried to nod his sunglasses back up from the bottom of his nose.

Gavin gave out a sudden scream as he tripped on the base, causing him to lunge forwards. Emma turned swiftly to see Gavin heading for the floor and the contents of the glasses heading her way.

"GAVIN!" she screamed as the cocktail hit her full in the face and over her head, drenching her in ice cold sticky cocktail. Gavin tumbled to the floor glad he was using plastic glasses.

"Oh Emma, I am so sorry, are you ok?" ann embarrassed and concerned Gavin asked.

Emma sat there motionless for a moment before laughing at the slapstick comedy that had just befallen her. "What the hell, Gav; oh I'm drenched and my hair! It's all matted!"

Gavin couldn't apologise enough and struggled to contain his laughter causing them both to roar with fits of laughter as Gavin tried unsuccessfully to lick the cocktail off Emma's face, saying it was too good to waste.

Emma said she would have to shower and wash her bikini now, Gavin showed her to a bathroom and told her to use whatever she needed adding that if she washed out her bikini, he would put it in the dryer so it would be ready to put back on.

Emma did as suggested, wrapping herself in a bath towel and handing the washed bikini to Gavin, Emma stood in the shower washing her hair repeatedly, laughing at the image in her head of what just happened, noting that she never even asked Gavin if he was ok. After her shower, wrapped in a towel, she called to Gavin for her bikini, Gavin entered the room with the item and looked adoringly at Emma who was apologising for not checking he was ok.

Gavin said he had a couple of grazes to a forearm but nothing major as he beheld the vision that he saw Emma as, Emma took his forearm to look at it as Gavin put the other arm around her and kissed her passionately.

The pair embraced and kissed each other with gusto and great intensity, they fell onto the bed where they continued the passionate entanglement between them.

Emma was the one now whose towel was slipping as Gavin kissed her neck all over repeatedly before lowering down to her breast, Emma wasn't sure how to react as Gavin showered her with tender loving affection.

The moment increased in intensity as the pair writhed together on the bed, Emma experienced electric type shocks across her body as Gavin stroked her inner thigh as her lower half was exposed.

Part of her wanted to stop before it went too far but she couldn't muster the courage to do it as a large part of her wanted it to continue. Gavin tenderly stroked her pussy that had become very moist with all the attention she was getting. Emma had an initial feeling of shock that was soon overwhelmed by feelings of pure pleasure and bliss as Gavin's fingers probed her inside, she squirmed with pure delight as he was thoughtful and tender with her.

Emma couldn't believe that she was actually about to make love for the first time in well over a year, almost two in fact; she reached down slowly to feel

Gavin's manhood; it was very hard and erect as she then teased his bathing shorts off him.

The pair were frantically kissing and touching, writhing all over each other, Gavin said that he didn't have any condoms and was afraid to go any further but he didn't want to stop. He felt relieved to hear Emma say that she had a coil fitted so it was ok.

As Gavin was about to enter Emma, she suddenly stopped him almost freezing up as the realisation of everything hit her. Gavin told it her it was ok if she didn't want to and that he understood but Emma said that she wanted to but was afraid for some reason.

Emma asked Gavin to try again and as she closed her eyes, she could feel his hard rigid cock touching her very wet pussy, Gavin very gently and slowly entered Emma until he had his whole shaft deep inside her.

Emma groaned with pleasure as Gavin made love to her and tears of joy slipped from her eyes, Gavin kissed her sweetly checking she was ok and asking if she was happy.

Emma wrapped her arms around him, holding on to him tightly as she experienced feelings long forgotten, Gavin started to increase his speed as each penetration seemed to go deeper and deeper into Emma who had raised her legs up around him.

Emma could sense the big moment was about to happen for him as she herself was experiencing amazing and unbelievable emotions, then in an explosion of pure love the pair reached a tremendous orgasm together causing Gavin to call out Emma's name in ecstasy.

The pair laid there in each other's arms for a few minutes, not really talking with their mouths; they let their eyes do it as they looked at each other so lovingly between the kissing.

Having sorted themselves out in the bathroom, the pair dressed and returned to the pool where they sat with a glass of wine talking about what a wonderful moment it had been for them and all come about because of a silly accident.

Gavin told Emma that she was a special girl and that he now felt she could move on with her life saying that he hoped he would be a part of it, Emma agreed on both points saying that Gloucester was not that far away and she hoped now that there was a chance they could make something of it.

Emma stayed at Gavin's until just after 5 pm and then headed back to hers to get ready for the party later that evening. Gavin thanked her for an amazing afternoon before seeing her off in a taxi.

The captain announced that the anchor was being drawn and that they were heading back to Kalkan, everyone made themselves comfortable as the yacht made its return journey. Matt and Giles joined Kelly and Inga, offering them a coffee, Giles said that he and Matt were saving it for tonight and that they had drunk very little as there was a bit to do back at the villa.

Lacey and Tristan were engrossed as ever with each other back in their seats, laughing and joking at each other's stories of past nightmares in their profession. Alice and Jeremy lay out on the lower front deck where Jeremy was caused to smile looking up to see Jen gazing down his way from the upper deck.

The steady cruise home was relaxing and enjoyable for all on board, everyone complimented the captain and crew for a most memorable and fantastic day out. Once in port, it was around 5.15 pm, Matt told everyone to arrive from 8.30 pm onwards. Jeremy asked if they needed any help as he was close by but they didn't and thanked him for the offer.

The port was full of people going about their business to and fro, many envious eyes looked on as the group disembarked the yacht to the port side, Kelly had rung Memhet and he was on his way down to collect them.

Lacey thanked Tristan for entertaining her so well and said she looked forward to seeing him later, Tristan smiled saying he looked forward to it as well thanking her for her company and making everything that little more enjoyable before leaning forward and kissing her on the cheek.

"Oh thank you," a smiling, slightly shocked but very happy Lacey replied. "I'll see you later then, bye," she added as her taxi arrived and whisked her, Kelly and Alice back to their villa.

Emma had not long arrived back herself and was making a coffee when the girls entered. "Hi Emm, how you doing, how was your mountain adventure then? Come on tell us before I tell you what an old tart Lacey has been!" Kelly laughed out apologising to Lacey saying she was only joking.

Emma had a look on her face the girls had not seen for some time; she looked like she was living in a dream world. "Right Emma, a face like that says there is much to tell so come on then, spill girl, how was it?" Alice said rather authoritatively to a bewildered Emma.

Emma sat down with her coffee and told them all about the journey up to the restaurant describing the scenic views on route and what it was like when they arrived, she enthused over the delightful views and ambience of the place before detailing the immense breakfast, showing them pictures from her phone.

The girls were clearly impressed and more so when Emma said she was arranging for them all to go next week some time when Gavin went back. Emma continued with her story about the trip back and the route they took, stopping at the mountaintop carpark, again showing them the pictures.

"Oh wow Emma, it sounds like an incredible experience; what did you do the rest of the day?" Lacey asked.

Emma beamed with delight saying they went back to his place and sat by the pool giving them the full account of how he drenched her in cocktail, falling over. Emma was laughing with joy as she recalled how she sat there dripping with sticky cocktail all over her.

"Oh Emma, that could only happen to you, you poor sod, what did you do then; come home, did you?" Alice asked feeling a little sad for her friend.

"No not straight away. I had a shower and washed my bikini out, Gavin was great, he tumble-dried it for me so we could continue outside." Emma's face lit up as she spoke his name, giving a little sigh as she recalled what happened next. Kelly looked up at Alice and both turned to Lacey before gazing back at Emma who was lost in the moment before suddenly snapping out of it and asking them how the yacht trip went.

Kelly turned to Alice and Lacey asking, "I don't know if it's just me but do you girls think there is something Emma is not telling us, I'm not sure what it is but have you two seen her like this lately or before?"

"I haven't seen her this way since she first met that toerag who was married," Lacey said.

Kelly stood there nodding. "And what happened then, do you remember?" she asked knowing the answer well.

Alice piped in, "Oh yes, I do. I remember her telling us that she had just had the most amazing sex ev—" Alice paused before finishing the word. "Emma, you filthy tart, you have had sex with Gavin, haven't you?" she blurted out as Kelly stood by smiling and still nodding away, Lacey looked on open-mouthed.

"Emma, is it true?" Lacey asked.

"Oh come on Lacey, of course it is; look at that bloody face! My goodness, you could write a bestseller romance novel of that any day!" Kelly said.

Emma tried to compose herself, she had known since getting home that they would find out at some time; she had just hoped that it wouldn't be this soon though. Emma sat there and told the girls everything as they had always done together, there was no judgement upon her; they all said that Gavin was probably going to be the one from the start as they looked well matched.

Alice asked her if she had any regrets but Emma simply replied that she didn't then laughing said if she did, it would be that they hadn't done it sooner.

The others joined in laughing with her, Kelly giving her a massive hug telling her she hoped that everything worked out well for them both as they both deserved it.

After a few moments, Lacey suggested they take a shot in celebration of Emma being back to something resembling her old self before filling her in on their day out on the yacht. The girls toasted Emma's joyous return to normality of a sort then Emma asked why Lacey had been like an old tart.

Between Kelly, Alice and Lacey, they filled Emma in on the day's proceedings, Emma was intrigued to hear more about this Tristan chap and asked Lacey if she had a photo of him, Lacey said no but Alice and Kelly almost in unison said they did and scrolled their phones.

"You two been spying on me or what, I never saw you take our picture!" Lacey said a little shocked but then not totally surprised.

Alice was first up with a couple of snaps, some looking rather intimate. "Oh wow Lacey, he is gorgeous; what's the catch? He must be taken, he has to be," she said excitedly as she grabbed Alice's phone back for another look.

Lacey explained his situation and said that he was a very nice man that was talented, kind and caring as much as he was like just fallen from heaven and so handsome.

The girls had a few more minutes catch up before getting ready, Lacey said this was their first official glam night out and they should pull all the stops out, Alice was up for it saying she was looking forward to a great night and may not be coming back anytime soon, planning on partying until the sun came up and then sleep all day Sunday.

Kelly got some music going as the girls returned to their rooms to get ready and over the next hour, they flitted between rooms to ask advice on their choices of everything from hairstyles to lipstick colours.

Around 7.30 pm, Kelly popped into see how Alice was getting on and ask how she looked herself, Alice was in the bathroom and said that she had a little stomach cramp and thought it may have been caused by the shellfish on board the yacht.

"You're not expecting your monthly, are you, Al?"

"No, not for a few more days yet and I'm always on time, it was probably the prawns or something not agreeing with me."

Alice appeared out of the bathroom to see her sister stood there smiling and asking what she thought. "Wow sis, that shade of blue really suits you, honestly you look stunning."

Alice said that she would be ready in a jiffy as a smiling Kelly went to Emma's room, Emma was almost ready just needing to fix her hair and do some make up, Kelly sat her down and helped her with her hair then she stood her up and told her that Gavin would be knocked out when he saw her.

The two girls walked to the lounge where Lacey entered behind them. "Well girls, how do I look?"

Kelly and Emma turned to see Lacey wearing a figure-hugging mini dress off the one shoulder and her beautiful brown hair up, looking a little like Audrey Hepburn; the pair praised their friend who looked so glamorous. Kelly asking her if she was auditioning for 'Stepmom' by any chance, they all enjoyed a good laugh as the stunning Alice made her entrance.

Alice stood there in a mostly white with black trim sleeveless trouser suit, the pants were flared and fitted her pert bottom perfectly. The top was unbuttoned rather low, Kelly thought, especially given the fact that she was bra less. Alice had fashioned her hair to curl to the one side over her shoulder and wore bright red lipstick that gave her the magic finishing touch.

Kelly asked her if she was sure about the top being open that much without a bra but Alice responded she had been showing more in her bikini earlier.

There was plenty of time before they needed to leave and Kelly suggested they go into town first and have a cocktail so they can have a little parade beforehand and show off how good they look. Lacey laughed agreeing that she was out to make a statement that night and apart from Tristan, there wasn't any other heads she had met out there she was bothered about turning.

Emma was harbouring desires of being back in Gavin's arms as quick as she could be but went along with the girls' wishes knowing that once at the party, she would hardly see them.

Lacey was checking herself in the large mirror fussing with her dress and shaping her hair. "Well, I think it only fair we let the rest of Kalkan know what they are missing, don't you think, eh girls!" Lacey chuckled pulling a funny face at them. Kelly said she would call Memhet to collect them at around 8 pm and then said they should arrive a little after 9 pm at the party by which time most people will be there and they could then make a grand entrance.

Memhet had arrived and was on his phone outside of his car talking when the girls descended the steps down to the road.

Memhet was lost for words as he looked at the girls. "Wow ladies, you all look like movie stars, so beautiful, I am taking you to the king's palace yes!" he asked smiling at them.

"No, just our usual cocktail bar for now please, Memhet, then at 9 pm we are going to a party at the villa we were at the other night," Kelly told him as they got into the taxi.

"Then maybe after I bring you home, probably no tonsils I think tonight, eh looking so beautiful." They all laughed together.

"Maybe these three will but not me. I am the only one not to meet anyone yet, as to picking us up later, this party may go on until very early hours so maybe not," Kelly answered him.

Memhet told them he would finish around 1 am in the morning but he would give them another number of his sister's husband who could collect them later when they were ready, Kelly joked that he was keeping it in the family.

Arriving at the taxi rank, the girls exited the car and were greeted by looks of admiration and pleasant smiles and nods from the drivers who were stood chatting and smoking by the side.

Memhet said he would be there at 9 pm to take them to the party and give them his brother-in-law's number, the girls strolled down the short distance to their favoured cocktail bar relishing the attention they were receiving from passers-by and people sitting at the bars en route.

Giggling like schoolgirls, they were shown a table by a young waiter who was mesmerised by them, the manager who recognised them came over complimenting them on how nice they looked and took their orders.

Emma had a text message from Gavin saying how much he was looking forward to seeing her again soon, adding that he and Jeremy would be there bang on 8.30 pm, he asked her when she thought she would arrive and that he couldn't stop thinking about the wonderful day they had spent together.

Emma almost blushed as the thought of that afternoon's romantic interlude played again in her head, Lacey asked her if she was ok, sensing her fragility by her body language.

Emma beamed, reassuring her everything was perfect saying that Gavin had messaged her and that she was just thinking about earlier, the others smiled and Lacey commented that she bet it was a lovely thought.

Emma texted Gavin back saying they would be there around 9 pm just as their drinks arrived, the girls sat there sipping away, pausing for light conversation about how good the party may be and if anyone new would be there, causing Kelly to say that she hoped so as she was the one left out.

The time came for them to attend the party and they made their way to the awaiting Memhet's taxi, they were not short of envious and approving looks as they took the short stroll back.

At the villa, many guests had arrived and there were a few new faces that were not on the yacht earlier, Matt and Giles introduced people to each other as the party was underway getting started, Giles asked Gavin where the girls were thinking they would have come with them. Gavin replied that they should be arriving at any time just as the taxi pulled up. Jeremy was standing on the edge of the front terrace looking down as the girls exited the taxi and informed Gavin that they were here and the pair made their way to the side door to greet them.

Gavin felt a rush of adrenalin as he saw Emma approach, looking as beautiful as she did, Jeremy meanwhile was lost for words as Alice came into full view. Brushing his hair back over his head, he let out a wow as he witnessed the vision get closer to him, Alice smiled in acknowledgement at his response then saying hi, she leant in and kissed him, causing him for once to be a little overwhelmed.

The group went in and joined the rest of the party-goers; Matt came over to greet them saying how spectacular they all looked closely followed by Giles who was full of praises and then said that they would introduce them to some new guests and proceeded to show them around.

Lacey was looking about casually, hoping to spot Tristan who was slightly hidden by a marble pillar, Tristan however had seen her and was really impressed by her look. Walking over to her from slightly behind, Tristan asked her playfully had she seen a young lady by the name of Lacey by any chance as he was looking forward to reconnecting with her. Lacey with her hand to her mouth laughed. "Oh Tristan, stop it."

"Oh my, wow, I am not sure what to say, this afternoon I met an adorable young lady and hoped to see her again tonight but instead a young woman of beauty and loveliness in the form of this exquisite vision that stands before me has taken my breath away. Honestly Lacey, you look absolutely stunning; how any of those former boyfriends could give you up is beyond me."

Lacey was a little overcome with such praise coming from Tristan as Matt, who had witnessed his words, nodded and winked at Lacey over Tristan's shoulder, Lacey felt her heart race as Tristan kissed her on the cheek telling her how happy he was to see her again.

"Thank you Tristan, I think that is the nicest thing anyone has ever said to me. May I say that you look very smart as well tonight and very handsome too, if I may be so bold?"

Tristan smiled and took her by the hand saying that he hoped they would get to know each other well over the coming days as he encouraged her to get a drink with him. Kelly commented to Matt that Tristan's words were beautifully put to Lacey and revealed that Lacey had taken a real fancy to him. Matt said that Lacey could not be in better hands; having known Tristan for many years, he said that he was the genuine article.

Two of the new faces there were Kevin and Jack in their late thirties, both working in the city and friends of Matt, the pair were both single having been divorced over recent years and they had taken a keen interest in Alice. Jeremy had need of the bathroom, leaving Alice momentarily abandoned on the front terrace, seizing the opportunity, Kevin and Jack were quick to introduce themselves. These two predators thought that they were in for a little fun with Alice as they talked themselves up about their high-ranking positions in the companies they represented back in London.

The two felt really encouraged upon hearing that she and Jeremy had only met on Tuesday just gone and were not an item as such but had enjoyed each other's company recently, Alice enjoyed the attention; after all, she had certainly dressed for it and she couldn't wait to see how Jeremy reacted to the competition he would now be facing for her attention.

Jen had dressed in yet another rather flamboyant designer outfit that was bright and dazzling full of colour, garnished with various rocks on her fingers and bejewelled necklaces; she stood sipping on her mojito watching the drama before her unfold as Jeremy emerged from the bathroom. "Now look, young man, looks like someone else wants to feather the nest you have been preening,"

Jen said raising her glass in the direction of Alice. She had no idea that Jeremy wasn't one to let things like that bother him as he had been a player long enough to know how to handle these situations. Jeremy smiled saying confidently that Alice would not be swayed by a couple of miniatures that had little to offer.

He had meant in stature as he was tall and muscular with a very fit body and those two were considerably smaller; what could they offer that he couldn't, he asked her.

"Well, they are both rather wealthy you know working in the city no less, a very good catch for the right young lady," she smiled giving him a discerning look.

"No, not Alice, she is way above that, she doesn't care about the size of your wallet," he quickly pointed out.

Jen just puckered her lips thinking to herself he was right it wasn't the wallet you cared about when it came to size, then with a cheeky slap on his backside she told him to go and regain charge of his conquest savouring his every move as he walked away.

Jeremy picked up two glasses of wine on his way back and casually walked back to Alice. Handing a drink to her, he greeted the two men. "Hi guys, I am Jeremy, how you doing?" he said with a broad smile full of confidence.

The two men introduced themselves as Alice said that they worked in the city, Jeremy said he knew already, explaining about being accosted by Jen. Alice laughed. "Oh no, poor you, I think she has it in for you, Jez, be careful not to drink too much tonight she may take advantage."

"Same old Jen, she never changes; we have both suffered her in the past; we sympathise with you, eh Kev?" Jack grinned shaking his head.

"Nice meeting you guys, will you excuse us a moment, I want us to go over and see Matt," Jeremy casually said putting a leading arm around Alice's waist and leading her over towards where Matt was standing.

"Hmm, that was rather smoothly done and why do we need to see Matt?" Alice said as Kevin and Jack looked on, helpless to stop Jeremy whisking Alice away and knowing in their minds that she was definitely out of their reach with Jeremy in the equation.

Jeremy held on tight to Alice as he said that they didn't, he just wanted to have her to himself as selfish as that may be; he said that that the time they had left was precious little as it was and he had no intention of wasting it with a couple of guys perving on her open cleavage.

"Ooh Jeremy, there is a definite change in you of late that I am starting to like more and more; maybe I should look at you a little differently in the future eh."

"How about you start tonight and stay with me at my place when all this is over then yeah what you think, come on we both know; we have skated around this long enough; no holds no promises, just be ourselves yeah?"

Alice was a little surprised at his sudden outpouring of honesty and found herself thinking that she just might take him up on it; as she turned to put her arms around his neck and agree with him, the stomach cramps hit again.

Jeremy asked if she was ok seeing her discomfort, Alice said that she thought she may have eaten something dodgy earlier on the boat and that was the third time she had experienced that feeling.

Kelly appeared, having seen Alice's discomfort from across the room and asking if she was ok. "Those damn prawns are taking their revenge on me again," she said rather bitterly.

The party was going very well; some people were dancing while others were talking away in quiet corners, Lacey and Tristan had gotten really close this evening hardly spending a moment out of each other's company while Emma and Gavin only had time and eyes for each other.

As the evening went on, canapes and snacks were put out for everyone to soak up the alcohol, Matt and Giles reminding them that the party was to go on until dawn so pace themselves. Alice came out of the bathroom having suffered more cramps, vowing never to eat shellfish again and refusing any more alcohol that night.

Jeremy asked her what she had been about to say earlier when the cramps first hit, feeling rather disappointed that her evening was not going to plan, especially after the effort she had gone to; she just said it was nothing.

Jeremy's puzzled look suggested that he didn't believe that and Alice confessed to the fact that she was about to accept his offer of spending the night at his but now as she wasn't feeling so great, she said she didn't think she would make a good sleeping partner.

Jeremy found himself in a less familiar place, being sympathetic and understanding to Alice's situation offering his services to help her anyway he could saying it was ok, he fully understood, this made Alice want him even more and promised him she would make every effort to make his night memorable.

It was a little after midnight and Matt said that they would now take the party to the back terrace and turn the music down to a more acceptable level, considering the neighbours, half of whom were at the party.

Emma and Gavin smooched away on a far part of the rear patio kissing and cuddling, eyes only for each other, Emma took no time in accepting Gavin's offer at staying over at his later as he had no intensions of staying up all night; he said 2 am to 3 am would be his limit or tomorrow would be a washout and he didn't have many days left.

Alice and Jeremy joined Kelly who was chatting with Inga after they had a little saunter themselves on the patio dancing and kissing, Inga said that they made a lovely couple well suited.

Alice nodded in the direction of where Lacey was with Tristan dancing close together to the gentle sounds of the jazz music, Lacey had her arms up around Tristan's neck as he rested his hands around her lower waist, fingers interlocked and resting on the knave of her back.

Kelly looked across just as the pair kissed each other with sweet intent and purpose, Alice gasped as she looked at her sister to see her response which was one of joy and surprise.

The sisters showed much pleasure feeling elated for their dear friend who was caught in the passionate embrace that she had so longed for, Alice excused herself saying that the attack of the prawns was back and made her way to the bathroom.

Barry and Lester passed by smiling and nodding as they joined Liz, Mike and Harry seated around a large patio table as Jen moved with the music in what seemed an awkward fashion that she would say was dancing whilst firmly grasping her drink in hand. One of the older female guests that they had not spoken to before asked Kelly to go to the bathroom as her sister needed her. Kelly went to see Alice, soon returning and heading over to where Emma was now sat with Gavin, Kelly beckoned Emma to her watched by Jeremy and Inga and they saw Emma hold her hand to her mouth and shake her head before Kelly shot over to Lacey, who was still smooching away with Tristan.

Kelly caught Lacey's attention and apologising to Tristan pulled her to one side and whispered to her, Lacey's head shot up, shaking it with a look of sorrow.

Inga's womanly instinct kicked in and she rushed to Kelly to see what the issue was, Kelly explained all and Inga grabbed at her arm and told her to follow her, leading her off up to a fence that she was able to step over into her garden.

Alice's night had gone from bad to worse, she had been complaining all day about feeling unwell from the prawns she ate but it turned out that her monthly had started slightly earlier than normal, ruining any chance that Jeremy had with getting with her before he went home.

The girls soon returned, rushing to a desperately waiting Alice with the sanitary products she needed, Jeremy sat there thinking that she may have been experiencing some unfortunate bowel movements but he was soon put right as a devastated Alice informed him of her situation.

Jeremy tried to put a funny spin on it to hide his frustration saying it was no problem, he would wait for her to return to Bristol airport and they could pop to the toilets and do it there, Alice gave him a dig in the shoulder in disgust but couldn't help grinning at the thought.

"Don't stress, Al, it wasn't meant to be; no worries; we can still have some fun as we have been though, can't we? I mean, it's not the end of the world is it and who knows maybe we might meet up after the holiday eh!"

Matt came over to where they were all sitting; it was approaching 2 am and everyone was still enjoying themselves even the older guests that sat with little blankets across the shoulders, Matt asked Kelly why one of the prettiest and smartest women there that night had not had a dance.

"Oh careful, you old charmer you, statements like that might make me more interested in an older man like you yet so go steady with beautiful compliments." Kelly chuckled as the ever smooth and charming Matt stood grinning at her.

"Well, please don't stand on ceremony on my account; you get as interested in me as you like. You won't find me complaining," he chuckled back.

"Right, come on you get me on that that dance floor then and entrance me with your dancing prowess," Kelly demanded with a broad smile and a chuckle.

"It's funny you know, Kelly, I'm almost 54 years old and being considered an older man already at what I still perceive as a relatively young age is quite difficult to fathom."

"Oh no Matt, I didn't mean to imply that you were old as such just that there is a good seventeen years between us and I have never given thought to being involved with anyone with such an age gap before."

"Yes oh yes, I understand what you mean but they say age is just a number; it is the person behind that age that counts."

"I suppose you're right, yes that does sound logical." Kelly found herself with a bout of the hiccups and apologised to Matt, breaking away to get some water, feeling a little embarrassed.

Emma came over to where Alice sat talking with Inga and Jeremy, Kelly had just arrived with a large glass of water as Emma said she and Gavin were calling it a night as they didn't want to waste the following day sleeping in because Gavin only had a few days left.

Gavin was going around the other tables and seating areas wishing everyone a good night and thanking Matt and Giles for a lovely evening. Emma said that she would be staying at Gavin's and promised to be quiet when returning the next day, Kelly asked her if she was sure she was doing the right thing saying it may make saying goodbye even harder.

Jeremy listened on intently with a little concern that Emma may think she and Gavin may have a future together, something he thought was not on as he and Gavin had many discussions on the subject and he wasn't certain Gavin was at the same point as Emma.

"Oh well, the fortress has already been seized and plundered anyway so what harm can come from another fumble in the dark, eh?" Kelly laughed as she gave Emma a hug and a kiss goodnight saying she would see her later the next day.

Matt came over as Emma now joined by Gavin said goodnight to the friends and left. "I hope you're not all going just yet, are you?" Matt asked.

"I can't speak for the others but I am going nowhere until we have had our dance," Kelly beamed at Matt.

Matt had just been called over by Barry to their table and he told Kelly to hold on to that thought saying he would return shortly, Kelly laughed and then told the others about the conversation she had had with Matt moments earlier.

Inga said she agreed with Matt then confessed to having a crush on Giles some years back revealing how she had flirted with him and was a little intimate with him on the odd occasion but it never came to anything.

That admission certainly raised an eyebrow or two from the others, Inga added that there were sixteen years between them but it wasn't an issue and as much as there was an attraction to each other, their personal life choices and ideals were so far apart there was no chance of a real relationship happening.

"My advice to you, Kelly, is if you like what you see and hear then go for it, Matt is one of the nicest people I know. He has made his past mistakes and is not afraid to admit it; nobody is perfect I think, don't let something silly like a number get in the way of what could turn out to be something incredible and truly magical."

It was truly food for thought, Kelly mused in her head just as Matt returned with a skip in his step, turning to Kelly and asking where were they. Kelly stood up offering out her hand to Matt and leading him to a clear patch of the patio where they held on to each other and gently moved to the music, watched by those that were seated with looks of approval.

Matt and Kelly chatted as they danced and the longer they did, the closer to each other they became physically, Lacey and Tristan had joined them and a couple of others at the same time. Lacey and Tristan were really getting on well with each other as they danced so close to each other moving with a majestic sway that was quite sensual to watch, Tristan kissed Lacey on her neck before their lips met in a seductive passionate way.

Matt looked on, a little envious at Tristan's loving movements of great subtlety and prowess, Kelly had seen the same scene and thought what the heck as she glanced into Matt's eyes. Matt didn't need it spelt out to him and positioned himself to meet with Kelly's mouth on his. Jeremy sat upright in his chair nudging Alice who was engrossed in conversation with Inga and pointing Kelly's way.

Alice looked on in great surprise, cupping both her hands over her mouth, she turned to Jeremy open-mouthed and eyes wide open in sheer delight. The three sat there smiling and watching Matt and Kelly kissing and dancing for a moment before then commenting on Lacey and Tristan's show of affection for each other.

"If she carries on much more like this, I'm going to insist on them getting a room or they will be getting a bucket of cold water."

Laughter was coming from where Inga's brother Lars and Jake were sat and as people looked to see what all the fuss was about, Lars pointed over to the big swing seat, shaking his head with his hand over his mouth to muffle his amusement.

There sat, with one leg on and one leg off, Jen who had fallen asleep still clutching on to her glass with her head bowed and snoring away. Harry just raised his head tutting saying he had wondered how long it would take her.

Jen was her own woman who had her views and thoughts on how things should be, she liked haute couture and expensive jewellery. She was a lady of her own means and Harry topped her up nicely, quite the socialite in her younger years but now in her sixties, not that she looked it having undergone several procedures; she just wanted to enjoy life to the full refusing to let her age stop her as she believed herself to still have what it takes.

Giles couldn't resist taking a couple of snaps of her in her unfortunate state, saying to Harry that he would save them for the annual Boxing Day meet, Harry just nodded with a vague smile before joining his friends back around the table.

Matt thanked Kelly for the dance and the unexpected treat she had provided, Kelly said he was welcome and that she had enjoyed it adding that she was wrong to have prejudged him, saying that he was a good kisser.

As they were moving back to Kelly's table, Giles beckoned Matt over and after ribbing him about his little dalliance with Kelly, showed him the pictures of Jen and the pair crossed the garden where she still sat gently snoring away.

Kelly meanwhile was being grilled by Alice about her kissing Matt and was asked if she now thought any different about older men. Kelly said she had always held Matt in high regard saying that he was a true gent, the sort of person she wanted to be with but was still not certain if she wanted it with someone that much older than she.

"Please don't read anything into that, sis; it was just a kiss and nothing else; we are not decreeing our never ending love for each other, it was just two people enjoying the moment and that's not to say I wouldn't want to enjoy the same again or anything."

Alice looked at her sister mouth wide open in shock at what she had just heard her say. "Oh Kelly, you dark horse, you do really fancy him don't you, go on admit it."

"Oh shut up, Alice, don't be childish and no I don't fancy him like that, like what you mean, I just like him and the way he is with me, that's all; there is no budding romance to be seen here, ok."

Alice wasn't convinced, giving her sister a sly glance to say as much, Matt joined them and asked why Alice and Jeremy were not up dancing, having not seen them do so for some time he asked if they were flagging already; being the youngest there, he thought they would have plenty of energy.

Alice explained that she had some stomach issues that were preventing her at the moment but was quite happy sitting and chatting watching everyone else enjoy themselves especially those two, she said, pointing at Lacey and Tristan who looked like they were about to devour each other.

"Well, that did surprise me I must say, not that Lacey is not an attractive and intelligent woman but Tristan does not usually allow himself to be this full on with women so soon after meeting them; he is normally very careful how he lets any new prospective relationship go."

"Full marks to Lacey if she makes anything of this because I have said it many times before that Tristan is a one in a million catch, a true gentleman in every sense of the word that has an impeccable character, devout, trustworthy, honest and truthful as the day is long; broke the mould on that one, that's for sure."

Matt spoke proudly of his long-time friend, adding how a cruel blow had befallen him losing his wife as he did, but he said he remained strong for his girls and put them before himself on every occasion.

Having said that, they all witnessed Tristan and Lacey collapse together on a small sofa with Lacey laying across Tristan and resting her head on his shoulder as he wrapped his arms around her; the pair struggled to stay awake.

Giles came across to say the older ones had nodded off in the chairs adding that he was glad they chose the comfier high-backed ones, Giles said he would fetch some of the small blankets; even though the early morning was not overly cold, it still had a little freshness about it and he said that Barry was going to get the patio heater out just to be sure.

Everyone seemed to have had enough alcohol by now as Jeremy wondered what the purpose was of everyone staying any longer, Matt said that usually they were more active at this time but the yacht trip must have drained them of their energy.

"At 6.30 am, I have a chef from a local restaurant coming who will cook breakfast for us all, then we normally all disburse back to our own place and sleep until early afternoon," he said rather despondently.

Jeremy asked Alice how she felt and if she was happy to stay for another almost three hours for breakfast or make a move, Alice said she would give it another hour and see and asked if she could make a cup of tea.

Matt was very obliging saying he would show her to the kitchen as Alice asked if anyone else wanted one, there were several takers and Inga said she would help her. Matt asked Kelly what her plans were and she happily said that she was feeling fine and happy to stay until breakfast and commented that she had hoped that he had another dance or two left in him.

That comment brought a pleasing smile to his face as he replied that he would gladly dance the night away with her anytime. Matt showed Alice and Inga to the kitchen and explained where everything was kept and said that there were biscuits and cake if they so felt inclined.

Returning to Kelly who was discussing Gavin and Emma with Jeremy, Matt stretched out his hand towards Kelly, saying 'shall we'. Kelly stood up looking at Jeremy with some concern saying they would finish the conversation later.

"That sounded rather serious, Kelly, is everything ok?" Matt asked her as they stood there dancing really slowly with only a suggestion of movement.

"Well, it better had be; it has taken Emma an age to come out of her shell and now she has; if what Jeremy has just told me is true, I fear she may never recover again. She has been so resilient in her ways avoiding getting close to men for almost two years now that she built an impenetrable fortress around herself but Gavin somehow found a way through. Please don't get me wrong. I think Gavin is a lovely guy and he seems genuine, Emma cannot speak more highly of him as does Jeremy but he thinks Gavin won't be able to come through for Emma when they return home due to his work commitments and the distance; though it's not that far, it is far enough."

"What will you do; will you tell her, but then again what can you really say; it is after all only his best friend's opinion, not something Gavin has said. Maybe you should consider speaking with Gavin himself and ask him outright; that may do the trick but then I suppose you are still faced with the daunting task of having to tell your friend something that could decimate her and you will end up with that on your conscience for some time I should imagine."

"Yes definitely, I think I am in a no win position, I will speak with the others later and see what they think, now I need to try and forget this. I don't want it spoiling my night so how about one of your lovely kisses to take my mind off it eh?"

A smiling Matt was happy to oblige and the pair kissed again for the second time just as Alice and Inga made their way out with the tea and biscuits and a plate full of cake slices that Jeremy was happy to tuck into. Alice watched as Matt and her sister kissed while dancing; she nodded her head saying to the others, "She definitely fancies him. I know her, she would not go back for seconds if she were not genuinely interested.

"Tea up, sis, if you can pull yourself away, that is!" Alice called out giggling. Matt and Kelly joined everyone for tea as Inga passed it around with the biscuits to the others who were all flagging around the big table, She was eventually able to offer cake once she managed to prize it from Jeremy's grasp.

The hours slipped by slowly; most of them had a snooze at some point and the only ones to carry on were Kelly and Matt, the music had long finished and the only tunes to be heard now was the morning chorus of birdsong.

The calm melodic sound of birdsong was broken by the voice of the chef arriving to cook breakfast, something he had done the two previous years to earn a little extra cash. Matt got up to welcome him as he looked puzzled at all the people sitting in some state of slumber. "What has happened, Matt, normally you are still partying, why is everyone asleep?"

Matt explained that they had been out on a yacht earlier in the day yesterday and that it had taken its toll on them plus some had only arrived earlier that morning so no surprise there; the chef said he had some more things to collect from his car and would then start cooking saying he would need just under an hour to get everything ready.

Sunday Day 8

Matt gently woke everyone up saying coffee was on and fresh tea for those that wanted it, towels were available in the bathrooms for those needing to refresh themselves. Jen strolled forward wrapped in a blanket that she thanked whoever was responsible for it, oblivious to the humour she had created that night.

Matt and Giles arranged the tables ready for breakfast out on the front patio with help from Jeremy and a few of the other men, some of the ladies arranged the crockery and tableware between them watched on by Jen who was not one to get involved with that sort of thing.

Everyone was gathered around the tables as the chef brought out bowls of scrambled eggs, dishes of sausages and bacon, mushrooms, tomatoes and beans, Giles turned up with baskets of sliced crusty bread and some toasted, followed by Matt fetching out the tea and coffee pots on a large tray.

All were very appreciative of the breakfast but tiredness had gotten the better of them as they rather lethargically tucked into the spread as the first burst of sunlight appeared off in the distant east. Matt handed the chef a bundle of notes as he shook his hand thanking him for his efforts, everyone applauded him as he left to start his daily work.

Back at Gavin's, he and Emma were sound asleep cuddled up to each other, oblivious to the new beautiful day that was dawning over Kalkan; they had both stripped off and gotten into bed together, hugging each other and after several minutes of ravenous kissing and touching, they fell into a deep sleep.

At the end of breakfast, a weary-eyed Jeremy asked Alice what her plans were, she replied that she would return to her villa and crash until she felt replenished enough. Alice said that she felt the evening would probably be the quietest on record as she had no desire to drink anymore or even go out. Kelly sat close by said she agreed it had been a wonderful day and night but now she too needed to recharge adding that there was food enough in the fridge needing to be used up and there was always takeaway if no one wanted to cook, looking at Lacey in hope of a response.

Lacey and Tristan chatted together with Lacey saying that was easily the best 24 hours she had spent in a long time, Tristan thanked her for a most enjoyable and enchanting time and asked if he would see her again soon.

Lacey said that she hoped so and gave him her mobile number asking him to call or text after 4 pm later to allow her to get some much needed rest, Tristan said that he felt the same adding that he looked forward to seeing her again.

Kelly put a call out to Memhet to collect them as soon as possible as she and the other two girls helped clear the table. Matt said to leave it as he had arranged for extra cleaning that day.

Some of the guests had already left by the time Memhet arrived and so Kelly hugged Matt, kissing him on the cheek, and thanked him for everything as Alice cuddled Jeremy saying she was sorry for disappointing him adding that she wished she had been braver sooner. Jeremy said that he would see her later if she was up for it; if not, maybe tomorrow. Alice said she would have to see how she felt as she kissed him goodbye and then had to prise Lacey away from Tristan and march her off to the awaiting Memhet.

Back at their villa, the girls wasted no time getting themselves into bed and falling into a wonderful deep sleep, not a sound was to be heard other than the occasional snore from one of the rooms.

Later that morning, Emma awoke feeling a little tired still but happy in the knowledge that Gavin was wrapped around her as the memories of yesterday came flooding back, causing her to lay there with a huge smile on her face as she held on to Gavin's arm that was holding on to her.

"You awake, Emm?" Gavin murmured in a sleepy voice.

Emma paused before answering yes but wishing she wasn't stating that she was still tired and asked what the time was, Gavin said that he felt the same and that it was almost 10.30 am. Emma grumbled that she was going to have to get up as she needed the bathroom, then reaching for Gavin's shirt she put it on to hide her nakedness, even though she and Gavin had been naked together twice now she still had certain levels of self-preservation to uphold.

As Emma went to the bathroom, Gavin asked if she would like some tea adding that he had a spare toothbrush if she needed it as he brought it in case his electric one broke. Emma thanked him for that gesture aware of the amount of alcohol she had had the night before and said that a cup of tea would be wonderful.

Gavin asked her not to talk too loud as he was unaware if Jeremy had come back last night and if he had, he would probably be in a worse condition than themselves, Gavin gingerly opened Jeremy's bedroom door and poked his head inside to see his friend flat out on his bed then gently closing the door made his way back to Emma to say that Jeremy was sleeping soundly before going again to make the tea.

The pair sat up in bed, Emma still wearing Gavin's shirt and Gavin in his boxer shorts, Emma chuckled to him softly saying that it was like in the movies with her in bed wearing his shirt. Gavin just smiled nodding in agreement.

"Well, I don't think we will be seeing much of the others today, do you, Gav?"

"I don't know what your friends are like but Jez has a remarkable recovery rate, he will probably surface around midday if I know him, looking for a big fry up after he has had a swim."

Emma looked impressed by that then said that the girls would probably not get up until much later and then coffee in copious amounts will be foremost before a shower and then probably collapse on a sunbed for the rest of the afternoon. "I can't see them making it out tonight to be honest; it will be take-out unless Lacey decides to cook."

"She, I mean Lacey, seemed to be getting on rather well with that Tristan fella didn't she. I thought he seemed nice enough though eh Emm? What did you think?"

"Honestly, I thought he was a perfect match for her although he has two children I don't think that will bother Lacey; she has a very maternal nature about her, I think that's why she does most of the cooking and I must say she is an excellent cook; she could easily go professional."

"Oh wow really, you will have to invite her around to cook for us when we come down to visit sometime, what do you think?" Gavin asked with a little laughter.

It pleased Emma to hear Gavin mention that he would be coming down to see her, it was something that had been tormenting her inside that she was hiding from him. She didn't want to force the subject of how things would be when they were back home, she was happy just knowing that he did intend to pursue some kind of relationship with her and tackling the subject so soon might ruin something unnecessarily before it had a chance to happen.

The pair cuddled up together face to face just looking at each other at first before some gentle kissing that led to a more passionate situation, Gavin felt himself get aroused very quickly, something that didn't go unnoticed by Emma.

"I say, Gavin, for someone claiming to be very tired, you came to life rather quickly, didn't you, eh!" Emma giggled rather girlishly as she felt Gavin's erection through his boxer shorts before slipping her hand inside and taking a hold of it, asking what he planned to do with it.

Within moments, Gavin's shorts were off and Emma had been undressed of the shirt she was wearing, before she could contemplate if she was saying and doing the right thing, Gavin entered her with his hard erection, thrusting away gently as he kissed her all over her face and neck before suckling on one of her breasts.

Emma was in total delirium as Gavin made love to her with so much compassion, she stroked the back of his head and kissed his forehead and mouth as she raised up her legs, allowing him to penetrate her even deeper.

Emma could not help herself screaming out in absolute pleasure as Gavin brought her to orgasm over and over until he himself exploded inside her in a moment of total ecstasy. Gavin apologised for putting his hand over her mouth to drown out her cries of passion but he was afraid she would awaken Jeremy.

Emma didn't care about that; she was tingling all over from her momentous experience and at that point, nothing else seemed to matter, Gavin rolled back saying that was incredible and that he could feel Emma climax each time.

Emma confessed that was the first time she had more than one and that a lot of the times in the past, she had struggled to have any at all. Gavin said he hoped that they could enjoy many more together, which brought a warm glow to Emma's heart.

They lay there for a while before Gavin suggested he cook them breakfast and eat on the patio after taking a refreshing shower. Emma said she would love that asking if she could shower as well and if Gavin had a pair of shorts and a t-shirt she could put on as her dress was a little too much for the day eating breakfast on the patio.

Having showered and dressed first, Gavin laid out some shorts and told Emma to help herself to one of his t-shirts as he left her to shower and he made a start on breakfast. It was getting close to midday as Emma entered the kitchen wearing a pair of Gavin's shorts and one of his t-shirts, Emma said she hoped he didn't mind but she put on a pair of his boxers as well, showing him as she told him while Gavin was standing over the stove cooking the sausages. Emma was shocked at the amount he was cooking until he told her that it was almost midday and that the smell of the food cooking would be like an alarm clock call to Jeremy.

Emma helped lay the table as Gavin made the tea and started on the toast, Emma was about to ask if Jeremy would definitely be woken by the smell when a large splash in the pool out back was heard, Gavin smiled broadly just raising up his palms to suggest that it just happened.

"Jez's room leads to the pool; he will do a couple of lengths then come in probably dripping everywhere, looking for food."

Gavin had put the sausages with the bacon in the oven to keep warm while he fried the eggs and the foretold arrival of Jeremy occurred dripping wet as he dried himself with a towel, asking if there was any for him.

Gavin and Emma greeted Jeremy with Gavin telling him that he would get nothing if he didn't clean up the water and suggested he put some dry shorts on as well, Emma shook her head in disbelief at Jeremy as he dropped his towel on the floor and trampled it in, soaking up the water.

What Jeremy did next had Emma shocked at first and then in a fit of laughter. Jeremy bent down to pick up the towel whilst removing his shorts at the same time, revealing his bare buttocks before walking off chuckling to himself.

Gavin was not impressed at his antics in front of Emma and quick as a flash took a damp tea towel, twirling it and flicking it out at Jeremy's buttocks, a crisp cracking sound was heard as the towel made contact with Jeremy causing him to scream out in shock and momentary pain. Gavin smiled as retribution was made as poor Jeremy nursed his sore buttock, walking back to his room where he observed the large red mark in the middle of his butt cheek.

Emma felt a little sorry for Jeremy but Gavin said he deserved that adding that he had no doubt that he would be getting a revenge whipping himself at some time when he least expected it. Jeremy returned moments later full of apologies and telling Gavin that he got him good, again exposing himself to show him.

Gavin handed him a plate of food as they all sat down to eat and Jeremy filled them in on what happened after they left, Emma was happy she left when she did or the day would have been wasted, she claimed.

Jeremy asked the pair what plans they had saying that Alice reckoned the others would probably have a quiet night in once they managed to get themselves up. Emma replied that she had suggested to Gavin earlier that was probably what would happen, knowing them as well as she did.

Gavin said they had not made anything definite but was up for a chill day and night with Emma and was happy for him to tag along if he wanted, Jeremy appreciated the thought but said that they had only a short time left together and should make the most of it. Jeremy got to his feet having finished breakfast and gathering some of the plates rather cruelly but with purpose suggested that the holiday would soon be over for them both and once back home, who knew what might happen; it may be ages before they could see each other especially with Gavin's work on the farm so they should make the most of the time now alone together.

Gavin was not sure how to take the comment because Jeremy had spoken the truth but he did feel it a little harsh and perhaps uncalled for as he and Emma knew where they both stood or so he thought. Emma quickly commented that there were always weekends and bank holidays plus days she could take off as annual leave.

Jeremy asked Gavin had he explained to Emma how a farmer's life worked, causing Gavin to snap back at him to leave it there, saying that he and Emma would work something out and thanked him to say no more on it.

Jeremy walked away with the dirty dishes apologising saying he never meant anything by it but he did have a purpose that was more honourable towards his friend than Gavin could see. Emma held Gavin's hand smiling at him with reassuring words that they would sort something out.

Inside, Emma's head was spinning because she knew she had to make things work with Gavin after the holiday, she wasn't thinking marriage and settling down as such but she had given herself to him freely and could not bear the thought that it was just for a holiday fling as she had totally fallen for him.

Gavin suggested that he run Emma back to her villa where she could change into her own clothes and then suggested taking a little run out of town to a lovely beach further down the coast. Emma agreed and after clearing away the breakfast things, Gavin told Jeremy where they were going before leaving.

Gavin took Emma back to her villa where they entered quietly to allow Emma to change, putting on her swimwear under some shorts and t-shirt then packing a towel and some sun cream. The pair headed off to Kaputas beach, arriving there they struggled for a parking spot until good fortune came their way and they spotted a car pulling away just in time to claim the spot, much to the annoyance of other drivers that had been patrolling up and down, awaiting the very same opportunity.

The beach was far down below the main road accessed by numerous steps but it was worth it once they were down there. Having found a nice spot, they settled down putting on plenty of sun lotion as the day was warming up nicely then they lay back soaking up the rays.

It was around 2.30 pm that life stirred back at the girls' villa with Lacey merrily making a cup of tea in her nightie reminiscing the night before, she was lost in a world of her own, thinking about the wonderful man she had just met. Kelly made an appearance as Lacey made her way back to her room, tea in hand, they greeted each other in silence with just a wave of acknowledgement as a yawning Kelly headed straight for the coffee machine.

It wasn't long before Alice appeared, no doubt woken up by the aroma of freshly brewing coffee. "Morning sis, you ok?" Alice asked hugging her sister and telling her how tired she felt. Alice was glad she had stopped drinking when she did telling her sister that she couldn't have handled being hungover and tired as well, Kelly said that she wasn't hungover, just tired and a laughing Alice told her that she did look rather crap.

Kelly thanked her for her opinion before pouring out the coffee and saying she was going back to bed with it, Alice asked if Lacey was awake and Kelly confirmed that she was and so she went to Lacey's room.

Alice knocked on Lacey's door and entered her room that was filled with sunlight as Lacey sat up in bed looking aimlessly out of the window. "Hey Lace, how you feeling, got a sore head or just tired?"

"Hi Al, nah, I'm good, a little tired but getting there slowly, what a day eh, who would have thought it would turn out like that, I know we all came out here with that dream in our head but boy, I had to check my phone for the pictures to see he was real and it wasn't just a dream."

Alice smiled as she put her coffee down and climbed on the bed to hug Lacey telling her that she was so happy for her and then revealed what Matt had said about them last night. Lacey was so overjoyed to hear what Alice had to say telling her that it was early days yet but she thought there was a slim chance that maybe something would come of it.

The friends cuddled up talking about how their holiday had gone so far and what the remainder of the time may hold, Alice said that Jeremy would be leaving in a few days and that she really did regret not getting with him now, adding that perhaps had he not been so arrogant and full of himself initially, she may very well have.

Lacey glanced at her watch saying that she had asked Tristan not to call until after 4 pm but said she wished now she had said earlier as she couldn't wait to hear his voice. Alice then wondered about Emma if she had come back yet or was she still at Gavin's, Lacey rang her mobile but it went straight to answer phone. The girls sat talking for a few minutes more before deciding it was time for a shower and to take advantage of what was left of the afternoon sun.

The three girls sat on the patio around the pool with their chilled soft drinks discussing Emma and Gavin with Kelly talking about her conversation with Matt on the subject last night. Alice couldn't help tease her sister about Matt.

"So when you say Matt, you mean Mr lover boy Matt, don't you!"

"Oh shut it now you, please don't start your winding up stuff now; we are discussing Emma and Gavin, thank you."

"Yeah but you do love him now don't you because you snogged him how many times last night was it three or four now, I can't remember, Lace, can you remember."

Lacey asked to be kept out of it as she could see Kelly was not amused, Alice told her sister to lighten up as she knew she was only teasing her as she had always done over the years given the opportunity.

"Right, you finished now? Can we get back to Emma please?"

Kelly continued with her discussion with Matt and asked the girls what they thought they should do, Alice said that Jeremy had thought it would fizzle out after the holiday and suggested that Emma was perhaps a mere distraction for Gavin to get him through the holiday.

Lacey and Kelly did not like that assumption if it were true in any way and Kelly said that if it was then they had a duty as friends to tell Emma, irrespective how it rebounded back on them, Lacey was not up for telling her knowing how devastated she would be; she said she could not bring herself to do that to her.

Alice proposed talking with Jeremy later at some point and see if she could get something more definite out of him, she then suggested that they should even consider getting Gavin to one side and having it out with him face to face.

Lacey and Kelly agreed that it sounded a good proposition, adding that they would await Alice's findings first before doing anything rash; at that point, Lacey's message alert sounded on her phone that she had held onto in anticipation of Tristan's call.

"Oh my lord, it's him, it's Tristan, he said that he can't believe what an amazing day it was yesterday and that he hopes we can share a few more like that over the next week. Oh I can't believe it; he really does like me, doesn't he? I was a little worried that maybe he might wake up today and think he had made a mistake."

"Really Lace, why on earth would you think that, ok he is good-looking, charming and obviously a man of means but come on girl, you are more than good enough for him; he should feel himself fortunate to find someone like you." Kelly hastily jumped in as a nodding Alice agreed adding her support to her sister's comment.

"He is asking how I am feeling and if I fancy grabbing an early supper with him, an early supper, I have never been asked that before." Lacey smiled.

"That's breeding for you, Lace, the better educated people have supper," Alice giggled.

"He said to let him know soon and forward my address so he can pick me up later, oh my lord, do you girls mind? I mean what about you, Alice, are you going out to see Jeremy and you, Kelly, will that leave you on your own?" Lacey got herself in a bit of a state wrapped up in the excitement of seeing Tristan again knowing that he genuinely liked her, causing her to babble on until Kelly calmed her down.

"Don't you worry about me, my lovely girl, you just do what is right for you. I am happy to have a quiet night in alone, there are a couple of DVDs in there I can watch and get a takeaway later delivered so go ahead, message him back and tell him you would be delighted. Oh and say that it had better be somewhere very swanky and posh as you're not a lady to slum it, haha!" Kelly roared as Alice joined in the laughter, causing Lacey herself to giggle out loud squirming with excitement as she texted back.

Lacey asked Kelly for Memhet's phone number to pass on saying it would make it easier for Tristan to find her. Lacey put the name of their villa and Memhet's phone number in the message with instructions to call him as he knew exactly where they were.

Lacey received a message back thanking her and asking her to be ready at 6.30 pm with an added comment that he was excited to see her again, Lacey read out the message causing all of them to scream with excitement for her as then their attention turned to what she would wear.

"The outfit I wore last night was one of my best ones but I think the black shorts and top with the sheer sleeves would be great, classy and subtle. What do you think girls, maybe with my hair up and perhaps you could help me with that, Kell, eh?"

"I'm with you all the way, girl; sounds perfect to me and normally I would suggest you would knock him out when he sees you but you obviously have already done that last night." The girls sat around in the sun until around 4.45 pm when Lacey said she would take a shower and wash her hair. Alice sent Jeremy a text asking how he was doing and what plans he had for later.

Jeremy's response was prompt saying that Gavin had taken Emma to Kaputas beach for the day and didn't know what they were doing after, he said that they had had a disagreement that morning and that Gavin wasn't overly pleased with him. Jeremy said that a hotel down the road had a pool table and he was toying going down there around 6 pm and grabbing some food, he asked Alice if she was up for a thrashing on the pool table.

Alice laughed at the thought as she told her sister what he had suggested, Kelly grinned telling her to go teach him a lesson as Alice was quite an accomplished player that had been taught by a previous boyfriend who was an amazing player good enough to turn pro.

Alice texted back saying she would see him there later asking for the name of the hotel sometime after 6.30 pm, Jeremy sent back the information saying he looked forward to seeing her. Alice laid back on her sun lounger joyfully smiling to herself giving the thought of Jeremy thrashing her on the pool table a totally different connotation to its intended meaning, Kelly seeing her expression knew her sister had some wicked thought in her head but chose not to ask what.

Lacey emerged from her shower, wrapped in her dressing gown and saying she fancied a glass of wine and asked if anyone wanted to join her. Kelly refrained but Alice said she would have a small one. Alice took the opportunity to ask Lacey if she minded sharing a taxi down to town later when Tristan picked her up as she was going to meet with Jeremy. Lacey had no problem with that at all saying that she was very happy to help.

A while later, Kelly was helping Lacey with her hair and made a beautiful job of it; having trained as a hairdresser in her earlier years, she had not lost her touch. Kelly left Lacey to get dressed and bumped into Alice in the corridor wearing cut-off denim shorts and a see-through white t-shirt that gave a tantalising glimpse of her bosom being heaved up in her black bra. "Oh my, really Al, you know trying to excite him in your state is a waste of time, don't you?" a slightly disappointed Kelly pointed out.

"I know yes but it makes me feel sexy nonetheless and it is more for me than him, anyway I have him exactly where I need him to be so there." Alice strutted off to the kitchen for some water, head held high with a swagger as she felt justified in her decision to dress as she did.

Alice checked in on Lacey who had just put on some very sexy lingerie, Alice admired her saying that she looked really hot before questioning why so sexy, was she planning on letting Tristan see her wearing it?

"No it's not that. I'm not ready to go that far with him yet even though if I'm honest, the thought had crossed my mind. It just makes me feel good about me, puts me in the right mood to go out and enjoy myself, you know what I mean."

Alice offered up a high five saying she was with her all the way on that one before explaining what she and Kelly had just discussed about her choice of outfit.

Lacey looked perfect, Alice thought as Lacey buttoned up her blouse, having applied the last few touches of makeup, she asked Alice how she looked, Alice replied that she looked amazing as Kelly entered the room beaming with pride at her friend.

Alice complimented her sister on doing Lacey's hair saying that it made her look the part, time was getting closer to pick-up as Alice asked Kelly if she was sure she didn't want to join her but Kelly said she was happy to just relax and regain some strength as yesterday had wiped her out.

Alice couldn't resist a jibe at the fact it must have been Matt sucking all her energy out of her while they were dancing. Kelly just gave her a telling look with a big tut. Alice put her arm around her saying that she was only teasing as she and Lacey laughed at her suggestion.

The sound of a car horn alerted the girls to the fact that Tristan had arrived and they made their way to the steps. Tristan was stood at the bottom about to ascend as Lacey appeared followed by Alice.

Tristan's eyes were firmly fixed on the vision that was Lacey descending the steps, he had a look of a man that was about to receive a great award or prize.

Tristan greeted Lacey with a kiss on the cheek as he took her hand helping her down the final step, he told her that she looked really beautiful and that he was very pleased to see her. Tristan said hello to Alice and waved to Kelly who stood at the top of the steps, Lacey asked Tristan if he would mind Alice catching a lift down to town with them as she was going on to meet with Jeremy at a certain hotel near to where he was staying.

"Alice, you are very welcome to join us; in fact, we can drop you off first before going on to our venue if you like; it's no trouble really, we have plenty of time."

Alice thanked him as she turned to wave to her sister before getting into the taxi where the awaiting Memhet greeted them, he joked that Tristan was a lucky man having two of his favourite women in Kalkan with him.

Tristan asked Memhet to go to the hotel first before going on to their venue and so he did, dropping a grateful Alice off outside the hotel where Jeremy was waiting patiently, looking very happy to see her; especially looking so sexy with her long, shapely, toned and tanned legs walking towards him and her t-shirt creating the effect she had hoped for not only from Jeremy but other male customers in the bar also.

Alice made a huge fuss of greeting Jeremy, giving him an unexpected long seductive kiss. Inside Jeremy was gutted knowing he and Alice could not further their intimacy but he was not about to let that interrupt the pleasure he was getting from this embrace.

Lacey and Tristan had arrived in town and were making their way down to the restaurant he had booked for them, it was not a rooftop restaurant nor a sea view one but a delightful place at the top of a hill that led down to the harbour tucked away neatly in the corner.

Tristan was known well in this restaurant having visited many times over the past couple of years and was warmly greeted by the head waiter who led them to a specific table he asked for that afforded them great views out at that part of town.

Emma and Gavin had a lovely time chilling on the beach at Kaputas and had retreated towards Kalkan stopping at a roadside restaurant that Kelly and Lacey had visited with Matt and Giles.

They were enjoying a sumptuous meal together with a very slowly diminishing bottle of wine, Gavin was conscious about drink driving so limited himself to two very small glasses that he said he would be safe with. Emma found she had lost the taste for alcohol having consumed so much lately.

The pair talked about many things before Emma brought up the subject of them having only two full days left together, Gavin suggested that he didn't want to dwell on it and tried to change the subject but Emma found herself breaking her own taboo and started to talk about how they would carry on once they were both back home.

Gavin tried again to change the subject without success and so chose his words carefully so as not to upset Emma in any way; no matter how careful his wording was, he couldn't disguise his body language and demeanour.

Emma sensed that Gavin wasn't being open and honest with her and wanted to ask him outright how he felt but something held her back; fearing she may have misunderstood his reticent manner, Gavin then suggested that talking about leaving each other may spoil what little time they had together and suggested that they leave things as they were and see where it went on its own merits.

Emma felt that he spoke sense and then thought that he may be finding it upsetting at the thought of going home before her so smiled and agreed holding his hand and squeezing it for reassurance, Gavin's mood seemed to change not too untowardly but he seemed to have lost his spark as he suggested they head back and park the car before finding a quiet bar close by to his place.

Emma agreed and shortly after, they headed back to Gavin's place where he parked up and said he wanted to check inside to see if Jeremy was there. Entering the villa it was clear Jeremy was out as the silence was not something Jeremy was known for. Emma noticed that Gavin was not being as attentive to her as normal and asked if everything was ok and wanted to know why he was searching for Jeremy, who had quite clearly annoyed him earlier that day.

Gavin was harbouring some form of resentment towards him but he knew deep within, it was because Jeremy had faced him with a factual piece of reality that he was not yet prepared to deal with, the fact was that he now was struggling to put it out of his mind more so since Emma had raised pertaining questions to it.

Gavin told Emma that all was fine and taking her hand led her out of the villa and on to a small cosy café bar close by, where he ordered a large rum and cola with a cold beer for him and Emma said she would have a vodka and tonic as she wouldn't be able to taste the vodka.

Gavin soon put away the beer saying he needed to quench his thirst to a worried-looking Emma who thought something was definitely up but let it go, there were a dozen or so in the place some eating, some just drinking as Gavin put an arm around Emma and they leant back against the wall, listening to the chill out music being played. Emma started talking about the day out yesterday going for breakfast hoping that Gavin may respond to it in a positive way and that certainly did the trick, bringing back a smile to his face as they reminisced.

Alice and Jeremy were oblivious to the fact Gavin and Emma were sat only a hundred yards or so away as they took their turn on the pool table. Jeremy racked up the balls and cockily said that he would go gentle with her in the first game and said that it was ladies first, saying she could break.

Alice, cool as you like, stepped up to the table, bending at the hip and giving everyone in sight a wonderful view of her rear end. Jeremy felt rather hot under the collar and couldn't help grin as a woman seated close by reprimanded her male partner for ogling Alice's fine form.

With a thrust of her arm, Alice hit the cue ball smashing the pack all over the table with two spots and a stripe going down the pockets, Jeremy looked on in amazement as Alice chose the spot balls and proceeded to pot them all one by one before downing the black ball.

"I think that's game to me," she said gloating as she took a sip from her drink.

"Wow, well, you have obviously played this before, bloody hell I have never been seven balled before and by a woman! I won't ever live this down you know, thanks and I didn't even get a ruddy shot!" a very frustrated and shocked Jeremy said as he noticed several other customers grinning at his loss to Alice.

Alice said she would play him again but he could start this time and promised to go easy on him just as a female customer that had watched her performance congratulated her as she walked by to the bathroom. "Well done darling, that was one for us girls; you showed him alright," she said grinning at Jeremy.

Jeremy was even more devastated now having heard that but continued to play again, breaking the balls managing to pot one then another before Alice took her turn potting four balls in her first attempt, Jeremy had another go potting two more before Alice cleared hers and the black, to a round of applause from the same lady as earlier along with a few others.

Alice could not contain her laughter at the desperation on Jeremy's face; he was totally embarrassed by the second defeat saying that was enough pool for one night, Alice jokingly asked if there was anyone else in the bar that wanted a try but received no takers and the woman from earlier shouted that they were all too embarrassed.

Alice and Jeremy found a quiet corner to sit and Jeremy asked if she had eaten yet, saying that he was famished, Alice said that she thought they agreed loser pays rather jokingly but Jeremy said after that display, he insisted on it and suggested a nice restaurant a few doors down.

Lacey and Tristan were enjoying a glass of champagne as they perused the menu for their supper, Lacey joked that she was a little surprised at him terming dinner as supper in his text saying she had never been invited to such in the past. Tristan confessed that it was something that he had picked up from his wife and her family and that it had just stuck with him. Lacey said that it sounded so posh and said she would use it sparingly, raising a good laugh from Tristan.

"Well Lacey, this is only our second date as such and you already have me wondering what kind of spell you put on me because I'm already starting to think I would like to see a hell of a lot more of you; not just here but back home as well."

Lacey was genuinely flattered and a little overwhelmed even though she was harbouring similar thoughts but thinking it way too early to act upon them, she hesitantly said that she understood and that the thought did ring true with her own feelings but she had considered the distance between where they lived and wondered how that would work.

"Logistics is one of my strong points; don't worry about that, I think if this holiday continues in the same vein then I am sure we can arrange something. Anyway, you did say you would like to come to our head office to see the operation so there is a starting point, isn't there!"

Lacey smiled back agreeing that it would be and said that they should do as he suggested and see where they stand at the end of the holiday as the waiter arrived to take their order. After ordering their food, Lacey asked how he was coping without his children and he answered that he Face Timed them as soon as he woke up earlier and chatted for a short time before he texted her.

"Grandma is spoiling them with riding lessons as she and my father-in-law are keen horse people as was my late wife, they haven't time to miss their poor dad; they are being kept busy."

"Oh! I used to love horses when I was younger too and used to go riding over on Exmoor quite regularly with friends and sometimes my cousins. I haven't ridden for some years now but reckon I could easily jump back in the saddle and pick it up quickly again."

"Really, how wonderful! I have actually ridden on Exmoor before a couple of times with my wife Penny, we actually met the first time at a gymkhana you know about six years before we met again and got together."

Supper soon arrived and the pair began to tuck in chatting away between mouthfuls, Lacey mentioned the situation she and her friends were worried about concerning Emma and Tristan listened in with interest offering some cohesive advice.

Gavin was feeling the weight of his exertions over the past week and they were very telling as he yawned out loudly and then excused himself saying that he was ready for bed, Emma said it wasn't even eight o'clock yet, feeling a little sad that her day may already be over.

Gavin could see Emma wasn't ready to abort the rest of the evening just yet and pleased her by saying that he would struggle on and resist the temptation his bed was offering him right now—laughing as he said it. Emma said that she hoped she wasn't starting to bore him already, also laughing as she spoke.

Gavin ordered a coffee hoping a little caffeine would give him the spark he needed, not really wanting to end the night just yet. He asked Emma if she would stay overnight and she replied that she had packed her toothbrush, clean underwear and nightie in her beach bag hoping he would ask.

Jeremy and Alice were enjoying a nice starter in the restaurant down the road and Alice turned the subject to Emma and Gavin, she told him that she and the other girls were a little concerned about regarding Gavin's intentions after the holiday, an area they had already visited.

Jeremy filled her in on what took place that morning after breakfast and said that Gavin was rather off with him for raising the subject. He said he did not see how Gavin could commit to a long distance relationship with his commitments on the farm. He acknowledged that Taunton was not really that far away but far enough that you couldn't just pop over for a few hours, especially as he was up on alternate days at four-thirty in the morning and only took one day off most weeks with the odd half-day here and there unless he made arrangements well in advance.

Jeremy was convinced it was a deciding factor in why Jess left him because she knew what a commitment farmers had to make and she was not prepared to give up what she could have for that.

Alice said they were at a loss as whether they should say something or not because they were so worried how Emma might react having let down her barriers for someone that just used her for his own means to get over his loss.

Jeremy said he was not perfect and not someone with all the answers but he felt they should leave it for Emma and Gavin to sort out for themselves. He added that no one, not even themselves, could know what will happen after the holiday and to just let what will be.

Alice toiled over his words, admiring his few pearls of wisdom but still fretted over what to do next, they sat there silent for a while just looking at each other as their main course was served.

Tristan was entertaining Lacey with stories of some of the assignments he had worked on over the years; she sat looking at him in total admiration while not allowing herself to get carried away with fanciful school girl type dreams of where this might lead. Lacey was as intelligent as she was an attractive young woman; she was well grounded after past relationships had wounded her and was not easily taken in anymore.

The pair sat there engrossed with each other through the early evening smiling and laughing and growing ever closer as the night wore on. Tristan spotted Barry and Lester walk by and they both waved back to him and Lacey as Tristan said that they were nice guys but sharing an apartment with them was not his cup of tea.

"Oh so you are sharing with them; oh I didn't realise; for some reason, I thought you were at Matt's."

"Well normally, I am but he is hosting Giles obviously with Jen and Harry." After dinner, Tristan suggested a walk down to the harbour to help digestion and offering Lacey his hand, they walked slowly together down the hill to the harbour taking in the various sights of bars, shops and restaurants and the people milling around doing much the same as them.

Back at the girls' villa, Kelly was curled up on the sofa texting Matt who had messaged her earlier asking after her welfare following yesterday's adventure.

Kelly said she was relaxing alone at the villa explaining that the other three were on dates causing Matt to offer to send a car to collect her to join him and his guests as he hated the thought of her being all alone.

Kelly thought it very sweet and typical of his gentlemanly generous nature but declined saying it was her choice as she wanted to be fresh for Monday, they chatted for a while Matt saying how much he had enjoyed their dance and hoped for a rerun before her holiday was over. Kelly told him he was a soppy old romantic but thanked him for a great night, promising there would always be another dance for him, before she signed off.

About twenty minutes later, Matt texted back saying they were going to Saklikent near Fethiye the next day and asked if she cared to join them seeing how the others were probably making plans for themselves, he explained about the walk and the river experience they would be going on and Kelly jumped at the opportunity, thanking him and asked what she needed to do.

Matt returned a text stating all she needed to take and asked her to be at his for 9 am, he said they had a private minibus to take them adding that Inga would be joining them along with Harry, Jen, Lester, Barry, Mike and Liz and of course Giles. Kelly thanked him saying she would be there on time and sat back feeling rather jolly with herself before jumping up and searching through the mound of tourist brochures before finding one about Saklikent then sat back to read up on it.

Emma and Gavin had returned to his villa; she had sent Kelly a message letting her know where she was and that she was staying over with Gavin, Kelly was a little concerned but her feelings were somewhat muted by the excitement she had for tomorrow.

Gavin apologised to Emma for his moody behaviour earlier saying that a little gremlin had gotten into him and he couldn't shake it loose, Emma asked if he wanted to talk about it but he said he just needed to sleep and was sure he would be fine the next morning.

Having climbed into bed together, Gavin snuggled up to Emma saying he would love to make love to her again but sadly he had no energy, they kissed for a short while before tiredness got the better of Gavin and he drifted off, leaving Emma wide awake.

Kelly was back at the villa getting into bed herself and setting her phone alarm for 7.45 am when she received another text from someone saying they were not coming back tonight as well. Jeremy had persuaded Alice to stay the night with him knowing that they couldn't have sex; he just wanted the chance to spend the night with her and Alice feeling guilty after leading him on and not delivering had caved in to his constant pestering if for nothing else than just to shut him up.

Tristan and Lacey stopped at a little bar and ordered coffee and a brandy each to finish the night off, Tristan said that everyone was going to the river experience at Saklikent the next morning and he had declined to go having been twice before but hoped that if he stayed back, there may be a chance she would like to spend the day with him.

Lacey nodded enthusiastically. "Oh yes, yes please, that would be wonderful, Tris, thank you. What shall we do?"

Tristan said that there was a decent beach club down by where he was staying and suggested they went there where they could enjoy each other's company and get to know each other better, then maybe hire a jet bike for some fun and then grab some lunch before deciding how to spend the evening.

Lacey thought it sounded perfect saying if he gave her his address she would come down to him and asked what time, he suggested around 11 am saying he would call in the morning to reserve a good spot adding that they knew him well down there.

After they finished their coffee and brandy, they made their way to the taxi rank. Tristan said that he would take her back to her place before going home himself, Lacey said that she appreciated the offer but it made no sense as they lived in opposite directions; besides, she had spotted the grinning Memhet waving to her from across the way so she knew she would be safe alone. The pair embraced and kissed with much respect and tenderness but as they parted, Tristan pulled her in close and kissed her again but with more passion, much to her delight; finally parting, Tristan waved her off in Memhet's taxi before finding one of his own.

Jeremy and Alice were back at his and he offered her a drink but Alice was fine with water and said she needed the bathroom. Emma had heard her voice and wanted to see her but was afraid of disturbing Gavin who was practically wrapped around her.

Jeremy went to his room carrying the water as Alice was just coming out of his bathroom wearing only a pair of pants, grinning broadly at the sight of Jeremy looking very pleased with what he saw. Alice said she had hoped to get into bed before he came in but it didn't matter and then climbed in under the sheets.

Jeremy himself went to the bathroom and after brushing his teeth, emerged stark naked showing obvious signs that Alice had excited him somewhat, climbing into bed with her and a semi rigid hard on.

"Ooh we are a little excited, aren't we?" Alice teased as she took a hold of his cock, gently playing with it until he was rigid as a rock.

Jeremy said he appreciated they couldn't have sex but he asked her not to stop what she was doing just yet, Alice looked up at him with the filthiest of grins while she lowered herself beneath the sheets and much to Jeremy's surprise and greatest pleasure, performed an act of sheer delight allowing him to release much pent up pressure.

Alice surfaced with a smile of contention and asked how he liked that as she made her way to the bathroom asking if he minded her using his toothbrush; thankfully, Jeremy had a spare having had to buy a pack of two at the airport when he remembered he hadn't packed his electric one that was still on the charger. Jeremy freshened himself up once Alice had finished and then joined her back in bed where he told her that was very unexpected but he had no complaints. Alice was happy he enjoyed the experience and was quick to tell him not to expect it every time they got together.

They lay there talking quietly for a short time before falling asleep together with Alice cuddled up to his side resting her head upon his shoulder. Next door, Emma was finally asleep having wondered what on earth Alice and Jeremy had been up to with all the noises coming from his room, especially given Alice's current situation.

Back at the girls' villa, Kelly was sound asleep; she had heard Lacey arrive back earlier but was too rested to get up and go to see her, she knew if she were needed, Lacey would not hesitate to give her a knock. Lacey was as quiet as she could be as she made her way into bed; her head was filled with wonderful thoughts about Tristan and went to sleep with a comforting smile upon her face.

Monday Day 9

Everyone slept well that night; the previous day's events had made sure of that and Kelly was first rise at 7.45 am; after taking a shower, she entered the kitchen to make herself some breakfast and coffee before calling Memhet to collect her around 8.50 am as it was only 10 minutes to Matt's villa.

Having packed her day bag the previous evening and set out her clothes, she had plenty of time, Lacey came into the kitchen and Kelly apologised if she had woken her but Lacey said she had woken up about ten minutes earlier and could hear Kelly moving around.

Kelly asked how her evening went and Lacey, full of smiles and a picture of real happiness, was beside herself with joy as she briefly relayed what had happened. Kelly beamed at her feeling really happy for Lacey knowing how long she had waited for a chance like this.

Kelly then explained about Matt's text last night and that she was now off to a river gorge experience with him and his friends at Saklikent, handing Lacey the brochure, Lacey said that Tristan had mentioned it to her and was happy that Kelly would not be left alone as she said she has to meet Tristan around 11 am and that he was taking her to yet another beach club for the day and then out later in the evening.

"Well Lace, it sounds like we are all sorted at last eh girl, although I am not as romantically inclined with Matt as you three are with your men," Kelly hastened to add.

Kelly excused herself to dress asking Lacey if she wouldn't mind finishing the coffee and making her an egg sandwich, Lacey was happy to do so as Kelly took herself off to dress, returning a few moments later day bag in hand and saying she would just tie her hair back as it was wet, adding it wasn't worth doing anything with where she was going. Lacey handed Kelly her sandwich and poured out the coffee. "Right Lace, I have just over ten minutes before Memhet is here; shall I ask him to collect you later?"

Kelly eagerly tucked into her sandwich thanking Lacey beforehand as Lacey said that would be great saying about 10.45 am should be fine. Lacey asked about Alice wanting to know how she got on with Jeremy last night and if she had any more info regards Gavin's situation.

"Oh Lace, she never came back; she texted me saying she was staying with Jeremy at his place."

"Really oh my, that is a bit of a step for her, isn't it, I mean it's not as if they can have sex is it and oh it doesn't matter; it's her choice what she does. I'm not here to judge her. I am sure she has her reasons not that I'm sure I am interested to hear them."

"Well, she did tell me that whatever she did, it would be on her terms and that if anything did happen, it would be because she wanted it not because he did but as you say, that is off the menu at the moment so I suppose no harm can have been done."

Lacey agreed with Kelly as she sat at the dining table drinking her coffee before Kelly dashed to the bathroom to freshen up before Memhet arrived; bang on 8.50 am, a car horn tooted and Kelly grabbing her bag, hugged Lacey telling her to have a lovely day before going down to the awaiting Memhet.

Memhet was pleased as always to see any of the girls that seemed to be using him more on their own as opposed to all together, he said that they all seemed to be having a great holiday, something that Kelly was happy to agree with.

Kelly arrived at Matt's, thanking Memhet, she remembered to ask him to collect Lacey later. Memhet was happy to do so wishing her a lovely day out as she made her way up the steps to Matt's villa where he waited to greet her.

"Well, a very good morning to you, Kelly, are you excited about our little excursion out today?" Matt asked as he greeted her with a kiss on the cheek.

Kelly said that she was excited explaining that she had found a brochure on the place and read up on it, then holding up her bag, she said that she was all prepared with spare everything in case of mishaps.

Matt was amused with her way of thinking as he offered out an arm and led her inside to meet with the others, Giles greeted her warmly as he told Matt the minibus was on its way and due in about fifteen minutes.

Inga came over and greeted Kelly, saying she was so happy to have another girl nearer her own age on the trip as the other females were a lot older and not so interesting. Kelly gave her a hug and promised her they would have a great day and that she was looking forward to tubing down the river.

Lacey was back at the villa sorting out her day bag and considering what to take for later that evening, she thought it better to dress at Tristan's so she wouldn't have to come back later to go back out again and she knew he would be happy to let her use his facilities.

Once Lacey had sorted everything she needed, she had a shower before making herself a light breakfast, Tristan sent her a message asking how she was and said that she could come whenever she was ready, adding that he had slept really well, the best for a long time, and was keen to see her again shortly.

Lacey had received a message earlier from Kelly confirming that Memhet was booked to pick her up at 10.45 am, almost an hour away and decided she would call him herself and tell him to come as soon as possible and then abandoning her breakfast and coffee, she put everything ready by the door ready for Memhet's arrival.

With a bag strap over one shoulder, a bag in one hand and a mini dress on a coat hanger in the other, Lacey stumbled her way down the steps to where Memhet was waiting; seeing how overloaded she was, Memhet rushed to assist her halfway up the steps.

"Morning Memhet, thank you so much. I guess I should have made two trips but these steps can be a killer sometimes."

"No problem, my pretty lady, it is my pleasure, please take your seat," a very helpful Memhet told her as he opened the taxi door.

Lacey gave Memhet the address and they set off, Lacey texted Tristan to say she was on her way as Memhet asked what her plans were and where the other three girls were.

Lacey told him that she was going to the beach club with Tristan and that Alice and Emma were over at Gavin's villa having spent the night there, Memhet said that there would be no tonsils left for sure now and they both laughed.

Tristan was waiting at the foot of his apartment complex as the taxi pulled up, Memhet said that Lacey had a very excited looking man waiting for her and that he hoped everything worked out for them as he felt he was a really good man.

Tristan helped Lacey out of the taxi giving her a warm embrace and kiss on the cheek as he asked her how she was. Lacey smiling said she was happy to be in his company again as Memhet took out both bags from the boot then handed Lacey her dress on the hanger from inside the car.

Before Lacey could retrieve her purse, Tristan handed Memhet some cash, thanking him and asking for his card. Memhet was finishing early that day and said if they needed a taxi to ring the number he wrote on the back for his brother-in-law before wishing them a good day and leaving them.

Helping Lacey with her bags, Tristan asked her jokingly if she was moving in with him saying they were only going to a beach club so a swimming costume and a towel was all she needed. Lacey explained what her way of thinking was about changing at his later and asked if he minded at all.

"Mind? No absolutely not! I think it a terrific idea; in fact I wish I had suggested that myself, good thinking, Lacey; it means when we are finished at the club, we can relax back here as we get ready to go out later; yes, well done you."

Lacey felt rather pleased with herself and found herself drawn even closer to Tristan with the way he responded to her; he was so different to the men she had known before. Tristan said he had spoken with Matt earlier and he told him that Kelly was joining them on the trip out to Saklikent.

Tristan asked what Alice and Emma were doing and Lacey told him that they stayed over at Gavin's, he sensed that Lacey wasn't overly impressed by it but declined to pursue any digging on the subject.

Once inside the apartment, Tristan showed her to his room that was spotlessly clean and tidy; a little unlike her room that had clothes and things scattered about the place. Tristan had the en suite room and said that it would make things easier should the others come back earlier than expected.

Tristan asked if she had breakfast saying that he had picked up some pastries from the bakers down the road earlier and that he had put the coffee on when she texted him she was on her way. Lacey said that she hadn't had time for breakfast not wanting to say she had abandoned it to get to his place sooner.

Tristan set a table on the terrace in the shade of the hot morning sun and they sat down to a enjoy the adequate tasty pastries on offer. Tristan said they had plenty of time and would call the club to send a courtesy car to pick them up shortly.

Gavin was making himself and Emma a cup of tea when Jeremy walked into the kitchen. "Hey you alright, Gav? Look, sorry about yesterday, mate. I don't know what I was thinking, sorry mate."

"Yeah hi, don't panic. I know why you did it even though I wasn't happy about it you spoke the truth and I know you did it for me, not to hurt me. Emma said she heard Alice here last night; did she stay over?"

"Yeah mate, boy, what a night! I took her to play pool and you'll never guess what; she seven balled me first game! I didn't even get a shot!" The pair laughed at the disclosure and Jeremy asked how he got on with Emma at Kaputas.

Gavin said that it was a good day out but Emma kept talking about what would happen when they were back home and all he could think about was what Jeremy had said and it put a bit of a dampener on things. Gavin said the fact that he was tired didn't help adding that he didn't have the energy to make love to Emma last night.

Jeremy said that was sad saying he must have been totally knackered to pass up the chance, Gavin said well at least he had some earlier and that was more than Jeremy was going to get from Alice, smirking as he carried the tea off to Emma, Jeremy spouted that he was more than happy with what she gave him last night, winking at a curious looking Gavin.

Jeremy returned to his room having made coffee for him and Alice and he said that he had spoken to Gavin, telling her what he had told him. Alice sat up with the sheet wrapped around her, asking Jeremy what he made of it all.

The conversation was broken with Alice receiving a text from her sister explaining her whereabouts and that of Lacey saying she may see her later depending what time they all got back. "Saklikent; where the hell is that when it's at home?" Alice blurted out.

Emma and Gavin were planning their day together and Emma said she would need to go back and get showered and changed before anything else; she asked Gavin if he had anything he would like to do or anywhere special he would like to go.

Gavin said he would need time to think and suggested that he would have a better idea by the time Emma sorted herself out, Gavin said he would make them some breakfast before dropping Emma back at her place then got up, leaving Emma sitting there wondering how the day would turn out hoping for no recurrence of last night's mood swings.

Gavin tapped on Jeremy's door asking if they wanted some scrambled eggs and bacon, a resounding yes please came back very quickly. Gavin's bedroom door burst open and Alice dressed in one of Jeremy's t-shirts came bounding in and jumped on the bed, getting under the covers with Emma and giving her a big hug and asking how she was doing.

Emma totally surprised by Alice's actions laughed as she tried to scold her for making her jump like that, "I thought it was you last night! I could hear faint voices and what the hell were you two up to in there? I thought you were out of action?" Emma asked with great interest.

"How was your day, Emm; you and Gavin have a good time eh heard you went to some beach?" Alice enquired avoiding the question.

"Well, it was a bit of a mixture really; it started off ok except for breakfast. Jeremy made some comment about after the holiday; you know how he is and it seemed to eat away at Gavin all day. I didn't notice at first until we came back here and he was looking for Jeremy."

"Oh really, why; what did he say?"

"It wasn't so much what he said, it was what he didn't say, I tried to discuss after the holiday, you know, in a positive sense but he kept trying to change the subject before eventually saying that we should enjoy every moment now and not make plans or promises and see what fate had in store for us basically."

"Oh wow really, how do you feel about that, Em? Do you think he is interested in seeing you after the holiday or not?"

"Look, I know you girls are looking out for me but I am certain he does, I just think he doesn't want to think about us parting on Wednesday, it is probably making him think of his ex leaving him or something like that."

Alice so wanted to say something to Emma; she thought her dear friend was lost in some romantic notion that all was sunny and bright when in all probabilities dark clouds were looming on the horizon. Alice was about to make a badly timed comment when the sound of Gavin's voice calling everyone to breakfast was heard ending the conversation.

Gavin greeted Alice saying he was surprised to see her this morning but was very welcome before asking what their plans were, Alice told them where her sister had gone and that Lacey had gone to some beach club with Tristan.

"Beach club yeah that sounds like a good shout. I wouldn't mind another bash on those jet bikes; what you say, Gav?"

Gavin didn't answer initially; he just looked up at Emma who gave a look of agreement that suggested she was happy if he was, Gavin asked if they wanted to go to the same one as before or the one down the hill close by as they could call a courtesy car from there. The girls unaware this was where Lacey was headed with Tristan shortly said it would be nice to see somewhere different.

Gavin said that he would run the girls back after breakfast and then collect them later when they were ready but Emma said they would get a taxi back; she didn't want him running back and forth for them adding that the taxis were so cheap out there anyway.

Gavin was soon escorting the girls back to the villa in his car and asking Emma to call or message him when they were on their way back so he could arrange a courtesy car. Emma agreed and gave Gavin a big hug and kiss before going up to the villa with Alice who thanked him for the lift and said they would see him soon.

Inside, the girls took a shower and readied themselves for a day out at the beach club, Alice tried a roundabout way to extract more out of Emma to see how far ahead she was in her own mind about where she saw herself and Gavin heading.

Thankfully, Emma wasn't getting ready to call the vicar once she got home but she was pretty certain that she and Gavin had a bright future together, Emma turned the tables asking Alice if she was now contemplating making something of her situation with Jeremy having just slept with him, accepting that it was not in the full sense of the meaning.

Alice confessed that if they lived in the same town or very close to each other, there could be a chance but under his own admission, she said she felt she could not trust him with the distance between them. Alice then added that it was a shame as she had grown a lot fonder of him the last two days saying that he definitely had the qualities she liked in a man but it was a shame about his wayward and sometimes selfish nature.

Emma called the ever dependable Memhet asking him to collect them straight away to take them back to Gavin's, the girls collected their things and made their way down to the roadside to wait for the taxi that arrived moments later.

Lacey and Tristan were ensconced upon their sunbeds down by the water's edge at the beach club, Lacey was applying sun lotion to her now golden tanned skin as she showed off her fine figure in a skimpy black two-piece.

Tristan could but only admire how wonderful she looked even without makeup and her hair tied up at the back; she was a vision to him, Lacey caught sight of his admiring glance through her sunglasses that made her smile and feel warm with contentment.

A waiter brought them two large orange juices they had ordered after arriving there as Tristan moved his sunbed closer to Lacey's so that they could talk quietly. Lacey lay back soaking up the hot sunlight and sipping on her juice as Tristan lay twisted, gazing at her and admiring her whilst talking about some ideas he had for a project he would be working on when he got back.

The place was filling up nicely with various age groups seated all around on the various levels, out on the water all sorts of crafts motored to and fro as the whirring of jet skis and bikes thundered across the tranquil sea.

Swimmers in the safe zone screamed out with excitement as a giant turtle was spotted swimming beneath them, people entered the water and scoured the seafloor to catch a glimpse of the majestic creature.

Kelly and her party had arrived at Saklikent and were embarking on the long and enjoyable trek through the gorge, one of the deepest in the world dotted with bodies of water that led to the river. Kelly and Inga clambered along together closely followed by the watchful eyes of Matt and Giles just behind.

There was no surprise that Jen was first to lose her balance and get a little soaking, much to the concealed amusement of the rest of the party, Harry was the only one brave enough to laugh out loud, something he then thought he may live to regret.

Memhet's arrival at Gavin's was great timing as the courtesy car pulled up moments later. He gave the girls his brother-in-law's number saying he was going off duty at 1 pm until 1 pm the following day and then wished them a happy day together.

Everyone got into the courtesy car and made their way to the beach club a few minutes down the hill. On arrival, they were shown to a place with four sunbeds at the opposite end to Lacey and Tristan.

Once they had attended to all their needs with towels and stripping off down to their bathing costumes, Jeremy ran and launched himself into the sea from the platform making a neat entry into the water surfacing several meters out, meanwhile Lacey who was walking back from the bathroom that was further along past the dive school passed them by, not noticing them down below her.

Alice who had turned to Emma to ask her to oil her back thought she caught a glimpse of Lacey just before she disappeared behind a sun shade. "Eh Emm, that's Lacey over there. I'm sure of it; come on let's go over and say hi."

Emma and Alice fumbled their way barefoot across the wooden structure over to where Alice thought she saw her and just as she thought she must have been mistaken, Emma spotted Tristan about to dive in the sea.

The pair hurried along then creeping up on Lacey, surprised her with a shout of "hey what are you doing here"; the girls hugged in turn as Lacey asked them how they knew she was there and Alice explained.

"So Lacey, what you think of this dirty stopout staying over with Jeremy, someone she is not interested then eh?" Emma joked.

"Well, I must admit I was a little surprised then thought was I really, you're a big girl, Alice, you can make your own choices, can't you?"

"Exactly; my body my choice, I am in control; no one else."

"How was your day, Emm, with Gavin at the beach, was it as you hoped it would be?" Lacey asked.

Emma paused pulling a bit of a face before answering saying it was a mixed bag of fun while slightly behind her Alice was winking at Lacey while shaking her head to suggest not to go there, Lacey understood and before she could comment further, Tristan arrived back out of the water.

Standing there dripping wet in his bathing shorts, Alice and Emma could not help but admire his trim frame and tanned hairy chest; as he wiped his head with the towel, the girls gave Lacey the thumbs up before saying they would catch up later and pointed over to where they were sat if she needed them.

Alice and Emma returned to their spot where Jeremy and Gavin were about to order some drinks and said that their timing was perfect, the girls chose their drinks and settled back down with Emma about to apply lotion to Alice's back only to be halted by Jeremy who insisted that he did it and gave Alice a little neck massage as he did.

Alice really enjoyed the attention Jeremy was giving her, looking up and winking at her friend who looked on very impressed by Jeremy's actions. Jeremy scoffed that it was the least he could do after the special treatment Alice gave him last night. Alice swiftly slapped Jeremy on his leg as a slightly disgusted Emma turned away, pulling a face showing she was not impressed by his comment.

"Just when I think you have changed and are starting to be the man I would like you to be, you go and spoil everything," Alice sighed as she lay down in disappointment, telling him to hurry and finish. Jeremy apologised saying he wasn't thinking but it fell on deaf ears.

Lacey asked Tristan if he would mind putting up the sun shade as the afternoon heated up, she had been careful to apply lotion on a regular basis but was concerned that she may ruin her wonderful tan if she wasn't careful enough. As Tristan started to manoeuvre the stand, a helpful assistant appeared out of nowhere insisting that he attend to it; Tristan was very happy to allow him to do so.

When the assistant had finished, Lacey thanked him and asked to see the menu when he had a moment, the man agreed to fetch it for them immediately and returned within a few moments saying that snacks could be eaten where they sat but meals are only served in the dining area.

"How hungry are you, Lacey, personally I am happy either way; the lamb chops sound great but if you only want a snack down here, I will go for the toasted club sandwich."

"Yeah that club sandwich sounds like a good choice and not that I usually drink it but one of those large ice cold beers like they have would go down a treat right now." Lacey pointed to a group close by just being delivered a round of beers in large frosted glasses.

Tristan attracted the waiter's attention and ordered food and drinks for him and Lacey before settling back and making suggestions that they could do that evening. Lacey said she was happy to go along with any of the options he had proposed as they all sounded perfectly good to her.

The moment was interrupted by a message sent from Kelly, she had sent a couple of pictures of where she was with a caption saying that she was having a really great time and was wishing that everyone else was too. Kelly had sent the same message to Alice and Emma, unaware that all three were at the same venue.

Emma had just read the message as Alice just lay there soaking up the sun listening to Emma comment on the pictures and the message. Emma snapped a couple of shots of the boys in the water, Alice laying on her sunbed then a distant shot of where Lacey and Tristan were with an explanation to it all.

Jeremy and Gavin were treading water talking about the girls and Jeremy in particular was keen to tell Gavin how well he and Alice had been getting on saying that he wouldn't mind bumping into her again sometime when they were back home. Gavin said that he and Emma had come a long way in such a short space of time and that he knew he wanted to see her again after the holiday.

Gavin said that he felt this holiday was meant to be and that he and Emma were like two lost souls destined to meet given all the heartache each had suffered over the years, even all that bull crap the locals claim about the photograph they took on the boat he said was a sign that destiny had planned this to happen.

"Sodding hell, mate, when did you start getting all drippy and philosophical about all this romantic fantasy rubbish, you have been hurt and met someone that you like and get on well with and now you think it was written in the stars or some crap like that! Haha, wake up mate, it's just a holiday romance, nothing else."

Jeremy asked Gavin to swim back in with him and then sitting on the edge of the platform, he asked him if he really felt he could give Emma the time and commitment she deserved moving forward with his obligations back on the farm, He pointed out that with his father winding down his involvement, everything was falling down to him and Luke to take the reins.

Gavin said that he knew it wouldn't be easy but he was willing to give it a go. "Luke and I take it in turns having a Saturday or Sunday off and that has worked out ok up to now and dad would always cover for holidays and special occasions so I think Emma and I could work something out."

"Mate, I am not trying to talk you out of anything please believe me when I say I think you and Emma are great together and I know she is well into you because of what Alice has told me. Look, do you think going down to Taunton early evening on a Friday night knowing you have to head back later the following day because you have an early start on the Sunday is going to help you develop a meaningful relationship?"

"I know, I know, it sounds drastic but I'm sure we can sort something out and don't forget, Emma can come up to me on a Friday and stay through to early Monday morning and drive to work from mine."

"Oh that's generous of you! Emma gets up at five with you, travels an hour and a half straight into work; nice, have you run any of this by her yet? I think you should, you know, at least she gets time to think about it and weighs up her options."

"Yes you're right, Jez. I will talk to her later about it, what are you and Alice planning later?"

"Well erm, nothing and to be honest, she might have kicked me out of the equation now because of my mouth so I will have to grovel and beg now to get back in her good books so we will have to wait and see."

Later that afternoon, Jeremy sat on his bed next to Alice telling her how sorry he was for his big mouth, he put on a front of a man sorry for his actions desperately seeking forgiveness. He told Alice with a saddened face that she had been good for him to see the errors in his character and that he hoped he had not ruined what they had built together over the past week.

Alice told Jeremy that he had a weakness for selfish and childish behaviour that spoilt the side of him that showed great promise; she added that she still liked him but he needed to think a lot more before speaking.

"Oh and Jeremy, I have seen that fake wounded puppy look on so many faces in the past that it doesn't wash with me so if you want to apologise again to me, just do it with sincerity, yeah? Now you can start making up to me by getting me a nice cold drink, something long and refreshing please; go on, I'm dry and thirsty."

Jeremy got up and after checking with the others, made his way to the bar with Gavin in tow to help carry things back.

Emma pounced on Alice, "Oh my lord Alice, you really told him off there, didn't you!" An excited Emma laughed.

Alice said he needed bringing down a peg or two and her current situation probably made her sound a little more harsher than she would be, she added that he was his own worst enemy saying how nice he could be when he paid attention to himself.

The lads returned with the drinks and Jeremy handed Alice a long cocktail in a tall glass with all manner of fruit and decorations on it. "Sodding hell! Jeremy brought me lunch and a drink, thank you, it looks lovely," Alice said as she took a sip and squealed with pleasure at the taste.

Lacey and Tristan were tucking into their sandwiches and Tristan suggested they give it another hour before heading back to his where they could chill in the late afternoon sun in a bit of peace before getting ready to go out later.

Lacey said that she could probably do with a little kip before going out so agreed with his plans, the pair sat back enjoying their snack and cold beers under the shade of the canopy as the sun beat down on the resort.

Alice and the others were dining in the restaurant when Lacey and Tristan who were passing through after paying for their stay stopped to say that they were heading back to Tristan's. Emma asked what they were planning later and Tristan answered that they were heading into town for dinner around 8 pm. Having wished them well, Tristan and Lacey took a courtesy car back to his place, Tristan fixed them both a refreshing drink and laid out some towels on two sunbeds close to the pool with Lacey's in the lightly shade part.

Tristan asked if he could put some lotion on Lacey's shoulders as even though she had been mindful of the sun, her shoulders did look a little dry and sore. Lacey accepted his offer sitting there before him enjoying the relaxing and sometimes sensual touch of his fingers running across her skin as he gently moistened her dry shoulders.

"There, how is that now, how do you feel?" Tristan asked in a sweet and gentle manner.

Lacey was a little excited by his touch and said that he had wonderful sensual fingers that made her all tingly inside, Tristan smiled as he leant in to kiss her and the pair sat on the bed embraced for a moment of passionate kissing.

After a few minutes in each other's arms, Tristan took to his sunbed as Lacey lay back on hers, Lacey smiled to herself unable to believe almost that she was really experiencing what she actually was.

She glanced over at Tristan, admiring his form and good looks pondering if this meeting would lead them to a future of happiness together and although she stilled harboured great scepticism of men, she felt that he was somehow elevated above the normal everyday man she had encountered.

Tristan caught her looking at him with a sweet smile on her face and asked her what she was thinking, Lacey just laughed it off saying she was just having a girly moment with her thoughts.

Gavin and Jeremy paid for the afternoon and then headed outside to the awaiting girls and made their way back to the villa in the courtesy car, once back, Gavin asked Emma what she fancied doing that night—stay as a foursome or go it alone without the other two.

Emma as always wanted Gavin all to herself but was conscious of not leaving Alice alone, not knowing if she was planning on being with Jeremy at all. Alice and Jeremy were out on the patio. Jeremy had just put the kettle on to make a cup of tea for Alice and asked her if they were now friends again and would he get to share the pleasure of her company that evening, saying he had some interesting developments to tell her regarding Gavin and Emma.

Alice smiled at him saying that had better not be a ploy to get her alone with him and if it was, he may live to regret it, then laughing she pulled him near and kissed him saying that he was lucky that she was in such a forgiving mood.

Emma was on her way to find Alice to see what her plans were but upon seeing her embrace with Jeremy, she did an about turn and went back to Gavin saying she believed all was well with the other two. Gavin was pleased and asked if she fancied going back to the hotel restaurant that they had gone to on their first night out together after the sunset boat trip.

Emma gleefully jumped at the chance saying that she would love to but only if he allowed her to share the cost as he was paying for everything and that wasn't right. Gavin agreed reluctantly and called the restaurant to book a table for around 8.30 pm to allow him time to build up an appetite.

A knock on Gavin's door was followed by a voice asking if they were decent and could they come in, Gavin opened the door to Jeremy and Alice to see what they wanted. Alice said that she presumed they had made plans for later and that she and Jeremy were going to just go out drinking and snacking as they had enough of fancy meals of late.

Jeremy joked that he would be steering well clear of any bars with a pool table though, as he had no intentions of enduring another night of humiliation. Alice laughed, poking him in the side and agreeing with him that he was a wise man for once.

Lacey had taken a nap on Tristan's bed to energise herself for later that day not wanting to have to go back to her villa too early, Tristan relaxed outside and spent some time catching up with his two girls on his tablet. He spoke with his father-in-law at first who enquired how it was going for him, Tristan said he was having a good time as it went and that things were turning out better than he had anticipated.

Although he never said anything or pushed Tristan to expand any further on that statement, his father-in-law suspected that he may have met somebody, it was something he and his wife had hoped for a little while now knowing how hardworking and devoted to his family he had been since the loss of Penny.

Tristan eventually got to speak with his girls and it filled him with heartfelt emotion to see their happy smiling faces tell him all about the horses they had ridden on. Tristan enjoyed several minutes catching up with them before ending the call showered with loving kisses being blown at him by the twins.

Alice and Emma had taken a taxi back to the villa to freshen up and change arranging to meet the boys at what they called their cocktail bar around 7.45 pm, Alice had said they could enjoy a drink together before going their separate ways and perhaps meet up later at the end of the evening.

Alice said she fancied a long soak and so ran the only bath in the villa that was in her sister's room, Emma meanwhile sent a couple of text messages to her mother back home updating her on the holiday and one to Kelly explaining her and Alice's plan for the evening.

Alice was waiting for the tub to fill and asked Emma in a slightly awkward manner if she were planning on stopping over at Gavin's again that night. Emma said that she had little time left with him and didn't want to waste a moment of it and asked her why she asked in such a way.

Alice said it was nothing and that she was just curious but then confessed that she and the others were a little concerned that she was pinning a lot of trust on her relationship with Gavin and that she was getter ever closer to him each day and night; they were afraid if he didn't pull through for her, how she would cope.

Emma's head dropped and shaking it as she raised it back up, she said, "No please, Alice, not this again; look, I have told you Gavin said things would sort themselves out ok, he does have genuine feelings for me and I know it will be hard but we will try and if down the line, it doesn't work then so be it but at least for once I have had someone genuine in my life that did try for me and gave it their best because I know in my heart that is what Gavin is like."

Alice looked at Emma with a hopeful and sympathetic smile, reaching out and touching her on the shoulder before saying she needed to check her bath. Returning moments later, Alice said that she only wanted what was best for her and that she and the others would always be there for her if needed. Emma smiled back saying she understood and was grateful to have such caring, loyal and dependable friends but asked Alice to please stop worrying because she knew it felt so right.

Jeremy and Gavin were enjoying a cold beer on their front terrace, watching the early evening close in as the sun was setting over to the west. "So mate, you going to talk with Emma later yeah about life after the holiday? Have you planned what you are going to say to her yet or will you just wing it?" Jeremy asked out of the blue.

Gavin was a little surprised by the sudden question but quickly regained his composure and with some confidence stated that it was simple, he said he would just tell her not to expect too much too soon and see how things develop and that he would make every effort to see her and make sure she understood the nature of his work and how busy it can get.

Gavin added that he can't do or say any more than that and that Jeremy had unfortunately been right about his situation but he was determined to see her again, he said that he was sure Emma would understand and that she would make every effort to fit in with his lifestyle.

Tristan stood in the doorway of his bedroom looking and admiring the shapely form of Lacey laying on his bed sound asleep; he walked over quietly, resting down beside her and wrapping his arm around her giving her a gentle cuddle from behind. Lacey opened her eyes, feeling lost for a moment then smiling with great contentment, she rolled over to face Tristan putting her arm around him, the pair kissed gently at first before they found themselves embroiled with each other in a spontaneous burst of wild and ravenous lust for each other.

After some time had passed, the pair cooled their intensity for each other laying still and in silence just looking at one another, Lacey glanced at her watch saying that it was almost six and that she should start thinking about getting ready to go out but Tristan said that he would rather spend the evening there and carry on from where they had just left off.

Lacey sat up on the edge of the bed and Tristan sensed that he may have overstepped the mark a little, He asked if she was ok and if something he had said had upset her.

"Look Tristan, it has been a while for me, since I have been with a man I mean, and to be honest there have been few men in my life that I have been intimate with; please don't think me a prude but before I can give myself in that way to someone, I really need to know them well. It is just the way I was brought up, a good little Christian girl, that's me." She tried to laugh.

"From what I have seen and heard from you, I must say I find no fault and to be honest, I have become a little captivated by you, I just feel it is too soon to take things to that level, I am sorry if that has disappointed you."

"Disappointed? Oh my dear girl, no, quite the opposite in fact, you have no idea how refreshing it is to hear someone speak like that and I am sorry to compare but you have so many of the qualities that attracted me to Penny."

"Really? Gosh that does surprise me, I mean especially with her background and upbringing."

"You have no idea how many dates I have had over the past couple of years where the women were happy to sleep with me on the first or second date, that really shows you the calibre of some women but please don't get me wrong. I have a couple of friends that slept together on first or second dates and been happily married for years since."

Lacey nodded and smiled before laughing at Tristan telling her that Penny made him wait more than six months before they were intimate adding that they both knew by then that they had a future together, Lacey said that if they had a future together, she was sure she wouldn't make him wait that long.

Tristan seemed to enjoy Lacey's response as he sat beside her taking her hand in his and kissing it then saying she was turning out to be a real refreshing surprise for him that he was enjoying immensely.

Lacey said that she needed to shower and make a start on getting ready and asked Tristan to leave her while she used the bathroom, Tristan said that he would wait until she had showered outside on the terrace and give her time to sort herself afterwards before showering himself.

Kelly and her party of day trippers had a wonderful day out in the gorge of Saklikent and were finishing off their drinks and snack in the restaurant there before heading back to Kalkan. Kelly was laughing and joking with Inga about some of the day's highlights, especially the ones that involved Jen, when Matt interrupted asking the girls what their plans were for later.

Kelly said that she had received a text from Emma saying that she and Alice were out with the boys and that she presumed loved up Lacey would be enjoying herself with the charming Tristan. Matt then suggested that she and Inga join him and Giles for a late bite and some drinks once they got back.

Kelly said that she would need to shower and change first so would have to return to her villa, Matt said she was fine as she was and could always use his shower before Inga jumped in saying she was welcome to use her facilities if she wanted and they could get ready together.

Kelly thanked Matt, choosing to go with Inga adding that she had brought spare shorts and a top that she could change into, Matt a little deflated said that was fine and returned to his seat just as Giles announced that they should all head out to the minibus.

The sound of a hairdryer blowing away broke the silence at Tristan's place as Lacey sat at his dressing table sorting out her hair. Tristan tapped on the door asking if he could enter and upon receiving permission opened the door smiling and asking Lacey if she would like a coffee as he had just brewed a fresh pot.

Lacey smiled and nodded eagerly saying that would perfect and without sugar, Tristan soon returned putting down her coffee and asking if he could now take a shower himself as he was feeling rather hot and sticky at that point and was desperate to freshen up.

With a wave of her hand, Lacey ushered Tristan off to the bathroom saying that he should not stand on ceremony for her and that it was his place. Tristan, ever the gentleman, just wanted to be sure she was comfortable with him in there as she was sat just wrapped in a large towel.

Lacey knew with other men she had encountered the sight of her sat in nothing more than a towel would have been too much of a temptation for them but she knew deep inside, Tristan was unlike other men she had known. Tristan took himself off to the shower and spent a short time in the bathroom shaving and attending to his needs making himself as desirable for Lacey as he could.

Tristan exited the bathroom dressed in his bathrobe and brushed past Lacey, helping himself to some clothing from his wardrobe saying that he would dress in Lester's room. Lacey closed her eyes as she smelt a waft of Tristan's cologne pass her by, giving her a warm feeling inside.

Alice and Emma were well on their way to being ready for a night out with the boys, Alice had donned a simple short skirt with a vest type top and put a cardigan at the ready for later that night. Emma was a little more glammed up, bravely wearing a figure hugging mini dress that she rather worryingly asked Alice if it looked ok and asked if it made her look fat.

"Emma, you could wear a sackcloth and Gavin wouldn't notice; he only has eyes for you and you alone, girl, no you certainly don't look fat; in fact I would go as far to say I think you may have lost a little weight since being out here."

Emma looked at Alice in total disbelief as she ran to the full length mirror to see for herself, Alice was right behind her laughing at Emma's sudden shock at her words.

"Well, I haven't been eating so much as normal and with all this heat and that, I suppose I may have dropped a kilo or two. What do you think, Al?"

"Yep definitely but look Emm, you were never really fat before were you, it was just a few curves that was all nothing major; so you went up a size, big deal eh who doesn't from time to time."

Emma turned and twisted in front of the mirror as she looked herself over and ran her hands over her stomach and down her thighs, she was so pleased with what she saw and with Alice's encouraging observations.

Emma hugged Alice and thanked her for her kind words saying that this was definitely the best she had felt about herself for ages, Alice was pleased for Emma and suggested they have a little shot before going out saying she fancied getting well sloshed that night and throwing caution to the wind.

Lacey called out to Tristan asking him if he was ready as she put her final touch of lipstick on. Tristan chuckling said he been for about twenty odd minutes and was just waiting on her but there was no rush. Lacey emerged from the bedroom to find Tristan standing in the doorway of the terrace. "How do I look?" she asked softly.

Tristan turned to see her standing there, a vision of beauty in a midnight blue lace style dress that showed off her tanned legs wonderfully and her hair hanging to the one side over her left shoulder, the only issue he had was that her heels made her taller than he was but he was so blown away with her statuesque movie star look that issue was soon forgotten as he told her that she looked absolutely wonderful.

Tristan stood there in his tailored shorts and blue and white striped shirt opened to below his chest showing off his tanned body in part and with his tousled dark hair falling onto the brow of his handsome tanned face. Lacey again felt that warm feeling he often gave her.

Tristan suggested they take a short stroll to one of the nearby bars before taking a taxi into town later and finding a restaurant to dine in, a smiling and joyous Lacey was only too happy to go along with anything he suggested.

Walking hand in hand, Lacey and Tristan made their way to a bar and sat at a table where they ordered two gin and tonics, they made such a handsome couple just sitting there enjoying each other's company just as the day trip minibus flashed past.

Kelly joined Inga back to her place having agreed with Matt to be back at his in about an hour's time, Kelly said that she felt happier about coming back to hers as after such a wonderful day out, she may have dropped her guard and who knows what may have happened as she had become aware that Matt was showing a keener interest in her since their little snogging session the other night.

Inga asked if he had acted inappropriately towards her in any way but Kelly was quick to dispel such a notion saying that he had always acted in a respectful way towards her, Kelly added that she was just aware that he had grown more attentive towards her since that night and that in part she was just as much to blame for it.

Inga was happy to hear that as she had always enjoyed Matt's company and had never seen him in that light before, the girls got themselves showered and dressed and after some little refinements, made their way back to Matt and Giles.

Gavin and Jeremy had already arrived in town and making their way to the cocktail bar as the girls were just getting into the taxi, Gavin was able to secure a table right at the front and the lads ordered themselves some drinks while they waited for the girls.

Lacey and Tristan were just about to take a taxi into town when Tristan heard Barry call out to him. He had been dropped off down the road at the supermarket where he wanted to pick a few things up to take back to the villa.

Barry asked where they were off to and how their day had been before briefly saying that his day out had been interesting and that he would tell him about it at a later time. Tristan just said that they were heading into town and were going to find somewhere to eat as he hadn't booked anything.

Tristan and Lacey waved Barry off as they headed to town in the taxi with Tristan asking Lacey if she wanted to try anywhere in particular, Lacey said with so many restaurants to choose from, it was hard to decide but she fancied one of the many rooftop ones as they afforded a good viewing platform across the old town. The pair arrived in town a few minutes behind Alice and Emma who had now arrived at the cocktail bar to meet the lads; as Lacey and Tristan made their way down to the old town past the cocktail bar, they were spotted holding hands and looking like a couple very much in love.

Gavin and Jeremy let out a couple of loud wolf whistles that caught their attention and looking up over at where they sat, they waved to them as Emma and Alice blew Lacey kisses back and gave her the thumbs up with broad smiles. Alice commented that Lacey looked stunning and was so pleased for her, something that Emma was quick to support her saying she thought that they made the perfect couple.

Gavin asked if she thought they were more perfect than he and she were. Emma, slightly stunned by the question, said in all honesty she hoped not but would wait to see what his intentions towards her were when the holiday was over. Gavin said that he wanted to discuss that with her later over dinner but for now he just wanted to relax and have some fun. Alice gave a look of concern towards Emma who just smiled nervously back as she picked up her drink, wondering what he was going to say.

Lacey and Tristan were at the head of the old town deciding which route down they should take, Lacey noticed a restaurant's display boards to the side and stopped to look at it saying that it looked nice in the photos. Tristan told her to wait and he would go up and see if there were any tables available within the next hour, coming back down the three flights of stairs a few minutes later, he said that they could have a table in just over an hour and so he booked it and now he needed to get some cash and remembering that there was a cash machine just down the way, he suggested they went there before coming back up and having a drink in the nearby bar.

Walking past the few jewellery shops that were there, Tristan pointed out the cash machine and told Lacey who had her eye caught by all the glitzy jewellery on display to amuse herself there for a moment while he attended to his cash flow needs. Lacey gladly stopped there and scoured all the wonderful pieces that were on display until Tristan returned.

"Anything special catch your eye there, Lacey?" A returning Tristan asked with genuine interest.

"It's all beautiful but I was rather taken by that lovely gold bracelet with the semi-precious stones hanging from it, it is like a charm bracelet but with beautiful coloured stones instead of charms and they happen to be some of my favourite colours that I could wear with many of my outfits."

Lacey pointed out the bracelet to Tristan who in turn suggested that they should go in so she could try it on; at over 400 euros, Lacey said she was just happy to window shop it for now but Tristan insisted that she should at least try it on before walking away.

Lacey was adamant that she didn't want to, afraid that he might try some chivalrous act and buy it for her, she liked him very much and hoped that she could develop something with him long lasting but like the sex situation, she wasn't ready to accept expensive gifts from him yet either.

Tristan was bemused by her stance but respected her wishes and taking her by the hand, he told her she truly was an enigma to him, then after kissing her, he led her back up to a bar where they sat and chatted over some wine before going up to the rooftop restaurant close by for dinner.

Meanwhile, Gavin and Emma had left Alice and Jeremy to go back to the site of their first dinner date together, Jeremy asked Alice where she fancied going next and to his surprise, she said rather sharply, "You can order me another drink here and we are going nowhere until you tell me what the hell is going on with your mate Gavin."

Jeremy sat back down just laughing shaking his head, he called over the waiter and ordered two more drinks before turning to Alice and saying, "Look, I know I said I would tell you everything and I promised it wasn't a ruse just to get you to come out with me but look, things have changed and I think you need to hold off until the morning."

"Sod the morning; I want you to tell me now what is he going to tell her over dinner; he is going to dump her, isn't he? Come on Jeremy, don't spoil things between us now please just tell me please, I am right aren't I come on say it."

"Alice please, would you just please calm down and listen; you have it all totally and utterly wrong ok! Gavin doesn't want to end anything with her and to be honest, I am shocked as well as you but it would seem and please this is nothing to do with what he has said directly but I think he has genuinely fallen for her."

Alice threw her hands over her wide open mouth as Jeremy uttered those words to her; she was completely taken aback and quite close to tears as she flung herself at Jeremy wrapping her hands around him and hugging him before asking him if he was certain and not just saying that to get out of saying something else.

"Listen, I have spoken with him again today and I think you will appreciate it more hearing it from her tomorrow ok, I don't want to seem harsh but I honestly think you will enjoy her telling you more than me; fair enough?"

"Yes of course, no you're right, Jeremy, and thank you, oh dear god, there you go again showing how sensitive and adult you can be; why can't you be that way more often then maybe I would have come up to Gloucester at some point to see you and who knows what might have happened."

"Never say never, Alice, there is still time; you will always be welcome at mine anytime you want."

Alice kissed Jeremy in total admiration and appreciation of the way he dealt with her outburst and demanding nature, she whispered that she always got a little high and mighty when she was going through her lady issues and thanked him for being so tolerant with her.

Gavin and Emma arrived at the restaurant and was warmly greeted by Mohammad who held out his arms saying inadvertently that it was a pleasure to welcome back Kalkan's most wonderful honeymooners before reeling back in a contorted fashion with agony etched on his face as the realisation of his words hit home, Gavin just looked at him a little stunned before roaring with laughter as did Emma.

Mohammad was a picture of a man wishing a sink hole would open up and swallow him before Gavin extended his hand and told him it was ok and that it was an honest mistake, Gavin asked if they could have their same table but was told it had already been booked by a VIP client earlier that day and that they had reserved the next best table for them with a lovely view and gentle cooling breeze.

Gavin and Emma were seated at their table and given VIP service themselves starting with a complimentary glass of champagne, Gavin told Emma that she looked even more beautiful than the first time they ate there and complimented her on her outfit, apologising for not taking notice sooner saying that with Jeremy and Alice there, it wasn't the same.

Unknown to Kelly, she and her little entourage were on their way to the same venue as Gavin and Emma and turned out to be the VIP guests that Mohammad had mentioned earlier; as they were being shown to their table, Kelly spotted Emma calling out and waving as Emma looked up.

Kelly excused herself for a moment to go across to see her friend who she said she felt like she hadn't seen for ages, Kelly and Emma embraced with air kisses as an excited Kelly asked how things were going.

The three chatted briefly before Kelly returned to her table wishing them a wonderful night, Gavin was amazed that with over a hundred restaurants in Kalkan, they had booked the same as them at the same time, not that he had any issues with it.

Kelly asked if they minded her sending Alice a quick text to let her know where she was; no one seemed bothered as they were eagerly perusing their menu's and Matt was engrossed in the wine list.

Kelly told Alice that they were at the same restaurant as Emma and Gavin and that they looked really good together, Alice replied that she should keep an eye out on her as Jeremy had said that Gavin was going to drop a bit of bombshell on her tonight, not realising that Kelly would read that the wrong way.

Kelly tried to keep a cool head and waited to see what developed between Gavin and Emma whilst trying not to show any kind of sign that would give away her anguish that was building up within her. Matt ordered the wine after taking a consensus at the table and then they all ordered their meals as Gavin and Emma tucked into theirs.

Emma looked up at Gavin and asked him when he planned on telling her what he had to say as the suspense was ripping her apart inside. Gavin apologised and started to tell Emma everything he had been thinking about and going through that past week regarding them and after the holidays and true to his word, he told her the truth as agonising as it was.

Kelly kept an ever vigilant eye on their table as she tried to interact with her party best she could, she sensed that things were getting a little tense on Gavin's table as she saw him grab Emma's hand as if to comfort her then Kelly saw Emma appear to wipe a tear from her eye.

Kelly was visibly moved and Inga seeing the change in her face asked Kelly if all was ok, Kelly said that she thought Emma was looking a little upset by something Gavin was telling her and at that moment, Emma got up from the table and rushed towards the bathroom holding a napkin to her eye.

Kelly was up in a flash apologising saying she must go to Emma and didn't think twice at giving Gavin a filthy angry look on her way past him. Kelly burst into the bathroom calling out to Emma who was standing in front of the mirror crying and trying to stop her mascara running everywhere.

Kelly rushed up to Emma calling out her name as she hugged her. "Oh Emm, I am so sorry. I will kill the bastard with my own hands! Tell me what has he done, sweetheart eh, come on tell me."

"Oh no oh no, you don't understand, Kell." Emma sobbed as she tried to explain.

Kelly looked a little bemused as Emma freshened up her face and then eventually in what seemed like an age told Kelly what Gavin had actually said, "He told me that he thinks he has fallen in love with me and that he doesn't know how it will work with his commitments to the farm that will be part his one day but he said that now he has found me, he doesn't want to lose me and that he would do whatever it took to keep me."

Kelly embraced Emma again, saying how happy she was for her just as Inga came in to check all was well, Kelly explained all to Inga and said that they had better get back soon because Matt and Giles were thinking of giving Gavin a piece of their mind, assuming that he had just delivered some rotten news to Emma.

Kelly herself said that she had an apology to make to him as well because of the way she looked at him coming to check on Emma, they all returned to the dining area where Matt and Giles were stood over Gavin. The girls rushed to them fearing they were too late but found the men laughing and talking and they asked them what was happening. Matt said they had asked Gavin to explain what had happened and he had told them point blank that he had fallen in love and then then the rest just fell into place.

Some of the staff had been looking on with a little concern at what they were seeing and went to find Mohammad who came over to ask if everything was ok, Kelly said yes but was cut off by Matt who said no actually.

"Look Mo, there seems to be a problem here, a big one." Mohammad looked very concerned when he asked what the problem was.

"You see Mo, this young man has just told this young lady that he is in love with her and we want to toast that acknowledgement but we don't have any champagne so you see the dilemma," Matt smirked as the penny dropped with Mohammad.

"Oh Mr Matt, you are a very bad man, you know we love you here but you are very bad man. I am simple man not the cat with nine lives I have only one please don't make it a short one please thank you, I will fetch you champagne right away, six glasses yes."

Mohammad turned to get the champagne uttering out orders in Turkish to a staff member to clean six glasses ready. Moments later he returned still shaking his head muttering some words that made Matt laugh, Kelly felt sorry for him until Matt said not to buy Mohammad's fakery saying he had known him for a few years and that he was nobody's fool. Mohammad gave Kelly a sly wink to suggest he was kidding all the while that made her smile, Mohammad opened the champagne and shared it between the six glasses carrying two over to Gavin and Emma telling them that the photograph didn't lie and gave them a friendly smile and wink.

Matt raised his glass and proposed a toast to a wonderful holiday romance wishing it longevity and much happiness, Kelly found herself shedding tears along with Emma as they all joined in the toast.

Lacey and Tristan were sitting down to dinner at their roof top restaurant and Lacey said that the view was not as she had hoped but the place had a nice ambience and the food looked good that she could see on other tables, A waiter brought them menus and told them about the specials before taking an order for their drinks which came to no surprise to Lacey when Tristan asked for two glasses of champagne.

Alice and Jeremy were enjoying each other's company over some kebabs and a cold beer sitting in a streetside café off Kalamar road, Alice said that the chicken and vegetable kebab was totally amazing as Jeremy showed no mercy to his lamb doner kebab.

It was turning out to be quite a successful holiday across the board with Emma finding love in the arms of a man who had saved her not only from drowning but the dark and dreary world she had allowed herself to become entrapped in. Lacey had found herself a handsome and charming man that was totally smitten with her and found her virtuous nature very appealing to himself.

Alice though not looking for anything long term with Jeremy was happy to have met someone that she could enjoy some fun time with and a little intimacy that may have continued further if it had not been for unfortunate timing on her part. Kelly meanwhile had learnt that older men can still offer great companionship and fun as well as loving moments should they wish to take part; so all in all, the four girls had experienced something of what they had set out to find.

Emma and Gavin were finishing off dinner and deciding what to do next as it was still before 10 pm and they wanted to make the most of their penultimate night together. Emma said she fancied going to one of the music bars and letting her hair down until they threw them out, causing Gavin to laugh out loud and suggest he knew the exact place.

Gavin suggested that they take a gentle stroll into town first and let dinner settle and said that where he was thinking wouldn't liven up until around 11 pm, he advised they take a walk and find a nice bar for a drink before going on to the place he had in mind.

When it came time to leave, Emma and Gavin crossed over to Kelly's table to say goodnight and thank everyone for their kindness towards them, Matt asked where they were headed and Gavin told him the plan. Matt knew the place and said that they may venture that way themselves later but not to worry, they wouldn't crowd their space, Gavin said it was fine if they did saying that it would help make the night even more memorable.

Gavin and Emma headed off thanking Mohammad on the way out, declining a taxi saying they wanted a nice walk together. Mohammad wished them both well saying he hoped that they would return again one day together and that it had been a pleasure to have served them before. The pair set off on the pleasant walk back to town.

Tristan and Lacey were enjoying dinner together talking about past experiences and what potential the future held for them, Tristan said that he appreciated it was early days and boldly claimed that she would probably be bored with him by the time her holiday was over but he said he hoped whatever the future had in store for him, she would be a part of it.

Lacey smiled back at him, reaching out to clutch his hand and said that she knew that she could never get bored with him and that yes, it was certainly very early days but she felt the same as he did, she told him that he had given her a new perspective on men, something her past acquaintances could never achieve and that he made her feel valued and respected.

Tristan stood up from his seat and bent over to kiss Lacey in a sudden burst of passion he was feeling for her, Lacey was taken by surprise but welcomed the amorous gesture whole-heartedly by clutching at his face and kissing him back with a heart full of seductive nuances that filled her with tingling emotions.

Tristan sat back down and said while he held both her hands that he truly believed that they were both at the start of something truly wonderful, he said that he did not want to sound like an old cliché but felt they were at the dawn of a bright new future together and hoped that she felt the same.

Lacey felt her eyes water up as she listened to his soft endearing voice send ripples across her body as he spoke to her in his charming manner, Tristan offered up his napkin seeing the effect his words were having on her and asked her to wipe her tears, assuring her that he meant every word.

Lacey let out a deep sigh before telling him that he had said everything she had longed to hear from someone genuine for such a long time, she said that he had truly captivated her and that she hoped as he did that there would be something wonderful waiting for them down the road.

Emma and Gavin were enjoying a drink in a bar when Emma spotted Alice and Jeremy coming close to where they were; she asked Gavin if he minded her calling them over and he said that he was more than happy as he was now feeling relieved that he had made a commitment to Emma and felt all his burdens had vanished into the night.

Emma stood up waving and calling out to Alice who spotted her just as she called out, she and Jeremy made their way over to the bar and joined Gavin and Emma, Emma gave Alice such a big hug as if she had not seen her in an age, making Alice ask what was all the fuss about.

Emma made the excuse she needed the bathroom and enticed Alice to join her using hand gestures, Alice asked Jeremy to order her a vodka and tonic before following Emma.

Once in the bathroom, Emma again in a fit of excitement hugged Alice with great intensity squealing out with pleasure in her eagerness to tell Alice about earlier on and Gavin's promise to do whatever it took to make things work after the holiday.

Alice was overjoyed with the news so much so that she even shed a tear with Emma who herself cried again with much joy, Gavin was sat with Jeremy telling him everything about earlier and Jeremy sat quietly listening puckering up his lips and nodding in acceptance at his friend's decision.

"Well mate, if you are sure that you can fulfil that obligation then good luck to you and I mean that sincerely. Look, I know I have been a little hard on you about this but it was because I couldn't see you go through all that agony and pain again like after Jess you know."

"Oh Jez, yes mate, I know. I do understand we have been best mates for how long we know each other inside out, thanks mate, it really does mean a lot you know and to be honest it was your reasoning that woke me up and helped me think straight for once."

The lads chinked glasses looking at each other with great affection as they had been so close for many years like brothers almost, the girls re-joined them at the table and Jeremy quipped that it was great news that Emma and Gavin were going to give it a go and that maybe one day he may get to play the part of best man for real.

Jeremy laughed as he suggested that if in years to come, they did end up spliced if Alice fancied making it a double wedding, Alice laughed back saying yes she did to everyone's surprise until she added that she would be sure to invite him along, causing the others to burst into laughter. Jeremy actually enjoyed the comment as it was very much on his humour level and winked at Alice with a nod to say well done.

The four sat there drinking for a while before heading off to the music venue a short walk away to find it getting rather busy there, Gavin said that they had come just in time and then familiar voices called out to them above the drowning noise of the music; it was Matt and Kelly calling them to join them in their cosy little corner.

Kelly hugged her sister telling her what a wonderful day it had been and then suggested they go to the ladies room so she wouldn't have to shout everything at her, in the toilet, the sisters were joined by Emma and Inga and they all talked excitedly about the day's events and the wonderful news they never thought they would hear about Emma.

Kelly asked if anyone had seen or heard from Lacey and Alice said that she and Emma had seen her looking really loved up walking and holding hands with Tristan earlier in the evening going for dinner, Emma said that Lacey looked amazing really pretty and that she and Tristan looked made for each other.

Kelly was beside herself with happiness to hear that and Inga joined in saying that she had met Tristan twice before and said that he was a wonderful sincere man that was hard to find nowadays, that was something that the girls knew all too well and agreed with whole-heartedly.

The girls returned to the men, full of happiness and ready to party on through the night, Matt organised the drinks and everyone stood around dancing and laughing as they enjoyed themselves. Tristan and Lacey were walking around the old town and found a quiet corner where they sat listening to relaxing sounds and enjoyed a coffee and a brandy. Lacey snuggled up to Tristan as he talked to her about his daughters saying how much he would like her to meet them.

Lacey had always wanted children as she had a very natural strong maternal side to her nature but would never consider it before being married, she said that they sounded wonderful children and would very much welcome the opportunity to meet them.

They spent the next hour or so there just talking and slowly drinking their brandy before the time approached the midnight hour and Lacey asking to be excused started yawning profusely, Tristan said that he was disappointed that the evening had come to an end but at the same time it meant that he would see her sooner as the new day was approaching fast and he was hopeful that they could spend another wonderful exciting time together.

They got up and made their way up to the taxi rank walking slowly, holding each other close with arms around their waists, Tristan said that he looked forward to seeing her the next day and asked if there was anything special she would like to do but Lacey simply replied that she was happy to go along with anything he wanted and asked him to surprise her.

Tristan asked Lacey about her things she had left at his place and if she needed to collect them before heading back; Lacey was a little perplexed at the situation having not given it any thought being caught up in the moment of being romanced the way she was. Lacey smiled and said that yes she would need to collect them because she would need certain things for the morning, Tristan said that he didn't wish to come over improper at all but said that she could always stay the night and head back first thing; he suggested that he could always take the couch if she wasn't up for spooning, promising profusely that he would be honourable.

Lacey was quite surprised at how much she actually entertained the notion thinking to herself that she knew she could trust him, she said that she had no nightwear with her but Tristan said he had plenty of t-shirts she was welcome to choose from. Lacey suggested that they travel back and see how she felt when they got there, putting a keen smile on Tristan's face, having now arrived at the his complex, Tristan asked if he should tell the driver to wait and a smiling Lacey just looked at him, shaking her head having decided to take him up on his offer.

Tristan and Lacey were greeted by Lester and Barry who were smoking out on the terrace whilst enjoying a couple of rather large brandy's. They both smiled at the men saying hello and Tristan exchanged a few friendly words with them as they in turn gave him a few raised eyebrows with a wink and a nod.

Tristan asked Lacey if she fancied joining the others with a brandy nightcap but she declined saying smoking wasn't her cup of tea and disliked the smell but apart from that, she was feeling a little tired and preferred that they just settle somewhere together and talk until they fell asleep.

"So do I take from that I am not on the couch then?" Tristan laughed, looking at Lacey for reassurance.

"No, you don't need to stay on the couch. I think I am a good judge of character now and am confident that you will stick by your promises," Lacey spoke with great sincerity as Tristan showed her to his stack of neatly piled t-shirts telling her to choose whichever she wanted.

Having allowed Lacey to change in private, Tristan entered the room then popping into his bathroom changed into his night shorts and vest top before he joined Lacey in bed, cuddling up to her and kissing her sweetly telling her to sleep well. Lacey lay there with her head spinning with all manner of thoughts about what she was actually doing wondering if she would regret her decision, then thoughts of how she may react if Tristan became aroused in the middle of the night and tried something on flooded her mind.

Lacey spun around and pulled herself in as close as she could get to him, resting her head on his shoulder and wrapping her arm around him, Tristan asked if she was ok and she simply replied that she hoped she had made the right decision and Tristan said with much empathy that she had and not to let it worry her.

Kelly, Alice and the others were just leaving the music bar all feeling the effects of the day's events and alcohol intake that night as they struggled along up to the taxi rank that was quieter than normal with only a couple of cars in there at that point. Kelly asked Emma if she was coming back with her but she just held on tightly to Gavin and shook her head as Alice said that she would be, much to the disappointment of Jeremy who was hoping for a repeat of the last evening.

Alice apologised to him seeing his demeanour saying she wanted to go back and shower and take care of some personal things but promised him a nice send-off the following day. Jeremy soon adopted a different stance as he hugged and kissed her goodnight and Kelly gave Matt a big hug and a kiss thanking him for a lovely day and telling him to take care.

Kelly and Alice arrived back at the villa tiptoeing quietly so not to disturb Lacey who they assumed must be in bed by now as the place was in darkness. Entering the hallway, Kelly whispered that she wasn't sure Lacey was back as her door was ajar.

Kelly poked her head inside softly calling out Lacey's name to discover she was right; she wasn't there, Alice and her sister looked at each other in disbelief questioning what Lacey was doing as they were both well aware of their friend's stance when it came to men and even though they knew she was smitten with Tristan, this was so unlike her.

Kelly told Alice to check her phone to see if Lacey had messaged her as she checked hers for the same but there was nothing. "This is so odd. Lacey would never dream of sleeping with a man she had only just met even if he was eligible and drop dead gorgeous like Tristan, what the hell is she playing at?" Kelly said, sounding a little worried.

"Look sis, this is Lacey we are talking about and as weird as it may be, I am confident she is fine and come on, is there anything you have seen or heard from Tristan that would cause you any concern and look at what everyone said about him. No, I am sure she is fine, now come on bedtime but I need a shower first. I am stinking with all that dancing in that bar."

Tuesday Day 10

The next morning, Lacey awoke aware that Tristan was not there and could hear faint noises coming from the kitchen's direction; putting on Tristan's bathrobe, she went out in search of him and found him making coffee and setting things up for breakfast. Wrapping her arms around him from behind, she hugged him and wished him a sleepy good morning in a slightly croaky way.

Tristan said that she had gone out like a light last night and asked how she felt, Lacey said she felt wonderful and that she had slept well adding that she was glad she decided to stay as it had been so long since she had slept in the arms of someone special and that it made her feel special.

Her words were pleasing to him to hear as he had been concerned that she may regret her actions and it would sour their time together. It was only a little after 8 am and Lacey was surprised she was awake so soon having felt a little exhausted last night even though she had a nap earlier on. Tristan said that he thought he would hire a car for the day and take a trip out along the coast heading west down to Fethiye and asked how she felt about that; Lacey gave a pleasant smile as she nodded happily saying that it sounded great.

Tristan asked what she fancied for breakfast saying that they were fairly well stocked in the fridge, Lacey said that some toast would do for now and suggested that maybe they have breakfast out somewhere later on their way to Fethiye.

After their coffee and toast, Lacey dressed and gathered her belongings together and thanked Tristan for the loan of his t-shirt, then they shared a taxi up to town where Tristan got out to arrange a hire car and Lacey continued on to the villa to get herself ready before Tristan picked her up about an hour and a half later.

Entering the villa, Lacey was greeted by two very unimpressed looking sisters that stood looking at her as if she had committed the crime of the century.

"Oh hello Lacey, and what time do we call this then, you dirty little stopout!" Kelly called out to her trying hard not to laugh as Alice jumped in demanding to know if she had abandoned all her virtues with Tristan last night, failing to hide her joking nature.

Lacey took a deep sigh as she abandoned her belongings to the floor and flopped onto the sofa with a look of tranquillity that suggested she were in another world living the perfect dream, Alice and Kelly looked at each other before rushing over to Lacey, demanding to know everything.

Lacey very calmly and with a generous smile said that everything was just perfect and that no, she had not had sex with Tristan if that was what they were wanting to know, she said that they had slept together but only after he had promised that he would act like a gentleman.

Lacey went on to say about what they had discussed earlier that evening over dinner and that she truly believed that she and Tristan could have something together moving forward into the future.

Kelly and Alice were beside themselves with joy for her, hugging and telling her how fortunate she was to have found someone like him and then saying that everyone had spoken volumes about him and all very positive. Lacey asked about Emma wanting to know if there were any developments there.

Kelly jumped up excitedly having forgotten that Lacey wasn't in the know and told her everything that had happened at dinner last night. Lacey was so pleased what she heard and was really made up for Emma and said that they were both very fortunate this holiday to find some happiness at last, even though it were still early days.

"I guess I just wish you two had found someone as well and I know you have had some fun with Jeremy but it's not the same is it and you with Matt. I mean, it is just a friendship with the odd snog at the end of the day and I wish we were all going home together with some positive things ahead of us."

Kelly said that she thought her friendship with Matt had offered her a lot of scope for the future as she now had a new section of men to look at for consideration that she hadn't given any attention to before, she said that he had taught her older men could sometimes offer more than people of her own age group so she was taking that as a positive.

Alice also said that her holiday had been a success even though she didn't believe that she and Jeremy could have a future together; she never really came out here looking for a husband; she just wanted to meet someone different and have some fun and she felt she had certainly done that so Lacey need not worry herself.

Lacey then told the girls that Tristan was hiring a car and taking her out along the coast down to Fethiye for the day so she needed to get a move on as he would be there around 10.30 am, Kelly said that she had not made any plans and Alice said that she would see Jeremy at some point but not sure when as it was the boys' last night in Kalkan.

Kelly said she hoped that Emma would handle Gavin's leaving well and that she was unsure if they had arranged a definite time to see each other once she was back home herself. Lacey said that she had not made any definite plans with Tristan but she knew she would see him soon after he got back a week after they did.

Lacey went off to ready herself for her day out with Tristan as Alice and Kelly sat down to some breakfast, suddenly the joyful sound of good morning rang out as an ever joyful Emma appeared at the patio door, making her entrance.

Kelly and Alice beamed at the happy smiling face of Emma who was full of joy at her newfound love even though it was his last full day there. Emma grabbed herself a cup of coffee and sat with the girls and said that she had bumped into Inga in the local shop by Gavin earlier that morning and said she told her that her brother and his partner were doing a big BBQ at Matt's place around 8 pm that night and told her to make sure that they all came.

Emma asked if Lacey was there and the girls filled her in on Lacey's news mentioning that she slept at Tristan's last night that had Emma really shocked, Alice put her right on a few things before Lacey came into the room and went up to Emma, hugging her and saying how happy she was for her having heard the wonderful news then wished her well.

Emma returned the favour saying how shocked she was at first hearing that she had slept with Tristan knowing how she was about those situations and then said that she had found a true and honest man and hoped that things went well with him.

Emma said that she and Gavin had now planned to spend the day by his pool relaxing and making plans for when she got home, she said that he was going to FaceTime his brother and see what the situation on the farm was to give him a better idea of what lay ahead and then he would talk to her after and make plans from there.

Kelly was well impressed with his efforts to sort things before he left in the knowledge that Emma would probably handle the separation better being able to focus on when she would see him again. Emma asked Alice if she would be joining her at Gavin's but Alice declined saying that she wouldn't leave her sister alone and even though Kelly insisted she go, Alice was adamant that she would stay with her and see Jeremy later at the BBQ.

Emma took herself off to get cleaned up and changed ready to return to Gavin's as Lacey went off to dress herself, Kelly told Alice again that she should go with Emma because Jeremy would probably feel let down and very disappointed but Alice just said that he would appreciate her more that evening and that she was contemplating staying over with him for his last night, adding that she had promised him a wonderful farewell.

Kelly asked her if that was wise especially given her condition but Alice replied that she was virtually clear of it now and that she wasn't thinking of going that far just yet as she wasn't that desperate; smiling as she walked back to her room Alice quipped that there was more than one way to skin a cat leaving Kelly wondering what the hell she meant by that and fearing the worst.

Kelly could hear the laughter coming from her sister's bedroom and knew well that she was trying to wind her up with that comment. Matt had sent a text message to inform Kelly about the BBQ asking if she would do him the pleasure of being his date for the evening and with intent on getting her own back, she asked Matt if he was available for an all-day date as she was going to be alone.

Matt texted back saying it would be his pleasure and that he was delighted at the prospect saying that she should come whenever she was ready. Kelly feeling rather smug with herself went to deliver the message to Alice that Matt had asked her over for the day as he thought she would be alone and said that she had accepted so she may as well join Emma.

Kelly returned to her room smiling away to herself at getting one back over her sister who was now sat on her bed contemplating her next move as she really didn't want to go over to Gavin's for the day. Lacey looked a picture dressed in pink shorts and t-shirt sporting a pinkish baseball cap style hat and white pumps as she went room to room to say goodbye to the others.

Lacey said that she would see them all at the BBQ later then grabbing her beach bag and sunglasses headed for the door as she heard the tooting of a horn, Tristan was waiting at the bottom of the steps in a jeep-style car he had hired, looking very pleased to see Lacey as she jumped in the passenger side and kissed him with much school girl type excitement.

The pair headed west along the mountain road towards Fethiye, Tristan told Lacey about the BBQ planned for later and promised they would be back in plenty of time for it. Emma appeared dressed and ready to go back to Gavin's having packed some suitable clothes for later that day. Kelly said that Alice would probably go with her now as she had been invited over to Matt's for the day and so Emma went to enquire if Alice had changed her mind.

Alice was well known in her family for her stubborn streak at times and she told Emma that she hadn't changed her mind and that she was quite happy to stay there on her own and said she would see them all later at the BBQ, Emma was a little surprised at her attitude but decided not to push it and left her, returning to Kelly to tell her of Alice's decision.

"Oh my lord, what has gotten into that moody cow now eh? One minute she is full of joy and the next thing you know she is right up herself, this is so typical of her, isn't it?" a frustrated Kelly asked. "Never mind, Emm, give me ten minutes and we can share a taxi down eh, she can wallow in her own self-pity, silly sod."

Emma didn't want to get between the sisters and failed to comment on Kelly's reasoning; instead, she rather sympathetically went back to Alice's room to see if she could coax her into joining her. Alice was all out of sorts and in all probability didn't have a clue why she was behaving so but hugging and thanking Emma who she knew meant well, she reiterated her decision to stay put.

Kelly was ready to leave and had already called Memhet to pick them up when she called into Alice's room and not prepared to accept any of Alice's nonsense, she just said that she would see her later at the BBQ, she ushered Emma out saying that the taxi should be there any minute then collecting their things, they made their way down to the roadside just as Memhet pulled up.

Alice lay back on her bed twirling her hair around her finger and staring at the ceiling, she let out a big puff of air before covering her eyes with her hands wondering what the hell she was doing, time passed by and Alice had showered and put on her bikini ready to sit out by her own pool but only got as far as the sunbed before turning around and heading back inside, flopping herself face down on the sofa while letting out a scream of anguish.

Lacey and Tristan had stopped off at a town en route having spotted a rather attractive looking diner and went in for some much needed breakfast as Tristan's stomach had been growling furiously for the past forty-five minutes. Lacey said that it was a wonderful place to stop and that the breakfast was really good leading her to tell him about Emma's mountain breakfast experience saying that she had promised they all should go there before they left on Saturday.

Tristan said that he knew of the place though never had the chance to go even though they had planned to a couple of years back, Lacey suggested that maybe Thursday would be a good time saying the boys would have gone back by then but it would be a great experience for them, according to Emma.

Kelly received a warm welcome from Matt and then Giles and was shown into the villa where Matt said she could use his room for herself through the day as she saw fit to do so. Matt enquired after Alice and Emma and Kelly said that Emma was with Gavin and then told him about Alice, confessing to her little white lie earlier to him to get back at her.

Matt gave a broad smile and said that if it meant that he would get the pleasure of her company then she should feel free to tell fibs at her discretion, Matt was laughing as he said that women were truly a mystery to him but he did enjoy Kelly's company and as much as he knew there would be no romantic fairy tale ending to their friendship, he said that he hoped they could stay in touch and perhaps she would do him the pleasure of her company at one of his many parties that he threw throughout the year back home.

Kelly was overwhelmed by his generosity not only his words but his honesty and nurturing conduct that put her at ease with him, Kelly said that she would change into her bathing costume and join them on the sun terrace by the pool shortly as she walked off to the room that Matt had pointed out to her.

Emma had arrived at Gavin's to find him and Jeremy play fighting in the pool over comments that Jeremy had made regarding Gavin being all loved up, it was quite childish really but there was substance to Jeremy's claim that Gavin knew all too well and so the playful fight had some measure to it.

"That is quite enough of that now, you two, come along now, mama is home," Emma said jokingly with a little giggle but it somehow had the desired effect as the boys stopped their wanton behaviour and exited the pool. Jeremy looked around for Alice and was distraught that she wasn't there and Emma could see the disappointment etched on his face.

"She said she wasn't feeling too good and didn't want to spoil tonight so she decided to stay home until later," Emma blurted out lying through her teeth to try and appease Jeremy. Jeremy shrugged his shoulders as he walked back to his sunbed to dry himself off before saying that he was going to start packing to save doing it in the morning. Emma felt terribly sorry for him as Gavin asked what was wrong with Alice and was it something to do with her period but Emma confessed the truth to him. Gavin's thoughts towards Alice were not the best and kept them to himself, not wanting to upset Emma. He knew Jeremy could be awkward and a pain in the butt sometimes but he did not deserve this as he had changed over the past week since meeting Alice and was trying really hard to please her.

It was around 1 pm when Giles asked Kelly if she would like a drink of something, suggesting they had everything from soft drinks and beer to wines and champagne, Kelly said that a glass of champagne always did it for her but asked Giles to promise not to allow her to drink too much as she wanted to enjoy the evening.

Giles laughed saying not to worry as he was in charge of the bar and that she was safe with him around. Meanwhile, Lacey and Tristan had arrived in Fethiye and after parking up were walking around the town taking in the sights before finding a little café bar where they stopped for light refreshment.

Having taken care of as much packing as he could, Jeremy appeared saying that they still had quite a bit of alcohol to use up and asked if anyone fancied one of his special cocktails. Gavin was happy to see him shake off the earlier disappointment and gave him an enthusiastic yes to the suggestion telling Emma at the same time she should try one and she agreed.

Several minutes later, Jeremy appears with a tray carrying three cocktails towards Gavin and Emma who had a shocked look on their faces. "Bloody hell mate, it's only a cocktail! I have made you one before now, you know," Jeremy said looking puzzled at their expression.

"I hope you have one of them made up for me," a voice echoed from behind Jeremy.

Jeremy put the drinks down and turned to see Alice standing there with a beach bag in one hand and some clothes on a hanger in the other. "Surprise!" She smiled at a slightly stunned and bewildered Jeremy who didn't quite know how to respond. Alice apologised for not coming sooner and not messaging him but she said she had some demons to deal with; she asked Jeremy if she could put her things somewhere and he held out his hand, pointing her indoors then finally speaking said she could use his room.

As Alice hung her stuff up, Jeremy asked her what she was playing at with him saying that she had really disappointed him not showing up earlier and without a message or anything. Alice approached him and put her finger on his lips telling him to be quiet before saying that she was sorry and would now make it up to him then forcibly pushing him back on to the bed, she set about saying sorry in her own way.

Jeremy emerged out by the pool a while later looking like he was holding the winning lottery ticket asking if they were ready for another round of drinks. Gavin had a good idea what had happened but Emma was a little behind. Alice appeared moments later smiling wearing her sultry white bikini to questions of how she had cheered Jeremy up so quickly from Emma, Alice smiled cheekily saying that she should know that women always have plenty of ways to make men come around.

Jeremy returned with four more cocktails and settled down close to Alice once he had handed them out, he thanked her for showing how sorry she was and said that to be honest, he was just glad that she was there and that it had really hit home to him as he was realising how much he was going to miss her.

Alice told him that she was surprised herself how much she was starting to feel the same saying it was a shame they couldn't have another week together to see how they felt. Jeremy said that they could always catch up back home at some time in the near future but Alice said that she feared the momentum may be lost by then.

The afternoon rolled on as the sun beat down on Kalkan and everyone at Gavin's villa chilled out by the pool while at Matt's place, preparations for the evening BBQ went ahead slowly with everyone there helping to set up for the event later that day. Lacey and Tristan were finishing off a light lunch at a restaurant on the seafront in Fethiye and talking about how they may spend the next few days together. Soon after, it was time for the new lovebirds to take flight and head back to Kalkan, Lacey thanked Tristan for a lovely day out together and said that she was looking forward to what the rest of the week may bring.

The afternoon sun was now fading in Kalkan where Emma and Alice were busy getting themselves ready for the evening in the boys' rooms as they themselves chilled out on the front patio discussing going home the next day. Jeremy said he was virtually packed and it would only take him minutes to finish it off adding that he was going to make the most of his time left with Alice now that she had shown real interest in him at last in the hope that they may see each other at home sometime.

Once the girls gave the boys clearance to use their rooms, Jeremy and Gavin took to their showers and got themselves ready, Alice and Emma sat at the patio table putting on their nail varnish and chatting generally about everything and how sad it was that the boys were leaving the next day.

Kelly had gotten herself ready and was feeling pretty good about herself as she emerged from her allocated room to pleasant comments about her appearance from Giles at first who was passing by and then from an appreciative Matt who offered her a glass of champagne and kissed her softly on the cheek saying she looked good enough eat as he licked his lips in a joking fashion.

"Oh Matt really, the evening hasn't started yet and you're turning on the charm already, you old devil you." Kelly hid her enjoyment at hearing the praise, something she had lacked over the past year or so.

Inga came over to Kelly having just arrived with Lars, Jake and a trough load of food for the BBQ saying how lovely she looked. Kelly greeted Inga with a kiss as Matt offered her a glass of champagne that she politely declined saying it was too early for her and that she wanted to last out the night.

Lars and Jake came over having deposited the food in the kitchen with Jake saying he had prepped enough meat and fish for about twenty-five people, Matt said that he thought they would only be about seventeen or eighteen but not to worry as they could always use it up again.

The doorbell rang and it was the two younger men from Matt's party after the yacht trip, Kevin and Jack, carrying a couple bottles of wine, Matt greeted them saying they shouldn't have worried about bringing any wine as he had a fresh delivery to replenish his dwindling stock earlier that day but thanked them anyway.

"Oh no, not these two again; prepare yourself for some amorous attention, Kelly, these two are always on the lookout for single women," Inga warned Kelly as she nodded in the direction of the two new arrivals.

"Oh yes, I know; they tried it on with my sister Alice the other night until Jeremy flexed his muscles," Kelly laughed recalling the event.

Over the next hour or so, other guests started to arrive and were welcomed with warm and affectionate greetings from the party host and others as people mingled reacquainting themselves with each other; true enough, Kevin and Jake paid special attention to Kelly and Inga who were the only two women in their age category that were single.

Gavin and Jeremy arrived with Emma and Alice in tow as the party was getting warmed up, music was playing in the background almost drowned out by the noise of chatter and laughter, Alice made her way over to Kelly throwing her arms around her saying she was sorry for earlier and Kelly just gave her a big hug saying that everything was ok and that she should just enjoy herself with Jeremy on his last night.

Jen and Harry were making the rounds catching up with people when they came across Barry and Lester, Jen enquired to the whereabouts of the lovely Tristan and was told that he had taken Lacey out for the day but should be joining them anytime soon.

"They seem to have formed a rather strong bonding for each other rather quickly, don't you think, chaps?" Jen said almost in a disapproving manner.

Barry said that he had not had the chance to catch Tristan on his own to discuss how he and the charming Lacey were getting on as he was spending every waking hour with her at the moment, he then added that even his sleeping hours were being spent the same, letting slip that the pair had slept together recently.

A look of horror and disgust spread across Jen's face within moments, before she said rather bluntly that allowing a man into her knickers at the drop of the proverbial hat, she could hardly consider someone so charming as that, she said that she was very surprised by Tristan thinking that he was a man of better character than that.

Barry and Lester looked bemused at Harry as Jen turned to walk away muttering to herself, Harry said that they shouldn't mind her as they had known her long enough to know she had her own forthright opinions on everyone else but found it easy to dismiss her own failings in life before raising his eyebrows at them and turning to go after her.

Lacey and Tristan joined the party shortly afterwards and were greeted warmly by Emma, Alice and Kelly who rushed over to the pair to see how their day had gone. Tristan smiled and waved in acknowledgement to other party goers who shouted out to him as the girls said they needed a catch up with Lacey and that Tristan should mingle for ten minutes or so, almost waving him away.

The four friends stood talking and laughing as they all caught up with what was happening with Lacey and filling her in on their day. Matt came over to welcome Lacey asking what she would like to drink but Lacey said she was fine for the moment, thanking him before continuing with the girls.

After they had all caught up, Lacey made her way across to Tristan who was admiring Jake's handiwork on the BBQ something he was well known for back home in Sweden, passing by Jen on route she said hello to her with a pleasant smile and received a look of disgust from Jen and a remark that sounded like "TART."

Lacey was startled by what she thought she had heard and said pardon to Jen, looking for some explanation from her, Jen just gave Lacey the cold shoulder, looking away with a smug expression on her face. Lacey continued over to Tristan, a little shaken and visibly upset. "Hey, there you are, look at what this guy has got going on here; doesn't it smell—" Tristan cut off his sentence as he saw the distress on Lacey's face. "Lacey, what is it; what has happened?" he asked in a very concerned manner.

Lacey told Tristan what had just taken place and it incensed him greatly as he tried to comfort Lacey, Harry made his way over apologising profusely saying that someone had overheard what his wife had said and just informed him.

Tristan was furious and told Harry to stay with Lacey as he was not about to let Jen get away with this sort of behaviour any longer as she normally did. Tristan pulled Jen to one side and demanded an explanation from her but she tried to dismiss him with a pathetic excuse about it being a misunderstanding.

Tristan demanded to know what gave her the right to slander such a sweet and innocent person like that especially given her own past antics. "Sweet and innocent! I hardly think so, my darling boy, you have known her five minutes and she lets you into her pants. I would hardly call her innocent after that, would you?"

"For your information and not that it is any of your bloody business, Jen, I have not gotten anywhere near into her pants as you put it and as for Lacey, her integrity is fully intact as she was the one that said right from the start that she was not that sort of girl and told me quite frankly that she would not consider sleeping with any man without having known them well enough first and was in some kind of meaningful relationship with them.

"Furthermore given your past exploits you should be the last person handing out insults, shouldn't you, remember Italy eh, ring any bells with that young waiter?"

Jen was visibly shaken by Tristan's honest appraisal of her as he turned to return to Lacey who he took in his arms and hugged, apologising that she had been spoken to like that by someone that had been a long-time family friend. Kelly and Alice rushed over to Lacey having seen and heard the commotion closely followed by Emma who had missed it all having been in the bathroom and just informed by Gavin.

"You take no notice of that mean old sour puss, who does she think she is criticising you and your integrity, what the hell does she know about that anyway; whatever integrity she ever had was shot to flames several years ago and any remaining embers that may have clung on to her have certainly faded into dust by now."

Barry came over and said to Tristan that he felt a certain amount of guilt for Jen's comment having been the one that let slip that Lacey had stayed over last night, Tristan said it was fine knowing Barry as he did wasn't one to stir things up. Matt and Giles tried to get the party spirit back into flowing action as Jake said that the first round of food was ready, Jen told Harry that she wanted to leave feeling embarrassed to be there but was surprised when Harry said that he would gladly let her leave and go home alone as he had every intention of staying on.

Jen was no stranger to controversy and had courted much animosity towards herself because of her outbursts in the past but people seemed to allow her a certain degree of freedom to say and do as she did in the knowledge that she had once been the queen bee and the belle of many a ball in her heyday but the ravages of time had caught up with her as had her excesses and she struggled to accept her decline.

For once, Harry took a firm stance with his wife and suggested that as they had another week of seeing these people, she would profit by firstly offering a full unreserved apology to Lacey then to their hosts for putting such a dampener on the occasion and then suggested she moderate her drinking and just find somewhere to settle and allow things to calm down.

Jen was not accustomed to taking advice from her husband but on this occasion, she felt she had no choice as his wise words echoed in her ears. Jen with what dignity she could muster made her way over to where Lacey stood with Tristan and her girlfriends.

"Hello Lacey. Look, I just want to say that I am really sorry for judging you in the way that I did and as hurtful as it was to hear from Tristan what in the light of day is a fact I am the last person that should be calling people names, please accept my unreserved apologies and if there is anything I can do to make it up to you, please don't hesitate to ask.

"Tristan, my darling boy, we have known each other for so long please accept my apologies for insulting your young and very much intact virtuous girlfriend, you had every right to say what you did as hurtful as it may have been; please accept my apologies. I would hate for us to fall out over my stupid ways."

Tristan accepted her apologies as did Lacey saying that the matter was now forgotten and asked if they could get on with enjoying the BBQ. Jen made her way over to Matt and Giles apologising to them something that Matt said later was one for posterity.

The rest of the evening went well with everyone enjoying the BBQ that Jake had put together offering him a round of applause as he finished the last batch of food. Emma, Alice and Lacey were up dancing close together with their newfound love interests as the others watched on while they relaxed drinking and listening to the wonderful melodies filling the night air.

Matt gazed over at Kelly with admiring eyes as she chatted away with Inga, who spotted his gaze and alerted Kelly to it, Kelly beamed a smile back at him waving an encouraging arm at him to join her for a dance. Kevin and Jack were talking with Barry and Lester when Jack seized upon the chance to rather politely ask Inga if she would like to dance; pausing for thought, Inga responded positively saying what the hell might as well and got up and danced with Jack.

The evening was over all too soon for Gavin and Jeremy and with heavy hearts they made their way around the terrace saying goodbye to everyone and thanking them for including them in their activities; they especially thanked Matt and Giles who had thrown some really good parties with the yacht trip being the highlight for Jeremy.

Barry and Lester told Jeremy that they would be in touch when they returned and wished him well. Alice said that she would stay with Jeremy that night as it was their last together.

Kelly looked at Lacey who smiled back at her saying that she would be returning with her to their villa just as Jen stepped in to say that she hoped moving forward they could become friends as she had an inclination that they would be seeing a lot of each other over the coming months, pointing out that she and Tristan made a lovely and interesting couple when they were together.

Kelly kissed Matt goodnight thanking him for yet another wonderful day as she and Lacey waited on a taxi. Tristan told Matt that he fancied taking Lacey up to the mountain restaurant for breakfast on Thursday morning and asked if he fancied tagging along with him and the girls. Giles interrupted that he hadn't been for ages and would relish the chance and so Matt said that he would get something arranged the next day and let him know.

Everyone made their way home after a wonderful evening at Matt's place, some feeling happier than others. Emma desperately fought against her inner emotions as she tried with all her might to stop the inevitable realisation that her holiday romance with Gavin for now was almost over.

A sense of quietness came over Emma that was not lost on Gavin as he asked her if she was ok, Emma simply smiled, nodding her head as she fought back tears that were bursting to flood out of her. As they entered Gavin's villa, Emma rushed to the bathroom followed by a concerned Alice, Gavin went to his room to retrieve his phone that he had left on charge and found a couple of missed messages, one of which was from his brother Luke that he failed to link up with earlier that day in a FaceTime call to see what the work situation was like.

Luke had left a message apologising for not being able to make the call as promised stating that their father was ill again leaving him with all the work and adding that his eldest brother Harry would now be picking them up from the airport the following day.

The message also stated that as he had been away two weeks and dad not well, he hadn't had any time off himself, he told Gavin to forget having any time off for the next two weeks as he would have to cover for him until dad was fit enough again. Gavin didn't know how Emma was going to take this news and he was worried about telling her now, given the state she was in.

Gavin went in search of Emma and found her sobbing away with Alice as friendly support. "Oh I'm sorry, Gav. I have tried really hard to hide my feelings but it's hard! I am going to miss you so much, you know," Emma cried, trying hard as she may not to.

Gavin tried his best to cheer her up while he harboured the news that they may not see each other again so soon as he had hoped, Gavin said that he would make everyone a coffee and leaving for the kitchen he nodded to Jeremy to follow him and showed him the message on the phone from Luke.

Jeremy was questioning him about what he was going to do saying that he had to tell her know no matter what she was going through as she was already suffering and it would be better than waiting for her to get over this to have that dumped on her.

Alice walked into the kitchen and having heard Jeremy's last words asked what was going to be dumped on whom. Gavin was about to speak when Emma wiping her eyes entered and looking at the others' body language asked what was up.

"Gav, what is it, is there something wrong?" she asked looking around at everyone, feeling afraid of what she might hear back. "Gav, come on tell me please; there is something wrong, isn't there? Alice, what is it, tell me please."

Alice was about to speak up when Gavin said he would show her the message he had just received from his brother and handed Emma his phone. Emma read the message and quietly looked up at Gavin, shaking her head in disbelief as he threw his arms around her promising that he would try and sort something out as Emma sobbed her poor heart out on his shoulder.

Jeremy ushered Alice out of the kitchen so the two could be alone and he explained everything to her about the message and what it meant in reality. Alice said that at least Emma could go up on a Friday night and stay with him saying that at least they could have some time together.

Jeremy then explained that a farmer's life was not a nine to five job and that Gavin would be up 4.30 am every morning and in bed by 8 pm every night; he continued that it was very hard work that normally he shared with Luke and his father but now his father was ill and Luke was needing a rest himself, which meant that Gavin would be exhausted and not much company for Emma.

Alice fully understood Gavin's predicament and knew it was not something he could easily get out of but if she knew one thing about Emma, it was she would gladly have just an hour or two with Gavin rather than none at all. Alice told Jeremy that all was not lost and that she would speak with Emma in the morning once she had a chance to sleep on it.

Gavin and Emma joined them briefly to say goodnight and Alice hugging her friend told her that she shouldn't worry about anything as she was sure everything would sort itself out. The two couples parted and retired for the night.

Kelly and Lacey had arrived back at theirs discussing Jen and her comments as they were leaving earlier. Kelly agreed that they did make a beautiful couple and said that Jen may have had something when she made that statement.

Lacey tried to laugh it off saying that they hardly knew each other and it was way too early days to be making that assumption, then in a burst of laughter and excitement she hugged a cushion to her chest saying with great enthusiasm how wonderful it would be if it did really happen for her.

Kelly reached across, hugging her and saying she was sure it would before declaring herself absolutely cream-crackered and in need of her bed. Lacey agreed saying that she was looking forward to seeing Tristan later tomorrow but couldn't help feeling for poor Emma having to say goodbye to Gavin.

Wednesday Day 11

Alice was first to awaken on Wednesday morning with the realisation that Jeremy and Gavin would be going back home later that day; she lay on her side looking at the muscular torso of Jeremy laying close beside her, toying with whether or not she should give herself to him now that she thought she was over her situation but something held her back and she quickly put it from her mind, choosing to get up and make some coffee instead, laughing at the options she had presented herself.

It was shortly before 8 am and Alice felt wide awake having paced herself yesterday with her drinking and rested well during the day; she quietly set about making the coffee before being joined by Jeremy in his boxer shorts looking for some cold water.

"Hey you, what you up to then, making coffee eh, good girl, I woke up and thought you had gone then heard a little noise coming from in here."

"Aw, were you missing me then?" Alice teased him as she gave him a playful hug.

"No I wouldn't say I was missing you but ask me that again tomorrow and you will get a different answer," he replied as he hugged her back with his powerful arms wrapped tightly around her in an act of loving feeling.

Alice kissed him on the cheek, saying that she knew she would miss him also and offered that they may still see each other at some stage yet, Jeremy said that he hoped so too just as Gavin appeared.

"Morning guys, how we doing; anyone fancy a coffee, oh well done, you put it on," a slightly subdued Gavin said.

Alice asked if Emma was awake and how she had slept, Gavin responded saying that she took some time to get over the news from Luke and he tried his best to convince her things would work out but wasn't sure she believed him.

Alice said that she would speak with her shortly, adding that girls knew how to sort these things out best and was confident that she could reason with her.

Gavin said that she was still sleeping when he left her so asked Alice to leave her for now.

Back at the girls' villa, Lacey was lying in bed romanticising in her head about her and Tristan, Kelly was taking a shower having woken up feeling a little hot and sweaty and in dire need of freshening up. Lacey broke from her romantic interlude and sprang out of bed, throwing back the curtains full of joy and happiness, hearing noises from the kitchen she moved at pace to find Kelly making the coffee and couldn't resist hugging her with a screech of excitement bellowing out of her. Kelly laughed out loud wondering for a moment what the hell had gotten into her friend before the penny dropped. Kelly stated if those were not the actions of a woman in love then she didn't know what was.

Lacey walked into the lounge area flopping onto the sofa full of smiles and happiness while Kelly looked on in awe at her. Kelly said that Lacey had certainly been bitten by the love bug alright and it had taken big chunks out of her. Lacey hugging a cushion just beamed gloriously as she allowed her imagination to run wild with her just as she heard her phone's messaging tone go off. Running to her phone in great anticipation, she was rewarded with the notice that Tristan had messaged her.

Lacey read his message that asked if she was awake yet and that he had dreamt about her all night and couldn't wait to see her later. Lacey walked briskly into the kitchen skipping as she went squealing with joy as she showed the message to Kelly who smiled at her friend's joy and happiness.

Emma woke up to find Gavin gone and got up to see where he was and found him sitting with Alice and Jeremy on the front terrace watching the sun make its way over from the east for the last time for the boys; they all greeted Emma with a good morning and Alice told her to sit while she fetched her a coffee.

Emma sat next to Gavin holding his hand and saying she was sorry for getting so upset last night but Gavin quickly calmed her saying she had nothing to apologise for. Alice appeared with Emma's coffee and said that she had an idea that she thought would work for both of them.

"The way I see it, guys, is that you Gavin have work commitments that will tie you up most of the day while you Emma would rather have an hour or two as opposed to nothing, right? Well if you, Emma, travel up to Gavin for the next couple of weeks after work on a Friday, you will get to see him at least for 3 hours before he goes to bed and at least you are there when he comes in for breakfast and lunch, albeit rather mucky and smelly," she laughed, adding that beggars couldn't be choosers.

"So I know it is not perfect but is it any different for a farmer's wife other than when the farmer gets days off and I mean, at least you have something other than a phone call to look forward to; what do you think?"

"You are right, Alice. Farmers do have little time for family life at certain times of the year but on the whole, when we work together all day, it is nice to have a break from each other, our situation is different in the sense we are just starting in a relationship and that is the hardest time, probably why Jess decided to do one.

"Look Emma, if you are prepared to do as Alice said then I promise I will work extra hard to finish earlier and maybe I can get my father to help out in the evenings a bit more when he is better to ensure we have quality time together. I am just sorry that I won't be able to take you out so often and we will be stuck on the farm or finishing off my own house that was intended for me and Jess that I have not bothered with since she left me."

Emma said that it sounded a perfect plan to her and was more than happy to do whatever she had to in order for them to spend time together. Gavin looked pleased with her response as he thanked Alice for her words of reasoning.

Gavin suggested that he cook them up a lovely breakfast as they had plenty of stuff to use up, the others didn't object in the slightest and Emma suggested that she would help him get things going. Alice asked what time their transfer to the airport was booked for and Jeremy said it was 2 pm a little earlier than normal but the courier liked to make a toilet and refreshment stop on the way he said. Alice said that she would stay until they left and confirmed it with Emma, though she already suspected that would be the case for her anyway. Alice sent a message to her sister letting her know of their decision and received a message back moments later saying that she and Lacey would call down around 1 pm to see the boys off.

Lacey in the meantime texted Tristan letting him know of her plans adding that she would call in at his after and spend the rest of the day with him. Tristan came back with the idea that he would join them at Gavin's as he would like to wish them well and see them off with her and so they agreed to meet there later.

Gavin and Emma served up a wonderful breakfast between them and the four of them sat and ate out on the terrace whilst enjoying the early morning sunshine. Gavin said that he would miss that moment very much once home as it was one of his favourite times of day seeing the start of a new day and looking forward to whatever it brought.

Emma agreed, saying it was so peaceful and relaxing watching the sun move across disappearing behind the headland before rising again and warming them with its rays. Alice and Jeremy both nodded in agreement with Emma saying that she supposed the sun rises over the farm may have its own finer points but the smells may take the shine off a bit.

Gavin laughed loudly saying she had no idea how different it could be. "You look out the window at a beautiful dawn and step outside stretching and take a deep breath only to be greeted by the smell of cattle waste and other unpleasant farmyard odours, a little bit different to here, I think," he continued laughing.

Jeremy told Emma that she had it all to come and asked if she had ever spent time on a farm to which Emma replied that she hadn't but living in the west country she felt may have prepared her as the area is surrounded by farms and it was hard to avoid certain smells when the muck spreading season was upon them. The foursome sat laughing at the conversation they were having and continued eating up the breakfast as they discussed some of the highlights of the holiday. Gavin said without doubt it was meeting Emma for him as Emma quickly supported him in that gesture saying it was meeting him, especially the part where he saved her from drowning.

Jeremy glanced up at Alice looking for a similar statement but Alice said the yacht trip was her highlight, turning Jeremy's happy demeanour to a more sour one as he did not expect that, Alice laughed telling him to man up adding that if he thought she was going to boost his overly hyped ego any further, he was mistaken before saying that she didn't think it at first but she was really happy that they had met and thanked him for making the effort and taking care of her.

Jeremy's smile soon reappeared and he thanked her for that comment and admitted she had taught him a lesson or two about his ways and sincerely hoped that he could learn from them, he held Alice's hand and said with much feeling that he was going to miss her more than she would know, causing Alice to have a momentary emotional feeling pass over her with a little tear appearing in her eye.

Emma herself felt rather emotional listening to them openly admit to each other that their little holiday experience had actually meant something to them. Emma said that she would take a shower before helping Gavin pack his things up ready for later and Alice said that she would do the same, although Jeremy was already packed virtually.

The boys cleared the breakfast things away as the girls took to the showers and they chatted about going home with Gavin asking Jeremy if he and Alice had arranged to reunite at any time soon. Jeremy said that they had only loosely discussed the possibilities but had not made any definite arrangements.

After the lads had finished the clearing up, they set up on the pool patio for their last session in the Kalkan sunshine of the holiday. Gavin and Emma then sorted his packing out and joined Jeremy and Alice around the pool talking and laughing until it was almost time for Kelly and Lacey to arrive. A familiar voice was heard calling out to them from around the front and Jeremy was first up to go and greet Tristan who had arrived ahead of the other girls. Tristan greeted everyone in his normal warm way saying how gutted he was that the boys had to go before everyone else.

Ten minutes later, the voices of Kelly and Lacey could be heard as they made their way around to the back terrace, Lacey rushed over to Tristan who stood to greet her with a radiant smile and a kiss. Kelly was full of joy as she spoke to the others asking how they were and if they had prepared themselves well for the sad moment that was drawing ever closer.

Emma gave an unconvincing smile and a nod as Alice simply said that it was what it was, she said that it wasn't forever and that everyone could meet up again soon if so inclined to do so. Gavin and Jeremy said that they would have to shower and get changed ready and asked everyone to help themselves to a drink or snack as there was plenty to use up and that they should take anything they wanted with them as it would all be left.

Jeremy returned moments ahead of Gavin to find everyone enjoying a nice cocktail Tristan had made from what he found in the bar and kitchen. Tristan poured out two fresh glasses for the boys and proposed a toast. "To Gavin and Jeremy, have a safe journey home and don't be strangers, it was a pleasure meeting you and we have all enjoyed your company."

"Gavin and Jeremy."

The girls raised their glasses saying Gavin and Jeremy as Emma clung on to Gavin resting her head against his chest. Gavin said that things had certainly turned out a lot different to what he had imagined and thanked everyone, especially Emma for making it such a memorable occasion, Jeremy joined in supporting Gavin's words adding that they had all made such a difference to what he thought the holiday was going to be like, offering his thanks to them all; he received a generous smile of admiration from Alice with a kind wink and a nod.

The moment Emma had dreaded arrived as the airport transfer car pulled up to collect the boys, Gavin asked Emma to be strong saying that they would see each other again in about ten days and that the time would fly by and said she had promised him no tearful farewell as he was struggling himself.

With their bags loaded, Gavin and Jeremy said their goodbyes to each of them one by one wishing them well and thanking them, finally the boys turned to Emma and Alice, hugging them and kissing them goodbye with Alice saying that she was definitely going to miss Jeremy's kisses and told him to call her at some time.

Jeremy got into the car as Gavin almost struggled to break free of Emma's grip as she clung on to every second she could have with him, Kelly put her arms around Emma gently and with soothing words coaxed her away from Gavin to allow him to leave.

Gavin climbed into the car and winding the window down, he waved and shouted "I love you, Emma" as the car pulled away slowly and disappeared down the road. Emma collapsed into the arms of Kelly crying uncontrollably as the others watched on feeling overwhelming emotion themselves.

Tristan suggested that they walk to his place where they could settle themselves before doing whatever they planned after. Alice added her support to Emma shedding a few tears herself and feeling surprised that she was having these emotions as she threw her hands around her friend and sister.

Tristan supported Lacey who was completely moved by the whole drama and told her not to be so upset and that he was there for her but that only caused her more heartache as the reality hit her that she would be in the same situation in three days herself.

The girls sat on the patio at Tristan's apartment as he went inside to fetch some wine in the hope that it may help the situation. Barry and Lester were out with the others from their group for the day so he tried valiantly on his own to bring some calm and happiness to the girls' unfortunate dilemma.

Pouring out the wine, Tristan handed it around and Kelly apologised for landing him with four teary-eyed women struggling to hold it together. Tristan tried to laugh it off saying that this was nothing compared to how he would be having to let go of Lacey on Saturday when they all had to go back home.

Kelly laughed as did Alice but it had the opposite effect on Lacey who was becoming more and more emotional at that thought. Emma gradually settled down and asked to use Tristan's bathroom to freshen up and was shown the way by Lacey who confessed her own feelings to Emma about leaving Tristan.

Tristan received a message from Matt that he had arranged for a minibus to pick them all up from his place in the morning at around 8.30 am to go to the mountain restaurant for the traditional Turkish breakfast. Tristan relayed the message to the girls and that seemed to put a smile on their faces and helped Kelly cheer up Emma a little more. Tristan asked the girls if they had any plans for the rest of the day and Alice said she was just happy to go back to her villa and chill for the rest of the afternoon before deciding what to do later on in the evening. Kelly and Emma agreed that was a good idea as Kelly said she would call Memhet to pick them up.

On the way back in the taxi, Memhet could see the sadness on the faces of the girls, especially Emma who looked lost and dazed by the morning's events. Memhet was very kind trying to offer words of comfort to them all saying that many tourists find some kind of romance in Kalkan on holiday and face the same dilemma of having to go home just as things are becoming wonderful in their lives, he added that he felt that their journey was not yet over as they had shown so much affection and happiness in their new meetings and he was sure there was more to come for all of them.

Memhet got out of the taxi after arriving at the villa and told Emma that she must remember the photograph she showed him of her and Gavin on the boat, he said that that promised a happy ending for her as it was written in the stars.

Emma hugged Memhet and thanked him for his kind words saying that she hoped he was right and it caused her to cheer up immensely. Kelly paid him for the trip saying she would call him again later probably at some time as they had not made any decisions on what they were doing.

The girls made their way inside with Alice saying that things would seem strange now not seeing the boys but on the upside it meant she could finish the holiday spending a bit more time with her big sister. Kelly then joked that she could forget that option as she had arranged to spend the rest of her time with Matt and then burst into laughter and hugged her sister who had a dour look upon her face saying that she was just joking.

Emma said that Alice was right; things would be strange without the boys but she was determined to get on with things and look forward to seeing Gavin in about ten days. Kelly commended her for the turnaround in her demeanour and said that together they would finish the holiday with a big bang and that the time would soon pass until she and Gavin could be together again.

The girls changed into their swimwear and made for the sunbeds by the pool with Alice clutching a bottle of rose wine and three glasses. "That's the way, Al, come on let us drown our sorrows in alcohol and forget all the upset," Kelly giggled as she took a glass from Alice.

Lacey spent the afternoon with Tristan at his place by the pool and were joined later by Lester and then a little time after Barry who had stopped off at a local shop for some things. Lester said that there would be ten of them heading for breakfast in the morning up in the mountains and that he was very much looking forward to it as he had missed out the last time they went having been taken ill the previous evening.

That evening Lacey and Tristan carried on much as they had done the past few days, spending their time chatting about the past and getting all loved up together over dinner and wine in one of the many eateries on offer. Kelly, Alice and Emma went out to the kebab restaurant Alice had been to a few days earlier with Jeremy and ate a simple meal before deciding on an earlier night, thinking about the next morning's early start.

The girls arrived back at the villa around 10.30 pm and were surprised to see Lacey appear moments later alone; the girls all greeted each other and sat down discussing the day's events and Emma mentioned that she had been sent a lovely message from Gavin just before he boarded his plane home.

Thursday Day 12

All the girls slept reasonably well that night, even Emma who struggled initially trying to deal with her sadness of seeing Gavin leave; they all awoke the next morning looking forward to their trip out to the mountain restaurant and gathered in the kitchen where Lacey was preparing some coffee for them.

Kelly received a text from Matt saying that they would pick the girls up around 8.30 am as it was virtually on their way that gave the girls a little extra time to prepare for the trip and walking off with their hot coffee, they set about readying themselves. The four girls assembled at the foot of their steps awaiting the minibus arrival that was not long in coming, they got aboard to welcomes of good morning and Lacey was pleased to see the happy smiling face of Tristan who had reserved the seat next to him for her; he put his arm around her and greeted her with an affectionate kiss on the cheek.

Once on board, the minibus set off for the mountains with Matt, Giles, Inga, Lester, Barry and Tristan with the girls. Emma recalled all the beautiful things she had seen previously with Gavin as they made their way up the hilly terrain and past some of the little villages dotted along the way.

Matt pointed out one of the trout farms that he said had cooked up a lovely dinner for him once and suggested maybe they all go there at some time. Kelly who sat behind Matt said that the next day would be their last day to go out anywhere and it was a shame because she and Alice were very partial to trout.

Matt rather heroically suggested that they should go then as he would not see her miss out on a real treat before going home and said that he would arrange something later that day. Kelly put her hand on his shoulder and whispered thank you in his ear as he patted her hand saying it was his pleasure.

It wasn't long before they arrived at their destination and everyone alighted the bus, looking in awe at the far reaching views of the Taurus Mountains in the distance through the sunny garden way. Matt was warmly greeted by the manager who recognised him instantly, having served him many times before in the past and he was shown to their reserved place in a large pergola style hut across from where Emma had sat with Gavin. Emma pointed out the fact to her friends as she smiled with much happiness remembering that wonderful day.

Emma posted some pictures of her and her friends having breakfast on her media page and sent a private message to Gavin saying she hoped he arrived home ok and that she was missing him; the breakfast again was amazing with so much food and a varied type of dish presented to them in a continuous flow with each person finding their own favourite delicacy amongst the plethora of dishes.

Emma shed a few tears as she looked back on the selfies she had taken with Gavin the last time she was there. Alice put her arm around her to cheer her up having been silently prompted by Lacey who was sat across from her and noticed her tears. Emma gave a little laugh and assured her friends that they were happy tears and that she was fine, she said it had brought back so many wonderful memories even though it was a mere week ago but seemed so much further back.

Matt commented that she and Gavin seemed to have crammed an awful lot into a week given the place they were with each other, he said that many people after many months and even sometimes years don't reach the point that they had. Emma smiled back at Matt and nodded in agreement, saying that as much as she had hoped to meet someone special out there, she had never dreamt that she would feel as she did about someone after only a week but she did and that was that.

"The heart wants what the heart wants and there is no getting away from that," Giles chipped in. Matt agreed readily as did the others with nods and murmurs of yes, some of the group got up and walked around the garden looking at the various eating huts and the well where the fresh spring water was drawn from.

Kelly asked Tristan to take some shots of her and the other girls with the ranging mountains in the background, then he asked for the same but just with Lacey pulled close into his side. Matt took a stroll around the garden and was joined by Kelly who said that she thought Tristan had really captured Lacey's heart saying that she was totally mesmerised by him. Matt said that he agreed but it wasn't one-way as Tristan had confessed to him that he had become smitten with her and hoped that they might carry on back home. "So say nothing to Lacey; let them come together naturally if it is to happen, that way they will have a better chance of making it work, don't you think?"

Kelly nodded and agreed promising she would say nothing and knew in her heart of hearts that Lacey and Tristan would make it work. Tristan and Lacey strolled hand in hand around the garden capturing the odd picture and selfie in some of the beautiful settings.

It was soon time to leave and Matt asked everyone to take their places on the minibus, Emma showed Matt a picture of the clifftop carpark she and Gavin had stopped at and asked if they could go back that way. Matt said that he knew the spot and spoke to the driver, asking him to take a different way back so they could stop off for a few minutes to allow everyone to take in the view, after a few moments they were on their way and taking the route Emma had requested, she told everyone how wonderful and yet a little scary it was once they got there but assured them it was worth it.

Jaws dropped at the breath-taking scene as they pulled up almost to the edge of the carpark. Lester said he was worried for a moment if the brakes were working as they all alighted the bus and strolled around the carpark taking in the incredible vista before them. Everyone was eagerly snapping away at the views as the sun beat down on them, Matt suggested that they should all take some refreshment from the mobile van that was parked up selling cold drinks and ice cream amongst other things.

After several minutes of savouring the views, they all headed back to Kalkan and made their way to the girls' villa first where they parted company with them and Tristan who was going to wait for Lacey to change and pack her things ready to spend the rest of the day with him.

Matt promised to be in touch later once he had sorted out the trout farm restaurant for Friday night before leaving them to go back to his place. Tristan said that he had been before and that the food was simple but delicious adding that it truly was a real treat.

Tristan waited out on the terrace as Lacey went in to change and put together some things to spend the day with him, not wanting to miss a moment of the precious time they had left together. Kelly sat with Tristan and politely turned the conversation to how he was getting on with Lacey and asked him outright if he thought he would be seeing much of her once he returned home.

Tristan didn't mind the question and confidently answered her in a positive manner saying that he hoped they could see each other on a regular basis as much as possible given the distance between them and his family commitments, he added work was trying enough at the best of times, meaning he had little time with his girls some weeks but he always tried to make up for it at a later time.

"Look, I will be honest with you, Kelly. I never came out here searching for a life partner or girlfriend as such and to be quite frank with you, I am almost lost for words trying to explain how I feel towards Lacey after such a short space of time but she really has captivated me. I have been single now for some time, not to say I haven't had some short term associations shall we say but I can honestly say that even with the longest of those, I never felt as I do when I am with Lacey."

"Oh really, that is so nice to hear, Tristan, and for what it's worth, I know Lacey feels exactly the same, she is not one to fall very easily for someone and is quite discerning in her choice of men not that it has helped her out in the past though, if I know her as well as I think I do, I am sure she will do whatever it takes to see you as much as she can."

"Well, that is very good to know, thank you Kelly, but please don't read too much into this it hasn't been a week yet and the testing time will come when we are home."

Alice joined them and Kelly filled her in on what they had been discussing, Alice commented that them being apart may help them in the long term as he would not have to worry so much about spending time with her if she wasn't there and that would enable them to see if there was any future for them together.

Tristan said that Alice posed a very valid point suggesting that he and Lacey would have to plan their time together in advance around work and his family life and so that may be an easier option than having someone sitting close by wanting his time constantly. Tristan smiled with great enthusiasm at the thought just as Lacey appeared saying she was ready and asking what they had been chatting about as she looked at all the cheery faces smiling back at her.

"All good things, don't worry, oh sorry I forgot to book the taxi, I'll do it know," Tristan said slightly annoyed with himself.

Kelly said that it was probably her fault as she had distracted him with her chit chat and said that she would call Memhet for him before being reminded by Alice that he would probably be working at the market as it were Thursday. Kelly said that didn't matter as he would send someone else from his extensive family line and laughed as she made the call.

Lacey explained the humour behind the comment about Memhet and said that he had taken a shine to them from day one and always went out of his way to make sure they were taken care of and mentioned the help he had given them at the market the previous week, saving them a lot of money. Tristan looked on impressed with what she and then Alice had to say about him saying himself that he had always found the locals extremely friendly and helpful.

Kelly announced that a taxi was on its way and that Memhet sent his best wishes to them all. Alice asked what the plans were for the rest of the day for him and Lacey, and Tristan said that he thought an afternoon at one of the beach clubs followed by an evening of food, wine and music with beautiful company if Lacey was happy to join in that.

Lacey beamed with delight as the sisters looked on in admiration for her, so happy to see their dear friend as happy as she was.

As Lacey and Tristan waved goodbye in the taxi, Alice turned to her sister and said that she should mark her words that if Tristan didn't screw it up somehow over the next year or so, she was confident wedding bells would be heard there, Kelly pausing for thought nodded her head before saying that she thought Alice was probably right and that Lacey would have to solve the long-distance relationship thing first.

Emma joined the girls as they walked back up to the terrace saying that she had received a message from Gavin, he wished that he had been with them at breakfast that morning and that he was back into full swing on the farm although he didn't start until 10 am having gotten home after midnight.

Emma seemed quite calm and content having received word from him and her sadness had been replaced with a much happier and cheerier stance. Alice asked the others what they fancied doing for the rest of the day and got a muted response of shoulder shrugs and head rolls.

Kelly took the lead and suggested they chill by the pool as the town would be packed with the market on and then they could plan on the evening's entertainment, Alice quickly agreed saying she was ready for a glass of rose and to park herself up by the pool adding that they had plenty in the villa needing to be used up and little time to do it.

The three girls sorted themselves out and gathered by the pool in the hot afternoon sun topping up their tans as well as their glasses of wine before Kelly prepared a beautiful salad using up some of the items she found in the fridge.

Lacey and Tristan spent the afternoon down at the beach club where she had visited with the girls for the jazz evening the previous week with Gavin and

Jeremy and they enjoyed themselves talking and drinking with the occasional moment of intimacy kissing each other as their bond grew stronger.

That evening the three girls made their way into town stopping off at their favourite bar for pre-dinner cocktails before deciding to try one of the harbourside eateries. There were no end of offers from the attentive staff as they walked along, perusing the various menus that all seemed to offer much the same. A charming older member of staff at one of the restaurants managed to say the right thing and enticed them into a nice table with views looking at the various craft moored up in the harbour, the girls were just getting started on their dinner when Emma spotted Lacey and Tristan pass by on their way to dinner themselves at a place on an upper level and they called out to her waving and blowing kisses as she passed by, looking all loved up with Tristan's arm wrapped around her.

"Oh well, ladies, we may have a double wedding on the cards here; who knows eh with our Emma and Lacey all loved up like this!" Kelly joked as Alice joined in the banter laughing along with her sister and saying yes definitely with the way things were going. Emma sat there smiling trying not to get caught up in the suggestion by saying that it was not something she was even thinking about at that stage.

"Oh come on girls, really, what after a week you think we are going to get wed, stop it now and look, it is not that I wouldn't; I just think it crazy to be saying such things at this stage. Ok I do confess I have fallen in love with him but I have been there before remember and I know Gavin is totally different to the others but I think there is still a long way to go for us."

"Come on Emma, Kelly is only joking; we know you wouldn't marry him after a week even if you have fallen in love with him as you say you have, we are just having some fun with you ok; don't get all defensive now, come on girl, lighten up eh! But he did say he loved you, didn't he, I mean he actually shouted it out from the taxi, didn't he?" Alice continued to tease Emma.

Emma dropped her head to hide her smiles before looking up and saying with great delight that yes he did say he loved her and sent her a message to say he meant it. Kelly said that was proof if any were needed before giving Emma a friendly nudge and a wink.

Lacey and Tristan sat at their table gazing longingly at each other over their dinner as Tristan casually mentioned the chat he had with Kelly and Alice earlier, he said he wanted to wait for the right moment to raise the conversation as he felt it important that she should know. Tristan explained what had been said and what he thought of Alice's point in particular and asked Lacey for her opinion; she gave a sigh of relief fearing what he was about to say before answering.

"To be honest, Tristan, I am also at a loss to explain how I am feeling at the moment since I have met you, it has been a whirlwind of a romance type thing if you will and it has taken me by complete surprise. The only thing I can truly say is that when I am with you, nothing else matters and when we are apart, I long to be with you again, I have no clue where we are going with this whatever it is between us but I do know I do not want it to end anytime soon."

"Oh Lacey, it is as if you can read my mind because that is exactly how I feel about us, you know I hate having to say goodnight to you and I wish the night away moments after you leave my sight every night. You have brought something wonderful back into my life that I had thought lost forever and I don't want it to go away, I promise from my position that I will do whatever to keep this alive between us as long as I can and for as long as you want me to."

Lacey stretched out her hand to hold onto Tristan's as she gazed at him with much affection and a wonderful warmth flooded over her as she felt her chest heave with the deep breath she had taken trying to contain her joyous emotions, her eyes glazed over as she squeezed his hand tightly, fighting back the tears he had brought on with his loving words.

Tristan and Lacey sat enamoured with each other after their dinner on a comfy sofa for two they found in a little bar up a side street where they had coffee and brandy to finish the night off, their faces rarely more than a few inches apart, kissing and cuddling oblivious to the surrounds and the other guests that sat nearby.

Kelly, Alice and Emma had made their way up to the cocktail bar that Matt part owned and was greeted by Mussie who told them that Matt was upstairs with some of his friends and so they made their way up to join them and were welcomed with much delight from Matt and Giles who were sat with Lester and Barry. Matt asked if they had seen anything of Tristan and Lacey on their travels as no one had seen them since that morning. Alice said they had seen them walking together earlier that evening walking along the harbourside where they were dining.

Matt had sent out a message to Tristan to join them at the bar earlier but had received no reply, Kelly said that she had spoken to him before they left the villa and as far as she was concerned, Tristan only had eyes and time for Lacey and she thought that he was totally and utterly taken with her.

Matt sat back smiling to himself saying good for him then repeating it before adding that he was glad that Tristan had found someone special at last, Alice said that they all felt the same way about Lacey as she was a really good person with a big heart that deserved to be treated right for once.

Matt and his group discussed the morning's adventure and he confirmed that he had booked the trout restaurant for Friday evening saying that he hoped it would be a wonderful final evening in Kalkan for them. Kelly said she was looking forward to it and said that the holiday had turned out far better than she had expected and would definitely be coming back.

Lester said that once Kalkan was in your blood, you couldn't shake it off saying that he came out several years ago for the first time and always looked forward to returning the following year. Matt and Giles both agreed that it was a very alluring place that made you want to return more and more.

Tristan was finding it difficult to fight off the passion he was feeling for Lacey as the intensity of their kissing grew hotter and more involved, there was a part of him that wanted to bed her there and then such was the level of his desire for her. Lacey herself secretly started to have carnal thoughts towards Tristan as her heart raced along with her mind as she enjoyed his passionate attention.

Tristan suddenly broke away from their embrace suggesting they take a short stroll confessing to not being sure if he could contain his growing lust for her. Lacey giggled at his remarks and said that she had found herself at his mercy on more than one occasion as they were getting more and more involved with each other, adding that she was close to abandoning all reason.

Tristan thought for a moment that maybe he had stopped too soon but then decided that he had done the right thing knowing that if or when they were together on a more intimate level, the wait would have been worth it. Lacey took his hand as they strolled through the narrow cobbled streets lit up by the bright shopfronts.

Unfortunately, it was time for Tristan to see Lacey off back to her villa in a taxi before heading back to his alone again, with a saddened heart he kissed and hugged her goodnight and reluctantly let her go, saying he would call her in the morning.

Tristan was about to take a taxi when he heard his name called out from behind him and turning, he saw the approaching Matt and Giles with Kelly, Alice and Emma, he smiled at them but couldn't hide his slightly disconsolate demeanour having just said goodnight to Lacey.

Matt said that Lester and Barry were still at the cocktail bar failing miserably to chat up a couple of single ladies there. Tristan said that he had just seen Lacey off in a taxi, Emma asked him if he was ok noting that he looked really down but Tristan just replied it was normal after he had to say goodnight to her. Matt patted Tristan on the back saying that there was always tomorrow and suggested he come back with him and Giles for a nightcap; the men wished the girls goodnight saying they would pick them up around 7.30 pm the following day before heading back to Matt's.

Friday Day 13

The next morning, Lacey was up and showered and making the usual coffee before being joined by Emma and Alice who were eager to know how her evening with Tristan had gone and sat her down at the table. Lacey was honest enough to admit that she almost caved in to Tristan saying at one point he could have had his freedom with her.

Alice and Emma sat open-mouthed looking at each other before turning to Lacey for more of an explanation just as Kelly waltzed in asking what was going on with them all sat around the table looking so shocked. Alice brought Kelly up to date and she sat down swiftly, encouraging Lacey to continue.

Lacey took a deep sigh before explaining how she was overcome with passion and had carnal thoughts relating to Tristan with the way he was kissing and touching her, she said his every touch sent shockwaves of pleasure through her and his kissing was so sensuous she claimed that she felt she would cave in to his every demand of her without any thought to it.

The other girls were clearly moved by what she told them with Kelly and Emma both agreeing that if she went on much more, they may find themselves having some kind of special moment themselves. Alice said jokingly and with laughter that it was too late for her as she was spent at the shockwaves moment.

All four girls had a real good laugh and Lacey admitted that as much as she knew she wanted him, she was glad now that she had not and was sure he would feel the same way though the girls thought otherwise having seen him after she had left. Lacey said that she heard the girls come in last night but had gotten straight into bed whilst the emotions she was feeling last night with him were still alive in her and it helped her sleep wonderfully.

Kelly poured out the coffee and asked the others how they fancied spending their last day saying that they had the trout restaurant to look forward to later on. Lacey asked if they minded her spending it with Tristan as she felt guilty not having spent much time with them lately. Emma was first to reply saying she had nothing to be guilty about as they had come out with a mission to find some love and happiness and that she should continue to pursue that with Tristan. Alice agreed as did Kelly who said that she had a chance in a lifetime and should not forsake it for anything.

Lacey thanked her friends for being so kind to her just as Tristan texted her, bringing a wonderful smile to her face. "He said he has a big emptiness that he is waiting for me to fill and is asking when can he see me," Lacey read out wide-eyed and full of excitement.

Kelly said to tell him she would be there within the hour and that he could take her for breakfast as he had given her such an appetite with all that passion last night, the girls all laughed as Lacey texted him back asking if she could treat him to breakfast and suggested they meet in town by the taxi rank around 10 am giving her plenty of time then suggested that they relax back at hers by the pool until later that evening when they would go to the trout farm.

Tristan was delighted at the request and said that he would pack a few things into a bag and see her at the rank in just over an hour. Lacey asked the girls if they minded Tristan coming over saying she thought that way she could get best of both worlds with him and them at the same time. The girls were happy to oblige and said that it would be fun and that they could also use up the rest of the stuff they had, especially all the vodka that was left. Lacey said that if they wrote a list, she could pick up any mixers or things they may need for a snack lunchtime.

Memhet turned up later to take Lacey to town and said that he was sad that it was their last day saying that they had brought much happiness to the resort. Lacey said that the girls had asked for him to collect them the next morning at 9 am to go for their final breakfast together at the same place he had taken them on their first day and Memhet was pleased to confirm that it would be his pleasure.

Tristan was waiting at the rank for Lacey and Memhet commented to her that he could see much happiness between them in the years ahead, Lacey smiled and thanked him as she paid him her fare. Tristan greeted Lacey with a big hug and a kiss saying how much he was looking forward to seeing her all night long, admitting that he had hardly slept not being able to get her out of his mind, she held on to his arm with both hands as they walked to a restaurant serving breakfast, resting her head against his shoulder.

Back at the girls' villa, they were having their own breakfast and Kelly said that after she would start packing up her things so she could enjoy as much of the next day as she could. Alice and Emma agreed it was a good idea saying they would do the same and so once breakfast had finished, they all began sorting out their things, leaving out clothing for the night and travelling home.

Later that morning, just after the girls had finished packing and were making their way out to the pool area, Tristan and Lacey arrived with a few essentials Lacey had picked up at the supermarket. The girls greeted Tristan warmly who was then shown to Lacey's room so he could change into his swimwear.

Lacey put the groceries away as Tristan sorted himself out and she made a fresh pot of coffee, once Tristan had changed, she offered him a coffee and went to change herself, telling him to make himself comfortable by the pool until she was ready. The girls all smiled as Tristan joined them outside looking very smart and handsome in his shorts with his bronzed hairy chest on show but seemingly looking a little agitated being around three scantily clad women in their bikinis, especially Alice who had put on her most revealing outfit that allowed her ample firm breasts to ooze over and her bottoms barely covering her modesty that caused poor Tristan to gulp at his coffee as she turned and bent over to straighten her towel.

"Oh really, Alice, have some thought please darling, would you; poor Tristan almost fainted at the sight of your backside bent over in that excuse for a costume!" Kelly said sarcastically, giving her sister a look of disapproval.

Alice turned and smiled at Tristan, apologising for not thinking whilst hiding her amusement at the action she had taken. Lacey came out to join them looking stunning in her new gold and brown bikini that really complemented her shapely figure and with her hair tied back and her body glistening in the sunshine from the sun oil, she instantly removed all images of Alice's posterior from his mind.

Tristan looked at her in total admiration as she took the sunbed next to him, telling her how incredible she looked. Kelly looked up at Emma who was smiling at Tristan's comment and gave her a wink with a big grin.

They all enjoyed sitting around the pool, soaking up the late morning sun into the afternoon taking a breather for a spot of lunch and some cool refreshments, Kelly told Lacey that she and the girls had packed most of their things already to save time the next day so they could make the most of it and Lacey replied that she had been doing bits and pieces to that effect the last few days so she was not far off herself.

Emma was excited to receive another text message from Gavin who said that he was having his lunch a little later than planned due to work issues and said that he was counting down the days to when he would see her again, he gave some positive news that his father was a lot better and should be back to work soon, giving him more time to see her.

Emma excitedly told the girls her news as Lacey asked her to be a little quieter because Tristan had fallen asleep, the girls all gathered around Emma at the patio table and Lacey told them what Tristan had told her earlier about not sleeping well last night. Alice joked it was probably because she had made him so horny that he couldn't sleep and that she should be ashamed of herself for leaving the poor man that way before inadvertently saying at least she had taken care of Jeremy's frustrations.

Alice sat upright in disbelief at her own words, not intending to mention anything about what she had done with Jeremy saying that was it, no more vodka for her, Emma and Lacey couldn't hide their amusement at her disclosure as Kelly looked on in disgust at her sister, just shaking her head.

Alice then made an excuse of needing the bathroom and left the girls laughing quietly trying not to wake Tristan up, Kelly said that her sister never failed to surprise her and that in reality, it should not have come as a shock to her as it did.

Tristan soon joined the girls back in the real world apologising for dozing off as he had done so but they were not bothered, especially Alice who was glad he had missed her little revelation. Emma said that they should all soon start getting ready as the sun started to drop over to the west.

Lacey said to Tristan that she would shower first then he could use her bathroom to get ready and asked if he would need anything ironing to go out later. Tristan said that he was a careful packer and should be fine adding that he had hung his shirt up in her wardrobe when he was changing and said that it should be ok.

Everyone was getting ready and Lacey emerged from her room calling Tristan in to use her shower, Lacey was dressed in a loosely tied bathrobe and nothing else that didn't escape Tristan's attention. Grabbing his toilet bag from his travel bag, Tristan went into the bathroom and took a shower and having finished he stood in front of the sink having a shave when he thought he heard Lacey call out to him.

Opening the door and peering into the bedroom once he had finished to ask what she had said, he caught her in the process of putting on her knickers and gave himself a right eyeful of Lacey's wonderful assets; quickly apologising, he ducked back inside the bathroom with that incredible vision filling his mind. He called out saying he thought he heard her call to him; a little embarrassed, Lacey said that she had and not to worry, it wasn't his fault and she should have sorted things sooner.

Tristan came out of the bathroom in his boxers clearly excited by what he had seen trying in vain to hide his embarrassment with the towel he held in front of him as he reached for his shorts; unfortunately, without thinking Lacey grabbed the towel saying she would put it in the laundry basket and ripped it from his grasp revealing his excitement.

"I am sorry you had to see that, Lacey, but it has been a while for me seeing a woman naked, especially one as beautiful as you, it is a natural reaction. I am sorry though."

"Don't you be silly now, I think I would be more offended if I hadn't excited you and besides, at least now I know there is more to get excited about in the future for us eh!" Lacey said as she threw her arms around him and kissed him with much passion and vigour being highly aroused herself by the whole event but strong enough to resist temptation of taking it any further.

The pair finished getting ready and joined the other girls out on the front terrace who were sat with a glass of wine chatting away, Tristan received a message saying that they would be picked up in around twenty minutes and replied that they were all ready to go.

Matt arrived with the minibus bang on time and they all made their way up to the trout farm that they reached in no time at all. The setting was beautiful with a waterfall feature and streams stocked with live trout and a lovely terrace restaurant overlooking a lovely garden with stunning views better seen in the daylight but nonetheless still stunning.

There were ten of them in total and they were shown to a table prepared for them all, giving a great vantage point for the views. Matt suggested that they allow the owner to just feed them typical Turkish style as they had enjoyed the previous day at breakfast and all agreed.

The evening was an incredible experience with a wonderful array of salads and vegetable dishes along with the trout and even a few plates of hand cut chips washed down with some refreshing wine. Barry commented on the fact that it was such a sumptuous meal that he thoroughly enjoyed and was supported in his thoughts by everyone else. The girls took lots of pictures of the place, the food and of course the stunning views that they were told were even better during the day.

The girls thanked Matt and everyone for helping make their holiday a wonderful success and they all wished they could stay on and enjoy it longer with them but unfortunately, they had jobs to get back to and reality as well. Matt told Kelly that she had been a refreshing change for him and that he had enjoyed her company very much and suggested they stay in touch saying that he threw many parties back home throughout the year that she would be welcome to attend at any time.

Kelly promised to keep him updated on any developments with Emma and Gavin and suggested that he would probably know more about Tristan and Lacey before her so it would be interesting to see how things turned out; the pair hugged and Kelly gave him a big kiss on the cheek as he told her that she was going to make someone a lucky man one day and wished her well.

Alice was a little emotional at the thought of going home having had such a wonderful time and meeting some great people, she said that she didn't want the evening to end just yet as they readied themselves to head back a little after ten. Matt said that they should all head back to the cocktail bar adding that he would call Mussie to set some seating aside the best he could.

Barry and Lester decided to head back to the apartment and offered to take Tristan's bag back with them. Matt suggested after that perhaps they were worried that they may end up bumping into the two women that blew them out last night.

Arriving at the bar, Mussie greeted them showing them to a small table he was able to set aside with a few chairs that were available. He said that he would fetch more chairs as they became available but Matt said it was fine offering the seats to the girls as he said to the men that they could stand around chatting for a while. Lacey and Tristan stood to one side wanting to spend as much time together as they could before the night was over. Tristan asked if he could see her in the morning before she left and Lacey said that he should join them for breakfast and if he liked, he could come back to the villa after until their transfer arrived.

Tristan was pleased to hear that and nodded with enthusiasm saying that would be great, the pair stood close to each other holding hands and kissing as watchful eyes looked on in approval. As the time approached midnight, Kelly said that they should think about making their way back so they were able to get an early start to enjoy the last few hours before heading to the airport.

Lacey and Tristan led the way up the hill to the taxi rank, wrapped around each other as the others followed behind. Alice was talking to Inga saying how much she had enjoyed her company and wished she'd had time to have gotten to know her better and then said that she was welcome to join them for breakfast in the morning if she fancied it. Inga was pleased to accept and said that she would arrange to come down with Tristan in the morning saying that it was nice to meet some girls of her own age for once, adding that she especially enjoyed her time with Kelly at Saklikent.

Lacey found it hard letting go of Tristan as the others called to her from the taxi but finally, she reluctantly let go, kissing him one last time before getting in after everyone said their goodbyes to each other.

Inga made arrangements to meet Tristan the next morning before saying goodnight and headed off to her villa. Matt asked Tristan how he was feeling now knowing that Lacey was returning to England the next day and he simply answered that he was gutted. Matt told him that he thought the pair of them could have a bright future together if they could work something out about the distance between them and of course, his other commitments.

Tristan looked a little lost and down as the words Matt spoke hit home with the reality that they held, he waved goodnight to Matt and Giles as he headed to his place, Lester was sat on the patio finishing off a nightcap and asked how Tristan was as he trudged along the path looking very solemn indeed.

Tristan and Lester sat together for a short time as Tristan confessed his feelings towards Lacey and saying how utterly gobsmacked he was that he came out there and not only met someone wonderful but had genuinely fallen for her. Lester said that it was obvious for all to see and that everyone thought them to be a perfect match.

That night was hard on Tristan and Lacey who both found it difficult to sleep with the pending departure between them drawing ever closer. Emma was the only one counting the hours down to getting back home because that was where her head was, with Gavin who had sent her a loving goodnight message that evening.

Saturday Day 14

The next morning, Kelly and Alice were up and about just before eight finishing off the packing ready for later, coffee was made and Emma appeared full of the joys of spring as she helped herself to a cup before looking in on Kelly who said she could guess why she was looking so happy.

Emma said that the holiday had been wonderful and that she never expected Turkey, and Kalkan in particular, to be so beautiful and friendly, the holiday had given her more than she could have ever imagined and now she was ready to go home and see if there was a fairy-tale ending to it all.

Alice appeared asking if anyone had seen Lacey yet as it was unusual for her to be last in bed, Alice made her way to Lacey's room knocking her door gently before entering to find her looking very sad, curled up in her bed.

"Oh Lace, you poor thing, are you ok, look, I know it is going to be hard but at least you have something and more importantly someone too look forward to now, don't you eh? It's only a week before he will be back and I am sure that it won't be long after that you will see each other again." Alice hugged her friend as she coaxed her into getting up saying that she had a breakfast appointment with him over some crispy bacon.

Kelly and Emma appeared asking if everything was ok and Alice simply replied that reality was hitting home hard for poor Lacey. Kelly then basically said exactly what Alice had said moments earlier with regards to it only being a week or so before she would see him again, much the same as Emma.

Emma joined in with the rallying cry saying she knew exactly how Lacey was feeling but now she was going home, it was less than a week away before she would see Gavin again, all the girls encouraged Lacey up out of bed and Emma fetched her a cup of coffee and said that she should make the most of these last few hours with him, talking positively about seeing each other again as she thought that he was probably feeling a similar way too.

Lacey sorted herself out and dressed ready to go to town as Tristan sent her a loving text saying he was looking forward to having breakfast with her shortly and spending the rest of her time there with her; the message put a smile on her saddened and tired looking face as she came to terms with the situation and taking a deep breath, she told herself to sort it out as she looked in the mirror.

Kelly had called Memhet to check that he was collecting them at around 9.30 am and it wasn't long before he arrived and they were on their way to town. Memhet dropped the girls off saying that he would return for them around 11 am as the restaurant was quiet and they should be ready by then.

Tristan and Inga were already waiting for them and upon seeing him, Lacey ran into his waiting arms hugging and kissing him apologising for looking so rough as she put it, saying she hardly slept all night. Tristan said that she looked perfect to him and that a few hours of a sleepless night could never change that.

The group sat down to a good breakfast enjoying the peaceful views out over the harbour where the boats were being made ready for that days excursions, selfies were being taken as a wonderful reminder of their holiday there and the waiter kindly obliged taking many group shots with the individual phone cameras. After breakfast, Kelly asked Inga if she wanted to come back and spend some time with them at the villa and she jumped at the chance saying she needed as much girl chat time as she could get, she said she had no idea what she would do once they were gone as she was surrounded by men and older women that she was not overly fussed about.

Lacey told the girls to go ahead with Inga and that she and Tristan would follow on shortly after because she wanted to pick up some things to take back and have a little alone time with him. Tristan smiled at her feeling pleased that she was thinking that way and said that he welcomed the opportunity to spend the time with her.

Memhet arrived a little after eleven to collect the girls and took them back to the villa as Lacey and Tristan walked amongst the various souvenir shops, looking for a few things to take back for family and friends. Arriving at the villa, Memhet got out of the car and thanked the girls for all their business and wished them a safe journey home just as Kelly pulled out an envelope with his name on it from her bag and handed it to him saying it was a little something for all his kindness and help, not forgetting the wonderful service he provided.

Memhet was a little overwhelmed by the kind gesture and tried to refuse saying that it was his pleasure to be of service to them but the girls insisted thrusting the envelope containing a sizeable tip into his hand. Kelly gave him a big hug and thanked him as Alice and Emma followed suit before he left them, feeling rather humble in himself.

Lacey and Tristan joined the girls about an hour later sat out the back in the slightly shaded area drinking tea and coffee, Lacey took her newly bought trinkets to her room and carefully packed everything away after showing the girls and then sat with Tristan at the table holding his hand.

Kelly said that she had checked the safe was empty and she had also checked the tickets and passports were all together in a folder in her flight bag ready for the airport and then suggested that everyone check their cupboards and under the beds for anything that may have been left behind; the girls laughed at her with Alice saying yes mum as Inga supporting her said that she was right, having often found the odd shoe and piece of lingerie hidden away somewhere.

Lacey was constantly checking her watch trying in some way in her mind to slow time down but it was soon almost pickup time. Tristan helped the girls out with their cases and down to the roadside and when Lacey disappeared back into the villa, he asked Inga for a small package she had in her bag and quickly hid it in Lacey's handbag.

Alice spotted what Tristan had done and gave him a quizzical look with a wry smile; Tristan put his finger to his lips as to say to her to say nothing just as Lacey returned. The sound of their transfer people carrier roared up the hill and around the corner into sight, causing a feeling of nausea and emptiness in Lacey's stomach, she clutched at her midriff searching for a breath as the vehicle pulled up next to them knowing that this was it; she was going to have to say goodbye to someone that had given her a new purpose and belief in life.

The driver put all the cases in the back of the vehicle as the girls said goodbye to Inga and then eventually Tristan once Lacey was finished herself with him. Lacey hugged him one last time saying that she would message him once she was home and said that she could not wait to be in his arms again as the tears flowed down her cheeks, looking at him through the window blowing a kiss at her as the transport pulled away.

The girls supported Lacey who was terribly upset for most of the first part of the journey back to the airport where they stopped for the toilets and refreshment, they were all enjoying a nice snack and refreshing drink when Lacey spotted the package in her handbag and asked what it was as she took it out. It was a small square-shaped package that had been carefully wrapped with a little gift card stuck to it. Lacey took out the card and upon reading it held her hand over her mouth and in a flood of tears said it was from Tristan.

The other girls looked on in excitement urging her to open the package to see what it was as Lacey said she had a good idea what it may be adding that she hoped he hadn't, there before her was the bracelet she had seen with him one night at the jewellers in the town and she lifted it up in front of the others who were sat there with envious eyes, cooing and gasping with delight.

Alice was first to comment, "Oh wow Lacey, that is really beautiful; you are so lucky, it looks really expensive."

Lacey said that it wasn't cheap and that he shouldn't be spending that sort of money on her at this stage of their relationship but Kelly said that she would be happy to have it on a first date adding that it was absolutely stunning as she looked on in awe and asking what the card said.

"Dear Lacey, please accept this a token of my affection for you, forgive me but after seeing your face when you first saw it, I had to. Love Tris xxx", Lacey read.

Emma, Alice and Kelly sat silent as Lacey put the bracelet on as she tried to hold back her tears, Lacey then took out her phone to message Tristan thanking him for the present and telling him that he shouldn't have but she was very happy that he had done so; she said that she would hold it close to her every day until they were together again.

The girls finished their break and were soon on their way to the airport just under an hour away; once they were checked in they made their way to the departure lounge then eventually boarded their plane and flew back to Bristol Airport. The girls managed to grab a reasonable amount of sleep or rest on the flight and arrived back shortly before eleven; having passed through passport control and collected their luggage, they made their way out of the arrivals lounge, hoping that Emma's dad was waiting to pick them up in the carpark.

Going through the nothing to declare section and out the exit door, Alice spotted an older gentleman holding a large poster with what looked like the photo she had taken of Emma and Gavin on the sunset cruise; making her way over to get a closer look, she could see it was and called to the others to look with her and then she asked the man who he was.

"Oh hello, my lovely, you must be Emma, is it?" the old man asked, smiling at Alice.

"No, this is Emma; where the hell did you get this poster from and who are you?" Alice asked him with great mystification.

"Oh sorry, it was my son you see but he had a toilet emergency and asked me to wait in case we missed you."

"GAVIN!" Emma screamed as she saw him approach and dropping her bags ran and threw herself into his arms hugging and kissing him as the tears streamed down her face. Emma said that it was a wonderful surprise and told him how much she had missed him as the other girls looked on, feeling so happy for her.

Alice glanced around wondering if Jeremy was about to jump out of the woodwork but she was left disappointed because he had not come with them.

Gavin's dad said that his boy had been working like a Trojan since coming back and that he was due back on the farm in six hours and so he didn't want him driving late at night not having had much rest.

The girls all introduced themselves to him and told him what a wonderful son he had and that pleased him immensely. Emma's phone went off and answering it she said it was her father waiting out in the carpark and asked Gavin and his father to come out and meet him. Gavin took Emma's case and they all went out and met with her father who was surprised to hear that she had met someone on holiday, knowing how she was with men normally. Alice said that Gavin had saved Emma's life and that their love had grown from there.

Emma's dad looked a little shocked at Alice's statement and asked what had happened but Emma said she would tell him all about later and not to worry but Gavin did save her and in more than one way; her father embraced Gavin and thanked him for saving Emma however it was and said that he hoped to see a lot more of him in the future.

After several minutes, they all said goodbye with Emma hugging and kissing Gavin saying she would call him the next day and looked forward to coming up to see him the following Friday.

Over the following weeks, Emma made the Friday trip up to Gloucester where she spent the weekend with Gavin on the farm and was welcomed by his parents as one of the family; she learnt a lot about farm life from his mother, especially about how to feed a hungry brood. Over the following months, she met his elder brothers and their families as she and Gavin grew closer and closer together.

Alice made the odd trip up to Gloucester and met up with Jeremy where they were able to satisfy their curiosity of each other at last but it wasn't to last as they were not really suited to a full-blown relationship. Alice soon met someone closer to home that she felt may be her Mr Right and started a casual relationship with him that became serious in no time at all.

Kelly had kept in touch with Matt and been to stay up at his place on a couple of occasions when he was hosting the odd party and met up with some familiar faces; having taken Matt's advice, she now found herself in a comfortable relationship with a new accounts manager that had moved up from Exeter.

He was divorced with no children and seven years older but had looked after himself and was a very decent, honest, hardworking chap with a great personality; things were going steady and Kelly was in a happy place and that was all she had ever wanted.

Lacey and Tristan made every effort as and when they could to spend time together; the first couple of months were the most difficult for them but they persevered and had made it through forming a strong bond together.

Lacey had met his children and they took to her immediately and even his late wife's parents warmed to her charms and gave Tristan their blessings on their relationship.

The girls' lives all seemed to change somewhat after the holiday, each going their own way finding relationships that kept them apart most of the time; they all messaged each other from time to time but the regular meet-ups just faded into memory as their lives took new turns; even the sisters seldom saw each other.

It was around late spring the following year when Emma was up at Gavin's and he was having the Sunday off and feeling rather excited at a surprise he had planned for her, causing him to get up early that morning; there was a lot of activity out in the fields and the yard, giving rise to Emma asking what he was up to.

Gavin said he had a surprise for her and that she should wait for him to come back in around an hour or so. Emma lay in bed excited wondering what Gavin had arranged for her as her head filled with all manner of notions.

Soon enough, Gavin was back encouraging Emma to get dressed and have some breakfast before he led her out past his rather pleased looking parents into the yard where they made their way in his Land Rover out to one of the nearby fields. Emma gushed as she saw there in the middle of the field a hot air balloon getting ready to take her and Gavin up in the air.

Gavin said that he wanted to show her the extent of the farm that was best viewed from the air and then she would see what he wanted to do with the house that he was finishing now with her help and input. Emma smiled with joy as she climbed aboard and the balloon master proceeded to take them up slowly.

Once they were up at a certain height, Gavin put his arm around her as he pointed out all the various parts to the farm on the one side, he pointed out to the house that he said he would be eventually moving into once it was finished and asked Emma if she fancied sharing it with him, saying she wouldn't have to keep travelling back and forth anymore that way.

Emma said that it was a lovely idea but she had her job to think about and didn't know if she would be able to find the same around there as it was so rural; Gavin replied that if she was a farmer's wife, she wouldn't have to worry about that and then said that she should look over the other side. Emma was a little confused by that last remark as Gavin turned her to look the other way; looking down there on the field below spelt out with all manner of farmyard bits and pieces were the words EMMA WILL YOU MARRY ME.

Emma's knees almost buckled beneath her as she read the message over and over hardly able to process it all as she became overwhelmed with loving emotions and gripped hold of Gavin with all her might, saying, "Yes! Oh yes please, Gavin, thank you, oh my God! I can't believe it, oh Gavin!" she cried as she hugged and kissed him before he got down on one knee and pulled a ring out from his pocket and put it on her finger.

Once the balloon descended, Gavin thanked the balloonist and took Emma back to the house where his parents and his brother were waiting to hear the news. Gavin's mother rushed to Emma giving her a big hug having seen the big smile on her face and she knew she had said yes.

They all sat around the kitchen table drinking tea and Emma said that she had better call her parents and tell them, saying they were going to be shocked for sure. Gavin said that he had spoken to them two weeks ago when he made one of his rare visits to Taunton and they had given him their blessings.

Emma made the call and spoke to her very excited parents who were overjoyed for her, wishing her and Gavin every happiness; next she took a picture of her hand with the ring and sent it to Alice, Lacey and Kelly asking if they thought it was the right colour nail polish for her.

A minute later, her phone rang with Alice screaming down the phone in total excitement and happiness for her as the tone for incoming calls could be heard over her as Lacey and Kelly tried to get through. Emma put Alice on hold and spoke with Kelly and then with Lacey and promised to call each of them when she got back later.

The four friends all got together three weeks later at Kelly's house to share some sparkling wine and toast their friend's wonderful news; everyone was happy for Emma and they all caught up with where they were with their lives and in particular, their new romances. Alice said that she and her new fella were getting on well and she could see herself settling down with him in the near future, no problem. Kelly said that she too was heading that way and asked Lacey what was new with her and Tristan.

Lacey said that she was going to say something sooner but didn't want to steal Emma's thunder but Tristan had asked her to move in with him. Alice beamed with delight as the other two applauded her and said that they were so pleased for her. Alice jokingly asked if the house was big enough having already seen plenty of pictures of the beautiful place. "Well, I think it is big enough for two adults and three children, don't you, Alice?" Lacey replied with a wide grin.

Alice was about to say I thought he had two children when the penny dropped. "Oh my lord, Lacey, you're pregnant! No, get away, really!" Alice jumped up with joy, hugging her friend and shedding a few tears as she told her how happy she was for her.

Kelly and Emma joined in on the celebration as they all had a friendly group hug asking how far gone she was, Lacey said that she was around ten weeks and couldn't be any happier as was Tristan and his girls who said that they were looking forward to having another sibling and a new mummy.

Tristan said that he didn't want to rush her into anything but he had every intention of marrying her at some point and that he wanted everything done in a proper manner and planned on coming down to see her parents in a couple of weeks who by the way were over the moon with the news, despite it being out of wedlock as they put it.

Emma and Gavin were married later that year in the July and enjoyed a fabulous wedding with Kelly, Alice and Lacey as bridesmaids and Lacey's two beautiful soon-to-be stepdaughters as flower girls; there were no surprises when the happy couple said that they would be honeymooning in Kalkan where they met up with their dear friend Memhet.

Dining at their favourite restaurant, they were sorry not to have seen Mohammad who had been promoted to a senior manager's position at one of the company's other hotels; the elder waitress that had told Emma about the meaning of that now famous photograph was there however and now the new restaurant manager. She was happy to see the newlyweds and pointed out that the legend was true and never failed. Emma was so happy to agree and told her that she and Gavin had an enlarged copy of the photo on their bedroom wall, showing her a picture of it on her phone.

The friends all got together again just before Christmas with a heavily pregnant Lacey only a couple of weeks away from giving birth, she knew she was having a boy and said that she hoped they didn't think it too corny but they were going to call him Kalvin, "Kal" for short.

Alice said she loved it and that it was perfect, saying out loud, "Kal Cannington, yes, it has a perfect ring to it."

They all smiled and enthused over Lacey as Emma said she had some news of her own to share, her face was a picture as first Kelly and seconds later Alice said, "Oh my God, Emma, you're pregnant."

Emma's face was radiant as she beamed with excitement before disclosing that she was having twins, the place was in uproar as the friends rallied together sharing in all the joy and happiness that abounded there.

Lacey gave birth to a very healthy 8lb 6oz baby boy in the January to the delight of all that knew her well. Tristan and his daughters were over the moon with happiness with the new addition to their family as were Tristan's former in-laws who would look upon him as they did the girls. Tristan and Lacey married in the June of that year and the whole family honeymooned together in Kalkan, of course, a couple months later. Matt had generously donated his villa to them for the duration as a wedding gift and was out there to greet them and settle them in before heading off somewhere else with friends, looking at some investment properties.

Alice was now sporting a delightful single diamond engagement ring on her finger of some size that she enjoyed showing to her friends; she had now moved in with her love interest and was happily settled and in no rush to tie the knot just yet. Kelly was also engaged and living with her chap who was now also her boss having been promoted at work. Kelly didn't take any issue with it as she told all that needed to know with some degree of humour that he knew who was boss at home and that was all that mattered.

The friends all stayed in touch and tried to see each other as time would allow them. Emma gave birth to twins, one of each sex, a boy she called Martin weighing in at 6lb 4oz and a little girl 6lb exactly, she called Kali; something she said she could not resist after Lacey had called her son Kalvin.

All the friends and their partners enjoyed a wonderful BBQ at the farmhouse where Emma and Gavin lived just after the birth where Alice met up with Jeremy and was surprised to learn that he was going steady with a fitness instructor that had seemed to tame his errant ways. Sat around a large table, the friends reminisced about the time they had all spent in Kalkan that wonderful summer a couple of years ago and where it had brought them.

Emma stood up and thanked her friends for being who they were and for all the support they had given her over the years; she said that without them, she doubted that she would be here now happily married with two beautiful children. Emma thanked Alice for recommending Kalkan in the first place and said that it had lived up to being the magical place where miracles could happen; she said that she and Gavin would always hold the place dear to their hearts and be regular visitors there.

Before the evening was over, they all pledged to do a group holiday out there the following summer; the new partners were intrigued by all the fuss over this place and one asked was it really that special, and in unison, all that had been there gave a resounding "OH YES!"

The End

Printed in the USA
CPSIA information can be obtained
at www.ICGtesting.com
LVHW011416090324
773945LV00001B/167